The Empty Throne

J.F. Gomez-Rivera

outskirts
press

Act I

Chapter 1
The Eager Student

V essel Silvus, a twenty-four-winter-old silver-scaled Raptor with light-blue stripes sits at his brown wooden desk reading a textbook in order to prepare for a final exam. With his big blue serpent like eyes, he reads through a topic about the mystery of ancient colossal trees called the wellsprings. As a student of Monastery, an organization dedicated to teaching Mistcraft, he is expected to learn, practice, and study the art. Lucky for him, he enjoys it greatly due to the fact that he has always loved to read since he was very young. He reads the chapter with a confident smile on his long snout. He is so confident, his long tail lies calmly on a clean carpet.

Silvus reads the book with candle wall lights off thanks to the sunlight that shines through a glass window, giving his bedroom light. Finishing a page, he lifts his left claw covered in a leather glove to turn to the next page until he gets interrupted by a knocking sound from his door. In annoyance, he makes a soft groan, showing his sharp teeth, and at the same time uses his uncovered claw to brush back his short dark-blue mane. He turns around to face the door and shouts, "Come in!"

The door opens to reveal a younger male with teal scale color wearing his blue-colored nobility scarf. His name is Vessel Ico, Silvus' younger first cousin who is looking at him with his brown serpent eyes filled with enthusiasm.

Ico drops his smile at the sight of his cousin still studying. He puts on a disappointed face and the same time crosses his claws. "Are you seriously still studying? It's almost been at least an entire month!" he complains with a huff.

"I'm sorry, Ico, but this is literally my FINAL exam, and this exam is going to determine whether or not I become an official Mistcaster!" Silvus tries to explain how important his exam is. It is true that he has been studying for the past three months, since his professor back at Monastery announced it. Ico makes an annoyed eye roll, not looking amused, followed by smirk on his snout.

"Oh, really? I thought you wanted to be a Mistcaster in order to qualify to become the next Beta-Lord?" Ico mockingly retorts, scratching the messy yet trimmed dark-blue mane on his head.

"Ha ha, very funny—true, but when I become the next Beta-Lord I could use my powers in order to help the Betadom as much as I can--perhaps even the kingdom." Silvus gets up from his desk with utmost enthusiasm to run up to a big bookshelf on the wall filled with books to take out a particular black-colored book with a silver symbol of the kingdom of Avalonia, one of the three Raptor kingdoms of the continent of Cretatia, on the front cover. He taps the book with his ungloved claw with glee to explain, "Perhaps, maybe, I could be as good as the great hero Ultamar Magnus, the first Alpha-King of Avalonia who led an army to defeat the evil Necros and his minions!"

Ico's only response is to lean against a wall, getting smug. "I could imagine you being the best Beta-Lord in the world."

"How so?" Silvus asks him with a brow raised, knowing what his younger cousin is going to say.

"Because you will be too stuck on your books and performing Mistcraft instead of doing your duties!" Ico laughs wanting to mess with him.

Silvus starts to get a bit annoyed, making a small growl at Ico's hatchling-like remarks. He always questions how an immature brat like him even passed any grades at Monastery at all, and he is a Seventh year! Ico further laughs, then he starts to slowly make a saddening expression, making Silvus worry.

"I'm sorry, man; life has not been the same since my older sister Sulphie went off and married the Beta-Lord of Tricia." Ico looks back up at Silvus. "I came here hoping that you would be done studying so we could do something fun, like old times."

Ico moans about the time when Sulphie, Silvus' other cousin, was around. Growing up without any siblings, Silvus considered his two cousins as such. With Sulphie now living in Tricia, it is only him and Ico. Silvus walks up to Ico, putting a free claw on his shoulder in comfort.

"Listen, when I become the Beta-Lord of Maglo, I promise I won't let that change me, and besides, I'm going to make you my steward," Silvus tells him, hoping to shed some light.

Ico's expression softens a bit, moving his gaze toward Silvus. "I hope that's true, and as your future steward, I'll make sure you don't end up like them snobby ones." Ico jumps up back on his feet in laughter, earning a nudge from Silvus, who turns around to return the book he took out. Ico's eyes widen with a gasp, because he suddenly remembers why he came.

"Oh yeah, your mom sent me here to collect you for dinner!"

Silvus stops in his tracks, looking freaked out, making Ico laugh once again as he starts to walk toward the door. "Guess I'll wait for you outside." With that, he leaves and closes the door.

Not that he does not like to have dinner, but Silvus really does not like being interrupted for anything. With a disappointed breath, he looks at the book he is holding. Distracted in thought, he remembers another great hero. So he walks up to a window to see a bright sunny day outside the courtyard.

In the center of the courtyard filled with flowers is a large statue of a Raptor wearing robes, holding a staff. Silvus gazes at the bronze plaque that reads "Vessel Atheros, founder and first Beta-Lord of Maglo." Silvus looks at the statue of Atheros with lots of admiration. He remembers from the old story that Atheros was one of the mighty four companions of Magnus who aided in the founding of third Avalonia.

As Silvus admires the statue, he thinks about what he could do if he becomes a great Mistcaster. Aside from being a great Beta-Lord, a part of him wishes he could go on at least one adventure. Discover more about the kingdom, save the innocent, rescue a damsel in distress, or the biggest dream that all young Raptors dream about is being a hero just like Magnus and his ancestor Atheros. Since he is First-Delta, it is expected for him to succeed his mother, the current Beta-Lady to be the next Beta-Lord, making him sigh in disappointment.

"SILVUS, HURRY UP! WE CAN'T KEEP DAD AND AUNTIE SILVIERA WAITING!" Ico calls out from the closed door, snapping Silvus back to reality.

"Hold on!" he shouts back, putting the book away, and rushes to his wardrobe to open it up. In the wardrobe are robes and fancy scarves that nobles of the kingdom wear. In the center is a big mirror on top of a dresser in the middle. He opens the first drawer, filled with a collection of left clawed gloves made out of crocodon skin.

Silvus raises his left glove, gazing at it for a moment. *Well, here goes nothing,* he thinks as he uses his right claw and slowly takes off his left glove, making him wince in pain. He takes off his glove to reveal that his left claw is burned. He throws the glove that he took off into a basket filled with dirty gloves and reaches into the second drawer to take out a clean glove to put it on. Putting the new glove on slowly makes him wince into even more pain. As soon as he puts on his glove, he walks out of his bedroom, wearing his own blue nobility scarf, to see Ico leaning back on the stone wall waiting for him.

"About time you showed up. I almost thought you went back to your books."

Silvus chuckles at Ico's comment, and the two cousins begin to walk along the stone hallway filled with portraits and armored mannequins.

As the duo trot along the candle lit hall, out of the blue Ico asks Silvus a question, looking uneasy.

"Hey, cousin, you notice Dad and Auntie have been talking about the rumors lately?"

"What sort of rumors?" Silvus asks him without turning his head.

Ico stops in his tracks, looking at his cousin as if he has been sleeping under a rock and shrieks, "Are you serious?!"

Not that he hasn't been paying attention. Silvus knows that Alpha-King Ultamar Sulthur died without an heir before he was born. He remembers reading some articles from *The Nosy Locust* about various instances ever since he got into reading at the age of eight.

"Is it another riot against the Mistatorium?" Silvus asks.

"That's very common, but nope." Ico squints his eyes expecting Silvus to know what he is talking about.

"More bandit attacks?"

"Part of it, but no."

"Than what is it?" Silvus stops right in front of a wooden door facing Ico.

In response, Ico snout palms in annoyance. "Damn, Silvus, you are so glued to your studying, you missed the fact that bandit attacks have suddenly stopped in Monchester."

"Isn't that a good thing?" Silvus asks, placing his claw on the door knob.

"Well cousin, from the way every Raptor is taking it," Ico shrugs, "it kinda sounds more like a conspiracy theory to them, so I guess we should just head to dinner and find out."

Silvus opens the door, allowing the two cousins to go through and have dinner, hoping to take their minds off the kingdom's issues.

Chapter 2
The Tale of Three Avalonias

T hrough the door, the two cousins are greeted by the throne
room, made of white stone pearl with dark-blue banners with
a silver star in the middle hanging proudly from the ceiling. Silvus
looks around the room from the archway and spots two teal-scaled
Raptors talking to each other around the throne place in front of a
large, glowing pine tree sprinkling mist from its branches.

The one sitting on the throne is his mother Beta-Lady Vessel
Silviera who wears a white and blue long cloak in all her might,
along with a silver crown on top of her head, filled with a long, light-
blue silky mane. In her fisted claws with silver jeweled bracelets is a
pendant that she holds against her chest as if her life depended on
it. In front is her younger brother and steward, Vessel Orezyme, who
wears a dark- blue scarf and amulet in panic like a crazy old man. He
seems to be ranting about the current state of the kingdom.

———— ◈ ————

"First the Alpha-King dies without an heir, then riots erupt due
to rumors, bandit gangs appear out of nowhere, and now Monchester
goes dark! By the spirits, it feels like the end times!" Orezyme rants

with a voice of one in his early forties, stopping in his tracks to brush back his dark-blue mane with grey threads.

"I agree with your worry, Orezyme, but I fear there is some dark presence at play," Silviera explains with a sweet voice despite her middle-aged appearance. She understands her brother's concern, as she believes there is a more sinister threat happening.

"What do you mean by a dark presence?" Orezyme looks back at his older sister, wanting to know what she means. To him, she speaks as if there is a hidden agenda among the kingdom in the brink of collapse.

"I was in communication with the Mistatorium about such matters during the years of my son's hatching. My mentor, the arch-sage, claims that he has been sensing unnatural Mist growing around the shadows." Silviera slowly opens up her pale silvery eyes halfway and gets up from her throne and approaches Orezyme, still grasping her pendant.

***

From the archway, Silvus listens to his mother and uncle talking, looking worried. Even though it is not right to listen to conversations, he cannot help but listen in order to know what is going on. He puts on an uneasy face, knowing what they might be talking about.

"They are talking about the rumors, aren't they?" he hears his cousin whisper uneasily.

"Yeah, they are... let's just go to dinner and act like we did not hear them. Wouldn't want to get in trouble, would we?" Silvus whispers back.

Silvus slowly climbs down the stairs while Ico follows suit. Silvus puts on a blank face, walking normally to pretend he did not listen as

Ico just walks up stiffly. Approaching the two talking adults, Silviera notices the boys and shushes Orezyme to stop talking.

"Hello, boys. Glad you both could make it to dinner. Let's head to the table, shall we?" She speaks up and leans to the side of Orezyme, who seems to stop panicking, and whispers, "We will talk more about this later." She guides them to a long burgundy wood dining table in the center with rows of lighted candles on top.

Once they are seated, Silviera tucks the pendant inside a hidden pocket in her cloak and claps. A guard who wears a chainmail chest armor and a metal helmet with blue feathers, guarding a wooden door, opens it to allow through a few servant drones with black dots on their snouts, carrying dishes. Once dinner is served, the family begins to feast.

While they feast, Silvus sees his mother, who sits beside him, eating her soup slowly with her eyes closed. Her face looks uneasy, making Silvus worried about her. He can guess that it has to do with the conversation she had with his uncle earlier.

"Is everything alright, young Silvus?" he hears his uncle call out. Silvus turns his gaze away from his mother to see his uncle looking at him with an inquisitive brow raised above one of his silver eyes.

"Oh! I'm okay, just excited to pass my exam," Silvus explains, dodging his uncle's question to go back to eat his Tritop (Triceratops) steak while his uncle in front moves his head side to side with eyes looking up and turns his attention to his son Ico, who is rushing his meal. With a frown, Orezyme uses his tail to slap a whip at Ico's head to get his attention.

"Ouch! What was that for?" Ico demands, very irritated.

"You're eating way too fast! You need to learn proper manners just like your cousin here!" The old steward points at Silvus making Ico grunt in annoyance.

Silvus hears a chuckle coming from his mother, making him turn his gaze back to her; she now wears a small smile. Silviera opens her eyes halfway and tilts them to Silvus. "So, how go your studies, Silvus?" she asks him, taking a sip of her soup from the spoon.

"Great, Mother. I was actually reading the part about the wellsprings, the source of Mist!" Silvus replies in excitement. During his time in the Monastery, he loved to give lectures on what he had learned to his friends and family. Sometimes he would get so carried away his friends and family would get annoyed or simply beg him to speak of something else.

He hears Ico making a grunting sound, looking annoyed, putting a fisted claw under his chin with an elbow on the table. Orezyme, glaring at his son's improper posture, makes a threating growl, scaring him back to normal stance.

As soon as the family finish their meals, Silviera requests only her son to stay with her as Orezyme and Ico head up the archway to the private quarters. Silvus wonders why his mother requested him to stay. Is it to tell him privately about what is going on in the kingdom? For sure, his hatch day is not next sunrise.

Silviera gets off her dining chair and gestures her claw for Silvus to follow her to the giant pine tree behind the throne. The mother and son stop in front of the throne and gaze at the tree with awe. The guards who are guarding the throne room entrance door look at each and back at them, wondering what they are going to do.

"So tell me, Silvus, how much do you know about the wellsprings?" Silviera asks with gleam in her eyes, still glued on the pine tree.

"The wellsprings are mysterious trees said to be planted by the spirits to grants us the gift of life and Mistcraft," Silvus replies, looking confident, turning his gaze to the side at his mother instead of the tree.

Silviera moves her gaze at her son with a smile, proud that he answered correct decides to quiz him about his studies.

"Can you name all six Betadoms? And what are they named from?"

"There are Suaronian Heart, Maglo, Tricia, Monchester, Sherrasic, and Creston. And some of them were named right after the Wellsprings like the one in front of us!" Silvus points at the tree with his claw and guides to the fountain streams. "The Miststreams are rivers of recycled mist that connect to the wellsprings in order to nourish each other to produce even more Mist."

"Even though I did not ask for you to explain Miststreams, explain what a Mistcaster is?" Silveira asks her final question.

With a deep breath, Silvus proceeds to answer the final question. "A Mistcaster is one who can tap into the Mist to perform supernatural powers if one chooses to, all thanks to our ancestors who learned. When a Mistcaster performs too much powers, he or she would start to get mentally exhausted, meaning that the Mist energy is depleting. When Mist energy depletes, the caster would be unable to perform more spells until he or she recharges, allowing the Mist around us to flow into us like a magnet."

His mother smiles, proud of him, knowing that he will pass the exam just as she did in her time, so she decides to tell him a story by starting with a question.

"Very impressive, my son. How much do you know about the history of our kingdom?"

"Well, according to the story that you used to tell when I was a hatchling, this kingdom was founded like three times! One by a mysterious champion, one by Necros, and finally Magnus himself."

His mother flinches, closing her eyes shut at the same time held her pendant tight close to her at the mention of Necros. Both the guards and the drones also react with a gasp. At first Silvus does not know why they reacted as if he said a curse, but then realizes whom he mentioned.

"Oh yeah, we don't like talking about Second Avalonia." The young eager student forms an apologetic face, tapping his talons, hoping he did not offend. Silviera calms down a bit and opens her eyes, looking at him to procced with her story.

"Well then, for the sake of your studies let me tell you a story my old mentor used to tell me. This story is called 'The Tale of Three Avalonias.' It is what we Raptors called it due to our history of our kingdom being remade at least three times. It all started with the first civilization, the Precursor race as we call them, were chosen by the spirits granting them the ultimate gift, the ability to tap into the Mist for the purpose of worship. With the gifts, the Precursors were able to establish a unique kingdom in their image. We Raptors today do not know who the Precursors were, but it is known that they eventually turned their backs on the spirits for false promises of power.

"They made contact with the evil spirits, enemies of the benevolent ones, in a realm called the Netherworld. The Netherworld is a realm where all the wicked go to be tormented for their wicked deeds, as well as the home of the evil spirits. The evil spirits bestowed a curse upon the Precursor race within their hearts. An act of using this dark seed in the heart as a source rather than rather than natural mist is called Dark Mistcraft.

"Returning to our world, the Precursor race carried the darkness within their hearts, allowing it to spread around and infect every soul of this realm. Corrupted by the curse, they used it to rule over those whom they considered lesser beings, like our ancestors.

"Our ancestors, the Raptors of old, were once mere nomadic tribes living in peace with the mighty Precursors before the corruption of Dark Mist. Lacking the ability to tap into Mist, our ancestors were vulnerable, allowing the Precursors to use their wicked powers to enslave us. That was until a hero among us rose up.

"We call this hero the Champion, because we do not know who

he is. The stories tell us he was beckoned by the spirits to grant him the ability to tap into the Mist like the Precursors to fulfill his destiny. The Champion was to teach the old Raptors how to tap into the Mist and unite them against the Wicked Precursors. With the newfound knowledge of Mistcraft, the Champion and his followers vanquished them and forged the kingdom of First Avalonia. The Champion became its ruler, with Patalot as its capital."

While Silviera tells her story, some of the guards are starting to sleep, bored by her long lecture. Even some drones are snoozing in boredom. Silvus, on the other claw, continues to listen with great interest until he sees his mother start to look gloomy, making him gulp in fear, knowing what she is going to tell next.

"From the royal capital of Patalot, the champion ruled first Avalonia right and just until a Raptor by the name of Necros started to dabble in Dark Mistcraft just like the Precursors. Our scriptures say that Necros was a trusted ally of the champion who felt jealous toward him. With the forbidden arts, Necros led an army of other corrupted Raptors in order to take control of the kingdom by killing off the entire royal family, thus starting Necros's tyrannical rule with the founding of Second Avalonia.

"Second Avalonia is also nicknamed the second dark age because the kingdom had become a reflection of the tyranny of the Precursor rule. There was hope, however; not all of the royal family were killed. One young Alpha-Prince was rescued by a member of the old Mistatorium, an organization of Mistcasters made by the Champion in order to teach proper use of Mistcracft. The young Alpha-Prince who survived was the hero we all know and love, Ultamar Magnus."

Silvus brightens up as he hears his mother begin to mention the hero. It reminds him of the good old times when his mother read him the story about the hero. He looks around the throne room to see that all the drones and guards have fallen asleep. Silviera, who notices them sleeping, makes a groan in annoyance and coughs into her claw.

"AND I BELIEVE BY THE END OF WAR, MAGNUS HAD TO LAY OFF SOME MEN FOR SLEEPING ON THE JOB!"

Her shout was so loud that the echo of her voice woke up the guards and drones to drive them back to work. Silvus could not help but laugh at the reactions, along with his mother, who did a softer voice.

"Well then, where was I? Oh yes, so the young Magnus--" She gets interrupted by large doors opening very fast, making a thumping sound, getting the old Beta-Lady and Silvus' attention. From the doors, a male Raptor wearing a leather chest guard and a dark-blue cape and hood comes through, looking like he is out of breath.

"Scout?! Explain why you burst in here!" Silviera demands with a hint of annoyance in her voice, showing that she really hates to be interrupted. She taps her foot, waiting for an answer.

"Lady Beta, I came from the southern camp near the royal army border with dire news!" the scout rapidly explains, at the same time kneeling with one knee.

The other guards guarding the entrance look at each other dumbfounded and the drone froze in place looking paralyzed. Silviera makes an exhausting breath before turning to Silvus who is wondering what is going on.

"Meet me at the war room. I am going have to deal with my son here and collect my brother along the way," Silviera demands, turning her gaze to the scout.

"But m'lady?" The scout tries to explain the urgency, but the Beta-Lady insists he wait in the war room. With a bow, the scout runs up to the eastern arch stairs to head to the war room as instructed.

Silviera walks up to Silvus, placing her two claws on his shoulders with a disappointed face. "As much as I want to continue the story, it looks like I have an urgent matter to take care of, so go back to your quarters and study for your final even though I know for sure you will pass it, okay?"

Silvus, shocked by what happened in front of him, wants to say something, but he nods, looking uneasy, and heads back to his bedroom, leaving his worried mother behind.

It is almost nightfall. Silvus tries to sleep in his queen-sized bed, but he can't, and his eyes are still open, looking up at the ceiling. He tries to think about passing the test, but what worries him is how his mother and uncle were acting. It wasn't only his family; he heard talk from the staff about the problems the kingdom is facing, as if it is the end of the world. All because the Alpha-King suddenly died without an heir.

Suddenly he hears footsteps from the door, along with a voice of his uncle. "I bet it has something to do with Monchester. You did tell me the scout came from the southern encampment, right?"

"Correct, dear brother. I fear something terrible might have happened at the border. We'd better head to the war room; I ordered the scout to meet us there," the voice of his mother speaks back.

As he listens, Silvus leans his head back on the pillow and slowly closes his eyes to sleep early, hoping whatever the news is, it can be resolved soon.

Chapter 3
A Testing Moment

As the sun rises above the white stone city of Athera, Silvus wears his monastery robe along with a bag filled with writing supplies to prepare for his special day. After one whole month of studying, he is confident that he will pass the exam and become an official Mistcaster.

Leaving the private quarters hall, he enters the throne room to see it more brightly lit thanks to the sun's rays shining through the mosaic glass windows. The shine gives him a good positive feeling about the test, as if the spirits themselves are giving him a sign. He climbs down the stairs to approach the large iron doors being opened by the two guards nearby. Now in the flower-filled courtyard, Silvus approaches the castle gates until a voice calls out to him. Silvus turns his head to see his mother approach him with a smile, along with Orezyme and her bodyguard carrying a big spear with a shady expression.

"Attempting to go to the big day without us wishing you luck, Silvus?" His uncle Orezyme speaks with his claws behind his back, looking stiff.

"Guess I got a bit too excited." Silvus scratches the back of his head and looks to see that his cousin is not around. "Where is Ico?" he asks.

"Probably still sleeping late, as usual," Orezyme complains, and shrugs, "but that is my son being my son, however annoying he could be."

Silviera gives a quick laugh before speaking to her son. "My dear only son, listen to me. I want you to know that whether you pass this exam or not, just know we will always be supportive of you; however, if you do pass, we are going to start with your training to become the next Beta-Lord." She explains as Orezyme behind her whispers something in his snout, catching Silvus' attention for a bit. He could have sworn his uncle whispered, "If we survive another day" with a hint of fear in his voice. He decides to ignore it for now, as he needs to keep a positive attitude if he wants to pass the final exam.

"Thanks, Mom, but I know for sure I am going to pass this test. I've been studying since it was first announced! When I pass, I will use my abilities to be the best Beta-Lord of Maglo I can be!" Silvus boasts, full of excitement.

Silviera walks up to him to give him a big hug, and Silvus hugs her back in return. As the mother and son have their moment, the latter decides to give her blessing.

"May the spirits help you succeed, my son."

"Same with you, Mother," Silvus replies back as he starts to hear a bell ring, alerting him that the Maglo Monastery is opening. Not wanting to be late, Silvus breaks off the hug and tells his mother and uncle that he has to go and waves as he leaves. Behind him, Silviera and Orezyme wave back, only for them to make worried faces knowing that the worst is yet to come.

"More like spirits have mercy on our souls," Orezyme whispers to Silviera.

Now in the Monastery district, located at the west part of the city, Silvus sees that the campus is crowded with students and teachers alike swarming into a large circular tower where all the final exams are going to take place. With a deep breath, the eager student proceeds into the main building to see a lot of guards patrolling around, keeping an eye out. He wonders if it has to do with the rumors going around. Makes sense that his mother would order a heavy guard presence.

Silvus shakes off the thought to continue through the crowd of students all the way to a big arching staircase with a big portrait of an old female Raptor with a plaque that reads "Vessel Avera." He climbs up all the way to the third floor where his classroom is located.

<hr />

Inside the auditorium-like classroom, fifty students sit around the rows of seats talking with each other. Silvus, sitting straight around the front row, keeps to himself to think about what he has studied for the exam. He hears a nearby door open gaining the attention of himself and the other students as an elderly brown male in a grey robe enters, pushing a cart filled with papers. The professor heads to the large desk belonging to him, places the cart right by it. The professor turns around looking just as excited as Silvus, who just sat to listen.

"Good morning, class! Today is the day that you all are going to be tested as to whether or not you will become official Mistcasters!" the professor announces in pure happiness.

While the other students make small whispers to each other, Silvus looks excited and eager to take the test. The professor in front explains the rules of the exam, like no looking at each other's papers, and those who finish the exam early uhjare not talk to the students who are still taking the exam. Once he is done, the professor takes out a big packet of fifty exams for fifty students with his levitation spell to pass them around quickly.

"Remember class, take the exam slow and steady. We have all day and if any of you fail, I will be eager to see you all next time, may the spirits guide you." The professor makes his final statement as the students receive their exams. Some students who read through the exam got nervous hinting that they did not study as hard. Silvus on the other claw made a big grin on how easy his test is. At least to him that is.

The exam that Silvus is taking are mostly essay questions and some multiple choice. For example, he has to name all six schools of MistCraft. First, He writes Elemental: the school that involves controlling the elements of fire, ice, and thunder. Gravitation: the school that involves bending gravity and physical forces. Illusionary: the school that involves bending one's mind. Life Mend: the school involving healing powers. Spirit Bind: the School that involves summoning guardian spirits and objects. And Enchanting: the school that involves creating enchantments, curses, and hexes.

Being very prepared, he prepares his writing quill and speeds through the exam without a sweat. He only pauses for one particular question. It reads:

"In a paragraph or more, explain Dark Mistcraft and why it is considered forbidden."

Silvus wonders if the professor is expecting future Casters to know about Dark Mistcraft. He thinks back in the defense against the evil arts class when a teacher would give a big lecture about Dark Mist. Ironically, his mother told him about it yesterday in a story. So he just wrote his answer in two paragraphs with his quill pen. In one paragraph, he writes that Dark Mistcraft is an evil source of power from the Evil spirits in one's heart. The other writes that using Dark

Mistcraft not only corrupts the soul of a Raptor but also turns into a monstrosity.

Finishing the exam in thirty minutes, he is the first to turn in his test to the professor, as always. Some students who notice made small grunts in annoyance as the professor is not a bit surprised that Silvus, whom he considers his best student, finished the final exam first.

"First to finish as always, young Silvus? You should look over your test," the professor advises, but Silvus assures him that he did great and goes back to his seat.

The professor immediately grades Silvus' exam and as expected, he passes it with a perfect score. He gets off his seat to his cart to search through a list of files for each student. The files are test records that the students have completed. One file in particular belongs to Silvus.

Silvus, sitting in front, watches the professor, looking a bit nervous. He sees him look around his test scores one by one for all the years he has been in school.

The professor gets off from his desk to announce, "Attention, class, I am going to head to the top floor for an important matter, so if any of you are done, place your papers on my desk. As for you, Silvus, come with me." He points at Silvus, freaking him out.

Silvus wounders why he would want him to follow him. Is he in trouble? Did he fail his exam for the first time? Whatever the truth is, he does as he is told and follows the professor.

⸻ ◆ ⸻

The top floor is a big lobby shaped like a half circle with a big wooden door in front. The professor stops his tracks to tell Silvus to wait for him outside as he enters through the doors. To pass the time, Silvus gazes up the ceiling, which is painted black with white stars. The brightest star painted on the ceiling is believed to be the very first spirit that created the universe and planted the wellsprings across the kingdom. That is what the legends say.

Silvus' thoughts are interrupted by the pair of doors opening by the professor, who peeps his head out, telling Silvus to come in. The curious student walks in to be greeted by a room lightly dimmed by blue flames on the walls. In the room, he sees a row of seven fig-ures wearing robes lined up across the half circle on separate circular platforms. Behind him, two armored knights close the doors as four more knights come out of the shadows from the sides.

"Are you Vessel Silvus?" The center figure in a hologram-like state speaks with a voice of an elder male.

Silvus nervously nods yes. His nervousness is due to knowing who they are: the most respected Mistacasters to ever live, and over-seers of Monastery.

"Step forward!" commands the head figure, making Silvus walk forward as commanded. When he steps into the center mosaic floor with a picture of a big star, he is commanded to stop and kneel on one knee.

"I assume you know who we are?" the figure asks.

"Yes, Lord Sage, you are all the legendary Mistatorium, the coun-cil of seven of the best Mistcasters of all the kingdom who oversee all practice of Mistcraft, my lord," Silvus formally explains to them.

"Do you know why you are here?"

"No, sir, but I had thought that I was in trouble."

The seven members of the council looked at each other as if Silvus had another head and whisper to each other. They assure him that he is not in trouble, as they want to tell him about an important matter.

"To start, young Silvus, you have perfectly passed the final exam," the head one explains, making Silvus beam up with a satisfied sigh, only for the head figure to tell him, "Don't get too comfy yet, as we have some questions."

"What do you mean?" Silvus asked

"Since the day you enrolled, the professors have been informing us that you managed to learn Mistcraft at a rapid pace. You even managed to pass every exam that was given to you!"

The figure's voice sounded neither critical nor appeasing but had a tone of hopeful praise. Silvus couldn't help but make a nervous chuckle and twiddled his talons like thumbs.

"What can I say, Arch-Sage; I just like learning Mistcraft and reading my books." Silvus shrugs his arms.

"I am surprised that you did not notice your uniqueness. According to legends, one family posed that same unique gift to learn Mistcraft without much training like a real master. Curious." The leader, the arch-sage, scratches his chin.

"We the Mistatorium shall look into this matter, but regardless, I want to be the first to say congratulations on passing your exam; however, there is one more test we reserve for special Raptors like yourself."

Silvus makes a nervous gulp as he listens to what the final test is. The arch-sage commands him to step back away from the center. In the center a hole opens up, followed by a pedestal rising up with an orb.

"This orb that you see here has the ability to transport your soul into the netherworld, where you must confront an evil spirit! Touch it when you are ready, young one, and the final test shall begin!" the arch-sage explained.

"What will happen if I fail?" Silvus asks, looking more nervous.

"We will simply pull you out from the realm in disappointment. You will not be allowed to perform Mistcraft ever," the arch-sage answers with a serious tone

Silvus walks up to the orb on the pedestal and gazes around it.

He wonders what it is supposed to do when he touches it. Whatever the final test is, he can only pray that he will be ready. He grabs it with two claws and waits for something to happen. He is about to ask until the orb starts flashing in front of him, blinding him with bright light in the process.

Silvus slowly opens up his eyes to see that he is lying on black, rocky ground. He gets back up onto his two talon feet and checks himself to see that he still is wearing his uniform, thank the spirits. He looks around to see that he is in some kind of wastleland with tons of black horrifiying towers that surround him. The sky above is colored bright red, instead of blue with clouds that thunder.

Silvus starts to walk along the narrow path to see statues of Raptors in agony. *Is this the netherworld?* Silvus thinks to himself. The strange realm indeed fits the description of the mysterious netherworld that he has heard about. From a distance on the path, he sees a big black castle of some sort, probably made for the lord of the realm.

He hears a demonic voice call out to him, making him turn around to see a clone of himself, except his eyes are serpent red, indicating that he is evil. Looking at him with an evil grin, the fake Silvus begin to walk forward. making the real Silvus walk back in fear.

"Don't be shy; I came here to see you! It's been awhile since we had any guests in this realm." The fake Silvus speaks with mockery in his demonic voice. "Maybe we need to be somewhere private." Evil Silvus snaps his claw, followed by a flash, making a boom sound, teleporting them on top on one of the evil towers.

"This is the netherworld, is it?!" Silvus demands as he tries to regain his balance after teleporting.

"Smart one, aren't ya?" Evil Silvus speaks from behind, making his good twin turn to see him walk slowly. Evil Silvus explains to him that the trillions of towers that he sees is a private sanctuary housing all the evil spirits, as the head evil spirit is inside the lone big castle to oversee all evil within the realm.

"So the towers are more like eternal prisons," Silvus describes, making his evil spirit clutch his heart like a drama queen.

"Ouch, that hurts so much—but to explain further, this tower that we are on is not just any tower." He begins to walk up to Silvus, keeping his sinister smile on his face "This is my personal tower, as I am not just any evil spirit that your kind describe me as."

The evil spirit looks right into Silvus' eyes to say, "I am your evil spirit, and I have a proposition for you!"

Silvus steps back with a glare. "What deal can you give me?! It's not like there is big price for it?!" he demands, knowing about trickery from the evil spirits. Silvus' evil spirit only laughs in return.

"Kid, you want to learn Mistcraft in order to become the best Beta-Lord, right? What if I say I could grant you Dark Mistcraft in order for you to pursue that dream that you desire?!" it further tempts, keeping his smile on.

"I think I'm doing pretty well without the forbidden art, wouldn't you say?" Silvus retorts, folding his arms and looking confident as he gets over his fear of the evil spirit.

The evil spirit is now starting to look angry at the mortal's petty defiance. It tries to find a way to get him to accept the evil gift. "True, but the gift could grant you your claw back! And more importantly, it could bring you to your father! Don't you want know who your father is?"

Silvus flinches at the question about his father. The evil spirit thinks it got him, so he pries further. "Isn't it sad to grow up without knowing who your father is? I wonder if your father is a useless drunk or a snobbish noble. There is only one way to find out."

Silvus thinks back to his hatchlinghood. It is easy to think about his life without a father, and only for him to think about a certain uncle who is like a father figure to him. Having an uncle as a father figure blessed him with two first cousins whom he would consider to be own siblings he would never have. If his real father was still alive, his mother probably loved him enough for him exist at all. A flash booms in between him and the evil spirit to see a white glowing figure with his hood up. The figure looks at the evil spirit with a glare. "WHAT YOU DOING HERE SPIRIT?!" the evil spirit demands.

The third guest, the good spirit, looks at a shocked Silvus with a smile, ignoring the evil spirit's demand. "You might not know who I am, young Silvus, but I am here to tell you that your father is way more special than you think! He watches over you from the heavens, guiding you through your own blood."

Silvus gazes at the spirit whose voice had a sound of a trust-worthy male. The spirit's face had a smile on its silver face with an eye color identical to his. The evil spirit tried to pounce at him for interfering only for it to be hit by an invisible wall.

Suddenly Silvus sees himself beginning to fade, as his time in the world is up. He looks back at the spirit with worry. "Wait! Please tell me who you are?!"

The spirit only looks down to explain, "Just know that I will always be with you, guiding you and your family even in death. Just promise me to always be on guard against any temptations of the influence of evil and also...take care of your mother?"

Silvus does not know what to think at this point. After he fades, the spirit, with a tear leaking through his eye, sayd, "Spirits guide you and your family, my son," and he flashes back to the heavens where he belongs, leaving the evil spirit unconscious on the ground.

Chapter 4
An Orca-Colored Maiden

S ilvus wakes up on a wood-trimmed bed to see that he is now inside an infirmary filled with various healers treating other patients. He slowly sits up, thinking about his experience in the Netherworld—the evil spirit that tried to tempt him to accept Dark Mist and the good spirit that appeared out of nowhere to save him from its influence. A middle-aged female voice calls out to him from the right side: "You're awake; we were worried that you weren't going to make it."

Silvus looks to his side to see a burgundy female wearing a purple cloak looking at him, sitting on a stool, at the same time holding a pocket watch with her tail. She is Headmistress Clara. A Headmaster or Mistress are caretakers appointed by a member of the Mistatorium to oversee a Monastery chapter spread across the kingdom.

"We have been watching you during your final test, even though the appearance of an actual spirit was not part of it. But again, you managed to resist the temptation. I say congratulations, young one; you passed."

"REALLY!" Silvus shouts in glee, hearing that he had passed the very thing he had been studying for. Clara in response makes small chuckles, like a kindly old lady who saw her own grandchild doing something special.

"Ho ho ho, of course, young one, but you are going have to wait till next moon for your license to arrive so we can have a proper ceremony." The female explains, "I advise you to rest for a few more minutes, then maybe have some fresh air while you are at it? Folks don't call me Headmistress Clara for nothing."

Clara gets off her stool and turns around for Silvus to see her long orange mane tied up in a ponytail as she walks out of the infirmary. Silvus lies back on his bed with a smile to embrace his success. All the years of studying have finally paid off for him. He remembers of course that his mother told him that the next step is to train to become Beta-Lord.

— ◆ —

After his rest, Silvus pays a visit to the market district located near the city entrance in order to find a place to relax for the rest of the day. Walking through the white stone streets and buildings resembling pointed towers and domes, he sees more guards are patrolling around the district, keeping an eye out for anything suspicious. He could only guess that, like the Monastery, his mother might have ordered more guards due to what might have happened last night. The other Raptor residents, on the other claw, keep to themselves in fear, hoping nothing bad is going to happen. He can't say he blames them though. Like them, he keept to himself, and approaches a local tavern, resembling a mid-sized dome.

The tavern proves to be perfect for Silvus to get a cup of tea for himself. For a tavern, the inside is best described as a nice clean circular stone room, with the bartenders in the middle serving drinks to the guests. He sits in a table with a bench chair to read a book about spirits to learn more about them. He reads through the book until he hears a young female voice.

"Excuse me? May I sit with you?"

Silvus looks up to the side and blushes at the sight of a nicely cloaked female looking at him with a cute smile on her snout, gazing at him with her white serpent eyes. Looking at her scale color, he sees that she is mainly black, with white patches like an orca. Her white mane almost resembles his mother's, only a bit shorter. Scanning to her busty chest he sees a strange-looking green amulet with a serpent eye in the middle, which he finds odd.

The female makes a cute giggle as if she enjoys him checking her out, followed by, "Well, can I?"

Silvus breaks his trance and nervously lets the new female sit in front of him. As she sits, the female moves her tail beside her, sticking it inside the table.

"You should move your tail inside as well. Don't wanna have it stepped on, do you?" the female advises him, tilting her head like a curious puppy.

Silvus looks around the tavern to see her point. It is filled with lots of guests having a good time, way overboard, like an Olympadonian. One middle-aged male got drunk and accidently stepped on a nearby tail, making the other male jump off from his chair in pain. The other yet older male, who looks more muscular, glares at the drunk with a threatening hiss and began beating him up, causing the other nearby males and some females to cheer on. Silvus only ignores the commotion as he takes the young female's advice and moves his tail into the table to avoid being stepped on.

"My name is Ocia, by the way, and by looking at your robes and book about spirits, are you a Mistcaster?" Ocia asks him, looking interested.

"I am about to graduate from the Maglo chapter of Monastery, so yeah, starting tomorrow I am going to get my license delivered to me by the Mistatorium!" Silvus replies with enthusiasm, which Ocia seems to find cute.

"That is amazing! It must be very hard to study there. I heard it takes a lot reading to do so!"

"My experience there was actually very easy," Silvus calmly retorts
"How so?" she asks.

Silvus explains to her how since he was young, he has managed to learn Mistcraft very easily, passing every test laid out to him. Ocia is a bit amazed yet skeptical at the same time. Silvus further tells her that learned about it from the Mistatorium themselves before giving him the final test which piques Ocia's interest.

"What was the final test?" She leans forward and puts her claws under her chin to listen.

Silvus, with all his knowledge, tells her that he had to face an evil spirit who looks like him and tried to tempt him to perform Dark Mistcraft, which scares Ocia a bit, only for her to calm down as the latter assures her that he did not take the bait. What gets more interesting to her is when he mentions a spirit coming in between them and saved him.

"What did the spirit look like?!" she asks him now eagerly; she wants to know about the spirits themselves.

"He had a glow around him and wore white robes. I could not see his face, as he kept his hood up. Facing a spirit for the first time is the reason why I have this book here, in order to learn more about them!" Silvus lifts up his book with his gloved claw.

Ocia sees his gloved claw with a gasp and points at it.

"Forgive my sudden change in topic, but what's with the glove you are wearing on your left claw but not the right?"

Silvus looks at his gloved claw that she is referring too. He puts his book down on the table and holds his glove claw with his free right. As much as he wants to tell her about a certain accident with a spell, he has just met her. He worries what she will think of him if she knows.

"I am not comfortable in telling you that yet," Silvus tells her with hint of pain in his voice.

Ocia in return feels bad that she might have poked up a sensitive topic too personal to him. Silvus, now looking a bit better, stares back and asks if she is a student of Monastery.

"Me, a student of Monastery?" She points to herself. "I would love to be a student, but I come from another Betadom. There is a chapter there, but my brother suggested private tutoring from an official Mistcaster, though."

"What Betadom are you from? Did your brother not trust Monastery?" Silvus asks, now very curious to know some things about her.

"My brother told me not tell any Raptor where I am from, but I don't know why." Ocia shrugs. "But I myself want to learn Mistcraft in order to learn its history. So I begged my brother to at least hire an official member of the Mistatorium to come tutor me in order for me to get a license without leaving his presence. Very overprotective, I say," she further explains with a huff.

"What about your parents?" Silvus asks her, looking interested.

"My mother died when I was still an egg and my father passed away just recently, so my older brother took up the role to protect me. And one day I was reading one of my own books--"

Ocia gets cut off by the sound of a window getting shattered by a Raptor being thrown. The pair turn around to see the crowd gathering around the shattered window to see if the Raptor is okay.

"Wanna get out of here and maybe walk outside somewhere more quiet?" Silvus asks her, and she agrees, so the two get off their table and pays for the Tea.

Leaving the tavern, the pair leave they noticed a large gathering of Raptors, who are mostly omega castes, gathering in a big circle, listening to a young male standing in front of a statue of the founder of the Betadom, rambling anti-Mistatorium rhetoric.

"OPEN YOUR EYES, CITIZENS OF MAGLO! THE MISTATORIUM ARE PLOTTING TO TAKE OVER OUR LIVES! THEY ARE OBVIOUSLY THE ONES WHO KILLED THE ALPHA-KING TO SEIZE POWER FOR THEMSELVES! THE SUPPOSED BANDIT ATTACKS APPEARS OUT OF NOWHERE AND THE ROYAL ARMY DO NOTHING! DOSENT THAT MAKE YOU SUSPCIOUS? THOSE BANDITS ARE REALLY MERCENARIES HIRED BY HOSE CORRUPT FOOLS IN ORDER TO DISCRACT US!"

Some members of the crowd cheered in agreement with him. Silvus, on the other claw, fees disgusted at the ramblings. In his heart, he knows the Mistatorium were not to blame. He cannot not help but clench his claws, wanting to step up. He is so mad, sparks of electricity burst out both his claws.

"It so sad to see so many buy into crazy rumors in a time like this." Silvus hears Ocia state her concern as she holds his free claw and looks at him with sympathetic eyes. "Their fears could be justified, as according to royal law, the Mistatorium takes over as regent during an Alpha-King's absence. The only time that ever happened was when Alpha-Queen Ultamar Ciri III died with only one son too young for the throne, so the Mistatorium stepped up until the heir was ready. But the death of Ultamar Sulthur with no heir?! It never happened before!"

Silvus is surprised by Ocia's great knowledge of history. He wonders if history is her specialty. Not wanting to be around anymore, Silvus decides to take her somewhere else as long they don't have to listen to the rubbish fool.

In the quiet park area located in the East Delta district, Silvus and Ocia learn more about each other. For example, Silvus learns that Ocia loves to read as much as he does. As he suspected, her favorite subject is history. To him, it is beneficial, due to the fact he knows some history himself. She tells him that she reads a lot back home in her own private library, making Silvus perk up in excitement. As the pair speak more, it seems like they really enjoy each other's company due to having so many interests in common.

Each time Silvus gives a lecture about what he knows about Mistcraft, Ocia always listens to him, especially when he talks about history, like the origins of the wellsprings. In return, Ocia also gives him lectures that interest him a lot, like what she tells him about the royal Beta families, which intrigue him. The residents who notice them give stares, debating whether they are actually dating or simply tutoring each other.

"You know, you seem to be the only Raptor I have met with silver scales?" Ocia asks out of nowhere.

"Really?" Silvus looks around the park to see all the Raptors in different colors. None of them are silver like him. He never really thought about it since meeting up with Ocia. Thinking back to his own family, his mother, his cousins, and his uncle are all teal colored with different shades, except for him. From a nearby fountain he looks at his reflection while Ocia follows suit. Silvus looks at his reflection, now thinking about it.

"You know, I never really questioned about it." He turns to her. "I think my scale color might have been inherited from whoever my father is."

"What do you mean by 'whoever your father is'? Don't you know him?" Ocia asks him, very surprised he questioned who his father was.

"I never met my father, so my mother raised me alone, growing up with my uncle's help. He treats me like another son to him," Silvus explains, calming Ocia, who is still a bit uneasy. Then she snaps up as if she has an idea.

"Were you around when the Alpha-King died?" she asks, rising up on tiptoe to look Silvus directly in his blue eyes.

"My mother told me I was still an egg in her womb not laid yet when he died--why?" Silvus answers, dumbfounded at Ocia's sudden outburst. Ocia turns around back in normal stance, thinking to herself until a male authority's voice calls out, "My lord!"

The two turn their heads to see a pair of guards with a carriage attached to a Stego (Stegosuarus).

"Your mother is calling out for you, First-Delta. She said it is urgent," the guard commands.

"First-Delta?" Ocia turns her head, facing Silvus. "You did not tell me you are a noble!"

"That did not come to mind. I hoped to tell you a bit sooner, but it seems the guards beat me to it." Silvus struggles with explaining, scratching the back of his head. "It was nice meeting you. I really enjoyed your company, but I better head to my mother. She is the Beta-Lady here."

Silvus starts to head to the carriage but Ocia stops him. "Wait! I just realized I never got your name."

"Oh, right!" Silvus bops his forehead. "My name is Vessel Silvus, but call me Silvus; Vessel is my clan name."

Ocia giggles, with her cheecks turning red, and walks up to him to whisper, "Can you keep a secret?"

Silvus whispers sure as Ocia goes on. "I know I told you that my brother told me not to tell, but I am from the Monchester Betadom so if you ever wanna come see me again, I will be in Rookingrad. I really enjoyed being with you, too."

As the two are saying their goodbyes, the guards by the carriage are getting impatient.

"Looks like our young lord has already claimed a future wife," one guard states, earning him smack in the back by the other guard.

"Don't be such a smart-aleck, wise guy. They probably just met each other, so don't get your hopes up," the other guard scolds as Silvus began to approach them.

"Let's go see what my mother needs of me," Silvus commands as he get into the carriage.

While the two guards climb up into the carriage, Silvus peeps through the window to see Ocia one last time as she waves back to him with a wink, making Silvus feel his heart race. He leans back with his arms behind his head while the carriage begins to move, heading to the Beta's palace.

Chapter 5
The Last Party

As he is being escorted back into the castle, Silvus cannot help thinking about the girl-Raptor Ocia. Never in his life did he think he would ever find a girl-Raptor who took a lot of interest in him. Remembering his times in the Monastery, he tried talking to other female Raptors, but all they did was break conversation with him, even if he stayed on topic or didn't lecture, which annoyed the tail feathers out of him. Not Ocia, though. Unlike many others, Ocia actually listened to him and did not at some point try to shut him up or make any attempt to break the conversation. What she did though was kept on talking to him, and he liked it.

Another train of thought Silvus has in his mind is the strange amulet that Ocia wore around her neck. He remembers during their supposed date, the amulet would glow bright green as if it were enchanted by Mist. If he remembers correctly, under the Mist school of Enchanting, a Mistcaster could enchant an object to do almost anything. His thoughts are interrupted by the movement of the carriage stopping, making him wobble a bit. One of the two guards on the carriage gets down from his seat to open Silvus' carriage door.

"We are here back in the front courtyard, my lord. I must escort you to your mother at once!"

The guard speaks with a voice of authority. It makes Silvus worried, and he wonders if something bad might have happened.

"Is my mother okay?" he asks the guard in front of him.

"Lady Beta is doing absolutely fine in this glorious hour."

The guard's tone of voice switches from being serious to excitement. In relief, Silvus climbs down from his carriage to be escorted by the guards leading him into the castle.

———⟫⟪⟨◊⟩⟫⟪———

Back in the throne room, no Raptor seems to be present except for the guards at their posts, with one blocking each stairway and two lower doors on each side. He is escorted to one wooden door located on the wall next to the wellspring, which is supposed to lead to the back courtyard. The guard then orders Silvus to wait as he walks through the door, leaving Silvus alone in the throne room.

To pass time, Silvus walks toward his mother's pearl stone throne placed in front of the wellspring. As the future Beta-Lord, he knows that he will sit on it one day to help his citizens within the Betadom. With curiosity, the new young Mistcaster walks further and hops onto it. Due to the blue leather cushions on both the seat and the back rest, it is very comfy. He looks up, gazing at the luxurious ceiling, lying back on the throne, and closes his eyes to daydream about himself as the new Beta-Lord.

———⟫⟪⟨◊⟩⟫⟪———

In his dream, Silvus imagines himself as an older male Raptor, dressed in robes almost fit for a ruler, wearing his Beta-Lord crown. In front of him is a line of citizens coming for weakly pensions. The first one is a male Delta caste, escorting a young female with her hood up.

"Lord Beta, for what you have done for your Betadom, I traveled from Monchester to give you my sister in marriage."

The Delta tells the maiden to put down her hood and she complies to reveal the familiar beautiful she-Raptor, Ocia. Silvus comes down from his throne to walk toward her to give her claw a kiss, like a gentle male. Dream Ocia giggles with blush in her checks as she walks toward him seductively.

"My dear Silvus, I would be honored to be your wedded wife, if you accept?"

Dream Silvus wraps his arms around dream Ocia, full of confidence. With a smile on his face, he is about to give his answer when the entrance doors burst open, interrupting him with a guard running in, shouting, "My lord, wake UP!"

⸻◉⸻

Silvus wakes back up from his daydream, freaking out as he looks side to side as if he heard a ghost screech at him. To his right, he sees a guard right next to him. "My lord, come with me to back courtyard," the guard commands, still standing.

Gazing around one more time, Silvus gets off his throne to follow the guard to the back courtyard to be greeted by a large crowd of Raptors gathered in the middle to shout, "SURPRISE!"

Silvus is taken aback by the sight of a nicely decorated back courtyard that blends well with the flora present. Tables with food are set up, a platform with a band prepares to perform, and most of the crowd are various nobles from across the kingdom. They probably want to try to make connections with him. He is the future Beta-Lord of Maglo, after all, so it makes sense that Deltas and

Betas would come and try to appease him. Among the crowd, his mother Silveria walks up with a joyful expression.

"Is this party for me?" Silvus asks her, still looking surprised as one of the guards behind him snickers at such an obvious question.

"Oh, Silvus, watching how dedicated you are, I knew in my heart you would succeed, which is why I organized this party for you," his mother explains as she looks down, looking sad. "You are just like your father," she whispers.

Silvus feels himself blush. His heart warms at the feeling of being compared to his father, whoever he is. Growing up, he always wanted to ask her who he was, but when he did, she would make ways to dodge every question. He is going to ask about who his father is again, until a familiar voice of a certain cousin comes into play.

"Are you guys just going to stand there, or can we get this party started?" Ico shouts out, earning a smack from behind from his father Orezyme.

⸺⸻◈⸻⸺

During the party, most of the guests speak to each other, dance to the music being played by the band, or eat snacks from the tables. The hatchlings who were brought around played with each other--childish games. Silvus, on the other claw, stands around looking at the crowd, hoping to see familiar faces. Most of the crowd, as he guesses, are nobles looking all snobby. The males wear fancy scarves and the females wear short cloaks, jewelry, or both. From behind, a pair of claws grabs him, making him do a small flinch.

"Did you miss me, Silvy?" a young female voice asks from behind. He turns around to see a familiar teal-colored female with semi-long blue mane, wearing a purple Tricia Cloak with a necklace made of seashells wrapped around her neck. It was Vessel Sulphie, his cousin—or Sidon Sulphie now, since she is married to a higher-ranking noble male.

"OH MY GOSH! Sulphie!"

Silvus is going to hug her back, but she raises her arms, telling him to stop. With a confused face, he makes a few steps backwards with claws raised. It is not like her to refuse hugs from him. He continues to scan around her pale silvery eyes that are looking at him guarded until she speaks with a hushed tone.

"Don't take this the wrong way! I have…a special condition to tell Father, so will you mind being gentle?" Sulphie speaks in a voice with small hint of nervousness.

Silvus curiously tilts his head owl-like, wondering what she is talking about. He gets worried that something happened to her health. So he asks her if she is okay. Sulphie starts to look uneasy when he asks. She grabs Silvus by his ungloved claw to take him to a corner of the courtyard to be out of earshot. With both cousins hidden by a post, Sulphie takes a deep breath so she can spill the news.

"Dear cousin, I'm gravid." Sulphie speaks quitely as she places her claws onto her torso to reveal her bulging belly.

"Sulphie…. That's amazing!" Silvus exclaims as Sulphie grabs his snout, making a hush sound. Silvus apologizes with a blush of embarrassment, making a toothy smile.

"Yes, Silvus, I am so excited and nervous at the same time to become a mother. I mean, it's my first time!" Sulphie begins to freak out like a worrywart. He stops her by placing his claws on her shoulders gently. He looks around the party, scanning for someone he might know.

"Where is your husband, the father of your eggs? I'd thought he be happy to be here!" he asks.

"I'm afraid he could not make it due to the tons of bandit activity lately back in Tricia. You know as Beta-Lord it is his job to look after the Raptors who lives in his Betadom on behalf of the Alpha-King," Sulphie replies with an annoyed huff, implying that something else is going on. Silvus sighs in disappointment. He was looking forward to see the Beta-Lord of Tricia.

"HEY GUYS, WHY AREN'T YOU HAVING A GOOD TIME?!"

The two cousins turn to see Ico approaching them with two young females who are giggling in his arms. Turns out he has been flirting with girls. Silvus cannot help but move his eyes side to side while Sulphie facepalms in embarrassment. The two older cousins also think to themselves that Ico's immaturity is the reason why he does not have many friends.

"You have not changed a bit, have you, little brother?" Sulphie sternly asks, placing her claws to her hips.

"Change? Oh, please; the only thing I see changed is your weight problem, BIG sis. Hahaha!"

Sulphie snaps at Ico's immature insult with a hiss, causing the females to run off in fear. Ico begins to walk back with a nervous grin as Sulphie slowly stomps up toward him with an angry look. Silvus is like, *Oh boy,* knowing that a big rule is to never insult a gravid female due to sensitive mood swings. To prevent further trouble, he moves in front of Sulphie and points with his two claws into her eyes making them glow greenish-yellow.

As Sulphie stares at Silvus' finger claws, she start to get a bit sleepy. "Relax," Silvus commands, calming his older cousin back to sanity. He turns around to face Ico with a glare and whispers, "You owe me big time!"

Ico, now looking guilty, walks up to his sister to say sorry. Sulphie accepts his apology a bit reluctantly, knowing that he is still immature.

"Well then, male of the hour. Now that you are an official Mistcaster, can you show us some cool tricks you learned, like that calming spell you just did?" Ico asks, turning his attention to Silvus.

"Why, yes! You gotta show us some cool spells you learned! Please?" Sulphie states in glee, holding her claws together.

Nodding with a smile, Silvus aggress to show them a spell he learned. He raises his right claw and it starts to get wrapped around by misty ice like a blanket. Then he moves his claw slowly in a circular position, causing the mist to form a big ball of ice, only for it to morph into a spike, and grabs it.

"This spell is called the ice spear!" Silvus explains and throws it up into the night sky, thanks to the back courtyard lacking a roof. Sulphie is amazed, but Ico only has a smirk in his face.

"Is that all you got? Show us a more awesome spell," he dares his cousin.

Silvus thinks about what spell to perform next as he taps his chin without realizing the guests are slowly approaching him eager to see after noticing the ice spear spell. Among the crowd are three hatchlings, two males and one adorable female, looking at him. The little female walks up to him and tugs his robe to get his attention.

Silvus turns around and looks down to see the little girl-Raptor in a cloak with a bow on her head holding her teddy-Rex in her arms. "Can you make a flower out of thin air?" she asks. He looks up to see the guests looking at him. They are probably wondering how he is going to responed due to rumors about how good with hatchlings he is.

Looking at the noble girl-Raptor on one knee he tells her, "I am afraid there is no such spell, but--" Silvus looks around to see a damaged candle bulb on a pot. He lifts his gloved claw to use telekinesis to bring it closer, making the crowd gasp in awe.

The pot flies into his claw and shows it to the girl-Raptor and asks her, "Do you know what this is, young lady?"

The girl Raptor scans the potted flower, wondering why he asks her.

"It's a candle bulb, and I think it looks hurt!" she answers with worry in her voice.

Silvus then points at it with his right claw and a white glow shines around the talon and gently touches the flower, making it glow, healing it good as new. Being healed, the candle bulb opens up to blooms with glitter around it. The girl Raptor and the crowd are amazed that he used a healing spell on the flower.

"That is the healing touch. It can heal any living thing as long it is still alive," Silvus explains as he gives the potted flower to the girl-Raptor, making her happy. She is so happy she latches him into a hug, making him blush as the crowd makes an "aww" sound with warmed hearts. Behind him, Silvus can hear Sulphie squee at his kindness as Ico makes a snickering sound.

———※———

From a distance, Silveria watches her son get swarmed by the guests hoping to have a chance to know him along with Orezyme, her bodyguard, and a hologram of the arch-sage.

"I am more surprised you are having a party at a time like this!"

Silveria turns her head around to see two noble Raptors with bodyguards wearing different colored capes and cloaks. One is the Beta-Lady of Sherrasic, who is a curvy, light-blue female dressed in a green cloak. The other is the Beta-Lord of Cretson, a slightly overweight golden male with a red fur-trimmend scarf and a puffy hat on his head. The two Betas are giving the old Beta of Maglo concerned looks about her decision to have a party.

"I believe my son deserves to have some enjoyment before the inevitable happens." Silveria defends her decision. Not that she is ignoring what is going on, but she is trying not to drag him into it.

"Dear Silveria, does the young chap even know what going on

behind the scenes around us?" the jolly Beta-Lord of Creston asks, sounding like an artist performing a play.

"I have to agree with Beta-Lord Davinchio Shakespear. I fear that one day you will regret not telling yer hatchling!" the Beta-Lady of Sherrasic says in a sailor accent, sternly crossing her arms and tapping her talon foot.

Silveria looks at her brother, who shrugs, and the arch-sage, who just floats. She looks back at the Betas so she cab explain by stating, "It's not that simple, I'm afraid."

The Betas exchange looks than back at her now, wanting to know what she means.

Silvus now sits on a chair to tell stories to a gathering of hatchlings who seem to be very interested. The grown ups are also intrigued as they stand listening. The two cousins, Sulphie and Ico, also pull chairs to sit between him.

"And then the Alpha-Prince defeated the evil Dark Mistcaster and brought peace to the entire kingdom!" Silvus finishes his short story. The crowd in front gives him applause. The hatchlings sitting in front of him start begging for him to tell them another story.

As Silvus tries to think of another story, he spots his mother having a conversation with the other two Betas present. The only Betas missing are from Monchester and Tricia. The way she spoke makes him worry that something bad is about to happen. He is aware of what is going on, and his mother did not need to tell him otherwise. His train of thought gets interrupted by his robe being tugged.

"Mr. Silvus? Are you okay?" the same girl-Raptor who is now sitting on his lap asks with a nervous tone.

Silvus snaps back to her frightened face as the crowd and the other hatchlings look at him with concern. Sulphie and Ico also give him concerned looks.

"Oh nothing, I just thought I saw something—so where was I? Oh yes!" So Silvus tells his stories for the rest of the night. It is the last peaceful night he will embrace before his unexpected adventure.

Chapter 6
After-Class Invasion

The party finally ends. Silvus makes his goodbyes to all the guests who were present. One by one each guest showers him with invitations to come visit them. Wanting to be an example, he politely states with a forced smile that he will consider it, as the guests leave through the entrance hall. After saying his goodbyes, he turns around in relief to see his mother Silviera standing behind him. She looks at him with a proud smile on her face, seeing how polite her son is to the guests.

"Starting to become popular, I see? It is always important to maintain the support from your subjects, both the Omega and the Delta. It is very important for a Beta to keep in touch with his or her subjects. Consider it part of your first lesson," Silviera excitedly states, waving her finger like a schoolteacher.

Silvus makes a big smile and poses as if he just got another A on his test by putting his talons on the sides of his torso. His tail even starts to wag slowly, as he is feeling very proud of himself from the comment made by his mother. Then he sees her expression change to a more serious one. He fixes his posture back to normal to listen with a face of confusion as he prepares to listen what she is going to say.

"When your subjects begin to recognize you as the Beta, they are going to expect you to take great care of them by solving different issues."

"What sort of issues?" Silvus asks her.

Silviera tells him to follow her to a better place to continue with the first lesson. She leads him to a dimly lighted yet spacious library.

Of all the rooms of the castle, the library is personally Silvus' favorite place, where he can just read any of the books placed in the sea of shelves. Remembering his hatchlinghood, he used to run into the wonderland of knowledge to spend time reading. Now he is with his mother lecturing him on the first lesson of being the Beta-Lord while sitting down on one of the two leather chairs that are placed in the middle.

"As Beta-Lord, you are to be expected to take care of your subjects in Maglo on behalf of the Alpha-King. Each day when you ever sit on the throne, you will be visited by many who seek your guidance, called petitions. When you receive petitions, it is up to you how you will deal with it, but remember! Whatever you decide will have an impact."

"What sort of impact? Can you give me an example of a petition?" Silvus asks with eagerness in his voice.

"Will do." Silviera sips some of her tea that is placed in front of them on the coffee table. Silvus gets himself comfortable and takes out parchment along with a quill pen from his carrier bag to take notes. She giggles, believing that intense note-taking is not necessary.

"Let's say around ninth hour of sunrise, an Omega folk comes into your throne room to complain about bandits, petitioning you to deal with them. After the request, you will make a decision. Will you send some guards to deal with them? Will you go yourself? Or will you dare ignore the request, which puts you at risk of upsetting the petitioner, which a Beta-Lord or Lady should not ever do. But because you are the Beta-Lord, your choices must not violate the royal law."

"So all I do is petitions? Sounds a bit easy," Silvus clarifies, sounding a bit disappointed by how boring the job sounded. His mother continues on with her lesson.

"It might look easy, but don't be fooled, as doing a request for one subject might upset another. For example, one Delta requests for you to approve ownership of a farm without knowing you just helped him or her steal property from another, tarnishing your reputation in the process. What I am saying is to be aware that many Raptors, regardless of caste, are mostly out for themselves and will not hesitate to exploit you."

Silvus makes a nervous gulp in his throat, with a chill going down his spine. Even for a good listener like himself, politics is definitely another world. He needs to get used to it, though, since he will be the new Beta-Lord one day. To imagine the idea of a simple Omega using him to gain power would be a nightmare.

With a yawn Silviera looks at a window to see how dark the sky is. She must have realized that it is late by the way she gasps.

"Oh dear! Look at the time! I am going to end this lecture for the day. So I need you to get some rest."

"Really, Mom? I was actually enjoying it!" Silvus sounds very excited, holding his collection of papers with notes in it. His mother looks surprised that her son has not gotten bored at all. Most hatchlings of his age mostly get bored very easily, to the point they would fall asleep. But not Silvus; he shows time and time again that he has a will of steel.

"Are you okay, Mother?" Silvus asks her with concern. Never has she stared at him so awkwardly. Breaking her gaze, she tells him it is nothing—only for her to levitate the chair behind her and sat on it. Her expression changes to concern.

"Silvus… during your time at Monastery, did anyone speak with you about your unique gifts?"

"My unique gifts?" Silvus starts to get suspicious. Never has his mother asked such a question. True, he remembers that during his time in Monastery, many students who knows him from his classes gave him awkward stares. Never once did they confront him about why. Then he remembers his meeting with the Mistatorium.

"Actually, Mother, after I did my exam, the professor took me to the Mistatorium and they told me that I have some unique ability to learn Mistcraft quickly like a master. Do you know about it?" Silvus sits up, with eagerness in his voice. His mother in front only takes a deep breath. He sees her turn her head to the side looking up at the ceiling with the sky painted above, avoiding the chandelier at the same time. The one thing the new Mistcaster can figure out is that his mother knows something, yet is very hesitant. He sees her slowly looking down with her eyes closed.

"In due time, I will tell you everything. But for now you need to rest up for the next day." His mother moves her head to him, looking very serious, even though her eyes are half open.

Silvus gets up from his chair and tells her that he understands, so he can walk out from the library to head to his bedroom. By the library entrance door, he turns his head to see his mother sitting in her chair by herself. She takes out the same pendant to gaze at it with a tear in her eye. The sight of his mother in a sorrowful state makes him worry. Not wanting to bother her, Silvus continues off to his bedroom.

———— ◆ ————

Silvus is still asleep despite the sunrise until a guard bursts into his room. He lifts himself up fast to see the guard by the door looking at him. The guard's expression lookeds as if he is being chased by a Tyranno (T-Rex) trying to eat him. Taking a few breaths, the guard explains with a salute, "FIRST DELTA! I HAVE BEEN ORDERED BY YOUR MOTHER TO COLLECT YOU NOW!"

"What's going on?! Is she okay?" Silvus demands as the guard just grabs him by the gloved claw and rushes him out of his room. As he is being dragged through the castle, Silvus can hear bells ringing in a pattern that means danger is approaching. He can even see all the drones panicking as the guards too are running out of the castle from the entrance.

———— ⋙⟨⟨◍⟩⟩⋘ ————

Rushing through the streets with the guard, Silvus sees the city folk of all castes being told by the other guards to remain in the buildings. Looking closely, he can sense fear on their faces, knowing that danger is ahead. He can even over hear some hatchlings asking their parents what is going on, looking scared. Whatever the danger is, it must be grim enough to start the panic.

The guard eventually leads Silvus up the wall above the main gates to see the crowd by the city guards, with weapons ready. Silvus finds his mother standing in the middle with a staff in claw as his uncle stands to her right, wearing long-sleeved chain armor with the familiar white metal plate over it, with a blue cape around his neck. His mother Silviera stares at the pine tree countryside with a stern face, along with Orzeyme ranting how he knew that certain danger was bound to happen.

"Lady Beta! I have collected your son as requested!" the guard shouts as soon as he and Silvus get near her. The guard gently pushes Silvus close to his mother, making him want to know what is going on.

"Mother! What is happening?!" he asks her, but in response she points for him to look. He turns his head to see a massive army of Raptors gathered in front, wearing the same set of armor as the guards, except the feathers on their helmets are orange, which represents the Betadom of Monchester.

With a closer look, Silvus can see that they have orange Monchester flags with a black rook in the middle raised up high, along with catapults prepared deep behind the army to breach the city. Coming from the invading army is a heavily armored male Raptor with an orange cape. He is assumed to be the leader of the group.

The leader is followed by seven other heavily armored Raptors, who are the officers, along with a shady figure wearing black robes, keeping the hood up to hide his or her identity. As they all approach the main gates, some of the Maglo guards look scared due to being intimidated by how outnumbered they are compared to the massive army led by their better-equipped superiors.

"ANVAR TARGON! WHAT IS THE MEANING OF THIS?!" Silvus hears his mother shout, demanding an answer of the leading soldier, Anvar Targon.

Anvar Targon? The Beta-Lord of Monchester? Silvus guesses to himself. It makes sense that the leader of the invading Monchester troops is the Beta-Lord. What is more surprising to him is that he thought Beta-Lords or Beta-Ladies are not allowed to form private armies. Silvus tries to get a closer look at the invading Beta-Lord Targon, but his steel helmet covers his entire face. However, he can see his white-colored Serpent eyes and black scales due to his legs, feet, and tail still exposed, which look kind of familiar.

Silvus is so focused on Targon that he fails to notice that the hooded figure beside is examining him from a distance. The hooded figure moves toward Targon to whisper into his ear, making him nod. Targon turns his head back up at the main gate directly at Silviera.

"The Alpha-King's throne have been empty too long! Our fellow Raptors are suffering due to the lawless savages who are taking advantage by preying on them, yet the Mistatorium does nothing!" Targon speaks with a voice of authority and frustration. Silviera takes another breath and tries to counter.

"I assure you, Targon! The Mistatorium are still seeking a new Alpha-King as we speak! As much as I want to help the Raptors now, the best thing we can do is be patient! What you are doing now is not the answer!"

"TWEENTY-FOUR FRICKEN WINTERS WE HAVE WAITED!!!! OPEN YOUR EYES, BETA-LADY OF MAGLO, YOU ARE DECIEVED BY THE MISTATORIUM, WHO ONLY SEEK TO GAIN POWER! IF YOU CAN'T BE CONVINCED THEN I HAVE NO CHOICE BUT TO..." Targon gets interrupted by the shady figure putting his or her claw on Targon's shoulder to get his attention once again.

As Targon and the figure speak privately, Silviera turns to Silvus, placing her talons on his shoulders.

"Silvus. Come with me! And Orezyme." She turns her head to her brother and whispers something to him. The tone is so quiet that Silvus cannot hear what she is saying. As soon as his mother gives a guard captain an order, Silvus feels himself get dragged by her through the crowd. He does not know where his mother is taking him, but whatever it is must be important.

Back in the castle, Silvus is led through the bedroom hall all the way to his mother's quarters, looking surprised. It surprises him because he remembers that his mother never allowed him nor any other family into her quarters. At first he thought it is because of private female stuff, but with the invasion underway, his mother must think that it is the best time.

Silvus' mother tells him to come inside her bedroom to be greeted by a larger-sized regal bedroom. Silviera takes him to a big bookshelf located toward the right side of the king-sized bed. She looks around the books to stop at the golden one. Silvus is going to ask what she is doing until she reaches her claw to pull the book back, making a clicking sound. The bookshelf starts to sink down into the ground, revealing an entrance to a secret room surprising, the young First Delta.

"Follow me," Silviera tells him, and motions with her claw. The mother and son walk through the tunnel all the way to a square dungeon room with a pedestal and chest in the middle. On the pedestal there is a wrapped long object. Silvus looks around the room in amazement while his mother approaches the pedestal.

The room itself has stone walls that do not match the castle. He notices a black banner with an elegant silver border of the kingdom of Avalonia hanging on the walls. He walks up to one of the banners for a closer look. The banner has a silver elegant line on the border and a silver seal that looks like a hanging plant with six leaves sticking out from the top.

His gaze is interrupted when he feels a tap on his shoulder, making him turn to see his mother holding a strange outfit she took from the chest.

"Put it on," she tells him.

Silvus takes the outfit to see that it is black hard leather chest armor with a dark-blue hooded poncho with silver lining. As much as he wants to admire it, his mother slams the staff, making sparks and getting his attention.

"Quickly, son! We don't have much time!"

Silvus turns around and quickly puts on the armor and poncho, feeling very comfortable. He turns around to see his mother looking at him with admiration while holding the wrapped object from the pedestal.

"Vessel Atheros, the founder of Maglo wore that same outfit during the war against Necros," states his mother, walking up to Silvus. "But now I need you to listen to me very carefully. You must go with your uncle and cousin to Atlantra, and from there you must journey to Patalot with this."

She gives Silvus the object. He looks at the wrapped object, wondering what it is. He is going to open it, but Silviera stops him and explains, "Open it only when you head to Patalot with Arkus. You can trust him."

"Who's Arkus? And why can't open this now?" Silvus asks her.

"Arkus is my mentor and the arch-sage of the Mistatorium, and this object I am trusting to you is a powerful relic that will be the key to saving Avalonia! If fallen to the wrong claws, it could also mean our doom. But right now we must meet with your uncle!"

Silviera tells Silvus to follow her out quickly. As they run into the throne room, an explosion is heard, making the castle shake below their feet. A guard captain wearing a blue cape runs from the castle entrance to them in panic.

"LADY BETA! The Monchesteons are attacking! Targon noticed you fled and started to attack--" The guard captian gets cut off by another explosion.

"Head back to the entrance and hold the line! I need to take the First Delta somewhere safe!" Silveira orders the captain but he looked a bit worried.

"But Mlady-"

"I SAID HOLD THE LINE! THAT IS AN ORDER!" Silviera cuts off the guard captain so loud she slams her tail on the ground to show she is serious. The guard Captian nods in under-standing and heads back out leaving only her and Silvus.

———)«(◉)»(———

They continue up to the east wing where the War room is lo-cated. By the entrance, Silvus and Silviera spot Orezyme, Ico, and a pair of guards waiting right by the fire place located to the north. She turns around to face Silvus as another explosion is heard making the castle shake again.

"Alright, son, this is the part that we must go separate ways!"

"What do you mean? You are not coming with us?" Silvus asks her in panic.

With a tear in her eye she explains, "As Beta-Lady of Maglo, I must assist the guard at any cost. As I mentioned back in my room, you must head to Patalot and find Arkus with the object. He will help you find a way to save the kingdom."

It does not feel right for Silvus to abandon his mother, even if it is voluntary, as she is going to face a bigger army that outnumbers hers.

"I…I can't just leave you here! You will get killed!" Silvus panics as another explosion is felt.

"Son… it is my duty. I must protect the Raptors here! You as the heir are too valuable to die, so I need you go with your uncle and do as I say!"

Silvus looks down at the object he is holding as more explosions are heard. He struggles in his mind to do what she is telling him. A part of him still fears for her life; at the same time, he hopes he can trust her judgment. With a tear in his eye he hugs her with one arm to whisper, "I will come back you after the task, I promise!"

They break from the hug and Silveira opens the door, allowing

Silvus to run up to Orezyme and the group. While Silviera watches him escape with the group through a secret escape tunnel behind the fireplace she whispers to herself, "This is where your destiny begins. Be strong…my hatchling." With that, she runs off to join up with the guard.

———※◎※———

Running outside eastward from the castle, Silvus is seen running along with Orezyme, Ico, and four guards, carrying the object on his back. Silvus makes a brief stop to turn around to see Athera from a distance. He helplessly watches his home being attacked by the Monchester army as they clash swords with the Maglo defenders and more fire bombs are thrown from the catapults. It tears his heart apart at the sight, and he feels a tear come from one of his eyes.

"I will keep my word, Mother. I will do as you ask. And I will save you no matter the cost!" He shouts his declaration to save his mother. He turns around to catch up with his uncle and cousin, who are now approaching for Triteria.

Act II

Chapter 7
The Swamp of Nightmares

Silvus has been looking forward to learning more about becoming a Beta-Lord after becoming a Mistcaster. He would rather be reading another book to pass another day, but he cannot. Instead he is carrying an important object strapped on his back, following his cousin and uncle on the wet road surrounded by a foggy swamp of Tricia. It is all thanks to the unsuspected invasion that came from Monchester which forced him to escape. The current destination is the Betadom's capital, Atlantra.

Looking up at the sky covered by the thick branches that came from the fern trees, Silvus sees the rays of sunlight that pierced through are starting to fade. It makes him a bit scared due to the books he read about the dangerous predators that lurk around. The four guards who joined also look up to see the fading sunlight. Ico, on the other claw, starts to shake next to his father due to his fear. He knows how dangerous the swamp is at night.

Lucky for them, the road is built right by the Miststream--glowing purple light leading them to one of the Beta-Capital cities due to them being built around the wellsprings that connect them.

Silvus looks to his right to admire the purple glow radiating through the fogging mist, hoping to ease his worry while walking. Catching his eye is a lone Ankylo (Ankylosuarus) standing right by a lake, eating the tall grass that grows from the drought. He wants to call out his party about it until an unknown predator from the lake snatches the Ankylo from behind, dragging it into the lake, making a splashing sound. Silvus flinches back as he feels his heartbeat rising in fear. He does not know what the predator is, thanks to the blanket of shadow not covered by the fog's glow.

"WHAT WAS THAT?!" he hears Ico shout, showing that he is very paranoid. Ico shows that he really hates being in the swamp like an open book. Orezyme grabs Ico by the snout to tell him to be quiet so they can continue walking along the road without attracting attention. As they continue on, Ico backtracks to Silvus' side and asks, "You heard it too, did you?"

"I did," Silvus answers, still holding onto the strap that is holding the object.

"What is it?" Ico further questions, as he really wants to know if a predator or two are stalking them. He has every right to be scared in the middle of the night and of nocturnal creatures that hunt down Raptors at night. It makes Silvus want to question in his mind how any Raptor could live in a place like this.

Silvus looks to his right again to see the great swamp lake, to check if they are being followed. He notices a pair of objects swimming in a pack, only for them to submerge. He gulps, hoping that the mystery predator is not what he thinks it is. He looks to Ico, who still has a fearful face, waiting for a response. He is going to answer until he sees Orezyme and the guards make a stop at a three-way crossroads with a signpost placed pointing directions leading to other nearby settlements.

It is weird to Silvus for the group to stop for directions; because they don't need to read a signpost to find the capital, thanks to the Miststream.

Silvus and his cousin walk up to get a closer look to see what the guards and Orezyme are looking at. It is not the sign they are looking at, but a dead Raptor, missing a tail, bitten off with bugs flying around. The dead Raptor might have been an Omega caste due to lacking the nobility scarf. The guards gaze at the corpse as if they have seen something supernatural. Orezyme keeps his cool examining it, Ico feels himself about to vomit, and Silvus cannot help looking shocked.

"By the spirits. What happened here?" one guard asks.

"It looks like this poor sod was trying to get away from something before his... tail got bitten off," another guard states.

Taking a closer look at the bite mark, Silvus thinks back his Beastology class. It hits him. "I think this guy might have been attacked by a--"

An arrow comes out of nowhere, cutting him off, striking at a guard's eye, making him wince in pain. Two of the other three guards run up to help the wounded as Orezyme and the other guard get into defensive positions. Ico freaks out as Silvus runs up to Orezyme, hoping to help fight, but he stops Silvus and tells him to stay behind with Ico and the three guards.

From the bushes, a gang of ten Raptors dressed like savages emerge from the bushes, holding weapons. Among them is one large Raptor dressed in heavy spiked chest armor, holding a large steel claymore, with an evil grin on his snout. He says with a mocking mid aged tone, "Well, well, look what we have here? I thought you pesky noble snobs don't like to travel in this place at night."

The other members, who kept their weapons drawn, made small laughs after their supposed leader.

"Bandits, at a time like this," whispers Orezyme as he looks back to see Silvus and Ico helping the two guards tending to the wounded one. He looks back at the bandits, scans all ten of them, and looks to his left at the avalible guard and tells him, "Stand back, I'll deal with them."

The guard looks at Orezyme, surprised, hoping he rethinks what he is doing. Silvus too gets up after using his healing spell on the wounded guard and approaches Orezyme.

"Uncle, you crazy?! You can't possibly fight off ten bandits by yourself!"

"I know what I am doing, Silvus! So get back with your cousin," Orezyme commands his nephew. Silvus hesitates to walk back, not wanting his old uncle to face the bandits on his own. He eventually walks back to Ico and the guards while Orezyme walks a few steps toward the bandits.

"Looks like the old fool wants to face us alone. This will be an easy plunder for us, eh boys?" the leader mocks, followed by manic laughter from his crew.

The guards, Ico, and Silvus can only stare at Orezyme from behind. They all wonder if he is going crazy due to his age. Ico is the most terrified by the fact his father is putting his own life at risk. Not to mention Orezyme has no weapon in claw. Orezyme raises his arm straight, making his claw engulfed with an aura, the Mist. The glowing mist begins to form into a long spear making Orezyme grabs and twirls it like a baton. He gets into battle position, freaking out all the Raptors present.

Silvus watches what his uncle did in amazement. He has never seen such a spell that would allow a caster to conjure up a weapon out of thin air. Why Monastery did not teach him this, he does not know, but all he can do is keep an eye on the surroundings, hoping Orezyme knows what he is doing.

"What are you sods waiting for? Get him!" the bandit leader shouts, jabbing his finger to point, growing impatient. The three bandits who carry a sword charge at Orezyme and try to strike him. Orezyme parries one bandit strike and makes a counter strike at the chest, followed by another bandit, only to be back-kicked, sending him flying into a lake. The third bandit tries a jump attack, only to be swatted by the misty spear.

As Orezyme fights the other bandits, Silvus focuses on how well his uncle fought.

"Dude! It is so hard for me to imagine how awesome my father is right now!" Silvus hears Ico cheer for his father. As Orezyme fights, he takes a closer look at the bandit leader, who just stands there, getting angry.

Taking a closer look, Silvus notices a strange purple badge on the left side of the leader's chest. He remembers back home during the invasion that a shady figure with Targon has that same badge—both purple and a carved skull.

Silvus further watches his uncle picks out the grunts one by one with his misted spear. The remaining bandit grunts are too afraid to face him, as they watch their comrades get slain one by one. The leader is boiling in rage about how one old Raptor could take out his men. He takes out a pocket crossbow to shoot a dart, only for Orezyme to deflect it with his spear, shifting back to his battle stance.

"WHAT THE HELL ARE YOU DOING, OLD MAN?!" the leader demands as he jabs the crossbow to one of his men, to draw his large claymore.

Orezyme points his Mist spear at the bandit with a confident smile and replies, "You face a mighty KNIGHT OF THE MIST!"

"Did my dad just say he is a knight of the mist?" Ico whispers to Silvus, who nods with a surprised face. He has heard stories about a secret order of knights who serve the Mistatorium as their own private army. It is said that they are trained to use unique combat spells in order to fight Mist- related threats. Silvus hears his cousin squee in excitement, knowing that his father is one them.

"YOU ARE SO DEAD!" the bandit leader fumes, and is going to charge, only to be attacked from the side by a large carnivore reptile that jumps from the lake. It grabs the bandit with its large jaws as the latter screams in agony. The predator swings side to side, making crunching sounds with its jaws to eat its prey. The bandit grunts in fear and tries to make a run for it, only to get attacked by two other reptiles that are a bit smaller.

Orezyme rushes back with the rest of the group, making the guards draw their spears, pointing directly at the strange predators that attacked the bandits.

With further inspection, the creature is a large crocodilian with feathers around its neck, a big snout with sharp teeth, and a very long tail. It uses its webbed claw feet to turn around, facing Silvus' group.

"By the spirits—Crocodons!" Silvus clarifies in fear as he prepares a lightning spell. Ico only hides behind the group due to a lack of a weapon.

The large Crocodon starts move slowly toward the group while the other two follow behind. Even more Crocodons emerge from the sides of the wet road to join up for their meal.

The lead Crocodon is going to prounce until a Trident is thrown from above, striking between its eyes, staggering the beast. From above, an unsuspecting figure in leather armor with a purple cape and hood up jumps down to grab the trident and continually stab the Crocodon, hoping to slay it. The large Crocodon falls to its grave, making all the smaller Crocodons run away in fear. The one who just slayed the Crocodon jumps off and walks up toward Silvus' group. He puts down his hood to reveal a familiar bronze-scaled face with a scar around one of his light-brown serpent eyes.

"Arrgh, what brings you guys in my Betadom? Yer know it is dangerous to be here at night!" The hunter says with a sailor's accent. From the bushes, a team of at least fifty guards come out of hiding with harpoons. Unlike the Maglo guards, their helmets have purple feathers for Tricia.

"Bless my soul! Beta-Lord Sidon Tritus!" Silvus shouts out, approaching his rescuer, and gives him a bro claw shake, grateful for being rescued from becoming Crocodon chow.

Chapter 8
The Noble with a Pirate's Heart

Rescued from being Crocodon food, Silvus gratefully walks up to Sidon Tritus, the Beta of Triteria, giving him a high five followed by a shake, as they are the best of friends. Despite becoming a Beta and marrying his cousin, that did not stop the young rebellious pirate at heart from going on hunting sprees that led to saving Silvus and his group's life. Tritus looks around Silvus' group, who are not in a good condition.

"If yer trying to start a crew, six mates isn't the way to start, especially one of them lack any fightin' spirit!" Tritus jokily speaks with the Triterian sailor accent and laughs, making Ico go "HEY" in annoyance, failing to hear a snicker from Orezyme.

Silvus could not help but laugh with him, and at the same time is glad that Tritus did not forget their friendship. However, he snaps, remembering about the task given by his mother, "Actually, Tritus, we are here on the run and are in a desperate need of help!"

"On the run?" Tritus raises a brow. "Did sometin happen to ya?"

"Let me explain," Orezyme calls out, walking up to the two young adults with his claws held together behind his back. "What my nephew is trying to say is that Maglo has been taken over by Monchester forces, leaving us on the run. We were hoping to meet up with you at Atlantra to discuss it."

Tritus gazes at rest of Silvus' group to see that they aren't in the best of positions with their run-down equipment. Turns his gaze to his guards, making the captain shrug.

"Well then, what about ya explain what happen to ya home at me castle back at Atlantra, shall we?" He looks at his guards and commands them like a pirate captain. "Let's go, mateys; tonight's hunt is over, so let's take the lads from Maglo back home."

"What about the dead Crocodon, Lord Beta?" one of Tritus's own men asks, concerned about the Crocodon corpse. All eyes land on the lifeless large creature with blood dripping from its forehead. Tritus looks to his men, who await his command.

"Head back to the camp and get a wagon. This here dead creature is going to fill up some bellies for our town for at least the month," Tirtus commands. Some guards salute and rush back into the wild areas of the swamp for their camp.

"Thanks for helping us out, Tirtus. I knew you would not let us down!" Silvus gleefully thanks him. Spirits bless him for having a great friend in a Beta-Lord like Tirtus.

"Anything for my first mate!" Tritus laughs heartily, giving Silvus a pat on the back.

The extended group of guards and leading nobles continue to walk across the road, with a dead Crocodon on the large wagon being pushed by three of the Triterian guards. Ico sits on the side of the wagon, due to not wanting to step on the wet road. In front of the group, Silvus walks alongside Tritus to his right, while his uncle Orezyme walks to Tritus's left.

"So how is Sulphie, by the way?" Silvus asks Tirtus, concerned for his cousin, remembering what she had told him during his graduation party. Orezyme moves his eye to the side to look at them and listen, wanting to hear about how his daughter is doing.

"Oh, she is fine, good lass she is. Except when she gets mad at me for hunting from time to time."

"Maybe it is due to you becoming a father yourself. My duaghter does not want you to die or else my grandchildren will be fatherless!" Orezyme butts in, earning some growling annoyance from Tirtus.

While Tirtus turns his attention to Orezyme, Silvus thinks about his mother and what she wants him to do. *This object I am trusting to you is a powerful relic that will be the key to saving Avalonia!* He hears her voice echo in his mind. He looks back at the supposed relic still strapped onto his back. He really wants to know what is inside the wrapping, but his mother told him not to look—only if he is alone with Arkus. It must be so important that his mother believes that it could potentially save the kingdom or bring it to further doom if brought to the wrong claws. For the rest of the trip, he keeps his mind on the relic.

⸺⧫⸺

Eventually the trio makes it to their destination: Atlantra, the Betadom Capital of Tricia. Silvus looks at the city in front placed on the edge of a beachside. Unlike back home, the city is made of wood: both the walls and the buildings. It is probably due to being a harbor town. Regardless, the young Raptor relieved that he has made it to one of safest towns in the Betadom. As Tritus leads both the guests and his guards in, Silvus looks up at the main gates to see a waving purple flag with the golden trident in the middle that matches his best friend's weapon.

Walking into the market district, Silvus can smell the tasty fish inside the market stalls in place. One thing to know about Triteria is that they are the biggest supplier of seafood products. Many Raptors that crowd around the district are mostly hunters or fishermen themselves, making them unique compared to the other Betadoms.

"By the spirits, this city smells like rotten fish!" he hears Ico complain, who is trying to cover his nose in disgust.

"Oh! I thought you loved fish?" Silvus teases his cousin with a smug look on his face.

"I LOVE THEM COOKED, THANK YOU VERY MUCH," Ico shouts back defensively.

"Okay, cousin, whatever you say." Silvus shrugs, still walking with the group. Ico huffs behind him and follows along.

Silvus looks around to see that the Raptors who live in Atlantra are very carefree. The hatchlings are playing and the adults are either fraternizing, maintaining their homes, or tending the market stalls where all the seafood is. They don't look worried about the impending invasion. He guesses that Tirtus has not told them about it yet, due to not knowing himself.

"LOOK! THE BETA-LORD IS BACK!" Silvus hears one of them shout, making his group stop in their tracks in the middle of the street. Almost all the Raptors turn their attention to his group as they flock right in front of them. Their attention is mostly for Tritus as he sees a group of females looking at him dreamily despite his marriage.

From the crowd, three male hatchlings run up to Tritus with wooden sticks.

"OH MY GOSH, YOU'RE BACK!" one hatchling says in glee, like a fanboy.

"Did you slay another Crocodon?!" the second hatchling asks as he uses his stick like a spear.

"I bet you're not afraid of anything!" the third hatchling shouts out in the traditional Trician attitude.

Silvus hears Tritus make a jolly laugh at the hatchlings. They are not wrong. Tritus is indeed a great hunter, just like all the past Betas of Triteria. To demonstrate, Tritus points at the large wagon with the big dead Crocodon making, all the Raptors ooh and ahh.

"That, my mateys, is food and leather for us all to last us another month!" Tritus turns his head to the guards holding the wagon, making the crowd cheer. He turns around to his guards and commands, "Take it to the butchery district so we can distribute that meat to the merchants."

The guards nod and begin to move the wagon westward to the butchery.

"And for the rest of ya!" Tritus turns his attention to the rest of his guards, "Get back to watch duty while I escort our guests to the castle!" The guards salute as they disperse to assist the other guards present in the city.

"The Raptors of Tricia are lucky to have a Beta-Lord like you," Silvus compliments his friend. It is great to see his friends and family doing well in times like this—especially Tritus, who is like a big brother to him and also family by the fact he married his cousin.

"My pa always told me that the first duty of being thy Beta-Lord is to always look after your Raptors as if they are your own crew," Tritus brags with a grin.

Silvus cannot help but laugh in agreement. "So true, buddy, so true."

He hears his uncle clear his throat, turning his attention to him; he has his arms crossed with Ico, who just stands there, bored. So the two friends decide to cut conversation short, continuing to head to the castle district to the north.

Silvus continues to follow the group all the way to a big wooden wall with a metal gate. He sees Tritus approach the guards to tell them to open up so they can head on in.

Silvus looks around the castle district where the Beta lives. Like the city itself, the castle is made of wood but with lots of decorations. One decoration that interests him is another statue placed in the middle posing like a hunter with the same trident Tritus has. The plaque reads: "Sidon Atlantra, founder and first Beta-Lady of Triteria."

Coming out of the castle, Silvus sees his cousin Sulphie, who spots them with a gasp and runs up to them. He thinks she is going to give Tritus a kiss, only for her to stop and smack him in the snout. Both Silvus and his group are taken aback at the sudden strike at the dumbfounded Beta Pirate.

"WHERE HAVE YOU BEEN, TRITUS?! DOING YOUR RECKLESS HUNTS WHILE I AM ALONE WITH EGGS?!" Sulphie accuses Tritus. She is really mad at Tritus for leaving her behind.

If Silvus remembers correctly, marriage is a very complicated commitment. He remembers that when he was a hatchling, Tritus and Sulphie got along pretty well when they first met. Not to mention that Sulphie always loved adventure and was drawn to Tirtus's nature in being adventurous with his hunts. Regardless, Silvus just stands around listening to his cousin and best friend bicker about their future as parents.

"Easy, my dear lass! You know as Beta I have to commit to my Raptors!"

"You are a Beta-Lord, I get it, but that does not mean you have to go recklessly to your dangerous hunts only for me to find out that I have become a widow and my hatchlings will be fatherless! By the spirits, your Betadom has a reputation of having the most rates of death!" Sulphie rants, completely ignoring part of Tritus's plea.

Sulphie takes a deep breath and latches Tritus into a hug, followed by a peck on the lips.

"Oh, Tritus, I am happy that you take your role seriously, but please don't forget that you are going to be a father and our hatchlings need a good model to guide them." Sulphie takes Tritus's free claw and places it onto her rounded belly filled with eggs.

"Oh, my dear Sulphie…maybe yer right, but right now we have guests!" Tritus points behind him at Silvus and his group. She tilts her body to the side to see her family behind him.

"By the spirits! Daddy, Ico, Silvus! What are you all doing here?!" Sulphie gasps in shock.

"It's a long story, but we should discuss more inside the castle out of earshot," Silvus recommends.

"He is right. We will need to discuss it private inside the castle. Not only to prevent a panic, but I fear there could be rebel spies around here," Orezyme says, in agreement with Silvus.

Tritus first looks around the courtyard to make sure no shady figure is spying on them. Once it is clear, he and Sulphie escort the family and the following Maglo guards into the wooden castle.

<hr />

The family gather around in the middle of the harbor-style throne room by a coral throne in front of the wellspring of Triteria. It is a giant palm tree that gliters purple-colored mist.

Silvus tells his story to Tritus, who is sitting on the throne while Sulphie stands next to him. Orezyme and Ico stand near Silvus, listening along. He tells them about Targon's claims, the army's appearance, and how his mother dragged him to her quarters to give him an important task.

"So you're saying Targon came to your doorstep, your mother gives you that package to take to Patalot, and you escape with Orezyme and Ico?" Tritus asks him. Silvus takes out the package off his back and explains.

"She told me that this could save the kingdom! Whatever this is, my mother believes it could convince Arkus to send the royal army to help us take back Maglo! As soon as we settle here, we are going to head to Patalot right away!"

"Whoa there, wait just a minute!"

Orezyme cuts in, earning attention from all the Raptors, including Silvus, who looks at him in shock at his uncle's sudden objection. Orezyme walks past Silvus, ignoring him, to instead present his own idea to the pirate Beta.

"The invasion of Maglo allows Targon's rebels to gain an edge at the border here. It means that at any time, they will try to take Triteria next. With the bandits dwelling around your Betadom, I believe that my nephew, son, and I should remain here and help with your Bandit problem to buy you time to muster your defences, hmn?"

While Tritus thinks about Orezyme's offer, Silvus still cannot believe that his uncle would rather stay put than honor his mother's request. Either that, or his uncle has become paranoid due to their battle with the bandits and the Crocodons.

"I accept your offer, Orezyme. Anything for family." Tritus agrees to the offer, making Silvus more upset that now his best friend just agreed to his uncle's plan to be sitting ducks.

⚬

Escorted to the living quarters at night, Silvus marches right to Orezyme, who is attempting to get into his guest quarters. He shouts his name with an angry tone to gain his attention.

"Were you seriously going to stay here while Mom is back there possibly being tortured?!"

"Listen, I understand your mother gave you a task, but we need to ensure the safety here first, unless you want the rest of your family to be in harm's way."

Orezyme counters Silvus with a shout of his own. Silvus gives him a hiss that reads "Are you serious?" Orezyme takes a deep breath and places his two claws on his nephew's shoulders with an apologetic look.

"You are a very smart hatchling, Silvus. I have known your mother long enough to know that she is a very strong-willed lady. She can handle anything thrown at her."

"Are you really sure about it?"

"Yes, Silvus, by the spirits—she is my sister! I love her dearly just as you do. I promise you that we will head to Patalot, but you need to remember that she isn't your only family. You don't want your cousins to perish, do you?"

His uncle makes a good point. Even though he still wants to head to Patalot to save his mother, he also has his cousins to think about, surrounded by bandits and predators as well as an invading army that will take over. He shivers at that the thought of the remainder of his family being harmed.

"I guess you're right, Uncle," is all Silvus can say before he turns around slowly to find his guest chambers.

"Silvus!" his uncle calls out, making him turn around halfway to listen.

"I promise you that we will save your mother. Once we finish here, then we will make the trip to Patalot. Which is why I am going to request that Tritus trains you to use a sword."

"Really?"

"Oh yes, really. I know you used to train with Tritus and two of your old friends when you were a hatchling. I thought you could use your skill in both Mistcraft and sword to help us. You'd better get some sleep. Good night, Silvus."

After listening to his uncle, Silvus parts ways feeling a bit better as he continues to his own guest chamber. Inside he puts down the package right by the bed. He walks up and flops into the bed to drift to sleep, still thinking about how he will be able to save his mother in time.

Chapter 9
The Mistcaster and the Sword

The next morning, Silvus wakes up half asleep, thinking about his fight with his uncle last night. Placing both talons on his forehead, he makes small growls of frustration. As much as he wants to head to Patalot, he cannot, because his uncle holds him back to help stabilize the Betadom. Not that he doesn't want to, though. Silvus feels that he has no time and his mother could possibly get killed at any moment. Whether his uncle is doing it for his daughter-in-law or is simply paranoid, believing the kingdom is too dangerous, it doesn't make much difference to him. What does make a difference is that he is being held back.

With a tired sigh, Silvus picks up the package beside the bed, to look at it as he drifts into his thoughts. He thinks about what will happen if he heads to Patalot without his cousins. According to Orezyme, with Maglo under Monchester's control, they could invade Triteria at any moment and the Triterian Raptors are not prepared, due to the bandits that dwell there. If he pursues Patalot now, there is a chance that the rebels will harm them too, leaving him with no family to return to. He shivers at the thought.

His thoughts are interrupted by the sound of knocking from the door to his right. "Who is it?!" Silvus calls out.

"I am a Castle drone m'lord. I have been sent by the Lord Beta to collect you to the throne room for breakfast," the voice of a professional female answers.

"Tell Tritus I'll come in a moment!" Silvus tells the drone through the door. Hearing the drone's footsteps walk away, he gets off the bed and heads to a wardrobe to change into his leather armor and poncho. He tucks the package away under the bed and heads off to the throne room.

Into the throne room, Silvus is escorted by the drone to see Ico, Sulphie, Tritus, and Orezyme all seated at the dining table enjoying their breakfast. He takes his seat right next to Orezyme, who seems to be chatting with Tritus about a group of bandits they encountered last night. The two stop chatting when they notice Silvus joining them for the feast.

"Ah Silvus, your uncle tells me you are going to help out deal with the group of bandits who had been terrorizing my Betadom, yeah?" Tritus asks Silvus with a jolly tone.

"Yes… he did," Silvus confirms, looking uneasy while he picks out a few crab biscuits, eating them slowly.

In front of him, Sulphie takes notice of Silvus' depressed behavior as she watches him eat a biscuit with an elbow on the table, at the same time resting his head on his folded talon.

"Are you alright, dear Couisn? You are usually happy to eat crab biscuits?" she asks him with concern.

She ain't wrong about that. Crab biscuits are Silvus' favorite food to eat for breakfast, especially when visiting Triteria.

Silvus looks up to Sulphie who is looking at him, worried. She does not know about his fight with her father, so he cannot blame her for not knowing. With a deep breath he tells her, "Let's just say I did not have a good night's sleep."

He turns his head at Orezyme, who looks back with an apologetic face in return, knowing what his nephew is talking about. Sulphie only turns back to her food as Orezyme turns his gaze back to Tritus.

"Well then, Tritus, when can you start training the young Silvus?" Orezyme asks him, hoping to change the subject.

"Whenever he is finished with breakfast. It better be soon, because a scout came by telling me that a camp is spotted near the settlement of Harpus." Tritus turns his attention to Silvus, who is still eating slowly. "You better hurry if you want to save your mother. Quick—do you?"

With that, Silvus eats up his fill and he is escorted by Tritus to his personal training room.

———◦◉◦———

Inside the candlelit castle basement hall, which almost look like a dungeon filled with doors, Silvus follows Tritus down with fear written on his face. He is not afraid of the dungeon layout. He is afraid of the small flames that are lit on each candle that hang on the wall. Stopping right by the large metal door, Tritus turns around with a smirk on his face.

"How long was it the last time you used a sword?" Tritus leans his back on the metal doors, listening to the sound of chatter from behind.

"I believe it is around four winters. I was busy with becoming a Mistcaster, so I had not been able to practice much," Silvus honestly answers his friend, turning to the side, looking suspicious, wondering what his friend is listing to.

"Well then, you better start remembering. I brought a lot guests for us to entertain!" Tritus opens up the doors with his two claws to reveal a large circular room filled with tons of guards cheering for their Beta-Lord to come in.

Silvus has his jaw dropped in awe at the sight of the guards sitting in the seats above to watch him and Tritus spar. Walking into the middle of the ring, Silvus cannot help but circle around the room, seeing all the guards chanting Tritus's name.

"Is it necessary to have all those guards?!" Silvus asks him. He feels uneasy at the sight of hundreds of eyes gazing at him. Tritus laughs as he himself turns around to a nearby male drone to order him to bring two wooden swords. The drone approaches a nearby cart with practice weapons and does what he is told to do.

"It is, mate. What better way to motivate your men than having their superior show them how it is done!" Tritus takes the wooden swords in glee from the drone. He gives one to Silvus. Then he takes off his cape and crown to give them to the other drone. Silvus follows suit by taking off his poncho, not wanting to get it dirty, and gives it to the same drone who has Tritus's cape and crown.

"Aren't ya gonna take that glove off, mate?" Tritus asks cracking his bronze neck and arms.

Silvus looks at his left glove with hesitation. He does not want to take it off due to his condition.

"You do remember what happened when we were hatchlings, right?" Silvus tries to reason, hoping his friend gets the message.

"Oh, right! In that case, keep it on." Tritus allows Silvus to wear the glove.

Telling the drones to back away from the ring, he gets into his battle stance with his wooden sword. Silvus follows suit, making the off-duty guards present cheer, while some of the guards chant Silvus' name. Silvus looks up to see the four Maglo guards cheer while the Triceons gave them stink eyes for cheering against their Beta.

"Are you ready, mate? If so, I'll let you make the first strike!" Tirtus tells him with a cocky look.

Silvus turns his gaze back to crack his silver neck and shoulders. He gets back into battle stance with a smirk. "With pleasure… mate!"

Silvus makes his first swing to the left, only for Tritus to block it. He makes another swing to the right, only to be blocked as well. He repeats the same attack while the guards cheer. Silvus makes one more swing to the left only for Tritus to parry it, followed by a kick to the chest, making his opponent tumble back almost losing his balance.

"Like old times, mate!" Tritus adds, recovering his balance, and begins his strikes.

"Oh indeed it is, buddy!" Silvus blocks each of his strikes. "You becoming Beta, me and my studies."

Tritus strikes one left, one right, one upward, one right, one left. Silvus keeps his focus on the bronze-scaled opponent as he struggles to keep balance with each block, due to having less muscle mass than Tritus. Tritus makes one upward strike, but this time Silvus makes the parry and thrusts his wooden sword at Tritus's chest, pushing him back. The guards gasp at Silvus' sudden counter. Tritus, on the other hand, only laughs as he clutches his chest in pain.

"HAHAHA! You have been practicing with your parrying, have you?"

"When I was around sixteen winters of age," Silvus spins a left strike, "I used to practice with two friends of mine when I was not with my books!"

The two best friends makes a few more strikes and lock up to face each other eye to eye.

"You practiced with two friends, yeah?" Tritus questions as he jumps back to perform a frontal only for Silvus to dodge it.

Silvus himself is starting to feel cocky with himself as he is getting the hang of his sword play, despite not performing for a long time, making little side steps still in the ring. He hears four Maglo guards continue to cheer for him, earning glares from the Triceons.

"The two friends were brothers who wanted to join the royal army."

"What happened to them friends of yours?" Tritus gets back up in position to start making horizontal strikes at Silvus.

"They ended up joining the royal army when I turned seventeen. Since then, I went to my studies." Silvus makes a hard swing at Tritus's claw, disarming his wooden sword off into the sky and grabs it. The guards gasp as they watch Silvus hold Tritus's sword on one claw while using the other sword pointed directly at Tritus's neck.

"Looks like I win, eh?" Silvus keeps a cocky smile with his head slightly turned to the side. He keeps his main sword pointed at his sparring partner as he slowly starts to circle around. The guards who have been spectating make nervous glances. Some have sweat coming out of their foreheads. Others are simply chewing on their claws. The Maglo Guards only cheer louder for Silvus, who thinks he has the upper claw.

Tirtus is impressed that his best mate managed to disarm him despite not practicing for a few winters. But he has cheeky smirk with one more trick up his sleeve. "Well, pal, there is one thing a Raptor warrior would rely on when losing his weapons!" He squats down and whips his tail at Silvus' legs to trip him, forcing him to drop down on the ground.

Silvus loses his own grip on one of the swords, flying up, allowing Tritus to catch it and pins Silvus on the ground with his foot and points his sword at his neck, making the guards go wild. "The Raptor warrior makes use of his natural weapons." Tritus withdraws his sword to show his sharp toe talon at Silvus' neck.

Silvus winces in fear as Tritus's toe claw gets closer. Once he sees Tritus retract, he helps him back up. Looks like Silvus is going to need more training than he thought seeing the guards around him cheer that their Beta has won the spar.

Silvus continues to spar with Tritus with sword combat during the next seven sunrises. Each morning he loses the fight to the ever unpredictable opponent. With each loss he starts to get very annoyed, questioning his supposed gift the Mistatorium told him back at the Monastery. He assumes the gift only works for learning new Mistcraft, not physical combat.

One day, Silvus rests in his guest bed filled with bruises by the beatings from Tritus. No matter how much effort he puts in, he can never outmaneuver Tritus. At the moment he begins to lose hope, he hears knocking to his right.

"Come in," he calls out, wincing a bit in pain on his head due to having a bruise.

From the door enters Sulphie carrying some soup, along with Ico who is trying to hold his laughter at the sight of his bruised couisn. "Looks like Tritus had been doing a number on you like a personal meat bag."

Sulphie glares at Ico's remark while Silvus only groans, keeping his head on the pillow.

"He does have a point, Sulphie…Tritus is just too good!"

"See, sis, even the book brain agrees with me!" Ico makes a big grin that his only cousin agrees with him.

Sulphie makes a small frown and walks up to Silvus' side to place the soup on the night stand next to him. Then she motions her right claw to call forth gravity mist to levitate a nearby wooden chair for her to sit on. She sits on the chair carefully, as she does not want to crush the eggs in her belly. She looks at the resting Silvus looking down. Perhaps, maybe, he can use some encouragement.

"With that attitude, you will never get better! Also, Father told me what happened between you two," she states, now knowing about the fight between her father and him.

Silvus gives his two cousins a raised eyebrow while Sulphie keeps her frown, waiting for what Silvus had to say. Ico only looks confused, wondering what his sister is talking about.

"Wait up? There was a fight between Dad and Silvus?" he asks.

Silvus gives Ico a quick glare and turns back to Sulphie with a softer expression.

"Oh yes, we fought. I really want to save Mom; she told me to head to Patalot to find Arkus, hoping he gives us help." He looks up at the ceiling with a worried expression. "But Uncle wants me to stay and help. Don't get me wrong; I love you guys too, but…"

Silvus pauses his sentence, shedding a tear. Sulphie places her claw on Silvus' shoulder and whispers, "If you really want to convince Daddy, you need to go beyond your comfort zone!"

"What do you mean?" Silvus asks her.

"There are other ways you could learn sword combat. Here is a hint." She leans near Silvus' head and whispers, "Use what you know best and adapt."

With that she gets up and exits the room, leaving Ico dumbfounded. "What did she tell you?"

Ignoring Ico's question, Silvus starts eating the soup, at the same time thinking about what Sulphie just said. He gets an idea with a smile.

"Dude, you're starting to get weird," Ico comments, looking creeped out.

⬤«(◉)»⬤

At night around the castle library, Silvus sits at a desk reading a book about sword combat. He hopes he can learn new skills just like how he learns Mistcraft. He flips a page to read about the defensive style. He knows how to parry sword attacks, but he needs to learn how to block or dodge the tail attacks. He puts the book back on the shelf and spots a strange grey-covered book right next to it. Catching his interest, he takes it out to read it.

The book shows a picture of a Raptor warrior using a sword like a wand. The book reads about the art of combat with Mistcraft. The art involves using the school of enchantment to one's advantage to gain boosts.

Silvus flips a page to see a picture of the warrior igniting his or her sword on fire, which makes him flinch. As he reads, a smile slowly forms on his face, learning a new skill that can put his Mistcraft to the test.

Back in the ring, Silvus spars with Tritus again, but this time he focuses on defensive stance. All he does is parry each attack Tritus makes. The spectating guards themselves are starting to get frustrated that Tritus has not hit Silvus yet. Tritus begins to feel himself sweat. No matter how well he swings, Silvus deflects each one. He wonders what his silver opponent is up too. The entire spar, Silvus does not even try to attack.

Silvus himself, however, is faring well as he continues to deflect each attack. Seeing Tritus very fatigued, Silvus gets his chance to deflect the sword to disarm him once again. Instead of catching it with his claw, he catches it with his tail.

"Big mistake!" Tritus taunts, believing he can trip Silvus despite his exhausted state. So he tries to do his tail whip again, only for Silvus to jump over it and kick him in the chest. The Triceon guards gasp as the Maglo guards jump up to cheer.

With a smirk on his face, Silvus twirls his wooden sword, forming a stream of ice, and flicks it. The gust of ice blows from the sword and freezes Tritus on the spot, leaving only his head unfrozen.

The spectating guards exchange confused looks with each other. Some of them question if that is allowed until they hear Tritus laugh with some burr in his voice. "You clever little grub! You learned some Mistblade style, have you?"

"I sure did. A wise lady told me to 'use what I know best and adapt'!" Silvus boasts, putting two fists on his sides.

From the crowd, a familiar middle-aged male voice calls out.

"SILVUS!"

Both Silvus and Tritus turn their heads around to the crowd of guards to see Orezyme climbing down with a blank expression, storming up in front of Silvus. At first Silvus gets scared, believing that he upset his uncle in some way, only for the older Raptor's expression to change from blank to shock.

"Where did you learn how to do that?" Orezyme puts his two claws on Silvus' shoulders.

Silvus looks at Tritus dumbfounded, who just mouths "Don't look at me" and turns back to Orezyme. "I found a book in the library last night."

"Show me this book!" Orezyme demands shaking his nephew up a bit.

"Mates! I am still frozen!"

Silvus and Orezyme turn their gazes at Tritus who is still covered in ice, shivering.

—◦《◉》◦—

Back at the library, Silvus shows his uncle the book where he learned how to use his wooden sword like a wand. Orezyme takes the book to examine it.

Orezyme flips through the pages, surprised that the book is still intact, while Silvus stands in his place, waiting for a response.

"All these years, I lost this book during my training with the knights." Orezyme looks at Silvus with joy in his face. "When I was squire, I came here with my mentor for a task with this book. Must have left it behind when the task was complete."

"What did the knights do when they found out you lost the book?" Silvus asks his uncle.

"They sent me to the Sherrasic chapter of the order to clean up the Stego stables for losing the book, with only a sponge and a bucket of water. It was not pretty, but there is a silver lining."

Silvus shivers his spine, imagining his uncle in his younger years scrubbing the entire stable of filthy dinosaurs.

"After I was done with the cleaning, I came across a village of Omegas, where I met your aunt."

"You mean Auntie Oria? Where is she?" Silvus adds, eager to learn of his aunt's whereabouts. Come to think of it, his Aunt Oria, Ico and Sulphie's mother, has been missing during his final week of studies for Mistcraft.

"I had her sent back to Sherrasic to be safe with her family. But never mind that! I'll tell you more about it another day. Right now, I have to say I am impressed that you managed to learn a skill supposed to be learned only between the knights!" Orezyme exclaims, shaking off the subject of Oria.

"The way I see it, your mistake allowed me to pick up a new way to defend myself!" Silvus adds, as he sees his uncle look at him with a smile.

"Well, nephew... I think you're ready to join us to hunt down those bandits so we can save your mother in time—what do you say?"

Silvus perks up and gives his uncle a quick hug. "By the spirits! Thanks, Uncle! I won't let you or Mother down!"

With that, Silvus runs back to meet up with Tritus to tell him the news without hearing his uncle whisper, "Why can't Ico be more like you?"

Chapter 10
The First Battle

Silvus finds himself saddled up on a grey-scaled Snaguana, a large four-legged snakelike creature that walks like an iguana, all dressed up in leather armor and poncho, with his hood up, during the next sunrise. On his left is Tritus, saddled on his Snaguana, while Orezyme rides his to the left of Tritus. Behind Silvus, Tritus, and Orezyme are an army of Triteria militia soldiers following behind, all lined up as they walk along the swampy road away from the city. Thank the spirits that predators don't really hunt much during the day.

Silvus looks at his sheath strapped on his belt to make sure that a steel longsword loaned to him is close by. He draws it out to admire it, then puts it away, looking forward to putting his skills to the test. After all his training, he going to have a taste of fighting the bandits, and more importantly, being a hero. His Snaguana makes a happy hiss due to liking him. In return, Silvus pets his loyal steed. "Oh yeah, girl, we are going to get em."

Traveling farther down the road, the battalion comes across a crossroads with arrow-shaped signs.

"Where are we going?" Silvus asks, very eager to know the mission at claw.

"We are heading to the settlement of Harpin to meet up with

the Delta-lord in charge of the settlement so he and some volunteers can join us for this hunt!" Tritus answers as they turn right, northward, marching deeper.

———— ((O)) ————

As they march on, Silvus takes his time to look around the scenery during daylight. The swamp looks calm rather than sinister at night. Instead of predators, he smiles at the sight of herbivore swamp animals like a herd of Guanadons, large plant-eating ornithopods, eating the nearby tall grass from the ground while others eat from the vines. It is very had to believe that a beautiful swamp like this is feared. His sightseeing gets interrupted when he hears Tritus shout "Halt" at the same time making the gesture with his arm, making Silvus and the rest of the battalion stop in their tracks.

Silvus looks up to see a big log wall in front of him. That must be the settlement of Harpin. The settlement is built in the middle of the clear fresh lake protected by large wooden walls like Atlantra, but a bit smaller.

"Beta-Lord! Delta-Lord Jons Davius is expecting you," a guard on the wall calls out.

"The better question is if he is ready?" Tritus shouts back at the guard.

The guard nods yes and turns around to jump into the town. The main gates open, revealing Jons Davius, Delta-Lord of the settlement of Harpin on his Snaguana, wearing leather armor, with a cutlass attached to his belt. Aside from his pearl-white scales and red mane, one of his red eyes is eye-patched due to being blind in one eye.

Behind Davius is a group of at least fifty volunteers from Harpin, approaching Tritus. They wear the same chain armor and helmets as

Tritus's own. The volunteers also have smiles on their faces, being just as eager for action as the rest of the group.

"Beta-Lord. Ready for the wild hunt, I see!" Davius boasts with a very jolly voice and notices Silvus and Orezyme in between Tritus.

"Who are they, I may ask? New members of your crew?"

"Oh no, mate! They are my extended family through marriage, volunteering to join us!" Tritus points to Orezyme and Silvus.

"Oh, really?" Davius scratches his chin. "A pleasure to meet you all. I assume you all are ready to hunt down some bandits?"

"Eager as ever, Delta-Lord!" Silvus adds with a boast, only for Davius to make a snobbish chuckle.

"Call me Davius, lad. Any mate of Tritus is a mate of mine," Davius clarifies.

"Guess we better not keep the bandits waiting then! They might as well get as smelly as your wardrobe!"

"BARG OFF!"

Davius nudges Tritus in a joking matter. Silvus gives his uncle a weird look, asking him what he meant by that. In response, Orezyme mouths "You don't want to know," while turning his head side to side.

⸺◉⸺

The battalion, now one hundred and four troops, including the leading four, venture deeper into the swamp off the road this time. According to what Davius has told the group, the bandits were spotted up north, camped near the sacred glow shroom grove. One militia male is jabbing wooden planks into the muddy ground to create a trail in case they get lost. The entire Tritarian forces halt their tracks when they spot the purple glow in their sights, feet away from them within a veil of trees.

"So this is where they are hiding?" Silvus asks Davius, who is in between Tritus and Orezyme to the left. Davius points up for the group to see a billow of smoke blowing out of the sky.

"In every camp there is a campfire, and with fire there is smoke. They must think the clow shrooms could cover up fire glow without knowing about smoke, eh?"

"Sure looks like it, Davius. I'll give them credit for that, but they have lots to learn," Tritus adds, keeping his eyes on the black smoke.

"So what are we waiting for? Let's go get them!" Silvus draws his sword with one claw as he uses his other to keep hold his Snaguana who in turn is getting ready to sprint happily.

"Easy there, nephew. An important rule when dealing with enemy encampments and forts is to not rush in!" Orezyme halts Silvus' advance.

"Why is that?"

"First off, we don't know how many there are. Second, we need to make sure there are no traps in place, or else we will be running into an ambush!"

Silvus gives a quick look to the glow in front and returns to his group. He sheaths his sword to await further instruction.

***

While the Triterian militia set up camp, Silvus volunteers to scout ahead with a telescope. Per his instructions, Silvus has to keep low by hiding behind the thick vines in between the leafless branches. Getting close to the glow, he spots the camp, built within the clearing from a slope.

Ignoring the camp, Silvus takes notice of all the Glow shrooms that surround it. Glow shrooms are actually a very common plant around all Avalonia, known for their enchanted glow that matches the color of the Miststream of a Betadom. Being in Triteria, the Glow shrooms in the grove are purple. They would be a beautiful sight if it weren't for the bandits that are defiling the place.

Silvus takes out the telescope to use it to scout the camp. What is interesting about the bandits is that they look very organized by the armor they wear, the weapons they use, and not to mention they look very clean. He looks around all the small tents to spot the big tent set up right by the edge of the slope. An armored figure comes out with his hood up. Silvus assumes he must be the leader. When the suspected leader turns around, Silvus notices a strange badge worn on the leader's chest. It looks like a terrifying skull, colored purple just like the black flags being hung around.

Where have I seen that badge before? Silvus wonders, until he sees two more figures approaching him on black Snaguanas, wearing the robes and hood along with the same badges. Whoever the other two figures are, they hitch their mounts to greet the bandit leader. The bandit leader in turn greets them and leads them into his tent.

"What do you see?" a voice calls from behind. Silvus turns around to see Tritus and Davius crouched slowly walking up to him.

"Well, it seems they might not be ordinary bandits."

"What do you mean?" Tritus asks Silvus.

Silvus gives Tritus the telescope so he can see for himself. While Tritus is looking around, Silvus explains what he knows. He tells them that the group numbers around at least fifty, the weapons and armor they wear look in good shape, and also the bandits themselves don't even look sinister at all.

"This here might be worse than I thought! I hope I am wrong, but I believe they are rebels!" Tritus lowers the telescope slowly with a hushed tone in his voice. Silvus looks toward Davius, who does not look amused, simply rubbing his chin like a snob.

"Rebels, eh? Kinda makes sense, since the Mistatorium have been getting bad rep for winters now."

Ignoring Davius's snobbish tone, Silvus adds to Tritus, "Do you think they are aligned with the Monchesteons?"

"I dunno. But all I know is that we better deal with them or else… sigh, this is one of them difficult parts of being a Beta-Lord."

"You're hesitating to fight them, are you?" Silvus asks his friend with a concern in his voice. He looks back to the bandits or rebels with sadness, questioning the course of action.

"We better head back to our camp; can't keep the troops waiting." Davius gets up and walks back into the camp hidden inside the trees.

Silvus too gets up but with an expression of disgust, watching Davius heading back like a snob.

"Don't mind his snobbish attitude; he is just focused on being a Delta-Lord." Tritus pats Silvus' shoulder and walks past him.

Even though it is true, what they are now about to do just does not add up. Silvus looks back at the camp to see the bandits or rebels having a jolly time. In a time like this, many Raptors would blindly follow any Raptor to solve their problems. It makes those who are innocent fall victim to those who would exploit them for personal power, like the bandit leader who comes out of his tent with a sinister smile, escorting the two figures out back to their Snaguanas.

Silvus growls at the sight of them and clenches his talons into fists. They have a lot to answer for, manipulating the innocent to commit horrendous crimes. He turns around to head back to the camp.

⟫⟪◉⟫⟪

All the Triterian forces gather in lines with weapons drawn. The Spearmen at the front lines, one-handed infantry behind the Spearmen, and the archers climb up on the trees, hidden. In front of it all are Davius, Orezyme, Tritus, Silvus, and some Snaguana riders with jousting pikes at the ready.

Tritus rides up a few steps and faces all his men to make a speech.

"Listen up, lads. Today we are going to show them bandits some Triterian justice!"

All the Triterian militia quietly chant "hoorah" at the same, thrusting their weapons up in a form of boast. Silvus keeps quiet. He looks at his friend, who has an uneasy look on his face. He makes a nervous gulp, knowing what Tritus is going through.

"I will not lie; turns out many of them are actually misguided rebels fed with many lies. But do not underestimate them. They do this for what they believe in and will not hesitate to strike you down. I don't want to hurt them as much as many of you, but we have no choice! They are going to tell you that they have families, but what about the other families, our families they destroyed for selfish gain!"

Tritus thrusts his trident high and proud. "I am Beta-Lord of Triteria! As long as I hold this family trident, I will bring order to this land by any means." He slowly points his weapon at the glow that shines through the trees were the rebels are.

"Which is why we fight until they surrender or we take care of the one that twisted thug they call leader! Are you ready?!"

Once again the militia cheers, but this time Silvus does too, with his sword. Tritus gallops back to the front lines with the cavalry and shouts, "SPIRITS, YE WILLS IT!"

They begin to charge, with Silvus holding onto his mount. He feels his heart pounding fast, with his sword drawn. This is the moment he has been training for. Tonight he is going to put his skills to the test.

At the camp, the rebels are getting ready to pilage another settlement. At the main tent, the leader comes out with two swords on both claws. The other rebels turn their attention to their chief to await what he has to say. He is going to give his speech, but he hears the sound of footsteps coming near. The bandit leader looks up with his pale white eyes to see an army of Triterian soldiers charging down the slope.

"BY THE SPIRITS! THE MISTATORIUM LEECHES FOUND US!" one rebel shrieks.

"THEN WHAT ARE YOU ALL WAITING FOR? BATTLE STATIONS!" the bandit leader commands desperately making the rebels form up a wall of shields despite being outnumbered.

The militia Archers fire their arrows at the shield holders to break defense, allowing the cavalry to charge through the barricade as the infantry clash with the others.

———•《❖》•———

Silvus rides around the battlefield, using his sword like a wand to shoot lightning mist at each rebel who dares try to attack him. His lightning attacks are not meant to kill the enemies but to knock them out cold. The same cannot be said for his comrades, who prefer lethal methods to fight. He can hear screams coming from both sides.

Still on his mount, he quickly scans the battlefield to check for familiar faces. First he sees Tritus, fighting with his signature trident. Second he sees his uncle, using the same mist spear that he used when they first encountered bandits. Finally he sees Davius, using his cutlass to make big swings, cutting through swarms of rebels.

The bandit leader, who was busy cleaving through Triterian milita, spots Silvus, too busy on his mount running around the grove shooting lightning attacks from his sword. With a sinister grin, he stabs another militia member and takes his shield to throw it like a disk, flying right at Silvus by the head, knocking him off his mount right onto the muddy ground.

Silvus gets up to see his mount running behind the tent. Rubbing his head, Silvus gets back on his feet to scan the battlefield while keeping his guard with his sword drawn. From the sea of soldiers, he spots the bandit leader running right at him with his two long blades.

"OH, CRUD!" Silvus crosses his arms like an X, creating a purple force field around him, blocking the bandit leader's attack, followed by a backflip away from Silvus.

"You must be Vessel Silvus, right?" the bandit leader says with a savage tone in his voice.

"How do you know my name?!" Silvus freaks out, keeping his sword aimed at the armored bandit.

The bandit leader chuckles like a buffoon and begins to circle around the young Mistcaster. Silvus keeps his eyes on the bandit, ignoring the ongoing battle between the militia and the rebels.

As the bandit leader continues to circle, Silvus has a lot of questions in his mind, like how he knew his name, does he know more about him, and who told him about him?

"A very special boss of mine seems to think you're some kind of threat," the bandit leader adds with a mocking tone. He makes a jump attack, only for it to be parried by Silvus, followed by a force push spell by thrusting the palm of his claw, pushing the bandit leader away.

"Who is this boss of yours? How does he or she know of me? And more importantly, how am I a threat?" Silvus demands, looking agitated. Perhaps he is starting to feel creeped out rather than afraid of the ongoing fight.

"Did I say boss? I really meant to say a group of pals of mine are offering a big reward of golden feathers for your head." The bandit leader's sword ignites on fire, making Silvus freak out. The former shows off, dancing his flaming blades in a cranelike movement.

Silvus keeps a fearful eye on the flames engulfing the swords. He begins to feel his claws shake, struggling to keep his grip on his sword. The bandit leader notices the fearful look on Silvus' face, making him grin.

"You afraid of fire, you Mist-wielding punk?" the bandit leader mocks as he starts to walk forward. Silvus steps back as the battle around him moves into slow motion. His heart beats faster at the sight of the flaming swords being used by the bandit, getting closer.

The bandit leader makes a horizontal swing, making Silvus jump back, followed by another swing to the right and another to the left. With each swing the bandit leader makes, Silvus dodges each one in fear. He attempts an ice mist attack to blow out the fire on the swords, but the bandit leader blocks it with his own force field. Turns out the bandit leader is a Mistcaster too. He should have known by the way he ignited his swords on fire.

"You thought you're the only one who could make some tricks, did ya?" the bandit leader boasts, making another leap attack, but this time Silvus blocks it with his sword, sparking lightning.

Both Silvus and the bandit leader continue to make more clashes with their swords. Silvus tries to keep his distance in order to avoid getting close to the fire. The best he can do is keep parrying as long as he could in hopes that the bandit leader will eventually get exhausted.

"SILVUS!" a voice calls out, making Silvus and the bandit leader turn around to see Orezyme galloping his mount and jumping off with his mist spear hoping to hit the bandit, only for it to be blocked.

"That spell? You must be one of them Mistatorium lackeys, the knights of the Mist, right?" the bandit leader asks mockingly, keeping his block locked with Orezyme's.

Instead of answering, Orezyme only hisses through his teeth, trying to save his nephew. Without hesitation, the bandit leader pushes him off and kicks his chest.

Silvus can only look in horror as he sees his uncle land on his back. The bandit leader pins him on the ground with one foot. The bandit leader is about to strike a finishing blow, only for Silvus to run up and slash his claw off.

"GAAAAAAAAHHHHH" the bandit leader screams in agony, dropping to his knees, trying to use his only claw to cover his wound.

Taking his chance, Silvus uses his frost spells with his sword to freeze the bandit leader in place. Silvus runs up to Orezyme and helps him up back on his feet.

"Are you okay, Uncle?" Silvus asks him, worried.

"I am good. Thank you for saving my life!"

The rebels notice their leader has been defeated and start to surrender to the Triterian forces by dropping their weapons on their knees. Tritus then orders his men to stop fighting and begin to restrain them with a smile, happy that no more blood will be shed.

The militia all cheer for their victory while Davius only pouts due to the battle being finished. Silvus and Orezyme, on the other claw, are both happy that the fighting has stopped.

"You did great back there, Silvus," Orezyme compliments Silvus' performance. "Holding your own against a bandit leader is no easy task, if I say so myself."

Silvus could not help but blush at his uncle's statement as he scratches the back of his head. Suddenly he hears the Triterian militia, Tritus, and Davius begin to cheer for him, as he is the one who captured the leader, winning them the battle.

Chapter 11
The Journey Begins

The militia marches back to Atlantra, escorting the rebels all chained up while the leader is still frozen on a wooden cart. The Omega folk rush out of their wooden homes to rejoice at the sight of the militia parading with the bandits in bonds. Members of the militia are showered in cheer while the bandits are showered with disgust due to the crimes they committed. Some Omega folk even throw spoiled fish at the bandits in anger.

Silvus looks around with a smile, mounted back on his Snaguana alongside Tirtus, Orezyme, and Davius at the front of the parade, very proud of himself that he took park of a campaign instead of being stuck inside a castle. He admits that it feels good to be outside once in a while, as his cousin Ico always pesters him to do. For now, he rides along the group to enter the castle district straight ahead.

The following night, residents of different castes celebrate in their respected districts. While the Omega Raptors celebrate in joy within the wooden streets of the commons and market districts, the Delta Raptors celebrate in the Golden Lagoon and the castle districts. The Omegas set up small gatherings with family inside households or taverns. The Deltas throw fancy parties with larger families and groups of friends inside their manors or estates. One thing that both Omegas and Deltas share is a sense of pride with their Betadom and nation, as both castes raise purple and black flags high.

⟿⟨◉⟩⟪

The same can be said for the Vessel and Sidon clans, who are hosting their own private party inside the castle built by the sea. Inside the castle grand dining hall, all the nearby nobility of the Betadom are invited to celebrate. Ico is seen flirting with females and making new friends, Orezyme chats with the grown-ups, and Sulphie stands by with Tritus, who sits at the dining table with his associated Delta-Lords and court members.

As for Silvus? Instead of mingling in the party, he sits at a table alone in the private library, reading a book—not for the purpose of being entertained away from the party, but for information. He seems to be reading about the history of Second Avalonia or the second Dark Age.

Flipping through the pages, Silvus spots the picture that he has been looking for: the purple skull that he saw on both the bandit leader's badge and also the flags the rebels hung. Placing a talon on the text, he reads,

"The flag of Second Avalonia

This symbol was carved out by Necros in order to symbolize his power with Dark Mistcraft.

It is said he choose the skull due to the connection with the undead Dark Mistcraft has control over."

Silvus gets into thought, trying to figure out what he read. He gets off his wooden seat and paces around the table, brainstorming some questions. Why would mere rebels use such an evil symbol to represent them? Do they know about it? And who were the figures the bandit leader was talking to? He even questions if they are somehow connected to the state of the kingdom. He stops in his tracks to hear knocking sounds to his left, making him turn to face the two wooden doors.

"Hey Silvus, are you in there? If so, why aren't you with us at the party?" This is Ico, who seems to be looking for Silvus.

"Just a sec!" He decides to put the book away on its shelf so he will not have to make his family worried. He rushes to the doors, opening them to see Ico with some Delta caste buddies between him. Silvus can tell due to the fancy scarfs they wear. He evens sees one of them holding a goblet in a fancy manner.

"Dude! Even at a party, you still like to glue your face in books!" Ico laughs along with his buddies, earning an eye roll from Silvus.

"What exactly are you reading about?" one of Ico's new buddies asks like a cliché snob, taking a sip of his wheat vine wine.

"Let's just say I am trying to…" Silvus slowly thinks how he is going to explain without mentioning the badge he saw on the bandit leader. He assumes they might not be interested. They look like the type of noble who would be too impressed with themselves to even care. Ico and the new buddies all look at him, waiting for what he has to say.

"Figure out some history stuff related to that bandit guy I fought." Silvus snaps his talons.

"Wait a minute! Are you Silvus? The guy who saved our Beta-Lord by freezing that weirdo's tail?!" one of the buddies perks up, looking excited, making his tail slowly wag side to side.

"That's right, guys." Ico rushes up beside Silvus to pat him on the back really hard with a cheeky smile. "This male of the hour is also my cousin."

Silvus flinches a bit from the pain felt. He has developed a bruise due to his hard fall after being knocked off his mount. The two noble juvenile males look at him like fanboys who are meeting a hero of legend.

"Dude, no way!"

"Our Beta has been telling us how you fought the big guy by yourself."

"Really?" Silvus turns to his younger cousin, looking surprised at the sudden outburst by the two young Deltas.

"What about you come with us and find out. Join the party, dude!"

Ico gently pushes Silvus down the hall with his buddies to guide him back to the dining room where the party is taking place.

⸻ ⚬ ⸻

Dragged into the dining room, Silvus can see all the party guests having a good time, dancing around as if they are in an Omega-owned tavern. The nobility in Triteria are not like your average noble. Being a seaside sub-culture, it is hard to believe they are of the higher castes at all. Maybe it is due to his being with Maglo nobles most of his life who are mostly intellectual Mistcasters. Speaking of Mistcasters, SIilvus notices a Triterian Mistcaster or two who came from the Tricia chapter of Monastery mingling with the crowd.

Silvus then hears a band begin to play accordion music to his right. The tone makes all the guests rush into the middle of the room to start square dancing around and singing like a bunch of drunken sailors. Silvus cannot help but make a small laugh at the sight.

Ico seems to notice, making a smirk, thinking up an idea what Silvus should do. He tells Silvus to stay where he is, and he and his pals walk up to a trio of four pretty females talking to each other. Ico coughs into his talon, gaining their attention.

"What can we do for you handsome lads?" one of the females asks with a flirtatious voice and look on her face.

"I was wondering if you ladies could do us a favor." Ico points to where Silvus is standing. The females seem to think Silvus is very attractive due to the way they gasp.

Silvus watches his cousin and his friends talk to some females. Seeing his cousin point at him, making the females gasp at the sight of him, makes his cheeks flush. *By the spirits, Ico, what are you doing?* Silvus thinks to himself, looking at the group very suspiciously.

The females all rush up to him with fan girl smiles as if he is some kind of celebrity.

"OH MY GOSH! YOU MUST BE THAT SILVER MALE WHO FOUGHT ALONGSIDE OUR BETA!"

"He is so handsome!"

"Is he mateless?"

The crazy females make Silvus want to stept back. Tritus must have told his Raptors a bit too much about his involvement.

"I'm guessing Tritus told you much about me?" Silvus looks to his cousin with an annoyed glare; he only mouths "Have fun" in return, with a smirk.

Suddenly he feels his talon grabbed by the fourth and the most attractive female, making Silvus' cheeks heating up even more.

"You look very swell for a Mistcaster. What about we dance together, shall we?" The female drags Silvus right into the crowd of dancing guests, earning him stares.

Silvus does not know what to do. He looks around the wall of dancing guests, trying to find a way out. Sadly he cannot find one, due to how crowded the room is. He looks at the female who dragged him starting to sway her hips and tail, looking at him with a flirty smile, trying to get him to dance.

Silvus closes his eyes, trying to fight off his nervousness. Never before has he danced with a female. Out of nowhere in his mind the nervous male starts to think about one particular female. The female Silvus thinks about is the one he met back home before the invasion.

He does not know why, but thinking about himself dancing with the orca-colored female eases his nervousness, yet still he feels his heart pounding while he slowly looks at the female still dancing.

Taking a deep breath, Silvus studies the guests' dancing pattern and begins to shake his upper body, followed by a bit of tapping with his big feet, just like the others.

From the dining table, Sulphie takes notice of her cousin dancing alongside a random female with the crowd. She turns to her left to see Tritus, her husband, having a bit of a jolly time talking with his court members, her father who just joined them, and the Delta-Lords. She taps her husband's shoulder to get his attention.

"What is it, my dear?" he asks. Sulphie points for him to look and see Silvus dancing with the crowd, having fun, making him laugh with his jolly sailor tone.

Orezyme, however, is surprised to see his bookworm nephew dancing with a female who looks way out of his league. Or that is what he thought.

Back on the dance floor, Silvus and the female begin to lock up talons to start performing the duet-style dance. The dancers take notice with smiles on their faces. Ico and his buddies begin to cheer for Silvus, only for them to be snagged by the remaining females onto the dance floor.

Silvus and the female continue to tango, making the crowd clap their talons at the same tap their feet without knowing that Silvus is really fantasizing about another female. The two make one big spin followed by a finisher pose, making the crowd go wild.

"You dance so swell! Maybe we should hang out one of these days?" the female suggests, but Silvus snaps back to reality. Despite her appearance, he is not interested in her, but not wanting to hurt her feelings, he plainly tells her that he will consider it and parts ways, still earning him a wink from the female.

Silvus makes his way through the cheering crowd, reaching the dining table where his family and nobles are seated; they are all look-ing at him with proud looks. Especially Tritus.

"You just became the talk of this night!" Tritus playfully pats Sil-vus on the back, making him wince in pain from the bruise.

"I did not know you are so good at dancing, cousin!" Sulphie adds.

The other nobles begin to butt in, hoping to get a chance to know him. One Delta offers him a blessing to marry one of his daughters. Another Delta, a female, asks if he is mateless so she can look him up, regardless of whether he is Omega or not. Poor Silvus feels a bit overwhelmed by the constant offers and praise by the Deltas; he just sits in his seat exhausted right in front of them.

Orezyme can't help but smile for his nephew socializing with the nobles. It reminds him of his younger days.

⸺◦《●》◦⸺

One night, Silvus tries to sleep. Despite all the sudden fame, he cannot get his mind off his mother. He is getting a bit of a nightmare of himself in the middle of an unknown dungeon. The dream felt so real. He questions if it's a dream at all. Silvus turns around to see his mother trapped inside one of the cells of the hall. He rushes right in front of it, only to run through like a ghost. He takes one glance back to make sure the bars are there, and back to see his mother chained up.

Despite being chained up, Silveria his mother still has her cloak on, but it is dirty. Silvus tries to call out to her, but she cannot hear him. Then he hears the cell door open, making him turn his head to see a hooded figure walk right at him with a black cane. With an-other gaze, he sees the same badge he came across back in the bandit camp. The figure walks right past him, facing his mother.

The figure kneels to her eye level and asks her, "Where is the boy?" with a tone of an old male as he lifts his mother's head by the chin with his claw.

Silveria puts on a defiant face, giving him a threating hiss, with her fangs being shown. In response, the figure jabs his claw on top of her head. The claw suddenly glows red, making Silveria scream with agony.

"MOTHER!" Silvus shouts as he tries to make a jump, only to be met by a flash waking him up back in reality.

⸺⸺((◦))⸺⸺

Silvus lifts himself up on his bed, making hard breaths with fear in his eyes. He looks around to see that he is still in the guest room of Tritus's castle. He looks to his left to see sunlight coming out of the window, telling him that the sun has risen. He decides to walk out of his bedroom, hoping to have a brief walk out of the castle. He plans to until he sees his uncle and Tritus standing inside the throne room, waiting. The two spot the young Silvus with smiles.

"Ah, Silvus, come here!" Tritus waves his claw for Silvus to join them.

With a sigh, he walks to them with a tired face. Orezyme takes notice. "Is something wrong, Silvus?" he asks.

Silvus makes a big yawn and tells him that he had a bit of a nightmare last night about his mother being tortured by some hooded figure. Orezyme and Tritus exchange a quick look and try to cheer him up until a guard bursts through the door.

"MY LORD! THE MONCHESTER FORCES ARE ADVANCING!" the guard screams with a salute.

"WHAT! How do you know?" Tritus demands.

The guard tells him that he was scouting around the border only to see the Monchester army coming through in full force.

The news is so grim that Orezyme turns around to walk up to the coral throne in front of the wellspring. Both Silvus and Tritus notice Orezyme's sudden change in behavior.

Silvus walks up to Orezyme to see that he is in a trance best described as shock.

"Spirits have mercy, I thought we had more time." Silvus hears his uncle mumble a prayer, kneeling at the same time. His uncle is devestated.

"Uncle? Are you okay?" Silvus asks him with a worried tone. His uncle responds by standing back up, still looking at the wellspring.

"Do you still have it?" Orezyme asks Silvus without taking his eyes off the wellspring.

"Still have what?"

"The package your mother gave you!" Orezyme snaps now, facing the startled Silvus.

Now knowing what his uncle is talking about, Silvus tells him that he hid the package under the guest bed. Looking grim, Orezyme tells Silvus to do what he has wanted to do the whole time.

"Go to Patalot. If your mother really believes that the Mistatorium could help, then I trust her!" Orezyme instructs his nephew in a tone of desperate pleading.

Silvus notices the sudden change of mind of his uncle and asks, "What changed your mind, Uncle?"

Orezyme turns around his gaze back at the wellspring with his talons behind his back. He takes a deep breath to explain, "To be truthful, Silvus, the real reason I wanted us to stay is not just for helping family, but I hoped to talk to your friend about requesting an army to take back Maglo."

Orezyme turns his head to face Silvus with a smile. "Seeing how you perform in battle, it is safe for me to assume that you could handle yourself, but promise me this." He walks up to his nephew and places his talons on his shoulders.

"Promise me you stay alive!" He pulls his nephew into a tight hug. "Do you remember me telling you that you like another son to me?"

Silvus tells Orezyme, "Yes"

Orezyme breaks off the hug and explains that he meant it. There was a reason that his mother picked his uncle to be her steward. It has always been obvious to Silvus that his mother and uncle are very close siblings. Silvus starts to feel a tear come out of his eye due to feeling his heart touched by his uncle's words.

"What about you?"

"I have to stay behind with my own family, of course—who else is going watch over that younger cousin of yours?" Orezyme gives Silvus a nudge on the shoulder.

Both the nephew and uncle share a laugh until they hear Tritus clear his throat, getting their attention. He has been standing around listening to them right next to the scout.

"Sorry to break your touching family moment, but I believe we have an upcoming war to prepare for."

With that, Orezyme gives the word, and Silvus runs to his guest chamber to put on the armor and poncho set. He straps the package onto his back. He runs to the main doors only to be briefly stopped by Orezyme once again. There are two more things he wants to give his nephew before he goes off. The first one is the steel sword for protection. As for the other, Orezyme tells Silvus to follow him to the same training room where he sparred with Tritus. This time, however, it is empty.

First Orezyme tells Silvus to but the package down for a moment. Silvus complies, still wondering what his uncle wants to give him.

"What I am about to teach you, young Silvus, is a spell that is meant only for the knights of the Mist."

"You mean?!"

"Yes, nephew, in these troubling times I am going to teach you the weapon Mist spell for when you ever find yourself losing your weapon. First, raise your claw in front of you." Orezyme raises his claw and Silvus follows suit.

"Think about the weapon you are best at, then use your mind to call the Mist to form the weapon."

Silvus does what his uncle tells him. He clears his mind and thinks about a single-talon sword. Next the young eager Mistcaster mentally taps into the Mist stored within himself, making his claw glow the same purple color. A sword begins to form Aura into his claw in a matter of seconds. It is a slow process, yet Silvus feels himself grow tired as he performs his spell.

The exhaustion that Silvus is feelling mentally is the sign of Mist energy stored in his body almost depleted. He tries to keep his mind focused but the spell is so advanced, the Aura sometimes halts its progress. His uncle in front begins to grow worried.

Silvus suddenly grabs the aura and it forms into the perfect sword onto his claw, earning a gasp from his uncle.

Silvus proudly looks at his misty sword with so much excitement. He makes a few practice swings to test it out. Orezmye, on the other hand, is surprised that his nephew just mastered the spell very quickly. That is, until the Mist sword just vanishes out of nowhere, making Silvus a bit dizzy. The Mist weapon is not supposed to vanish that quickly.

Seeing Silvus on the ground, Orezyme helps him back up on his feet and asks him, "How did you manage to form the weapon that quick?!"

"The Mistatorium told me that I have some unique unnatural gift to learn Mistcraft very quickly... well, it seems I still have to learn how to actually keep this spell active? And by the spirits, my body is going to need a recharge!" Silvus laughs it off as the Mist that dwells in the atmosphere begins to merge into his body.

Hearing Silvus laughing it off, Orezyme wants to ask him another question about his so-called gift. But he does not have time, so all he can do is get Silvus on his journey to Patalot.

Around the outskirts of Atlantra, Silvus begins to ride his Snaguana on the muddy road for Patalot. He stops to take one more glance at the wooden city of Atlantra and makes a mental prayer for his uncle, best friend, and cousins to be safe from the upcoming battle. He turns around to enter the swamp forest until he hears a voice call out to him, "SILVUS, WAIT UP!"

Silvus turns his head back to see Ico, wearing chain armor with a bow and arrows, riding on a red Snaguana toward him.

Silvus is a bit shocked to see his cousin run up to him at an awkward time.

"Ico?! What are you doing here? Why aren't you with Uncle Orezyme and Sulphie?"

"Dad being a Knight of the Mist, you being a hero. I thought maybe if I join up with you I could get a chance to meet the knights! Better yet, join them!" Ico beams at the idea, earning an awkward look from Silvus.

"In a time like this, you want to join the knights?"

"Remember when you told me you wanted to be a Mistcaster to be a good Beta-Lord?"

Silvus nods in reply, remembering what they spoke about back home.

"So I thought if I become a knight, maybe I could learn to grow up to be the adult my dad wants me to be! More importantly, I could learn new skills to help Raptors in the kingdom!"

Ico makes a good point. Without further ado, Silvus decides to let Ico come with him on the journey to Patalot. The two cousins ride into the swamp, staying on the road by the mist stream in order to reach the capital. What the two cousins do not know is that group of five figures, in black robes and armor, follow close behind them with their black Snaguanas.

While the two cousins ride along, Ico bombards Silvus with various questions. The common question is about the knights. For example, Ico asks him if he might be able to see the knights when they get to the capital. Silvus only tells him that it may be possible since they are the Mistatorium's private enforcers. It makes Ico feel giddy as he squeals like a fan boy.

"You know, cousin, if I'm able to join... you think I could learn that spell my dad fought bandits with?" Ico asks, remembering the spell his father used to fight bandits.

Silvus is about to answer until he hears a pair of footsteps behind him, making him look back. Ico looks back too, wondering what is going on. The two cousins gasp at the sight of five shady Snaguana riders running at them.

The riders are so fast they run past the cousins to block their path by making a line wall.

"Are you Vessel Silvus?" The head rider walks up, speaking with a dark mysterious tone, freaking out Ico. The Snaguana used by the cousins make threatening, hissing sounds knowing they are in trouble.

Silvus takes a closer look at the riders. Aside from the black robes and armor, he sees that they have the same badges he saw on the bandit leader.

"How do those guys know who you are? They're freaking me out," Ico whispers to Silvus.

"Ico, listen. I have a feeling those guys are up to no good, so when I shout 'run,' we must run for it until we lose them," Silvus whispers back and makes a few steps forward.

Silvus studies the figures further. He cannot tell what they look like under those hoods, due to the masks they wear.

"Who are you Raptors, how do you know my name, and why in the spirits' name do you want me?" Silvus demands with a hiss, not trusting them.

The riders respond by drawing their black steel swords. The leader points his or her sword at Silvus and responds, "You are coming with us by demand of Anvar Targon, future Alpha-King of Avalonia."

It is obvious to Silvus that the riders do not really work for Targon. If he remembers, Monchester soldiers do not wear black robes, nor do they wear the unknown badge.

The two parties are silent. Tension fills the air, bugs nearby make chirping sounds, and some nearby dinosaurs in the wild make moaning sounds.

Silvus turns his head around to see Ico starting to sweat, scared of what they are about to do. Looking back at the riders, he draws his sword, twirls it around, and jabs it into the ground to create a wall of ice, causing the riders to step back with their mounts.

"MOVE!" Silvus shouts to Ico, causing the two cousins to gallop off road into the wild swamp.

"DON'T LET THEM GET AWAY!" the lead rider commands, throwing a dark fireball spell, the corrupted version of the fireball, with a free claw, to shatter the wall of ice, allowing the riders to make chase.

Silvus and Ico gallop their mounts as fast as they can while the riders continue to pursue them. Silvus looks around through the vines and branches, hoping to spot a place to hide. Suddenly he spots a giant rock in the middle.

To distract the riders, he uses his sword to perform a lightning spell behind him at a nearby tree. The zapped large tree falls down, blocking the riders' path out of sight. With the riders blocked, Silvus and Ico take advantage to gallop around the giant rock, ignoring a strange banner with a Triceratops-like head as a symbol. Eventually the cousins spot a big opening to a cave, allowing them to enter.

In the middle of the cave, the cousins stop their advance to turn around to see that the riders are not chasing them anymore.

"Dude, you think they are still out there?" Ico asks Silvus with a worried tone.

Silvus wishes he could answer, but he can only guess that they might still be searching for them.

"We should make camp for the ni—augh!" Silvus feels his neck get pinched, then feels himself get so dizzy he falls off his Snaguana, who looks at her rider, very worried. Ico gasps at the sight of Silvus falling down out cold.

"SILVU--"Ico gets hit too as he too falls down out cold into a weird sleep.

The two couisns lie on the stone ground inside the cave, out cold. A pair of feet is heard approaching them. It is a group of at least five mini two-legged lizards wearing Oriental-style armor. They are reptilian due to the scales on their feet and little tails. Unlike Raptors, they have no feathers.

Turns out they blew sleep darts, as one of them still hold a blow pipe in its claws. The biggest one, the leader of the squad, checks out the sleeping Raptors who are much taller than them. The leader looks to his squad and tells them, "Get a cart ready; we better notify the king that we have some trespassers in our mist."

———————

The five riders who were chasing them stop by the entrance of the said cave outside waiting. One of the riders lean toward the leader and asks, "Should we go after them?"

"No. We have hidden agents in there who might be able take care of them. Just in case, we will make camp and keep an eye in case they come back out," the leader answers with a sinister tone.

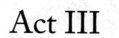

Act III

Chapter 12
Kobolds

Forced out of his home, helped clear out a band of rebels or bandits, being chased by shady riders…thing have gotten grim for Silvus. He is knocked out cold by some unknown force. The only train of memory he can remember are the mysterious strangers who wanted him for some reason. The better question? No. Two better questions are why do they want him and how are they tracking him?

His train of thought is interrupted by a bump bellow him. He feels himself lying on some wooden platform. Hearing pairs of feet and cranking wheels, Silvus slowly opens his eyes to see that his talons are tied up. He freaks out, trying to stand, only to get hit on the head by the ceiling, forcing him to sit back down. He uses his tail to rub his head.

Silvus looks around to see he is inside a cage being escorted by five strange little creatures who are as tall as a Raptor's hip. Four are walking along the carriage, while the fifth is on his seat driving it with two large skink-like creatures pulling. Aside from their small sizes, they also wear very strange Oriental-style armor with curved skinny long swords on their belts.

Silvus look behind to see the two Snaguanas are okay but are tied up to the carriage with their snouts muzzled. Than he looks back in front to see Ico trying to stand up, pacing around, rambling about their current predicament.

"This can't be happening, this can't be happening!"

His ramblings remind Silvus of his uncle back home who had also rambled with his mother. Makes sense, since Ico is his uncle's son. His cousin continues to ramble until one of the little guards up front walks up and pokes him with his small spear, making him go "ouch," and falls into fetal position.

"By love of the root, be quiet, trespasser!" The guard sounds very serious and annoyed.

The tone of annoyance from the guard makes Silvus wonder how long he has been unconscious. He slowly gets up and crawls up to the right of the cage and calls out one of the escort guards.

"Excuse me, sir? Where are we and where are we going?"

The guard looks at him. He cannot see what the guard's face looks like due to his helmet covering most of his face. What he can see is a pair of serpent slit eyes looking at him and a pair of horns. The guard only tells him to look for himself. Silvus looks around to see he is being escorted deeper into a cave, like a tunnel.

Inside the tunnel Silvus sees strange roots sticking out giving the tunnel lots of light. He even sees stone carved statues that look identical as the creatures who are escorting them. *They must be very artistic; I give them that* Silvus thinks to himself before turning his attention back to his wounded cousin.

Silvus crawls up to Ico still shaking in fetal position, holding onto his leg where the spear poked him.

"Ico, are you okay?" he asks him, looking worried.

Ico slowly looks up to Silvus with a scared look on his face and weakly asks him, "Do you know who these guys are? Please tell me you know something?"

Silvus tries to remember if he has ever read anything about the creatures. Of all the books he read, there is one book in mind that speaks about old fables. One in particular is about Kobolds, small two-legged lizards that live underground below them. Looking at one guard, Silvus calls out to him once again.

"Excuse me, guard, forgive our ignorance, but what are you guys called?"

"We call ourselves Kobolds, prisoner, now be quiet before I poke you like your friend!" the guard demands, very aggressively. He even shows Silvus his spear to show he is not joking.

Silvus walks to a corner of the cage to sit on until he notices that he does not have a strap on him. He hectically looks at his back to see the package is not with him. Looking around, he spots the package lying near the driver. As much as he wants to get it back, two things stop him: first, he is bound. Second, he and his cousin are stuck in the cage being escorted to wherever the creatures who call themselves Kobolds live. The best that Silvus can do is lie back and wait while Ico begs with one of the guards, who are just getting more annoyed. One of them makes small grunts, wanting him to shut the heck up.

<hr />

The carriage makes a stop. Silvus, who tried to sleep the entire ride, jolts up awake with gasp. He gets onto his feet to see a large grey gate in the middle, guarded by two more of the creatures or Kobolds guarding the gate.

One of the gate guards walk up to the driver and asks him, "What is this?"

"We found them in the middle of the tunnel. So we captured them to take them to the king so he could deal with them." The driver points back at the two bound cousins.

"WHAT?!" Ico freaks out while Silvus makes a small gasp.

"Sir, in our defense we did not know this cave is--Gah!"

"SILENCE!"

One of the guards now pokes Silvus with the spear, earning him a snarling hiss, only to be poked again. Not wanting any more trouble, Silvus stays silent while Ico beside him begins to sweat and shake in fear.

The gate guard nods with the driver and walks to back toward the gate. He opens up a secret little door to shout, "OPEN THE GATES!"

The stone gates begin to slowly open up to allow the carriage to continue its course.

Both Silvus and Ico both have their eyes wide open, looking amazed by the sight of a circular underground city with stone cylinder buildings with colorful curved rooftops. What is more appealing about the city are the strange roots sticking out from both the ceiling above and the ground below giving it lots of light.

The inhabitants, the Kobolds that dwell on the stone streets, are indeed reptilians walking on two feet like Raptors. Unlike Raptors, they are a bit smaller, with beaklike snouts, not to mention they have big frill on their heads, almost resembling a Tritop. The boys seem to be more muscular, having long horns on their foreheads with darker scale color, while the females are more slender but lacking horns, yet their scale colors are brighter.

The little Kobolds seem to be singing a cheerful melody while they work. They sing tending to their private little root gardens. They sing while cleaning their houses. And even guards are singing while they patrol the streets. Looking around the streets, Silvus notices a group of Kobolds are weaving a strange silky material he has never seen before, harvested from strange big worm like creatures, instead of cotton from the puffer plants.

A Kobold or two spots the carriage with faces of amazement as if they have never seen them for a long time. They stop singing to run up the carriage to check out the newest visitors or prisoners. Even the hatchlings stop playing in the streets to see the newcomers. Eventually more Kobolds begin rushing through to get closer looks, only for the guards that patrol to block their path, allowing the carriage to enter another district.

———— ««◎»» ————

They must be in the nobility's district, to judge by the fancy-looking buildings that look like towers with curvy rooftops, cleaner streets, and the Kobolds wearing silk rags and jewels that make them look like nobles.

In contrast to the lower class, the nobles sing a more soothing tone while some of them drink wine, play with instruments, paint pictures, and even walk strange shelled reptiles on a leash. The songs are so relaxing, Ico seems to have calmed down. Silvus can only think of the district, as it reminds him of the Creston Betadom by what he is taught.

Noticing their presence, the nobles stop singing and walk up to the carriage rather than rushing. The crowd whisper among themselves about the prisoners, while the carriage continues its course. More guards nearby join up to keep order. Eventually the carriage stops by a large, towering structure that is built right on a wall north of the district. Its mere size is so big, the cousins cannot help but admire.

"Dude, that must be where their ruler lives?!" Ico whispers to Silvus, keeping his eyes on the castle watching its gates open up.

Coming out of the castle gates is an elderly dark-blue Kobold male wearing a crown between his long horns, with a nice blue cape made of silk. He is followed by a bodyguard and two other Kobold nobles who might be his children or members of court. One is a young dark-blue male wearing the same Oriental carved armor, but black. He has a serious expression on his face like a soldier. The other is a pearl-white female with a flirtatious look wearing a purple short cloak, a necklace, and some rings.

All the nearby nobles bow to the crowned Koboldn confirming he is the king of the metropolis. The King looks very annoyed as he approaches the guard at a rapid pace.

"Guard, what is the meaning of this?" the king Kobold demands calmly of the driver as he examines both Silvus and Ico.

"We found those two trespassing into our entrance tunnel, so we decided to capture them, your majesty," the guard driver explains to the king, taking out the package at his side, making Silvus run up with a gasp of worry. "We also found this thing strapped on one of them."

The king takes the package for a closer look. With his green eyes, he looks it up and down. He gives it to the young blue male and turns to the guard and commands him, "Take them to the dungeon so we can prepare for trial."

"As you command, my king." The guard of the carriage salutes and takes the two cousins to wherever the dungeon is. Ico tries to plead innocence, only to be poked by the guard again. Silvus, however, could only watch the king and the other young Bolds looking at them as they are taken to the dungeon.

———— ✦ ————

For a stone dungeon, the place is very clean, according to Silvus, as he sits in his cell by the corner while Ico lies in fetal position on the stone bed, looking very terrified. Silvus walks up to his scared younger cousin, puts out a now unbound talon and tells him, "You asked for this, Cousin."

In response, Ico looks up giving Silvus a childish glare yet struggles to keep the face on, knowing that his cousin is right.

"How can you be this calm? We are prisoners to a bunch of little guys! So humiliating." Ico moans at the idea of dying by the claws of the small creatures.

Silvus walks up to the bars of the cell, hoping to get a closer glimpse of the dungeon. This kingdom must not have problem with crime due to cells being empty, except for one cell—a female walks up looking seductive toward him. She makes a wink with bedroom eyes asking him how a handsome male like himself got caught up. Silvus' face turns red, and he takes a few steps back toward the wall. Dragging his back down against the wall, he sits down with his arms around his knees.

Silvus worries that now he is in prison, he will not be able to head to Patalot. Even worse, the package that he is supposed to deliver is out of his grasp. Suddenly, a pair of guards walks up to the cell to bang the bars with their stubby talons, getting his attention.

"The king wants to speak with you," one of the guards says directly to Silvus, making the latter get up. Ico hopes to follow suit only for the guards to stop him, shouting at him, at the same time pointing at Silvus.

"Only this one! You stay."

"YOU KIDDING ME?!" Ico complains, only to be punched in the gut by one of the guards and knocked out cold.

"Did you really have to do that?" Silvus asks the guard, being concerned for his cousin's safety.

The guard only tells him to follow, as the other guard closes the cell, leaving behind an out-cold Ico on the stone floor.

Taken to a stone hall of the castle, Silvus follows the guard all the way to a bronze metal door. The guard escorting tells him to wait as he enters through the door. While he waits, Silvus thinks about why the king wanted to see him specifically. His train of thought is interrupted by a female voice.

"What a strange fellow you are."

Silvus looks around, trying to see who called out to him. The voice tells him to look down, so he does, to see the young noble female who is with the king, looking at him with her emerald-green eyes with a flirtatious look. He asks, ignoring the pretty face, "Who are you?"

The female laughs and begins circling around him like a Veloci getting ready to attack her prey. Silvus keeps his guard up as he begins to sense a dark aura around her.

"You may call me Cri Jin, Princess of this underground world, Shima," the female Kobold answers him like a scheming rich girl trying to get what she wants.

"So this city is called Shima? And if you're a princess, that means the king is your father?" Silvus guesses.

Cri giggles in response, clarifying his answer. Out of nowhere, she uses one of her stubby claws to grab Silvus by the collar to bring his head down so she can take a closer look at his silver face. She stares at his blue eyes for a few awkward seconds and places a kiss on his nose. Silvus flinches back up in response, turning red as a tomato, using his claws to wipe it off, making Cri laugh.

"Oh, you—you have some very interesting scales. Are there others with such a thing?" Cri stops her laughter to look at Silvus again.

"Not that I am aware of; but seriously, lady, what the heck!" Silvus snarls at her quietly.

"Well then, I better get to my quarters." Cri starts to walk away not caring about Silvus' reaction. She stops on her tracks to turn her head around to tell him, "Guess I will see you around, handsome."

With that, she leaves. Silvus just stood looking dumbfounded. *Spirits, that is the second female that flirted with me!* he thinks to himself as the door behind him opens.

"The king would like to see you now," the guard orders gruffly as he comes out, opening the door wider for Silvus to enter by crouching, since the door is a bit short.

———◦(◦)◦———

Silvus is greeted by a decent-sized office filled with small furniture. He walks up to a short yet long table, trying to sit on one of the three stone chairs. Being too short, he is very uncomftorble due to being a taller creature. In front, across the table, the bigger chair turns around, revealing the king himself not wearing his crown.

"What is your name?" the king asks him with an inquisitive look.

"My full name is Vessel Silvus, but call me Silvus, your majesty." The young Raptor makes a small bow to the king to show some respect.

"Interesting. I am Yi Jin. You probably figured that I am the king of what is left of my beloved Shima."

"What is left, your majesty?" Silvus tilts his head, curious about what King Yi Jin meant.

King Yi Jin looks hesitant to explain, probably due to the fact Silvus is a stranger to him. Yi gets off his chair, walking up to a nearby portrait of what looks like a Kobold queen, because she is wearing a crown with pearl white scales. As the king looks at the portrait, a tear comes out of his eye.

"By the Root--listen, we might look like we are a bunch of jolly little lizards, but in truth we are facing a crisis of our own!" King Yi explains to Silvus with a depressing tone.

"Kinda hard to imagine, seeing your subjects sing very happily to each other," Silvus states with a small chuckle, earning a small glare from Yi, making him stop.

"Long ago, this city was the seat of a mighty empire! Our kind throughout the years built Outer Roads that once connected this city to the Claves!"

"What are Outer Roads and Claves, if I may ask?" Silvus respectfully asks Yi about the weird names due to his ignorance of Kobold society.

"Of course you be ignorant. You Raptors live in the surface world. Lack of contact do make the perfect bait for one's ignorance." King Yi makes one more glance serious at the portrait.

"Is she…?" Silvus asks the king now concern about his fixation.

"That is my late wife, mother of my three hatchlings." King Yi takes a deep breath, with his eyes closed.

"Sorry to hear that, your majesty." Silvus feels guilty, looking away only to hear the king chuckle, surprising him. He sees Yi turn around back in good spirits as he fixes up his cape, shifting it side to side as if he is wearing a tie.

"It's alright, surface dweller; it has been years since then. At least I am happy with my eldest son and two daugh…" Yi pauses and shakes his head realizing that he is distracted from the point.

"Never mind that! Come with me; I'd like to show you something." Yi gestures his arm for Silvus to follow him out of the office.

⇒●《◑》●⇐

Led by King Yi, Silvus finds himself inside a large square room with a long glowing root sticking out. On the walls are different panels with a painted picture.

Silvus looks around the room as if he stepped into the heavens. Each panel seems to tell a story. One panel shows a big glowing root surrounded by Kobolds bowing to it. Another panel shows a Kobold with a crown looking high and mighty in front of a large crowd of Kobolds with the same root in the background.

"Welcome to the Hall of Stories. Since the beginning, our ancestors have recorded all they know on these walls. The first panel you see talks about how we are the children of the Mother Root. The second one you see is the crowning of the first king chosen by the root to be her voice, to guide her children along with the various Scions, the champions of our kind who founded the ruling clans."

King Yi guides Silvus to another panel, but this time the entire city is shining gold.

"Since then, the king and the ruling clans created the mighty Shima Empire living the golden age under the Mother Root's guidance. For example, we learned how to use large silky worms to produce our wondrous outfits!"

The king's expression turns sour as he walks up to another panel. Silvus gasps in horror as he sees the next panel shows different kings, queens, or other bureaucrats turning their back on the pleas of their subjects as they suffer at the claws of fearsome beasts and savage Kobolds who turn to curroption.

"Eventually, the ruling clans turn their backs on the Mother Root. They ignore the pleas of others and care not for the teachings of the Mother Root."

The king and Silvus shift to another panel, but this time it has squares of different underground villages with tunnels connected on one square; the city is on fire, with savage beasts and Kobolds acting like bandits.

"As if the Mother Root were punishing us, Shima collapsed. The Claves—or villages, in your speech—that connected this city by the underground network of large tunnels, the Outer Roads, fell to the feral creatures and the lost.

"The lost were Kobolds who submitted to a life of crime due to frustrations of the past kings and queens. As for the Kobolds who did not submit, they fled back to this city. This city you see here is all that is left of the once beloved empire of Shima."

Silvus feels a tear come out of his eye. Listening to the entire story makes him feel very bad for the little lizards. It makes him think the kingdom of Avalonia might be suffering the same fate.

"What about today? How have you been running things?" Silvus sobs a bit, hoping there can be some beacon of light. Yi turns around to face him.

"In my reign, the best I could do was help protect what is left of my subjects from the horrors of not only the Outer Roads but also the horrors of the surface world. Speaking of the surface world, you and your friend were not the only Raptors to have come here."

"Really?" Silvus questions, surprised.

"Oh yes. I called for you specifically because your scales remind me of the Raptor who calls himself the Alpha-Prince. Ultamar Sulthur, he called himself."

Silvus perks up at the mention of the late Alpha-King when he was Alpha-Prince. That sparks more questions into his mind. Yi continues.

"Oh yes! At some point, I sent scouts to navigate the surface world. Eventually they came across a group of strange tall lizards, Raptors they call themselves, being led by Sulthur. I have to say, Sulthur was a charming fellow. I showed him around and told him of our plight. Not to mention he promised when he becomes Alpha-King, he would help negotiate trade and possibly help us take back our old territory within the Outer Roads!"

That is a lot to take in. Silvus does not believe what the little king told him, at first—not only that the Alpha-King knew about the Kobolds but actually made a promise. In his mind, a question pops in. *Did others know about the Kobolds too?*

"Now that you're here, I assume you might be an envoy. So did he become Alpha-King yet so he could fulfill his promise?!" Yi asks in a form of plea. He must be very desperate, to assume that Silvus is some emissary for the Alpha-King, who is actually long dead.

Feeling uneasy, Silvus debates in his mind how he is going to spill out the old news. For sure, he isn't going to lie to foreign royalty. He better think quickly, as the king is staring at him, losing some patience.

"I hate to be the bearer of bad news, your majesty, but Alpha-King Sulthur died twenty-four winters ago."

"WHAT! How?" Yi demands, in denial.

Silvus explains to him that Sulthur died a month after his coronation, during a party. In response, Yi is even more devastated by the news. The broken king walks up to the panel of the golden-painted city, places a stubby claw on it, and falls to his knees.

Silvus does not know what to do at this point. He can only listen to the king rambling about how their only hope for survival is gone. Suddenly an idea comes into his head. Remembering about his destination, maybe he can try to negotiate. "My cousin and I were heading to Patalot, your majesty!"

The king looks at the Raptor behind him with one eyebrow raised, listening to what Silvus had to say.

"Even with the Alpha-King dead, the Mistatorium took regenary power, so maybe I can talk to them about that promise!" Silvus continues, hoping to shed some light for both the king and himself.

"You would do that?!" Yi gets up with glimmer of hope in his eyes.

Silvus nods yes and continues, "Indeed, your majesty! My cousin and I were on an important mission until we ended up here."

"A mission?"

"Yes, a mission that involves delivering a certain package I believe you gave to that other noble before you took me and my cousin the dungeon."

Silvus explains to Yi that he had a package with him. Then he proceeds to tell him how he could speak to the Mistatorium to see if he could convince them to fulfill a promise. That lifted Yi's spirits a bit, thinking about the offer. After thinking it through, the king gives his answer. "As much as I would love to accept your offer and as true as your story is, you and your cousin are still under suspicion. Don't get me wrong—you do seem like the fine sort, but you are still a stranger. Tomorrow we are going to hold a trial to decide what to do with you both!"

Silvus is disappointed by the response. The king does have a point; he and his cousin are strangers who somehow trespassed into unknown territory. So the king orders the guard to take him back to the dungeon into his cell.

Chapter 13
To Save an Underground Princess

Two guards escort Silvus back to the dungeons, to his cell. In the cell, he sees Ico trying to sleep on the stone bed, rocking back and forth, complaining how uncomfortable it is. He stops to see Silvus has returned, gasping in relief that he is back.

"By the spirits, you're back! What did you and the king talk about?" Ico asks, wanting to know what happened between him and the king.

Silvus grabs a nearby stool to sit on and explains what he and the king spoke about. He tells Ico the king's name, then about their plight, and finally revealing that their Alpha-King knew about them. Ico's face is jaw-dropping. He is shocked by the news explained to him.

"Dude, no way! The Alpha-King knew about this place?" Ico shouts, earning him a nod from Silvus.

"Correct, and he actually made a promise to help them."

"Did you tell their king that Sulthur is dead?"

"Sadly, yes I did, but I tried to negotiate with him by offering to speak with the Mistatorium on their behalf," Silvus explains in response to the hard question.

Ico gives Silvus an inquisitive look, sitting up on the stone bed that reads, "Were you really gonna do it?" Silvus tells Ico he will do it when given a chance. Still skeptical, Ico lies back on the bed try-ing to get comfy. He asks, "What do you think is going happen to us now?"

Silvus gets back on his feet to walk slowly to a nearby wall, lean-ing his back on it, and replies, "There is going to trial for us tomor-row. The best we can do is pray to the spirits that it goes well."

Obviously not satisfied with the answer, Ico huffs, then shifts his entire body on the bed facing the wall. Silvus climbs onto the other bed, hoping to sleep. He only gets another nightmare about his mother being tortured, making him toss and turn for the rest of the night.

Silvus wakes up to banging sounds from the cell bars. Ico wakes up too, as both cousins could see four guards standing in front wait-ing, carrying spears.

"Follow us! It is time for the trial!" one of the guards orders, as the other one opens up the cell with his key, allowing the couisns to walk with them out of the dungeon.

⟞⟝⟞⟝⟞ ⟪◉⟫ ⟞⟝⟞⟝⟞

Silvus and Ico are escorted to a large Oriental-style throne room filled with various nobles or ruling clans gathered around the sides near two large dining room tables filled with food, which is unfamil-iar meat and bugs. The males wear colored sleeveless silk Oriental vests, while the females wear jewlerly.

As the two couisns cross the light-blue carpets, in front of them is the throne, in front of a large glowing root with King Yi Jin on it. Between him are two of his hatchlings, one of them being Cri, whom Silvus meet last night and who looks at him like a flying predator scanning for its prey. Also with the king are higher ranking members of the nobility with their own guards standing with them.

One of the guards orders Silvus and Ico to kneel. Once on their knees, a Kobold servant wearing a puffy silk hat walks up with a parchment and reads, "Ladies and gentlemen, today is the trial of two trespassers from the surface world."

The present nobles in the room gasp with gazes glued to the cousins. At the same time, they whisper to each other quietly their thoughts about them.

King Yi remains on his throne turns his attention to Silvus and asks, "What are your names?" with a wink, letting him know that he knows his name but the court does not.

"My name is Vessel Silvus, and this guy with me is my cousin Vessel Ico, your majesty," Silvus explains very calmly, earning awkward whispers from the nobles, as if they expected him not to comply so smoothly. Ico, still kneeling, is just as surprised that his cousin spoke so calmly. With a smile, the king speaks once again.

"Do you deny trespassing into our territory?"

"No, sir, Ico and I did somehow end up into your territory, but--"

"THE PRISONER CONFESSES!"

Silvus is cut off by one of the elite nobles standing next to the king, wearing a purple coat, looking serious. The other noble, the one wearing a red coat, tries to calm him down.

"Whoa--easy there, Pi Wei!"

"Easy? You are always too soft on prisoners!" the noble named Pi Wei accuses.

The other nobles begin to argue with each other. Silvus and Ico can only cover their ear holes, because the arguing is getting loud, until the king shouts, "SILENCE!"

The crowd goes silent, including the two elite nobles. They all turn their gazes at the king, who looks annoyed to the core. He sits back down calmly to speak.

"First off, Sun Wu is right. Pi Wei, you really need to stop drawing conclusions. It is true that they confessed the crime, but we need to listen to why and how they ended up here." The king points to the two cousins, allowing Silvus to continue speaking.

"To be honest with you all, we were being chased by some strangers. We needed to hide, so we came across a cave, not knowing that it yours."

"So you came to hide?"

"Yes, your majesty—not because we are fugitives, but a lot of things are happing on the surface." Silvus bows once again and explains all he knows about the troubles happening on the surface.

The nobles continue to talk among themselves. King Yi sits up straight and announces, "So it is settled. The crime was unintentional! Which is why I have decided that the punishment will be to perform a task for community service!"

The two cousins are relieved that the punishment will not be harsh. Ico is glad that he won't be executed. Silvus himself is glad that it will be a chance to be able to continue on his journey after doing whatever task Yi wants them to do. The relief is short lived when a pair of doors bursts open, gaining the crowd's attention. A scout comes through, looking exhausted. Yi stands up from his throne, fuming at the sudden interruption.

"What is the meaning of this?!" he demands of the scout, who makes a bow along with a quick apology.

"Forgive me, your majesty! I have dire news concerning the whereabouts of Princess Fi!" the scout fearfully explains, making the crowd gasp.

"My youngest daughter? YOU FOUND HER!" King Yi demands further.

The scout runs up to Yi and whispers the news into his invisible ear. In shock, Yi sits down on his throne, slouching down. The male blue Kobold walks up to Yi and asks, "Father, is everything okay?" with a voice filled with concern. Cri, however, looks calm for some reason. Silvus notices it from a distance, giving her a raised brow.

What kind of a sibling would not be concerned for his or her own kin? he wonders.

The king looks to his son and then back at the male Raptors, giving him an idea. He stands up once again with a hopeful smile to proclaim the task at claw.

"Due to the turn of events, I have decided what the boys are going to do for community service! I would like them to join my eldest and only son Prince Ki on an expedition to the outer roads to rescue my youngest and other daughter Fi!"

The crowd go wild with cheering while Silvus and Ico gasp with diferent reactions. Based on the stories Yi has told him, Silvus makes a soft swallow in nervousness. He looks to Ico, who for some reason is making a big grin with gleam in his eyes.

"Ico? Are you okay?"

"Dude, we are going to save a damsel in distress!"

King Yi, who heard the exchange of words between the cousins, smiles and turns to Ki.

"My son, you would be so kind as to escort our esteemed guests to the royal forge so we can make some new armor and weapns for them?"

"I will be honored, Father," Ki replies with a bow. He walks down the steps from the throne and tells the cousins to follow him to the forge.

———⟨◊⟩———

In the middle of the streets of Shima, a pair of doors in the noble district opens up, with a battalion of fifty soldiers in blue coming out along with Silvus and Ico, both wearing the Kobold carved chest armor and helmet forged just for them in the same color. Silvus is given a curved sword, and Ico is given a long bow and steel arrows.

The two cousins march next to Prince Ki, who is leading the entire troop.

The lower-class Kobolds take notice and gaze curiously to see that all the troops are marching all the way to an enormous gate that, Silvus guesses, leads to the Outer Roads. Stopping them in their tracks, Prince Ki runs up and faces his troops.

"Listen up, soldiers! Beyond these gates leads the Outer Roads. You all might have heard stories of fearsome beasts and savage marauders, or the lost that dwell beyond!"

Silvus looks around to see the small soldiers are nervous, to judge by the way they shake their bodies. This shows that they probably did hear stories. Ico stands proud as if claiming he is not afraid of anything making him do a soft growl in annoyance, turning his eyes back to Ki.

"A while ago, my youngest sister Princess Fi was missing, but now we know where she is thanks to a scout, and it is our duty as the king's soldiers to go out there and save anybold in trouble, especially a member of the royal family! We are trained for this, men; this is the moment!"

Ki draws his curved sword up high. It is nbot just any sword—the sword Ki is wielding is pure gold. It must be an important symbol, as the soldiers behind Silvus all cheer, along with the peasants nearby who listened to the speech. The prince points the sword at the gate and shouts, "Open up!"

A loud clunk sound is heard. The gates slowly open up to reveal a big subterranean opening.

Ki runs back to the group and begins their march. Once they are in, the gates closes behind them.

The Outer Roads is the subterranean tunnel system built inside a cave deep underground. Silvus cannot help but admire the giant wide road built long ago. He even takes interest in the wildlife he never saw before, like the giant skink-like creatures he saw while he was inside a cage. He could have sworn he saw a giant insect or two crawl around the walls.

"Admiring the scenery?" Silvus hears the voice of Ki call out to him. He turns his head down to see Ki looking at him.

"I read about places like this in books, but to see it in the Scales!" Silvus beams around the cave filled with glowing roots, like a hatchling discovering wonderland. He looks to the right to see some geysers blowing from a lake. To his left, he spots a pack of large frilled lizards scavenging for prey.

"This road we walk was built by my ancestors long ago in order to expand our underground empire. My father explained what is actually going on, right?" Ki assumes.

"Oh, yes, he did. Must be rough to live in a society on brink of destruction." Silvus expresses his sympathy. He tells Ki what his father had told him when he showed him the wall of stories the other day.

"No argument here, soldier. Silvus, right?"

"Yup."

"Well then, what is it like to live on the surface?"

Silvus beams at the question. Ico, who sees his couisn's reaction, whispers "Here we go" and rolls his eyes, knowing what he is going to do.

During the entire march, Silvus gives a lecture to Ki all about the surface world, the open sky, how Raptor society works, and as well as their beliefs. They stop at a crossroad to rest. It allows Sivus to ask about bits of Kobold beliefs, especially this Mother Root they seem to keep bringing up, which is heretical to an Avalonian Raptor like himself.

"So Ki, what can you tell me about this Root that you guys keep mentioning like it is some kind of god?" Silvus asks the smaller prince, who in turn bursts out laughing, along with the soldiers who overheard. Silvus gives Ico a confused look not knowing why what he said is funny, only to earn him a shrug from his cousin telling him he did not know.

With his laughter dying down, Ki explains, "We Kobolds venerate the Root; we do not worship her like a god. We believe the Root is a living thing that we are born from, making us part of nature. When we Kobolds die, we are claimed back to the Root's embrace."

"So you guys believe nature is your afterlife?" Silvus takes out a scroll and quill from his carrier pack and writes up what he learned, earning an eye roll from Ico.

Ki, however, seems to be intrigued as Silvus continues to write.

"So you Raptors believe in supernatural stuff?"

"We Raptors have always liked to base our traditions around the concept of Mist, the source of power we use to perform some neat tricks."

"Tricks? What sort of tricks?"

"Let me show you."

Silvus lifts up one claw to demonstrate his Mist ability to form an ice ball to show Ki. Ki and his soldiers get spooked at the sight. Silvus twrils the ice balls with one talon, with a smirk on his face.

"This, my friend, is Mistcraft, the ability to tap into the Mist to perform powers that would make you question reality."

"And you could do this anywhere? Could all Raptors like yourself do it?" Ki asks him.

"As long as I have enough Mist stored within myself, I could do them anywhere. To answer your other question, any sentient creature blessed like Raptors could perform Mistcraft, but it takes a lot of practice to get used to it. The more you use Mist, the longer you can use it until it depletes. When Mist depletes, a Mistcaster needs to wait for the Mist to recharge."

"How do you recharge?"

"Because Mist is everywhere as long as the wellsprings exist, Mist simply flows inside us," Silvus states as his eyes flash blue, spooking Ki and the soldiers even further.

"Did your eyes just flash?" Ki asks him.

"That means I am fully recharged, since I did not really use much."

Ki is going to ask another question until a shrieking sound from the right side of the road is heard. The entire party jumps back on their feet and turn their heads to where the sreech came from.

"What the heck is that?" Silvus asks Ki, hoping he knows what they are dealing with.

"That is a shriek of a pack of Rantulas getting ready to attack. Better check it out." Ki motions all the soldiers to follow to the right side of the crossroad into a deep tunnel.

<hr />

The entire battalion come across a big opening with huge webs on the walls to see giant fury spiders, Rantulas are attacking a group of Kobolds who are fighting back fiercely. From side of the tunnel the battalion halt their tracks to observe what is going on.

Silvus peeks his head to take a closer look. He sees a party of at least fifty Kobolds engaged with a swarm of Rantulas by the hundreds, wearing black Oriental armor. On the armor is painted a dark- green, rotting Kobold head.

"Who are those guys?" he asks Ki.

"They must be 'the Rotting Ronin.' An army of criminals, those looking for a place in life, and dishonored nobles sentenced by the royal court in order to regain their honor."

"So you guys put criminals into an army? Just what we need," Ico sarcastically states.

"The Rotting Ronin are actually an order of the best warriors the Kobolds of Shima have trained to protect any threats from the Outer Roads. Look."

Ki points to the battlefield for the cousins to observe the battle. He probably wants them to see for themselves how special these warriors are.

————))⦿((————

On the battlefield, the Ronin warriors seem to be handling themselves pretty well against the Rantulas, thanks to being armed. Being armed with long swords keeps the Ronin safe distance away from the poisonous bite attacks.

One Rantula tries to swipe one of its thorned legs at one male Ronin warrior with a two-clawed sword pointed at it, only for him to slice through it, making the Rantula shriek in pain. The male Kobold takes advantage by sprinting toward it like the wind and makes a big leap, landing on its head. Then he impales his sword right through the head of the giant arachnid, squirting a lot green goo, Rantula blood spraying at the Kobold.

————))⦿((————

"By the spirits—did you see that, Silvus?!" Ico asks, looking very surprised. "That guy just leaped onto its head and plunged it like a monster slayer!"

"I did, Ico, and I have to say, that was amazing! They seem to have it under control," Silvus claims as he continues to gaze at the battle.

"I wouldn't count on that yet," Ki warns as he points at the holes to see more Rantulas coming out, while the Ronin Warriors can only watch, as they show signs of exhaustion after dealing with a horde.

"We better reinforce them. They might be good at fighting, but they can still get overwhelmed."

Ki draws his blade and orders the battalion to charge, with Silvus and Ico following suit. They run down the rocky slope like a raging waterfall, making the Ronin warriors turn their heads at the sight of the stampede of soldiers rushing to their aide.

"REINFORCEMENTS!" the leading Ronin warrior shouts out with excitement in his voice while thrusting his blade up in the sky. The others do so too, feeling just as pumped. They rush alongside the main army and clash with the remaining Rantulas that are crawling down the walls of the web-filled cave.

Both the army and the Ronin warriors tear through the horde of Rantulas. Silvus and Ico fight side by side, making sure neither of them gets killed. The Rantulas, for a horde of giant bugs, are determined to kill their prey.

Silvus uses his favorite lightning blast spell by wielding his sword like a wand, flicking it to shoot lightning at the head of each furious arachnid. Based on what he sees, he believes the head must be a weak spot. He attempts to make another flick of his sword covered in Mist aura, only to get struck by a pile of web from behind. Stuck in the web wrapping, he struggles to get out while the Rantula that struck him is about to pounce, only for an arrow to strike it in the head.

Silvus turns around to see that the arrow came from Ico, who is running toward him as he shoots a few more arrows at nearby Rantulas that tried to attack him or the other Kobolds in battle. Ico uses his claws to cut off the webbing, freeing Silvus.

The Rantulas eventually flee in retreat, crawling into the holes like a bunch of whimpering wolves. The Kobold army and Ronin all cheer for their victory, covered in Rantula blood all over. Silvus, being helped up by Ico, looks into the cheering crowd to see Prince Ki also covered in green, making sure his troops are okay.

Among the surviving Ronin warriors, one male takes off his helmet to reveal his brown-scaled face with a large scar crossed on one of his yellow eyes, looking very grateful. One of his horns seems to be cut off. He approaches the prince and kneels to show respect as the other Ronin warriors do.

"Thank you for the assist, your highness. You and your soldiers stormed in just in time."

"The honor is mine indeed, Commander. Glad to help with that giant bug problem."

The Ronin commander laughs at Ki's comment and gets up back on his feet to explain the current predicament.

"Not just giant bugs, your highness. We had come across one or two of the lost giant cresthead snakes. You could say the usual for us of the Rotting Ronin trying to get them uncivilized trash away from Shima."

"So the Rotting Ronin are frontier defense?" Silvus speaks up as he walks up to both Ki and the commander who drew his blade in fear not knowing who to larger creature is. Ki stops him before things go out of hand.

"Forgive my ignorance, but who or what are they?" the commander asks Ki, sheathing his sword on his back.

"They are our esteemed guests from the surface world. My father charged them to come with us to rescue my youngest sister Princess Fi." Ki turns his head to Silvus. "To answer your question, yes, they are primarily frontier defense, sworn to protect what is left of us from Shima."

"You know, for a bunch of little guys, you Ronin guys are pretty tough," Ico adds with a smirk, earning him looks from all the nearby Kobolds. One of them even demands what he meant by it.

Ignoring his cousin's smart-tail comment, Silvus looks back to the now calmed down commander and explains, "Well then, yes, we have been sent by your king to look for Princess Fi. Have you seen her?"

"We did see a Rantula carrying a maiden, which is why we are here." The commander points to a big ball of web sticking onto the wall.

Without giving orders, Ki gasps and rushes up to the ball. Silvus, Ico, and the commander follow suit. Ki takes out a sword and cuts the ball open to reveal an adorable bright light-blue female wearing a necklace falling into his arms. *That must be Fi*, Silvus thinks, without noticing Ico looking at the female with bright red face.

The female Fi slowly wakes up, revealing her light-green eyes. Confused, she looks around surrounded by members of both the royal army and the Rotting Ronin along with two creatures she has never seen. She turns her head to her brother and weakly asks him, "Where am I?"

"You are in the middle of Rantula territory of the Outer Roads! You had us all worried sick!" Ki softly scolds at her a bit due to her being gone for a long time.

"But I remember our sister telling me to meet her at an abandoned Clave, only for me to get taken by these things!" Fi tries to defend her action.

As much as Ki wants to scold her, there is something more important to discuss. "Wait a minute. Cri told you to be around here?"

"She did! She told me to meet her at a Clave, wanting to show me something. Then I felt something hit me on the head, and now somehow I ended up here." Fi looks around and spots the two cousins.

"Who or what are you two?" she asks.

Silvus makes a soft bow to her and tries to say, "My name is Vessel Silvus, milady, and...gah!"

Ico cuts him off by rushing past him. In front of her, Ico kneels on one knee with a flamboyant expression on his face and greets her. "I am Sir Vessel Ico, milady. Mighty hunter and future knight to be." He takes one of her little claws and places a kiss, making her cheeks flush.

"OH MY GOSH! A hunter, you say? And what is a knight? They must be really fab?" the rescued says in a peppy tone. Her tone seems to excite Ico a lot, by the way he smiles.

Silvus awkwardly watches his couisn's sudden...interest in the Kobold female. Of all the flirting Silvus remembers Ico doing, seems to be very interested in the smaller creature no taller than his hip. He turns his head to Ki and whispers, "I believe we have a damsel to escort back."

Nodding in agreement, Ki coughs into his claw, getting both the princess and the lover Raptor boy's attention. "I hate to interrupt this moment at first sight, but we better get back to Shima, pronto. I am going to have a big word with Cri when we get back," he tells them.

With both the royal army and Ronin marching back, Silvus takes one more look at Ico with Fi.

"Would you like to get to know each other while we head back, Princess?"

"That. Would. Be lovely of you! Ico, right?"

The Raptor in front of her makes a grin, nodding yes. It's obvious that he has a crush on the princess. Silvus could not help but snout palm and turn around, only to see the army has stopped in their tracks. Wanting to know what is going on, he walks through all the way to the front next to Ki, who looks like he is in a trance. "Whats going on?" he asks the crown prince.

Ki points for him to look, and he sees an army of at least two hundred Kobolds marching down the slope entrance, wearing green armor, with weapons drawn. Silvus' first thought is that they are possibly lost Kobolds in banditry, but he shakes off the thought, seeing the unknown army holding flags and organized. They seem to be led by the Kobold wearing a dark-green cape. They stop in their tracks once they are six feet away from the Allied army.

The Kobold leading the unknown army steps forward. He takes off his helm to reveal a white- scaled face with hues of dark teal. He seems to be in his late twenties, just like Ki. His yellow eyes gaze at both Silvus and the gang with utmost fury, seeking revenge. With his eyes landing on Ki, he says, "Ki Jin, you have fallen right into our trap!"

The leading enemy Kobold draws his sword, as do the others behind him. In response, the royal army and Ronin draw their weapons to prepare. Silvus too prepares his blade, filling it with Mist aura, while Ico draws his bow and arrow, trying to protect Fi, who cowers behind him.

"What is the meaning of this?! Identify yourselves at once!" Ki demands while standing his ground with his blade pointed at the green-armored enemy.

The leading Kobold raises his blade up and high and with a face of fury he shouts, "I am Jiang Shu! And on behalf of the Shu clan, we will have our revenge and restore our rightful claim to the royal throne!"

Chapter 14
A Game of Kobolds

After declaring who the green-armored Kobolds are, both sides kept up their guards. Swords, spears, and arrows aim at each other, filling the web-covered cave with an atmosphere of tension. Both sides are so quiet that the sound of flowing air is heard blowing through the tunnels.

Silvus, one of the two Raptors among the royal army side, hold his sword with the blade covered with Mist aura. He turns his head back to make sure his cousin is okay. Ico is seen standing among a row of archers with his bow and arrow drawn, at the same time protecting Fi by standing in front of her.

Silvus turns his head back up front, leans left to Ki who is standing next to him, and whispers, "Who are Clan Shu? And what do they have against you?"

Ki in return whispers back, "Shu was one of the major ruling clans until they tried to overthrow my clan in order to gain power. Because of it, my ancestor King Zhao Jin forced them into exile. As you can see, we Kobolds take honor among clans very seriously."

"For so long, we have prepared for this day. We knew the king would send you to rescue your sister, so we decided to kidnap her to use her as bait to take out both of you. I have to admit, I hoped the Rantulas would eat you all first," Jiang Shu of the opposing side mocks with a smirk.

"YOU KIDNAPP THE PRINCESS TO USE HER AS BAIT! HOW DARE YOU!"

All eyes go to an angry Ico, who shouted. He keeps his bow drawn, getting ready to fire at any momment. Fi, who stands behind Ico is holding onto his leg like a poor maiden needing her knight in shining armor. Obviously she is scared not only because she is young, but also she has no weapon to defend herself.

"Who in the Root's name is that abomination?" Jiang demands with a brow raised.

"That's my cousin!" Silvus snarls, followed by a hiss, gaining Jiang's attention. Jiang squints his eyes, getting a closer look at him. He seems to be scanning Silvus as if he has seen him before.

"You must be that silver-scaled surface dweller that our mutual ally is interested in!" Jiang states with a curious look.

"What mutual ally?" Silvus shouts, looking confused. He only earns a laugh from both Jiang and his army. Ki himself is also just as confused.

"This hidden ally of yours. Who is he?!" Ki demands, stomping his foot to show he is serious.

"It is not a he, pretender. The ally is a she and she wants you, your sister, and your tall friend dead as much as we do. She is the reason we manage to plan all this. Regardless, we all are going to get the revenge we wanted. Kobolds of Shu, ATTACK!"

Jiang Shu and his army begin their charge. They all run down the rocky slope like a stampede of angry Tritops. In response, the royal army, allied with the Ronin, charges with Prince Ki leading. Ico, Fi, and the archers, however, stay behind to give arrow support to their allies.

The two armies clash in the middle of the opening. Blades clashing, axes bashing, arrows being shot. Both sides fought intense. At the center, Ki is seen fighting one on one with Jiang clashing their swords.

Among the battle, Silvus is the only one seen performing elemental Mist spells at the enemy. The common spell he uses is the lightning shock spell with either his blade or claw, in order to zap them nonlethally. When one or two enemy Kobolds get close to him, he thrusts his claw forward to perform "force push," a spell in the Gravitation category, to push them off. He begins to feel his mind getting tired due to performing too many spells.

A nearby Kobold, thinking Silvus is weakened, tries to strike with his blade raised, only for his target to quickly spot him and parry his attack. Silvus deflects three blows from his attacker, followed by a stab to the chest. He kicks the enemy on the face, making him rag doll off his blade. Silvus turns around to see another enemy Kobold about to charge.

Silvus stands guard, only for the enemy to get shot in the back of the head by an arrow. He turns his head to see Ico giving him the thumbs-up with a bow on claw. He made the killing shot, saving Silvus' life twice.

Having the more numerous advantage, the royal army and the Ronin are prevailing against the Shu army. Seeing that they are losing the battle, the Shu forces begin to either run away like cowards or drop their weapons to surrender.

Jiang Shu, who is busy fighting Ki, notices his soldiers running or surrendering. In pure rage he shouts, "COWARDS!" only for him to get jumped by Ki. Ki takes advantage of the distraction, pinning Jiang on the ground with his foot, and pointing his sword to his neck.

Silvus, the royal army, the Ronin, and the surrendering Shu army take notice and begin to flock to the prince pinning Jiang.

"It is over, Jiang. Who is this ally of yours? And what is she planning? And don't you dare lie!" Ki jabs his blade at Jiang's shoulder, making him shriek in pain. The scream from Jiang slowly morphs into laughter, confusing the crowd.

"The enemy of my enemy is friend, they say, pretender! She was behind your tail before you came here! Betrayed by your own blood. Ahahahaha!" Jiang continues to laugh, still lying on the ground.

Silvus continues to stand in place thinking about what Jiang told Ki. Betrayed by one's own blood... Then it hit him, shouting the name "CRI!"

Eyes all go to him. Ki gets off Jiang, orders one of his soldiers to tie him up, and rushes up toward Silvus.

"You know something, Soldier?!"

"I do! Last night, your sister Cri came up to me before meeting your father. Then earlier, during the trial she was calm, too calm at the news of your other sister's situation!"

"WAIT JUST A MINUTE!"

Eyes all turn to Fi, who is storming toward Silvus and Ki with Ico following along.

"You don't mean Cri is really behind all this?"

"Did you not mention your sister telling you to meet her out here?" Silvus asks her with a serious tone.

"That's...true." Fi shyly turns her head to her eldest sibling and only brother. "What do you think, Big Brother?"

"I don't know. But if it's true, why would she want us killed?"

While the siblings debated why Cri would try to get them killed, Silvus is having his own debate about Cri in his mind. *Why did she want me killed? Obviously her reason to dare kill her siblings is to get closer to the throne, but why me as well?*

Silvus turns around to see Jiang bound, held by two of the royal army. He approaches Jiang to get some answers.

"What do you want, you tall freak?" Jiang growls at him.

"This ally, it's Cri, is it?"

"Why does it matter to you?"

"Because you said that she wants me dead. Well, of course it matters to me!" Silvus retorts at the bound prisoner and continues.

"What did she tell you about me?"

"She only tells me that you are some kind of threat to our plans after promising we would get married! From the way you fight with those powers of yours, no wonder she thinks you are a threat."

"How am I a threat to her?"

"Hell if I know. She just told me that you are a threat; that's all. You will get no more from me, friend of Clan Jin!"

With that, Jiang huffs and turns his head to the side, refusing to cooperate further. Silvus decides to just let it go, knowing that he can get more information from Cri herself. He walks back to Ki and Fi who, just finished debating, turn to him.

"Well, Soldier, if Cri is behind this, it means Father is in danger!"

"Big Brother is right! We need to save DADDY, QUICK! So not cool."

The royal siblings walk past Silvus at the same time Ki orders the Kobold army to start moving back to Shima with the Shu prisoners still bound. The Rotting Ronin bid farewell, wishing them luck before parting ways. As Silvus watches the army move, Ico walks up beside him and whispers, "Dude, getting your family killed! What kind of monster would want to hurt their own scales and blood?"

"It's part of the reality of politics, my young cousin. I have read many books about it."

"Like what?"

"Like the story of Alpha-Queen Ultamar Irona VIII. So obsessed with wanting a daughter, she would abuse her power to go through six husbands and abandon one of her sons." Silvus starts run to catch up with the army while Ico stands dumbfounded. Shaking his head, Ico too runs along.

Silvus finds himself marching fast along the caverns of the Outer Roads along with the royal Shima army. Based on the information what the Shu prisoners told them, a princess among the Jin clan is a possible traitor. If she is a traitor, King Yi is in danger.

They quickly come across the same gates they came to before, heavily guarded. Among the guards, the captain approaches them with a relieved smile on his face only to be ordered by Ki to open the gates ASAP. The guards salute, looking surprised that the prince is in a hurry.

With a loud clicking sound, the gates begin to open. The sound of opening gates makes all the Kobold residents in the city to rush up hoping to see if the army has been successful in rescuing the princess. The army, however, ignores the crowd, rushing to the elite district as soon as possible while half of the army takes the prisoners to a nearby city dungeon.

Silvus and the gang barge right into the throne room, slamming the doors right at the walls. The Kobold nobles waiting inside are startled by the booming sound as they watch Silvus' group of now twenty soldiers along with Ico, Ki, and Fi.

On the throne, King Yi looks at the marching gang, ignoring the sudden barging, seeing that they have succeeded in rescuing Fi. He smiles with lots of joy. Cri, on the other claw, gazes at them with a face of disbelief, as if an evil genius had his or her plans foiled.

"PRAISE THE ROOT! YOU ALL SAVED MY SWEET PRINCESS FI!" King Yi rises from his throne with outmost joy.

"Father! Stay away from Cri!" Ki tries to warn as his entire group, including Silvus, halt in front of the throne. "The entire thing with Fi was all a set-up for us to be killed!"

"Big Brother is telling the truth! Big Sis was the one who told me to meet her at the Outer Roads to give me a surprise for my hatch day!" Fi speaks up for Ki.

King Yi faces Cri, conflicted whether to believe them. He cannot fathom the idea of one of his own hatchlings killing the others. "Is it true, Cri?"

Cri looks around, trying to think of an excuse.

"Um… What proof do you have that I would dare lead my own family to their deaths?" Cri stutters a bit making a nervous smile. Silvus knows she is lying and gives her a threatening glare.

"Does the name Shu ring a bell, your majesty?"

"Shu?" King Yi turns around looking at Silvus. "Aren't they the clan that my grandfather King Zhao banished to the outer roads?"

"The guest speaks truth, Father! Perhaps we have some of them prisoner right now who would be great witnesses!" Ki confirms, with Silvus standing beside him.

"If it's true, I say bring them over; then we can learn the truth!" King Yi decrees without knowing that Cri is getting angry, taking out a dagger from her cloak, about to stab him.

Silvus sees her, shocked, and shouts, "YOUR MAJESTY—BEHIND YOU!"

It is too late. The moment King Yi turns around, Cri stabs him right in the chest.

"FATHER!"

"DADDY!"

The two silblings Ki and Fi calls out in horror while the rest of the nobles, servants, and guards all gasp.

"Cri….Why?" King Yi asks with his voice breaking, facing Cri in tears, only for her to remove the dagger from his bleeding chest and throw him down the steps, rag-dolling him. Ki and Fi rush to their dying father while the Raptor cousins stand glaring at Cri. Ico draws his bow and arrow while Silvus draws his borrowed sword with his gloved claw and activates his Mist aura on the other.

"You fools were supposed to get killed! I had great plans that would benefit this rotting rock that we all call an empire!" Cri rants with a shrieking hiss coming out of her beck snout, showing her teeth, confirming that Kobolds do have sharp teeth.

As he growls back at her, Silvus narrows his eyes toward the pommel of the dagger Cri used to kill King Yi. It is the same purple skull he saw back at Triteria.

"That symbol on your dagger!" Silvus points at Cri's dagger. "I saw that back home on the surface! You have been there, have you?!"

Cri takes one look at the dagger, and back at him with a smirk, and whistles. From the rooftops, twenty Raptor warriors armed with long swords wearing familiar black armor and cloak appear. To Silvus, they resemble the pursuers that chased him and his cousin. Whoever they are, Cri must be working with them.

The nobles start to panic, running out the throne room for their lives as the Kobold guards draw their weapons to engage with the mysterious warriors. Ico helps out by shooting arrows at each one, while Ki tells Fi to stay with their father, as he draws his own sword to deal with intruders as well.

Silvus sees Cri tyring to make a run for it at a nearby door as a means to take advantage of the distraction. Not wanting her to escape, he runs after her, knowing that his cousin, Ki, and the guards can handle the intruders.

Silvus chases Cri up the tower, hoping to catch her before it is too late. The climb is pretty long, but that does not tire the two. Into a hall, Cri knocks down one of the busts with her tail in order to halt Silvus' chase, only for him to jump over, thanks to Raptors having longer legs.

He continues to chase her all the way to a balcony that towers over the rest of Shima. Now cornered, Cri turns around to see Silvus approaching her slowly with his blade drawn.

"There is nowhere else to run, Cri! Those Raptors you called. Who are they, and why are you helping them?!"

"I only wanted to bring Shima back to its glory! I need to be queen to do so!" Cri hisses at him and continues, "When I traveled to the surface world, I came across those Raptors. They told me they could help me become queen if I promise to ally with them during this war you Raptors are in!"

"And what does that have to do with me? Your associate from the Shu clan told me that you wanted me dead?" Silvus demands, only to earn a sadistic chuckle from Cri.

"You? Ha! They know you are here. I don't know why my associates want you dead, but all they told me is that you would be a threat to their plans. If their plans are threatened, my plans are threatened!"

"What about your family? Why get them killed?! You could have worked with them!" Silvus makes a few steps forward, keeping his eyes Cri.

"My father is an old fool! He wants to place my airhead of an older brother on the throne! And Fi? As a princess, she could rally the clans against me!" She begins to climb up the edge of the balcony railing, preparing to commit a certain act.

"Cri...I know what you about to do! You could still come quietly!" Silvus tries to reason, but Cri is not having any of it.

"I spoke too much...I would rather die by my own claw than be sentenced by a bunch of fools!" With that, Cri makes a T formation and falls down.

Silvus rushes up, hoping to stop her, but it is too late. He can only watch in horror as he watches the insanse Kobold female fall to her death. The Kobolds below nearby rush up to her, shocked.

Family killing each other for power and shady deals. It is a lot for Silvus to think about. Makes him wonder if it's part of Kobold politics. Even worse, is it also part of Raptor politics? Thinking about it gives him a shiver down his spine. Shaking off the thoughts, he decides to head back to the throne room to makes sure everyone else is okay.

———※———

A funeral is being held around in the middle of the nobility district shortly after dealing with Cri. The body of King Yi is placed on top of a wooden platform in front of a giant root in the middle. Fi cries among the mourning crowd, being comforted by Ico. Ki stands with the members of the clan elites, with a torch in claw. Silvus stands next to Ico and Fi, observing the entire funeral.

Ki walks up to his dead father to give one more tearfull glance. The body of King Yi lies with arms crossed and a crown placed on top. With his eyes closed, Ki makes a prayer.

"Mighty Root and Scions of old. May you listen to my voice and claim my father King Yi Jin into your presence. May you all continue to watch over us and protect us, as one day we will join you."

Ki bows his head and uses his torch to ignite the wooden platform on fire. The flames burn along with the body of King Yi as a symbol of his ashes joining with Root.

As the king's body burns, Silvus turns to Fi and asks her, "What are the Scions?"

After a few sobs, she looks up to him; Ico still has his arm around her.

"The Scions are legendary Kobold heroes of utmost honor. To be a Scion, one most do something remarkable, like my ancestor Jin, who became a Scion for reuniting Kobold kind during the age of the three cities. All the ruling clans you see here are descended from many Scions before."

As much as Silvus wants to know what the age of the three cities is, he won't pry further, seeing Fi is cracking down tears again. He gazes back at the fire, trying to hold back shaking due to his secret fear of fire.

⚊⚊⚊◉⚊⚊⚊

The next day, the streets of Shima seem to be back to normal. The Kobolds go on with their daily lives, but without singing due to mourning for their king. Silvus and Ico find themselves being escorted to the main entrance of the city, since they are finally allowed to head back to the surface for paying their debt. Both have their original equipment on, along with the Snaguanas, who were taken care of.

Escorting the two couisns is Ki, or King Ki in this case. After the funeral he was crowned the new king shortly after. As king, he wears his crown along with his father's royal cape and sword to his waist. With him are two royal guards and a greenish-white female.

Silvus guesses she might be Ki's mate, from the way she walks with him side by side. He can only pray to the spirits that Ki knows what he is doing with her. That will be a story for another day. Regardless, they stop in front of the gates for King Ki to turn around facing the cousins, Silvus specifically.

"Well, boys, I have to admit these times have been filled with déjà vu. You two coming from the surface, youngest sister going missing, ambushed by members of a vengeful clan, other sister going mad, my father dying, and now I am king!"

"Tell me about it, King Ki; things are even more intense where my cousin and I came from!" Silvus clarifies with a small laugh, thinking back how his uncle ranted about their own problems.

"No argument here, my friend, but before you all go, there are two things we must cover." Ki claps for one of the guards to carry a familiar package.

"I believe this package is yours."

"It is, your majesty."

Silvus walks up to the guard looking very relieved and gently grabs back the package. He checks it out to make sure it is not opened. Thank the spirits it is not.

"When father gave it to me, I assumed it must be very important to you?" Ki questions.

"It is not just important to me, your majesty. My mother wanted me to take it to the surface city of Patalot to show it to the Mistatorium. She believes it is a key to saving my kingdom!" Silvus answers, showing the package's seal.

"In that case, there is one other thing I want to discuss." Ki looks back and whistles. Both cousins look around him to see Princess Fi approaching them.

Princess Fi is wearing a sleeveless chainmail curiass with bracers. She also has a crossbow on her back. With a smile on her face she greets them, "Hey boys!"

With curious looks, the cousins look back to Ki.

"I believe you promised Father that you would send us aid; am I right?"

"Your father told you?" Silvus asks, earning a nod from Ki and a giggle from Fi.

"Oh yes! Brother wanted one of us to join you on your quest to serve as a walking reminder of your promise. I always wanted to see what the surface world look like, so I decided to volunteer!"

"Are you sure it is not because of that guy?" Ki points at Ico, who makes a big grin, hoping it is the case.

"BROTHER! Don't embarrass me!" Fi's face turns red as a tomato.

Ki and Silvus share a laugh, while Ico only stares at how cute Fi looks when she is embarrassed. After the laughter dies down, Ki explains, "She is right about the reminder part. One last thing I want to say is that thanks to you two, my sister and I would have been dead. My other sister Cri, despite her best intentions, would have become unknowingly a tyrant." Ki looks at his mate, who puts a sympathetic claw on his shoulder, before turning back to the cousins. "What I am trying to say is that on behalf of Shima and Kobold kind, we all owe you."

"And so do we," Silvus clarifies, shaking claws with Ki; goodbye for now.

With that out of the way, the cousins and the princess make preparations. Silvus straps the package back onto his back, while Ico does not hesitate to suggest that Fi ride with him on his Snaguana, making Silvus chuckle at his obvious crush on the little Kobold girl.

With the guests and princess prepared on the Snaguana, King Ki orders the guards to open the gates. The gates slowly open, and the trio begins the journey out of the city and back to the surface.

While Fi rides behind Ico, she takes one more look back to wave goodbye to her brother, who in turn mouths "Stay out of trouble," making her huff, throwing her little arms around Ico's waist.

Ico makes a nervous grin with his cheeks turning red, enjoying it.

As for Silvus? All that matters now is for him to head back to the surface to head to Patalot. He can only pray that his mother is still alright.

Chapter 15
To Journey with a Small Princess

Silvus finds himself back riding along the road southwest on the surface, to continue on his journey to Patalot. Based on his surroundings, he is still in the middle of the northern swamp of Tricia. Lucky for him, it is still daylight, so no predators are around. One must still be on guard for those who hunt during the day, however.

Following behind Silvus is Ico, his cousin, who hopes to meet the knights of Mist to earn a purpose, and Fi Jin, the Kobold princess of Shima who decided to tag along in order to learn of the surface world as well as being a reminder of Silvus' promise.

Ever since she joined up, Fi gazes around as if she is in dreamland. Living underground most of her life, she is most fascinated with the bright blue sky above almost covered by trees. She turns her head to the purple glowing river with a gasp. "BY THE ROOT, that river is so sparkly!"

"That, dear Princess, is what we Raptors call the Miststream. It is said that whoever drinks from it will be granted the power to perform Mistcraft."

"You think I could drink from it and use those powers like your cousin?!" Fi peps up, looking excited at the thought of using supernatural powers.

"Would you like to take a drink and see if you could? It is literally right next to us right now," Silvus offers, pointing at the glowing river right next to them on their right.

"That would be so FAB!" Fi once again beams, making Ico smile, showing that he enjoys her high-spirited personality.

So the cousins decide to make a quick stop to test whether Fi, a Kobold, can attain the power of Mistcraft. First, they get off their Snaguanas and hitch them up to a nearby tree so they won't wander off. Then they look around to make sure no predators, bandits, rebels, or shady riders are nearby. Finally, they walk near the purple Miststream of Tricia.

Fi drops onto her knees and uses her stubby claws to cup up some of the Mist-filled water. "First Kobold to use Mistcraft, here I COME!" she boasts, then sips the water. The water must be very refreshing, from the way she reacts in relief after drinking. She stands up and closes her eyes to brace herself if something is supposed to happen.

Instead, they only hear cricket sounds from the nearby bushes. A flock of big dragonflies fly around a bush and eat a mosquito. Nothing happens to Fi, making Silvus sigh in disappointment.

"What is wrong?" Fi asks the Mist expert.

"Your veins and eyes are supposed start glowing immediately, but it seems the Mist can't adapt into your body," Silvus explains, looking down with a claw on his snout as if he is ashamed.

"What do you mean?" Fi asks him, worried; she really wants to know what is wrong.

"I believe my cousin means that you're one of the few creatures who do not have the Mist gene," Ico sadly guesses. He hoped that Fi would be able to perform Mist powers.

"There are many theories about how certain creatures are cut off. One popular theory is that there are some creatures who are never touched by Mist, like the Tritop, since the 'Growing period.' So I believe because your ancestors lacked a Mist gene, your bodies are incapable, so I am afraid at this point drinking Miststream to you is like drinking water," Silvus sadly lectures.

"Oh, bummer," Fi moaned sadly. She looks at Ico and asks him, "Can you do this Mistcraft?"

"I know a few spells, but I choose not to do them often. It's just very mind exhausting."

"Mind exhausting?" Fi asks Ico, wondering what he meant.

Silvus is about to answer until he hears the sound of banging drums deeper into the wall of thick trees, covered by a misty fog in front of them. "Do you guys hear that?"

"OOOOOO, it sounds like a party is going on!" Fi squeals, earning a nervous chuckle from Ico.

"I don't think it is the beat of a party, Princess; more like a beat of war," Ico nervously states, turning his attention to Silvus. "What do you think it is?"

"There is only one way to find out," Silvus clarifies and performs the "ice gust" with his claw in a soft motion. From his claw, a stream of ice blows into the Miststream to form a bridge so the gang can cross.

⸺◆⸺

Silvus and the gang travel deeper into the swamp until they come across a wetland opening. In their sight are two armies in a stand-off. Not wanting to be seen, Silvus has Ico and Fi hide behind a patch of tall green grass so they can see what is going on.

To his right, Silvus sees an army of Triceon militia lined up in formation, being led by a young Delta-Lord of another settlement he is not familiar with, standing in front. He can see the purple cape the Delta-Lord is wearing, compared to the lightly armored militia. Both the Delta-Lord and the militia behind him have weapons drawn at the ready, while keeping their focus on the enemy in front.

To the left, Silvus sees the Monchester rebels in greater number marching toward the militia. The rebels have their weapons drawn ready while the war drums continue to beat. Compared to the militia, the rebels are shown to be better equipped. Bigger weapons and armor in good condition make the defenders look outdated. Leading the rebels is a Delta-Lord, middle-aged, riding on a Snaguana, looking very proud, showing off his shiny silver steel armor, with a bushier orange mane on his helmet.

The rebel leader looks smug, believing that he can easily win the battle, since the militia are shown to have fewer numbers than his own. The militia leader tries his hardest to not look scared, wanting to be an example for his troops. He looks down at his troops to see expressions of fear by the way they shook their bodies.

Back in the middle of the tall grass, Fi asks, wanting to know what is going on, "Whose side are we supposed to root for?"

"The bad guys are the Monchesteons, wearing orange, while the Triceons, the guys we are rooting for, wear purple," Ico explains to Fi while pointing at each one to identify them.

While Ico continues to explain what is going on to Fi, Silvus continues to focus on the armies, feeling uneasy. In his mind he begins to question how long he and his cousin stayed in Shima. One thing he knows is that the civil war for Alpha-King's throne has begun.

"POSITIONS READY!" Silvus hears the rebel Delta-Lord command his troops, making the drumming sounds stop. Then the rebel troops get into sprinting position: swords, axes, and maces raised in the middle; spears, pikes, and halberds pointed in the front lines. Then the archers at the back lines aim their arrows toward the bright blue sky.

"SPIRITS WILLS IT!!!!" the rebel leader calls out with all his might, leading the charge while his troops make roaring shrieks as they follow suit.

While the rebels run like a stampede of Brontos (Brontosuarus) splattering the wet ground, Silvus turns his gaze back to the militia leader, who looks to his archers with a desperate face. "ARCHERS!" he fearfully calls out.

The militia archers draw their bows and arrows, with a captain telling them to hold, with an arm signal. They wait for the rebels to get to center. Then the captain thrusts his arm forward, commanding the archers to fire. The archers release their arrows to fly into the sky at the same time. The arrows fly like a swarm of GilgaWasps swarming in to make their sting.

The arrows fly down at the charging rebels, killing those who have no chance of protection, while those with shields block them.

Believing they have weakened them, the militia leader draws his own sword and points it forward with a thrust and yells, "SPIRITS WILLS IT!" making his militia charge back at the rebels.

From a distance, Silvus and the gang watch the two armies collide into the center, hearing the bashing sounds of each other's weapons. They see both sides are fighting with outmost brutality already seeing blood being spilled. Fi's bright blue face starts to turn green as she fells herself getting sick watching how barbaric the battle between the two Raptor armies is. She covers her snout with her claws and turns around, walking away. Ico follows suit, worried about her condition.

Silvus keeps his gaze on the battle ahead, still looking uneasy. He sees one Raptor get axed on the face between the eyes, while another is stabbed by a spear from behind. Not bearing to see it anymore, Silvus turns to his cousin, who is helping Fi vomit behind a bush due to seeing the barbaric battle.

"Come on, guys, we need to get back to the main road, and fast!" he tells them with a worried voice.

In agreement they decide to head back to the main road. Silvus takes one more peek at the battle, only to see the Triceons suffering more casualties.

Back on the main road, Silvus and the gang continue on their journey. While he continues to lead, he cannot get the battle off his mind. It shows him that he really needs to haul his tail not only for his mother's sake but also his uncle, other cousin Sulphie, and his best friend Tritus. The thought of them being harmed sends a shiver down his spine. Silvus turns his head back to check on Ico and Fi. He sees Ico riding his mount with his eyes on Fi, who is resting her head on his cousin's shoulder, still recovering from her vomit spree.

He turns his head back, refocusing on the road in front. Silvus looks up at the sky to see it getting dark, meaning nightfall is coming. As much as he wants to continue, the last time he checked, he is still in the swamp. He has three options. One, stop and make camp. Two, continue on and pray that predator or bandit will not ambush on the way. And three, hope to spot a settlement nearby so they can stay at an inn for the night.

A growling sound is heard, making Silvus stop his mount, putting both claws into his stomach as if he got a belly ache. He looks back to Ico and Fi also stop in their track looking at him. "Getting hungry too, cousin?" Ico asks with a desperate tone, showing he is hungry as well.

"Stopping for food and rest would be nice," Fi states, getting better and lifting her head up.

Silvus looks to his right and left. To his left, he scans around the tall trees, hoping to find a good place to camp away from danger. He spots one large tree with an opening at least twenty feet away and tells them, "I think I found a good spot for us to camp, guys!"

"Where?" Ico asks him, trying to find the spot he talking about.

"Follow me and you will see." Silvus turns his mount to gallop to the tree with Ico and Fi following suit.

In front of the tree Silvus tells Ico and Fi to wait and gets off his Snaguana. Slowly he approaches the opening, but it is too dark to see. As much as he wants to use a fire spell, he is too afraid. He turns around to call out for Ico, knowing he knows the spell.

Ico gets off his mount, telling Fi to keep watch while he walks up to Silvus, who somehow needs him for something.

"What's wrong?" Ico asks Silvus.

With a nervous smile Silvus asks back, "You know how to make a fireball spell, right?"

"Yeah, why? I thought you know a lot spe..." Ico pauses, seeing how Silvus is looking at him a paranoid look.

"You want me to do it for you, do ya?" Ico folds his arms, giving his older cousin a smirk, knowing why he wants him to do the spell.

"Yes, Ico, just do it!" Silvus demands quietly, desperate for Ico to do the act.

"Alright, then." Ico moves his right claw below and his left above. He moves his left claw in a clockwise motion, forming a ball of fire, making Silvus step back in fear.

Ico gives a small laugh as he moves his right claw holding onto the fireball into the tree cave to see a big empty space perfect for both them and their Snaguanas to hide for the night.

"How is it inside?" Silvus asks Ico.

Ico decides to make a little prank. With a toothy grin, he slowly moves out.

"It's safe, Cousin, but the better question is ARE YOU!" He thrusts his fireball at Silvus' face, making him fall back with a scream. Landing on the wet floor, Silvus gets up with his upper body, making a glaring hiss at Ico, who bursts into laughter.

"THAT'S NOT FUNNY!" he scolds his younger cousin.

"Sorry, dude, but you need get over this fear you have of fire." Ico does a counter-clockwise motion with his left claw, putting out his fireball. "Many years have passed, and you are still afraid of fire, haha!"

"I will do that only if you start to GROW UP!" Silvus gets up on his feet and nudges his cousin with a scoff. That only makes Ico laugh some more.

As Silvus approaches the Snaguanas, Fi, who sits on Ico's, asks him, "You sure you guys are cousins? You two seem to be more like brothers."

"No Fi, Ico and I are cousins. But we do live together because my mom and my uncle, who are sister and brother, do so as well," Silvus explains while he takes the leash of his Snaguana and guides it to the big tree, leaving Fi a bit confused.

"If your mom and uncle live together, are you two nobles?" she guesses while Ico approaches her.

"Correct, Princess. Silvus and I are part of an important clan of nobles. My dad actually works for his mom as a steward."

"So your aunt is like a clan leader of something?"

"Hehe, I think my egghead of a cousin could explain more about this political stuff than I can," Ico tells her while he takes the leash off his own mount.

—◈—

Nightfall is getting close. Inside the large tree, a campfire is set up in the middle, and the Snaguanas are hatched up safely inside, resting on the ground. Silvus is seen sitting at least seven feet away from the fire while he explains the political nature of his kingdom to Fi, who sits a bit closer, trying to listen. Ico, however, is not present due to volunteering to hunt food.

"Let me get this straight. You and Ico are part of one of the ruling clans that govern for an Alpha-King's behalf?"

"That's right. Ico and I are Clan Vessel, the ruling clan of the Maglo Betadom, with my mom as the Beta-Lady."

"That sounds interesting. Does that mean you are supposed to be the next...Beta-Lord?" Fi guesses with a snap of her fingers.

"That's right." Silvus gives her a thumbs up. "And I had planned to make Ico my new steward, but now with the war going on..."

Silvus leans back with a sigh, thinking about the war going on.

"Why exactly are you guys at war anyway?" Fi finally asks regarding the battle earlier.

With an uneasy face, Silvus struggles in his mind how he is going to explain briefly. He reaches a gloved claw behind his back and takes out the wrapped package. He gives the package a quick gaze.

"Do you really want to know?" he asks her.

Fi nods, eager to know about surface affairs. With that, Silvus tells her about the sudden death of the Alpha-King and the events that led to where they are now. The rumors, the riots, bandit attacks, the royal army doing nothing, and finally how he and Ico were forced out of their home. He even tells her why he has this particular package. Fi's face is priceless. She is a bit horrified, yet sympathetic at the same time. Fi is going to say something until the voice of Ico calls out.

"HEY GUYS, WE ARE HAVING ANKLO TONIGHT!"

Silvus and Fi turn their attention to see Ico enting their temporary campsite with a big bag. He throws it right by the campfire, allowing the wrapping to open up, revealing a big Ankelo corpse with an arrow hole to the neck.

"So what have you guys been talking about?" Ico asks them as he puts down his bow and arrows. He kneels with one knee, taking out a knife in his left claw. He is going to skin the meat until Fi latches him into a hug looking dramatically sad.

"You okay, Princess?" Ico asks the sobbing princess, who looks at him with tears.

"You poor thing! Forced out of your home at a time like this!" Fi sobs, making Ico look to his cousin, confused, earning a shrug in return.

The gang begins to feast on the cooked steak by the fire still lit. By the spirits or the Root, it is good!

As he ate, Silvus cannot believe a Raptor like Ico is capable of hunting a large, armored herbivore. Perhaps he remembers how good he was with a bow and arrow back at Shima. He takes one more bite from his steak and asks, "You know, Ico, how did you learn how hunt and cook?"

Taking one more bite of his own with a swallow, Ico answers, "My mother used to teach me when I was young. She thought I should learn some of her heritage as a means for me to survive if I ever get lost."

"You mean Auntie Oria? Your dad told me she is back in Sherra-sic right now," Silvus clarifies.

"OH OH! What is your mom like? What noble clan is she from?" Fi jumps in, eager to know more about Ico's family.

"My mom has no clan name, for she is an Omega, a commoner," Ico answers, taking another bite from his steak.

"YOUR MOM IS A WHAT!" Fi freaks out, making the two cousins shush her so predators, bandits, or unwanted guests won't hear them due to it being nightfall outside.

"Yes, Princess, my mom is an Omega, and yes, it is allowed for Raptor nobles and Omegas to marry, as we don't believe in this ridiculous claim of blood purity," Ico tells her trying to sound quiet.

Fi looks at Silvus with an expression demanding an explanation. Realizing he had not told her about how their caste system works, he decides to give a quick lecture for the rest of the night.

＝《◍》＝

The following morning, Silvus continues to lead the group in a rapid pace. While he rides, he can hear Ico explaining to Fi the caste system.

"So you Raptors believe having offspring with Omegas makes your bloodline stronger?" he hears Fi ask Ico, trying to get a better understanding.

"Correct. We believe noble blood hungers for weaker blood. When breeding with Omegas, who have the weakest blood, offspring always inherit noble blood; thus we inherit highest caste from one of our parents."

"And because your dad is the higher caste, you inherit his caste?"

Ico nods yes at Fi's response. "Indeed, Princess. It allows Mom to live with us, but because she is still Omega at the end of the day, she still is not allowed to dwell in political stuff."

Ico and Fi continue to discuss the Raptor caste system while Silvus keeps his focus on the road in front, starting to see large oak trees and neon-colored grass, hinting that they are getting near Suaronian Heart, the heartland of the kingdom. Eventually they come across a large stone wall with large gates blocking their path forcing them to stop.

"Why did we stop?" Fi asks.

"Look up," Silvus tells her, pointing upward on the wall showing two black flags of the kingdom hanging.

"That is the royal border—a large wall system built to divide the Betadoms so the royal army could be stationed to keep watch," Silvus briefly explains.

Ico scoffs and blurts out, "The way I see it, they are not doing a good job right now."

From the top railings of the wall, a royal guard captain walks up along with two other guards and calls out, "Greetings, travelers! If you three are seeking passage to Suaronian Heart, I am afraid we have orders to keep the border closed due to the war going on!"

The shout was loud enough to gain the attention of the gang. With all eyes gazing at the royal guards, they see the guards wearing plated armor with black feathered helmets. The one wearing the shoulder pads is assumed to be the captain due to the belief that higher-ranking guards are more heavily armored.

"Why so, Captain? We are on an urgent mission to Patalot on behalf of the Beta-Lady of Maglo!" Silvus tries to plead with the guard captain on the wall.

"Urgent mission?" The guard captain crosses his arms.

"I am the Beta-Lady's son! She wants me to deliver this package to the Mistatorium as soon as possible!" Silvus takes the package from his back. The guard captain only makes a small laugh, showing that he does not believe him.

"Nice try, kid. I heard news that Maglo was taking over by them lousy rebels. They have a new Beta now."

"WHAT!" Silvus shouts out. He kind of expected that the rebels would place a puppet Beta on the throne to support their efforts. He knows full well that his mother would never cooperate with her invaders.

"Is there any way we could convince you to let us through?" he further pleads, knowing that the guard might be too stubborn to argue with.

Back on the wall, one of the guards taps his captain on the shoulder and tells him, "You know, Captain, what about we have them take care of some bandits camped right by Sherrasic? I heard they captured a group of merchants."

The captain thinks about it, scratching his chin and tapping his foot. He walks up back to the ledge to tell Silvus and the gang, "Tell you what, kid. There are a group of bandits eastward of here with a group of merchants being held captive. You three look like capable fighters, so if you rescue the merchants, I'll let you all cross through. Deal?"

"DEAL!" Silvus blurts out without thinking. He so desperate to make it to Patalot that he would do anything, even take an opportunity to do some hero stuff along the way. His choice earns him stares from Ico and Fi that ask whether he is crazy.

"Well then, the bandits are seen camped right by the border of Sherrasic." The captain points eastward. "And be careful! They don't look like the typical bandits we have seen."

With that, Silvus leads the gang eastward in order to hunt down the bandits and save the merchants as soon as possible. To Silvus, it is for the sake of his mother, while Ico and Fi continue to catch up.

Act IV

Chapter 16
Bandits or Rebels

Desperate to convince the royal guard to open the gates, Silvus leads Ico and Fi east of the lower area of the great swamp alongside the border to rescue some merchants from bandits near Sherrasic. He does not take notice that the sun is starting to set, being focused at the task at claw.

Silvus continues to ride east, and still no sight of the bandits. Instead he sees various forms of insect life that fly away from either tall grass or bushes. While he continues to ride, he thinks about the guard telling him of the bandits being not the typical types. It makes him wonder if the bandits might be rebels, like the ones from Tricia. "Yo, Silvus! How far do you think we are from the bandits?" he hears Ico ask from behind. Silvus stops in his tracks, turning his head to him.

"I wish I knew, but we can't just give up yet!" Silvus answers loudly, giving his Snaguana a few pats on the neck. As much as he wants to stop and rest, he feels the pressure that he has hurry before the war gets worse. He checks on Ico, who has a face of uneasiness, making him concerned, and asks him if he is okay.

Ico looks side to side and gallops up to tell him, "Dude, we have been riding for like an hour or two. What if the guard lied to us? What if there are no bandits?"

"Why would they lie to us?"

"What do you think? Maybe just to get rid of us! Don't get me wrong, I understand you want to open up the gates, but dude, you really need to think through when making deals," Ico explains to him.

They can't be lying to us! Silvus thinks in denial. It does not make sense for any Raptor to use the bandit attacks as an excuse. As much as he wants to disagree, Ico might be right. So far, they have not seen any bandits yet, making him lose hope until he hears Fi speak up.

"Hey guys, look!"

Silvus and Ico turn their gazes to Fi, who is pointing to their left. Both heads turn to see thick smoke fuming through the trees. The sight of the smoke heightens Silvus' spirits. When there is smoke, it means a campsite is nearby.

"Good eye, Fi!" He dismounts his Snaguana to tie it to a nearby tree. Ico and Fi also dismount and repeat the same action Silvus did with his.

—————◦《◉》◦—————

Hiding behind the tall grass from a safe distance, Silvus sees a camp with at least five tents set up in the middle of the clearing. Scaning around, he spots the cages where the merchants are being held up, confirming they are the bandits the guard mentioned. He sees the bandits themselves, numbering at least twenty. With further suspicion, the bandits look like the same rebels he faced in Tricia. Same armor and same banners with the familiar symbol.

"Yo, Silvus! Whats wrong? Scared?"

Silvus turns his head to see both Ico and Fi looking at him concerned. In response, Silvus reaches a claw into a pocket of his robe to take out a familiar dagger he collected from Cri.

"Is that the dagger my sister used to kill my father?" Fi asks with a gasp, looking at the dagger Silvus took out.

"Yes, Fi, I requested your brother that I take it with me for study." Silvus raises the dagger to compare the symbols on both the dagger and the banners of the camp. His suspicion is proven true. The symbols match.

"What exactly are you looking at, Silvus?" he hears Ico ask him.

"Before Targon attacked us, there was this guy in robes wearing this symbol." Silvus shows the symbol on the dagger to Ico. "Back at Tricia, I saw the same symbol used by the bandits that Tritus and I took care of, the riders that chased us to Shima, this dagger used by Cri to kill the king, and now I see it again right there!"

Silvus points to the camp, specifically the banners, and gives the dagger to Ico to get a closer look at it. Fi too leans forward to see the symbol herself. While they study the dagger, Silvus turns his attention back to the camp.

In his sight, Silvus sees at least four Raptors keeping guard while the rest are just either eating grub or sparring with each other. They look more like organized rebels than mere bandits. Just like the ones at Tricia. He gazes at the cages to his left where the merchants are being held. They seem to number around at least ten.

By the spirits, they are scared. Obviously, they fear for their lives due to being captured by criminal savages. Among the hostages, one familiar female gets his attention. He narrows his eyes to the female wearing a leather cloak for a closer look. "What do you think it means?" he hears Ico call out, breaking off his gaze. He turns around to see Ico giving the dagger back to him.

Silvus takes the dagger, makes one more gaze at the banners of the camp, and tells them, "I think there is a group of Raptors out there behind all this. The death of the Alpha-King, the riots, the bandit attacks, and now this war might be some part of a conspiracy."

"A conspiracy? As in a shady group with an agenda?"

Silvus nods yes in response to Ico's question.

"If what you are saying is true, why would this group, cult, or whatever even pull a stunt like this? What do they hope to gain?"

"I don't know, Ico, but I think I know who might have some answers." Silvus turns his head around, looking at the largest tent. The leader of the bandits might be part of this group connected to the symbols.

"So what do we do now?" Fi asks.

"We do what we came here for." Silvus carefully stands up on his feet, posing like a hero with a grin on his snout. "We be like Ultamar Magnus and rescue those in need!"

"Ha ha, who is Ultamar Magnus? And why did you have to act like such a dork?" Fi teases, making Silvus drop down, looking embarrassed.

"Princess, this guy here was so glued to his books he would act like a total fanboy," Ico whispers to Fi, earning a glare from Silvus. The latter shakes his head to refocus at the task at claw.

"Jokes aside, I think I have plan. Who knows how to lock pick?"

Fi raises her claw. "I could use one of my bolts to pick locks."

Silvus give Fi an inquisitive stare, looking awkward at the idea of a princess picking locks. She makes a nervous giggle in return and scratches behind her head. "Hehe, there was a time I accidentally locked myself in my own bedroom," she shrugs.

"Alright then. The plan is I am going to face the bandits head on to distract them so Fi can sneak in and free the merchants, while Ico climbs up onto the tents to give me covering fire." Silvus looks back at Fi. "As soon as the merchants are safe, join Ico by using that crossbow to take out any bandit who will try to attack me. Got it?"

"Yeah, I have question." Ico adds it up. "Are you really that crazy, to deal with twenty bandits head on! Even with our help, it is still suicide."

Silvus puts on a smirk on his snout. He raises his claw to form a small surge of electricity to whisper, "Mistcraft."

As the sun gets closer to setting, Silvus marches out the safety of the trees to the marsh fields. As he gets closer to the camp, he feels his heart beat faster in his chest. It is his moment to be as brave as the heroes from the stories. In front of him four bandits are guarding the front camp.

Spotting Silvus, the four bandits begin to walk up to him with blank faces instead of stereotypical evil looks from the average bandit. They all stop six feet away from him, keeping their eyes focused on him.

Silvus stands his ground, trying to be brave, with his back straight. He slightly turns his eyes to his right see Ico sneaking up to one of the tents to climb up. To his left, he sees Fi hiding inside a pile of tall grass near the cages awaiting her signal. "What are you doing here?" one of the four bandits demands with a common accent, surprising Silvus. It kind of shows that they might not really be bandits.

"I am here by request of the royal army to tell you all to release the merchants you kidnapped!" Silvus points to the cages.

"Kidnapped?" One of the bandits raises a brow. All four give each other confused looks and share a laugh.

Silvus does not know what is so funny that made them laugh. He puts on a mad expression, staring at the four clutching their armored guts with their claws. "What's so funny?"

"Kid, we are not bandits. We are revolutionaries with a cause."

"Revolutionaries? Seriously?" Silvus raises a brow, looking skeptical.

"You heard us, hatchling. The Mistatorium were the ones who killed the Alpha-King. Those old Mistcasting farts are attempting a power grab!"

"How do you know that? And what makes this revolution of

yours any better by kidnapping innocent Raptors?" Silvus gets a bit aggressive toward the four fools who easily bought into the lie so that they would harm the innocent. However, he wonders if he can try to convince them that they are wrong.

"Our families were attacked by bandits and fierce creatures, and they did nothing! Our actions might be extreme, but we need to deliver a message to those power-hungry jerks!" one of the rebels rants.

"If you think harassing innocent Raptors helps your cause, then you all are being a bunch of fools! Think of your families—you all really believe they would support this needless violence?" Silvus pleads to the misguided Raptors in front. In truth, he does not really want to fight them. He never likes the idea of fighting possible innocents due to misguided sense of justice. The way he sees it, the bandits or rebels are not buying it. Looks like they would rather die for what they believe in.

All four draw their swords, getting impatient, making Silvus put a claw to his sword. "GET HIM!" one of the rebels recklessly declares. The rebel raises his sword and rushes to Silvus, only for his attack to get parried. In response, Silvus quickly stabs him in the chest and kicks him on the ground. Two other Raptors try to gang up on him, two on one. Silvus quickly uses his two claws to use the surge spell to create a stream of lightning to electrocute the two rebels at the same time.

The final rebel takes out a horn and blows it to alert the others. Throwing off the horn, the rebel raises his sword to attack him, only to be zapped at the head by Silvus' favorite lightning bolt attack, sending him flying across the field.

Dealing with the rebel, Silvus sees the remainder of sixteen rebels rush up, surrounding him in a circle with weapons drawn. He slowly turns around, keeping an open eye to wait for one of the rebels to make their move as part of the defensive stance from his training. One rebel rushes and Silvus parries three strikes and counters with a slice to the chest after staggering him. Two rebels rush with spears; Silvus uses the lightning bolt at one rebel and dodges the other and stabs him in the back. He uses his foot to kick off the rebel off his sword, landing his face on the wet ground, making a splashing sound. Three more rebels rush in with all swords; this time Silvus uses the surge spell to electrocute them.

While Silvus repeats the fighting routine, a rebel from behind tries to attack, but he gets met with an arrow to the head by the left. Another rebel who sees his comrade get hit frantically looks around to see where the arrow came from, only to get shot next by Ico, who is giving Silvus covering fire on a tent near the battle. On the other tent, Fi joins in and uses her crossbow to strike down the rebels who would dare attack Silvus.

With all the rebels dealt with, Silvus falls to his knees to catch some breaths. The fighting and the overuse of Mistcraft put him into an exhausted state. Taking a few breaths, he looks up to see Fi and Ico run up to him to make sure he is okay.

The Mist turns visible and flows into Silvus' body in order for him to recharge while catching his breath. Feeling the energy coming back, he slowly gets back up to his feet, taking a glance at Ico and Fi.

"I FEEL SO ALIVE RIGHT NOW!" Silvus shouts in excitement, earning small laughter from his friends. Silvus is going to ask about the merchants, but a gruff voice cuts him off. All three eyes turn to the source of the voice to see a large Raptor coming forth.

The large Raptor's scale color is grey as smoke, with tiger stripes. His eyes are blood red, with a scar to his right. He wears black-plated chest armor and gauntlets. On the left side of his chest is the same symbol that Silvus studied. He is The boss of the camp.

He looks around to see his troops either dead or out cold. The more he looks, the angrier he gets until he spots Silvus still recharging the Mist inside of him. Ico and Fi run up in front of Silvus with arrow and bolt drawn to protect him in his current state.

"You little brats did this?" the boss demands with an aggressive tone in his voice.

"You must be one who deceived these Raptors to throw their lives," Silvus accuses with a cough, still exhausted. Yet he can feel the Mist in himself almost charged.

the boss takes one step forward, making Ico point his arrow with a hiss, warning him not to come closer. The old rebel only makes a small laugh and uses...a Mist power to levitate Ico by the throat and throw him into a nearby tent.

"ICO!!!!" both Silvus and Fi shriek in horror. Fi runs into the tent to make sure Ico is okay. Silvus, however, turns his attention back at the leader snarling at him.

"You know who I am, do you?" Silvus accuses, pointing a claw at the rebel leader, who turns out to be a Mistcaster like him.

"How do you know?" the boss asks with a mocking tone while his eyes make a flash, indicating that the Mist in him is recharged.

"That symbol you are wearing." Silvus points at the badge while his eyes flash, fully recharged. "I have been seeing it almost every-where. Who are you Raptors? Are you all responsible for all this?"

The rebel boss only smiles and moves one claw up. A shadow aura begins to form into a large disk. "How about you catch this!" he tells Silvus as he throws the shadow disk right at him.

Silvus jumps to the side quickly, making the disc pass by, and cuts through the tall grass only for it to fade. He turns his face to the boss with a face mixed with horror and anger. He sees the boss look at him with a smirk. The young Mistcaster knows what he did. He points a talon at him and accuses, "That was a shadow disk spell. YOU'RE A DARK MISTCASTER!"

"That's right! Thanks to the power of Dark Mist, I can use it to deal with pests like YOU!" the leader taunts and uses another shadow disk.

Silvus draws his sword to deflect the spell away into the sky. He keeps his guard up to be aware of any more dark powers the leader might use. Raising a claw, he forms an ice spear and throws it at the rebel leader, only for him to catch it in his palm.

The rebel boss takes the ice spear out of his claw, allowing blood to come out, making Silvus sick in his stomach at the sight of blood. What is even more disgusting is that the blood from the boss's wound forms into a sword on one claw and forms onto another. The two blood swords harden when the boss grabs them to make some practice swings like an assassin.

Silvus starts to feel himself get scared at the sight of such abnormal power with blood. He is so scared that he can hear his own heartbeat while he watches the boss walk up with the two blood swords in claw. He prepares his sword back to his defensive stance, walking backwards.

"This is the power of the school of Blood Bend, the power to use your own blood to make any weapon you desire." The boss begins to swing his blades at Silvus.

SIlvus tries to parry the first strike, but the boss does a feint attack with the second blood sword to deflect the sword off of Silvus' claw flying. The boss makes confident smile and points his swords.

"Looks like you are out of luck," the boss taunts.

Without his sword, Silvus tries to use his Mist Powers. He shoots two lightning bolts, but the boss uses his swords to deflect each one. Then he tries using the surge spell by unleashing sparks of lightning, but the boss is able to block by crossing his arms into an X, forming the gravity shield. *By the* spirits, *this guy is too good!* Silvus thinks to himself, already getting tired.

He starts to lose hope, dropping to his knees. Poor Silvus tries to catch his breath as quick as possible while the boss walks up to him with sinister smile, like a predator who is about to catch his prey. The boss is about to strike Silvus only to be blocked by mist blades, putting the boss in shock.

"WHAT THE HECK?!" the boss blurts out while Silvus is seen using the spell that his uncle taught him to save his own life. He slowly gets back up and pushes the boss off and shows off his own duel- wielding skills.

"That spell! I thought only them pesky knights of the Mist could wield that!" the boss complains, but Silvus looks at him with newfound hope. With his newfound courage, Silvus gets back into the defensive stance, waiting for the boss to make a move. In fury, the boss tries to attack, but this time Silvus can use the second Mist blade to block any feint attack the boss might attempt.

The two fight fiercely at a rapid pace. One clash after another, Silvus is able to parry the boss's attacks more effectively. the boss shows no signs of exhaustion, but he is getting annoyed. Silvus does not give up, holding his ground as he keeps on parrying, hoping to expose a weak spot. With no weak spot in sight, Silvus begins to feel the Mist inside of him begin to fade. He shows it by the amount of sweat coming out of his forehead, and the Mist blades begins to fade.

Taking notice, the boss makes, a big smile, hoping to take advantage by making one jump attack, only for an arrow out of nowhere pierce right into his eye where the scar is stopping his attack. "GHAAAAAA WHAT THE HELL?!"

The boss screams in pain, letting go of his swords, which turn back into liquid blood. Silvus looks to his right to see that the arrow is shot by Ico, who is standing in front of the tent looking high and mighty, with Fi next to him with her crossbow drawn.

"SILVUS, THIS IS YOUR CHANCE! GET HIM NOW!" Ico calls out, allowing Silvus to de-spell his blades and use the blizzard spell to freeze the boss in place. Frozen in place, the boss tries to struggle his way out.

Silvus walks up to the struggling boss. He lifts a claw to the boss' eyes to uses the persuasion spell, which will force him to tell him the truth. "Tell me! Who are you Raptors?! Who are you working for?!" he demands.

The boss struggles to fight the spell in his mind. It shows that he is dedicated to whoever he is working for. He is unable to fight anymore and he is about to tell, only for another arrow to strike him at the back of his head, killing him, and freaking out Silvus.

Silvus turns to the side to see a shady rider in black robes with a red bow, only for the said rider to retreat back into the veil of trees. He turns his gaze back to the rebel boss pierced by the red arrow to see it reliquefy into blood. "Damn it," Silvus mutters to himself.

<hr />

"DUDE, THAT WAS TOTALLY AWSOME!" the voice of Ico calls out. Silvus turns his gaze to see Ico and Fi running up to him.

"Even for a dork, you fought like a total pro!" Fi jumps for joy. "My brother could learn a thing or two about your fighting style!"

"That spell you used. Did my dad teach it to you?" Ico asks him.

"He did," Silvus answers with a hint of disappointment, turning his head back to the frozen rebel boss. That makes Ico and Fi look at him with concern. He is still thinking about the rider he saw. The one who just shot the rebel leader before he could say anything. He shakes off his thoughts to another task at claw. He turns his head back to his cousin and friend looking okay now and asks, "Are the merchants okay?"

Lucky for him, a group of ten Raptors approaches him from his right, looking very relieved. The Raptor leading the group is a young golden male with a white feather mane and orange eyes, wearing a nice cotton coat and hat, looking at him with even more gratitude.

"By the spirits, I thank you and your friends for saving us in this dire time of need! What is your name, fabled hero?" the golden male asks, like a play director from Creston.

"I am Vessel Silvus, First-Delta of Maglo, and he is my cousin Vessel Ico, and she is Princess Fi Jin, Kobold from Shima" Silvus introduces himself and his companions.

"You're a First-Delta? By the spirits! As if they made it prophecy for us to meet at a most dreadfull time. The name is Davinchio Nardo, First-Delta of Creston and Owner of the great Conclave Company." The golden Raptor named Nardo makes the actors bow.

"You're the First-Delta of Creston? That means--"

"Oh yes, I am next in line to be the Beta-Lord of Creston, after my Uncle Davincho Anglos," Nardo answers Silvus.

"So if you're also the owner of one of the merchant companies, what are you doing out here? I thought all trading companies stop traveling town to town due to what is going on?" Silvus asks Nardo in concern, at the same time checking out the other merchants who are trying to collect their things stolen from the bandits.

"As the owner of Conclave, it is my important duty to see my company achieve its main goal, to spread all the creations of Creston throughout all Avalonia to admire the art we all put in! We were traveling to Patalot from Creston until my colleagues and I got captured by those brutes who killed our dear Snaguanas, and now we find ourselves in the middle of this dreadful swamp right by Sherrasic." Nardo turns around to fall on his knees, raising a claw to his forehead with a look of sorrow. "Oh, woe is me! How can we head to Patalot now?!"

"What a drama queen," Silvus hear Ico mutter to himself.

Hearing Nardo mention he is going to Patalot, he gets an idea and tells him, "Hey Nardo, we have Snaguanas that Ico and I would love to let you borrow until you guys get new ones."

"Really?"

"Oh yes! We too were going to Patalot, but the gates to Suaronian

Heart were closed. How about we journey together until we head inside the city?" Silvus offers, making Nardo beam.

"That would be superb! Where are your Snaguanas now?" he asks.

Silvus turns to Ico and Fi and tells them to escort the merchants to the Snaguanas. With that, Ico and Fi do as they are told and escort Nardo and the merchants until Silvus notices the female with her hood up, standing.

"Silvus? Is that really you?" she asks with a familiar sweet voice.

Silvus walks up to her and asks, "Have we meet before?"

The female puts down her hood to reveal a familiar orca-patterned face. She has the sweet smile on her face, making the latter gasp.

"OCIA?!"

Chapter 17
Journey of Suaronian Hearts

If the spirits are either playing tricks or rewarding him for his deeds, Silvus cannot believe the sight of the orca-colored female wearing a brown cloak and the same amulet from before standing in front of him. She is the same Ocia whom he met the day before the invasion, alright.

Silvus finds himself at a loss for words, struggling to say something as he sees her holding her claws together raised up to her chest. She even puts on a joyful smile as if reuniting with a long-lost lover. Ocia then runs up to him to throw her arms around him into a tight hug, leaning her face onto his chest, making him feel awkward.

Silvus feels his cheeks burn up and his tail springs up rapidly. He could not help but move his arms around to hug her back. He still looks nervous.

"Oh Silvus, I heard what happened at Maglo," Ocia says as the two Raptors gently break off the hug.

"You did?" Silvus replies with a questioning look, scratching the right side of his head with his claw.

"Oh yes! I heard there was fighting between Maglos and Monchesteons few weeks back! Thinking of you, I got worried that something bad had happened between your family and Targon. Is it true?" Ocia gives Silvus a concerned look, putting her claws back together, almost covering her snout.

Remembering she is from Monchester, Silvus struggles regarding what to say without hurting her. Whoever told her might be a member of the army with knowledge of what is happening to his old home. He nervously turns his head to the side to see Ico and Fi come out of the wall of trees, waving at him to hurry up.

"It's a long story." Silvus walks beside Ocia. "Tell you what. How about I explain everything after we leave this dreadful place?"

Silvus gestures his claws at the pile of rebel corpses for Ocia to see. With a nod of agreement, Ocia lets Silvus escort her back into the trees.

What Silvus does not know is that a group of familiar riders in black stands in the trees watching him escort Ocia from behind. One rider leading has a sinister smile. "The snake is set."

——◦◦◦——

Back on the main road, a two-carriage caravan is seen being pulled by two Snagunas. The back carriage is filled with boxes and bags of goods waiting to be sold, while in the front sit members of Conclave who speak with Ico and Fi. Taking the helm is Nardo, who holds two leashes to steer the Snaguanas on the right track. Sitting behind Nardo is Silvus, who is telling Ocia sitting in front of him about his adventure since leaving Maglo.

"So long story short, my mom tasked me with delivering a package, helped my uncle and Tritus defeat bandits, and even discovered a new society!"

"Wow, what an adventure." Ocia gleams. "You said something about a package. Can I see it?"

Without further ado, Silvus takes out the package from his back

—— 191 ——

and shows it to her. Ocia leans forward, taking a further gaze at the strange long wrapping with the familiar seal.

"What do you think it is?" she asks him, looking at the seal with a curious look.

"I don't know. My mother told me not to open it until I arrive to Patalot. She thinks it is the key to saving Avalonia," Silvus explains to her, putting the package back onto his back.

"Interesting. Things between the Maglos and Monchesteons must have been really bad, if your mother would entrust you with such a task," Ocia states with a talon to her chin.

The mention of Maglos and Monchesteons makes Silvus uneasy, leaning his back onto on the ridge of the carriage. In his mind, he really wants to tell her what actually happened.

Ocia, who notices Silvus' uneasiness, asks him, "Are you okay?"

Silvus looks up to see Ocia leaning toward him with a face of concern, pinning him on a corner. A part of him does not want to lie, and another part does not want to hurt her. He feels his chest clutching up in pressure, while hearing a heartbeat inside his mind. It is like one of those stories that he read involving heroes of old making the most difficult decisions.

"What exactly did you hear about the battle between Maglo and Monchester?" he nervously asks her to make sure they are on the same page.

"Well, according to one of my friends, Beta-Lord Targon attempted to negotiate with Beta-Lady Silviera, but things went sour, forcing Targon to take action. Do you know something?" Ocia leans back with a raised brow, wanting to know why he asks such a question.

Not holding anything back, Silvus decides to tell her, "Ocia…I don't mean to hurt your feelings or anything, but what happened at Maglo was a hostile invasion."

"THAT CAN'T BE TRUE!" Ocia snaps, gaining the attention of all the passengers, including Ico and Fi, all looking at her.

"Anvar Targon would never do such a thing!" Ocia defensively argues with hint of emotion in her voice. It is exactly what Silvus feared, yet he stays calm.

"I was there when it happened. I saw Targon with a large army behind him. Not to mention he had catapults hidden behind the forest."

"You gotta be under a lot of stress! I mean from what you told me...you...you..."

"Silvus ain't lying, miss," Ico calls out, gaining Ocia's attention. She gives him a questioning glare.

"And who are you? And how do you know that he is telling the truth?"

"I am his cousin Ico. He and I lived together as if we are brothers. Not to mention I escaped with him and my dad," Ico explains.

Ocia scans around the members of Conclave. They all have uneasy looks; it is obvious that they believe the two cousins. She looks at Fi who just tells her with a shrug, "What? I'm a Kobold who has lived underground most of her life. I know nothing of Raptor politics."

Ocia looks back to Silvus with a hurt face while he gives her an apologetic look, with his arms on his lap. She looks into his eyes to see that he is not lying, yet feels bad for telling her the news. A tear or two begins to come out of her eyes and she tells him, sobbing, "You're telling the truth."

"The day after we met, I was dragged out of my bedroom to the front gates of Athera. Targon was there trying to convince my mom that the Mistatorium is corrupt. My mother refused and tried to convince him the opposite. From there she took me to her quarters, giving me the package, then the catapults began to fire at the castle, forcing the Maglos to fight back. Since then, I left with my uncle and cousin to escape...that is all I know."

Ocia says nothing after Silvus finishes his explanation. He sees her trying to hold back from crying. Nardo, who has been listening, asks him, looking sympathetic, "Is the young lady going to be okay?"

Silvus looks to Nardo and tells him, "I think so; just give her some time to think about it. She'll be okay, I hope."

Silvus looks back to Ocia, who has her head lowered, sobbing into her knees. Seeing how devastated she is makes him wonder if telling the truth hurts more than lying.

⸻ ◉ ⸻

For the rest of the ride in lower Tricia, the passengers stay quite. Ocia is no longer crying, but she is looking at the side, gazing at the swampy wilderness, watching a flock of Meganearas buzzing around some tall grass trying to catch mosquitos. Ico is seen napping, with Fi laying her head onto his lap. The passengers speak softly among themselves. Silvus looks to the sky, watching the long yellow- green leaf-covered branches of the swamp.

He wonders whether he the right thing, telling Ocia the truth. He wonders what his mother would have done in his place. His thoughts are interrupted when he hears a sweet voice call out to him, "Silvus."

Silvus looks back down to see Ocia looking at him with an apologetic expression. He only looks at her a bit nervous about what she had to say.

"I wanna say I am very sorry for snapping at you like that. I get very defensive when any Raptor dares to say anything bad about Monchester," she tells him with an apologetic tone.

"You are?"

"Truly, because you and your friends did save my life, I'll forgive you this once," she tells Silvus, making him smile because she is feeling better, until her face turns serious and she folds her arms.

"However, I admit I am still having a hard time believing your story, because Monchester is my home." She looks up to the sky in thought. "To imagine Anvar Targon doing something like that...it is just not like him."

"Did he have any unusual friends or associates?" Silvus asks her, remembering a shady figure who was with Targon on the day of the invasion.

Ocia looks back down to his eye level with a small smile and responds, "Well, while I was in Rookingrad castle, not long ago Targon hired a new court Mistcaster after exiling of the previous one due to disagreements."

"Did he have a name?"

"I believe he calls himself Bylark. When I first met him, he had this dark aura which made me uneasy. Are you implying that he might be responsible for what Targon did?" she asks, looking oddly hopeful at the possibility that her Beta-Lord could be innocent.

Despite the unusual behavior, Silvus is glad that Ocia is better now. Perhaps, she seems to be a very forgiving she-Raptor. However, she did mention that she "was" in Rookingrad castle, which is odd. If he remembers correctly, Omegas aren't allowed in Beta's castle unless they make an appointment, get invited, or married to the family. Because she never mentioned having a clan name, he assumed she is Omega caste.

"You mentioned that you were in Rookingrad ca--" Silvus tries to ask her about the castle only to be interrupted by the sound of the carriages stopping in front of the border. He and all the passengers turn their heads to the border, expecting the captain of the border guard to return.

"WHO GOES THERE?" The captain of the guard walks up to the ridge along with two others.

"IT IS I, DAVINCHIO NARDO, FIRST-DELTA OF CRESTON AND OWNER OF THE CONCLAVE COMPANY

RESCUED BY THEM, GREAT HEROES IN NEED!" Nardo gestures his claw to Silvus and his friends.

The captain turns his gaze to Silvus and smiles, "TOOK CARE OF THEM, DID YA?"

"I SURE DID, CAPTAIN! NOW WOULD YOU OPEN UP THE GATES?" Silvus shouts back, looking proud. The captain honors the deal and orders the others to open up the gates. With a loud click, the gates of the border slowly open up, allowing the caravan to pass through.

———⋙●⋘———

Silvus takes his first glance at the northern area of Suaronian Heart, nicknamed "the Neon forest," a nice name for a mystical forest with large trees that glow neon shades of blue along with the light-blue-colored grass that covers the ground and rocky cliffs. Upon the tall grass that grows in between the trees are various colors of flowers and mushrooms glowing white, purple, teal, or blue, giving the forest a perfect blend.

It is exactly what Silvus pictured from his books. He continues to look around with wide eyes of amazement, with his jaw slowly dropping. He can see spores of white Mist wisps flowing under the branches like fireflies above. To his right, he sees the Miststream glowing white on the right side of the road, radiating the spores. Turning to his left, he sees large teal-green Luneth moths flying around the flowers hoping to gather nectar.

"This place is so...beautiful!" Silvus hears Ocia enjoy the remarkable scenery while the other passengers look around in opposite directions. Among them, Fi gets up, looking paralyzed at the sight.

"I know, right?" Silvus turns his attention to Ocia. "Did you know it is said that the reason why the plant life here is like this because there was an ignition of Mist when Patalot was first born, infusing the trees, plants, and some wildlife nearby!"

"Like an explosion?" Ocia turns her head, looking at Silvus with amazement in her eyes.

"Correct! It is what we call today 'the growing period.'"

Ocia gasps in response, putting her claws to her cheeks. "Wow! That must be one hell of an explosion! If so, I wonder if that is how the Raptors and Precursor tribes got their Mist powers."

"They did! During the ignition, nearby tribes were infused, thus gaining what we call the Mist gene. It is said the reason why the Precursors where able to tap in Mist first was because the spirits unlocked their Mist gene before our ancestors," Silvus further explains to her with a proud grin on his snout, putting his gloved claw to his hip while using the other to wiggle his finger upwards like a teacher.

"That is so amazing!" Ocia beams, turning her gaze back at the forest forward. "Is there anything else you know?"

Silvus is about to answer, only to be cut off from the sounds of moaning heard to the left of the caravan. He turns around to see a herd of at least ten tall reptilian behemoths with long necks trying to eat leaves from oak trees, making his jaw drop. Their scales are blend of various cool colors like blue or purple, with white glowing stripes, giving the forest a soothing blend. The height of such magnificent creatures is at least twenty-nine feet tall, compared to the common Raptors who are at least eight feet, while the Kobolds are six.

"Those, my friends, are Brontos."

Silvus and Ocia turn to Ico, who made the comment with a smirk and arms crossed.

"My mother used to tell a lot about the wildlife of Avalonia as part of my training to be a hunter like her."

"Is your mother from Sherrasic? Ico, right?" Ocia asks him with no aggression this time.

"That's right. My mom would take me to parts of the wilderness to learn of wild dinosuars that dwell like the Brontos." Ico points to the be-hemoths feasting on the leaves while the young ones feasted on the grass.

Silvus continues to look at the Brontos until he spots a large burgundy-scaled predator emerging on a cliff. It leaps down, latch-ing its large, sharp teeth right onto a nearby elderly Bronto. The rest of the Bronto herd begins to run away, not wanting to be food.

"Is that what I think it is?" Silvus freaks out, gazing at the beast holding its jaws onto the struggling Bronto. When the Bronto dies, the mystery predator gets onto its feet, showing it is bipedal. It has two stubby arms with three talons on each. On its back is a patch of feathers that grows from neck to back. Lifting up its head, it makes a big roar with its sharp teeth shown confirming its kill.

"That is the Tyranno Rex, my friends, the apex predator king of Suaronian heart." Ico beams at the sight. He makes it no secret that the Tyranno Rex is one of his favorite predators.

The Tyranno finishes roaring making five smaller Tyrannos come out of hiding from the cliffs or bushes to join in. The large one jumps off, letting the smaller ones feast on the corpse. The pas-sengers have expressions of either fear or amazement as they watch the Tyrannos have thier feast. It is not every day they see large ma-jestic predator's hunt. Fi, on the other claw, looks like she is going to faint, falling to the side to be caught into Ico's arms when he notices.

"I believe I remember that Tyranno Rexes hunt in packs?" Silvus asks his cousin, who is the wildlife expert at the moment.

"That's right. Unlike Crocodons from Tricia, a Tyranno's pack consists entirely of family." Ico gets up with a fainted Fi in his arms. "The others you see with him are either his sons, brothers, grand-children, or sons-in-law."

"Sons-in-law?" Silvus turn to Ico, surprised. Reading about Tyran-nos, they did not look the type who would not go well with other males.

"Unlike other territorial predators, the Alpha male's job is to keep his genes going. When they have daughters to spare, they find a worthy male who gets into his territory to challenge him to a fight. In that way, the Alpha male tests the intruder if he has the potential genes worthy of not only being part of his pack but also claiming one of his daughters to mate."

"Sounds like recruiting for an army," Silvus states, turning his head back to the sight as the caravan slowly moves away from the Tyranno Rexes still eating.

"I have to say, young Ico, your mother must be a great huntress, which is expected of an Avalonia Raptor from Sherrasic!" Nardo comments in praise without taking his eyes off the Snaguanas.

"My mother would take that as a compliment. Unlike those air heads of Tricia, the Sherrasic hunters are more careful at hunting," Ico states, sitting back down, carefully laying Fi gently down.

With all the passengers sitting back down, Ocia turns her head to Silvus and whispers, "Your cousin is not wrong about that."

"You mean how Tricia and Sherrasic were founded by a disagreement of the way of hunting?"

Both Silvus and Ocia shared a good laugh and gaze at each other into their eyes. After a short pause, both Raptors widen their eyes with smiles forming onto their snouts. Ico notices their weird behavior, making a nervous gulp, knowing what they are about to do.

"Is something the matter, sir?" one of the Conclave members who sat next to Ico asks him.

Ignoring the question, Ico makes a face palm in annoyance and mutters, "Oh spirits, no wonder Silvus likes her," as he continues to hold on to the out-cold Fi in his arms for the remainder of the ride, hearing his cousin and the She-Raptor begin to talk to each other like total nerds.

Venturing deeper, Silvus and Ocia find themselves lecturing each other non-stop, filled with energy. They cannot stop talking about stories of heroes, bits of what they know about the Betadoms they live in, and every time they come across a new creature they bother Ico for some information.

For example, the caravan has to stop at the sight of small turkey-looking biped reptilians with feathers covering most of their bodies, and long tails, rushing out of a bush filled with blue flowers crossing the road to get a drink of the Miststream for water. Ico tells them that they are Velocis, with a curious look, stating that they look like the miniature version of themselves. Nardo adds that they remind him of the Raptors that live in the kingdom of Fenheim to the deep north.

Silvus and Ocia continue to speak throughout the ride. The members of Conclave keep to themselves, either gazing at the wilderness or joining Silvus and Ocia's conversation, like Nardo wanting to give his knowledge about how his clan became the ruling clan of Creston. An hour or more later, the Caravan eventually comes to a crossroads with two arrows putting them to a stop. One is pointing straight, reading "Patalot" while the other points left, reading "York."

Nardo turns his head around to the passengers and tells them with a voice of delight, "By the grace of the heavens, if any Raptor is hungry, looks like we are in luck."

"You telling me? All this talking is actually making me hungry!" Silvus perks up with hungry eyes, looking at the arrow to York.

"By the spirits, I cannot remember the last time I ate Tritop steak," Ocia joins in, looking just as hungry, slurping her tongue with her claws held together.

The passengers all agree, eager for some food before heading further. Ico, who has been snoozing the entire trip due to boredom with Silvus and Ocia's lectures, wakes up at the mention of Tritop steak. He stretches his arms and cracks his back and says, "Did some

Raptor mention Tritop steak? Any meat coming from Suaronian Heart, Tritop or Bronto, is a luxury to the other Betadoms!"

Silvus rolls his eyes in response to his cousin's statement. Ocia makes a cute giggle at Silvus' reaction. Fi, who was lying on Ico's side hip, begins to wake up from her long coma with a yawn, stretching her arms.

"What happened?" she asks with a tired voice as she looks around, seeing that they are still in a caravan cart, with her eyes still opened halfway.

⊷⊶«◉»⊷⊶

The caravan make its way to York. It is one of the local meat farms and butchers spread across the kingdom for the purpose of producing and trading meat products. The farm itself is a cluster of spread-apart buildings resembling tree houses in the middle sur-rounded by large trees. From the carriage, Silvus spots four ranches with the Tritops themselves

The Tritops are quadruped dinosaurs with stubby tails, big frilled heads with three horns, and a beak-like snout being used to eat the blue grass for nourishment. The stone fence they are in has large pikes carved on top in case a predator dares to try to eat them.

Traveling further into town, Silvus could see a lot of Omega-caste farmers are very busy. Many are tending the ranches in order to lead some Tritops to a nearby slaughter building to begin the meat harvesting for the season. Some are shopkeepers with stalls, getting ready to sell goods for travelers or the ranchers for new ranching equipment.

Making a stop right by a large building with a sign that reads "York Butchery and Saloon," Silvus gets off the carriage along with the others. All fourteen, led by Nardo, enter the building to reveal a large tavern-like interior filled with guests seated at their tables, enjoying the taste of their Tritop steaks or drumsticks. Like the townsfolk themselves, they don't seem to be worried about the war going on up north.

The smell of the meat being cooked from the kitchens made Silvus drool, gazing at the cooks making the meat behind a counter. He debates to himself whether to have a cooked steak, drumstick, or ribs.

A waitress wearing a gown has just finished serving a few guests; she walks up to the party of fourteen followed by a bow. She seems to know that the lead, Nardo, is a Delta due to seeing the fancy red scarf and hat.

"Greetings m'lords, welcome to York Butchery and Saloon. Are you all here for feasting today?" she asks the trio with a polite tone.

Nardo walks up to the waitress and picks up one of her claws like a gentle male. "Me and my companions here are indeed in need of your brilliant Tritop delicacy." He places a kiss on her claw, making the waitress blush with a giggle.

"Oh, you flatter me, m'lord." The waitress turns her head in shyness.

"Oh, yes." Nardo points to his other thirteen companions. "Perhaps I'll pay enough Golden Feathers for each one!"

"Well then, right this way." The waitress guides Nardo and the companions to a nearby long table.

For the rest of the day, Silvus and the gang are eating up their meals, with Nardo paying, as he promised. During the meals, Ocia is seen talking with Fi, becoming fast friends. Finding out Fi is a princess, the inner history buff in Ocia wants to learn about Kobolds. Silvus, however, is focused on eating his Tritop drumstick, enjoying every bite of it. He feels a tap on the shoulder to see Ico already finished with his Tritop ribs, using a cloth to wipe his lips.

"Where did you find that girl?" Ico asks him with a smirk.

Silvus turns his head to Ocia, who is talking to Fi instead of eating her steak. Realizing that Ico is referring to Ocia, he turns his head back to Ico and tells him, "I met her back home after passing my test." He takes another bite of his drumstick.

"I have to say, man, you and that Ocia girl seem to have a thing for each other already." Ico leans back in his seat with his arm behind his head, giving him a teasing look.

Silvus can sense that Ico is trying to have some fun with his girl-related situation. He narrows his eyes, giving Ico a stern look with a smile, and whispers, "Says the lover boy eyeing a princess."

"I don't know what you talking about?!" Ico perks up with flustered cheeks, turning his head away in denial, making Silvus laugh. What better way to tease back than to poke fun at one's hypocrisy?

Chapter 18
A City Under a Tree

Inside the town inn, the members of the caravan slept inside the adventurers' special suite, consisting of twenty large beds located at the top floor. Nardo proves to be a wealthy Creston merchant with the benefits as a First Delta having enough golden feathers, the currency of Avalonia, to pay for such a room.

Upon the bed right by a window at the corner is Silvus. Instead of sleeping like the others, he sits up on his bed, gazing at the starry sky. He has always wondered what the stars are, ever since he was young. Reflecting on good times with his mother, he remembers that she used to take him outside for some stargazing. Closing his eyes puts him in a flashback to his past. He thinks about a time when he was young. His mother would take him to the back courtyard where she educated him about the stars being the spirits themselves and also when Raptors die, they become one of them. If makes him wonder if his father is up there, watching them.

———◦《◦》◦———

Silvus wakes up to see he is still at an inn around York. Turns out he fell asleep while he was reflecting on his experience with his mother. Taking a few gasping breaths, he looks around the suite to see that the members of Conclave, Ico, and Fi are still asleep in their assigned beds. The only one he does not see is Ocia, who is supposed to sleep on the bed in front of him.

Looking out the window next to him, he spots Ocia coming out of the inn, walking by the farm square. Curious what she is doing awake in this time of night, he decides to carefully leave his bed, not wanting to wake any Raptor. Leaving the building, Silvus carefully follows Ocia all the way to a hill, where he sees her sitting gazing at the stars.

Silvus slowly walks toward her for a closer look. She seems to be simply humming a strange tune while she continues to gaze. Taking a few steps forward he softly calls out, "Ocia?"

"Eeek!" She freaks out with a small hop. "Silvus?! You scared me."

"Oh, sorry." Silvus makes a cheeky smile. "I did not mean to startle you, but why are you still awake?"

"Well, I was dreaming about what Patalot might look like until I woke up unexpectedly, and instead of going back to sleep, I decided to go out for a walk and maybe stargaze for a bit," Ocia claims, shifting her body to the side and pats the blue grass beside her, signaling for Silvus to sit next to her.

Silvus walks up to the hill and sits next to Ocia, joining her in stargazing. After a short pause, he speaks up, turning his gaze back to Ocia.

"You said you were dreaming about Patalot?" he asks. Ocia puts on a nervous face, gazing back at the night sky.

"Yeah. Speaking of that, after we first met, I went back home to wait for my brother. When he finally returned a few weeks after... well, Monchester took over Maglo, oddly, he told me to head to Patalot."

"For what reason?"

"I don't know," Ocia shrugs. "He only told me that it is for an important mission. What is even weirder is that he wanted me to wear this amulet at all times."

Ocia grabs her green glowing amulet with a serpent iris. Silvus leans forward to take a closer look as the former observes it. That amulet she wears—he could swear he has seen it before, but he just can't piece it together.

"Where did you get this amulet?" He asks her hoping she knows something.

"It was given to me as a hatch day gift last winter. A Mistcaster gave it to me and told me that it is a good luck charm blessed by the spirits."

"Really?"

"Oh yes! He told me that it gave good luck to many girls of his family, yet--" Ocia looks back at the amulet with a skeptical face. "I am beginning to question this luck ever since my capture by those Dark Mist-casting bandits."

Speaking of that, a question popped into Silvus' mind. Come to think of it, he wonders how a maiden from Monchester got captured all the way to the border to Creston. Especially remembering that she mentioned that she was told to head to Patalot.

"Come to think of it, Ocia, how exactly did you end up captured with Conclave?"

"As I mentioned before," she takes her gaze off the amulet to Silvus with a blank face, "my brother wanted me to head to Patalot. He managed to hire a caravan to take me there until we were ambushed. I was the only survivor, but whoever ambushed me probably took me all the way there. I did not know who ambushed me, because my head was covered by a bag, blocking my sight. After being sold, the bandits or rebels as you call them took off the bag from my head and threw me into the cage with the others they captured. That is how I met them."

Ocia points a talon to the inn were the Conclave still slept.

"I have to say, Ocia, that is one strange tale. What about your brother—do you think he is worried about you at this point?" Silvus asks her, remembering that she told him that her brother is overprotective.

"I bet he is worried sick about me." Ocia looks to the side with a huff. "If I ever see him again, he is going to demand me to explain what has happened."

The two Raptors stay silent. As the wind blows by, they slowly look into each other's eyes. Cricket sounds can be heard, and Mist wisps fly around the sky above. Feeling awkward, they look away from each other with blushes on their cheeks.

"OOOOK, so how far do you think we are from Patalot?" Ocia breaks the silence.

"I think we are almost there! But I heard that the wellspring Patalot itself is so huge, it almost reaches to the stars themselves!" Silvus points up to the stars, making Ocia gasp in amazement, covering her snout with one claw.

"WOW. Really?"

"Oh yes, if we ever managed to climb up there, maybe our passed-away ancestors can get a closer look at us," Silvus adds with grin, putting his talons on his hips, looking macho, making Ocia giggle.

"Imagine our ancsetors looking at us right now!" Ocia adds, but this time the two Raptors on the hill share a big laugh.

After their little laugh-fest, they begin to feel strange not only in their chests but also behind them. They turn their heads to see their tails wrapped around each other. They even see themselves holding claws. Gazing at each other in the eyes, they start to slowly move their snouts closer to each other only to be interrupted by a roaring sound. Both startled back on their feet, the two worry that a Tyranno Rex or a Spino could be nearby. They turn their heads with red cheeks to see the town behind them.

"Um… we better return with the others… gotta rest up for Pata-lot!" Silvus awkwardly states.

"A-agreed," Ocia cheekily smiles.

With red faces, the two begin to walk back to York to rest up for the night, as they are getting closer to the city under the tree.

* * *

The next morning, the caravan is back on the main road. Silvus and Ocia sit in the same seats behind Nardo, who is back at the helm. Ico and Fi decide to sit near Silvus and Ocia, having a good time speaking with each other. Getting closer to their destination, all four decide to share their thoughts of the city.

"So this city, Patalot, that you Raptors speak of. Is it really under this giant tree? As big as a mountain?" Fi asks her Raptor companions with a hint of fear.

"It is what our family and friends tell us. It is said many lifestyles of all Betadoms came from here!" Silvus states, pointing down at no place in particular, referring to the forest they are in.

"It is so true. Monchester, Maglo, and Creston embrace a path of enlightenment while Triteria and Sherrasic embrace hunting. And it was all thanks to the mysterious champion who wanted to share the knowledge with all," Ocia adds, wanting to demonstrate her historical knowledge. "What really brings all the Betadoms together is the love of studying and using Mist and our faith in the spirits."

"Sadly, we don't really know who this champion guy is. When I actually try to read, they never really tell us who the guy is." Ico shrugs. "Might as well be some kind of myth."

"How can he be a myth? It is written in our history books! If he really did not exist, then the royal family would not exist either!" Silvus argues at his cousin.

"If I may add, my dear friends," the voice of Nardo speaks gaining their attention. He turns his head to the side and continues, "Did you know that Conclave was an inspiration by the many merchant guilds here? Like the more popular 'Golden Kingdom Company.'"

"Isn't the Golden Kingdom Company a trade company directly owned by the Alpha-King?" Silvus asks, now listening too.

"Indeed it is, my friend. Once we get to Patalot, the first thing I would do is--" Nardo pauses his sentence with a smile. "Speaking of, you better look at this."

Silvus carefully stands up in the carriage to move next to Nardo to see what he is talking about. In front of his view, he could see an opening leading to more sunlight. His jaw drops, with his eyes widened.

He sees a large circular metropolis built in the middle of the blue grasslands. The buildings are of Roman in style and shape, almost looking like cathedrals. The pearl white colors look like it is made out of blueish-white stone with bronze rooftops, all protected by a large wall surrounding it. In the middle of it all is the colossal teal-emerald oak tree the size of a mountain, with the royal palace built around it. That is Patalot, the largest wellspring of the kingdom.

Approaching the main gates, Silvus looks up to see a pair of long black banners with the symbol of Avalonia hanging above with an enormous gate made of iron in between. A group of at least six guards is seen guarding the gates. They draw their spears and slowly approach the caravan.

"Halt! State your business!" the captain of the guard demands.

"I am Davinchio Nardo, First-Delta of Creston on Conclave business," Nardo replies with a few coughs.

The guard looks to Silvus and his three friends with a suspicious look and then back at Nardo.

"What about them?" the captain asks, pointing at the four mentioned.

"They are my rescuers whom I offered to travel with me. I owed them that much," Nardo clarifies.

The captain orders the other five to further inspect the caravan, which annoys Nardo. Three of the guards inspect the carriage with goods, while the other two are inspecting the passengers. The two guards command the passengers to get out of the carriage and line them up with Ico, Fi, Ocia, and Silvus as the last four in that order. From right to left, the other guard inspects each Raptor for anything suspicious all the way to Silvus.

"Does your cloak have pockets? If so, hand them over!"the guard demands.

"If I may ask first, sir, is it really necessary?" Silvus asks looking at him suspicious.

"With the war going up north, we need to be on high alert for any Raptors seeking entry." The guard inspecting Silvus draws his short sword, pointing it at him. "I will not ask again. Hand over your cloak, now!"

One thing Silvus knows about members of the royal army is that they usually take their duties very seriously. So seriously, they would go through extreme methods like what the guard is doing to him right now. For the sake of not causing trouble, he takes off his cloak and gives it to the guard.

The guard inspects each pocket for any item that could be used by an assassin. Searching through cloak, the guard spots the dagger that Silvus carries with him. He takes it out and confronts Silvus. "What is this?!"

Silvus had almost forgotten about Cri's dagger. He sees the other guard draw his blade, getting closer to him. Sweat is coming from his forehead and his heart starts to beat fast. He'd better think of what to say, or he will be imprisoned for being an assassin.

"I... found that dagger during my travels on my way here for study."

The two guards look at him with skeptical looks. One looks to the captain, who gestures at him to keep questioning. As ordered, the guard asks, "If so, where did you get this dagger from?"

"I got it from a place called Shima, an underground city of Kobolds," Silvus tells them without taking a breath. In response, the two guards laugh as if he told a joke, even though he is telling the truth.

"What creature would name an empire with such a name?! And you really expect us to believe Kobolds exist!" the guard mocks, showing that they don't believe him until a voice calls out.

"HEY! DOWN HERE!"

The two guards turn their heads to Fi, who is of course the shortest of them all. With a huff, she stomps up to them to give a piece of her mind.

"Who and what are you? Where did you come from?" one of the guards asks her.

"While you were inspecting, you accidentally missed me because I am too small. To answer your first question, I am Princess Fi Jin, princess of the Kobold kingdom of Shima! And I could confirm for you dopes that I am pretty much real." She puts her fists to her hips with a huff.

One guard raises his claw looking dumbfounded and questions, "Does that mean he is telling the truth?"

"YES! That dagger you see belonged to a crazy sister of mine due to political stuff. For helping my people, my brother who is the new king allowed him to keep the dagger for study."

The guards turn their heads to the captain looking stunned; he only shrugs. Looking back at Silvus, one of them tells him with an apologetic look, "Apologies, citizen; please forgive our ignorance. We will let you go; however, I must warn you. Next time, don't have a small weapon like this hidden. Any Raptor who wishes to carry a weapon into the city must keep it exposed at all times so we can keep an eye on them."

The guard gives the cloak and dagger back to Silvus while the other three finishes inspecting the goods giving the thumbs up "cleared."

"Thank you, sir," Silvus nods with a smile of relief. However, there is another case that he must address. He walks up to the captain to show him a package on his strap.

"If I may ask, Captain, I was sent by my mother, Beta-Lady Vessel Silviera to deliver this package to Arkus. By any chance could I meet him as soon as possible?"

"You mean the arch-sage? I believe he is currently at the royal palace with the Mistatorium." The captain gestures one of his three talons like a thumb behind him at the gate. "Whatever that package you have is, it must be important since a Beta requested you to carry it all the way here."

The captain allows Silvus and the gang to return to the caravan. The captain turns his head up to the gates, shouting to open up. The iron gates in front slowly open with the sounds of roaring engines.

"Welcome to Patalot! The capital of Avalonia!" the captain announces, allowing the caravan to move in the bustling metropolis in front.

⊰⊙⊱

Inside, Silvus takes his time to admire the city up close. All the buildings, houses, and shops indeed look like stone temples neatly preserved, while the flower gardens and smaller trees grow in between, giving the city a nice forest theme. Looking up at the sky, he sees the branches filled with leaves from Patalot itself, almost covering the city like a large umbrella. From the branches he sees wisps flowing around its branches, giving the tree an enchanting look.

Crowds of Raptors of all castes are seen crowding the streets without a care in the world. Some Raptors play music in the streets. Some are tending to the market buildings, selling assortments of goods. Some Raptors are simply hanging around the various land-marks, like the big statue of Ultamar Magnus erected in the middle of the circular district center surrounded by more shops. Silvus can see more guards patrolling in groups, keeping an eye out for trouble.

Stopping right by a three-story building with a sign that reads "Conclave," the passengers begin to hop off, with Silvus hopping off last. He stretches his limbs after sitting on the carriage for too long. His cousin and two friends do the same. He turns to his left to see Nardo approaching him.

"Well, my friend, it seems this is the time we part ways. If you ever want to buy the greatest goods Creston has to offer, Conclave is the best shop!"

"Thanks for the offer, Nardo." Silvus extends his claw for Nardo to shake. "More importantly, I want to thank you guys for escorting us here."

"Any time, my friend. My associates and I do owe you our lives. But one more thing!" Nardo walks up to the caravan of goods to take out a big bag and throws it for Silvus to catch. "For your help, I give you 1,000 golden feathers for you to enjoy this majestic city."

Nardo waves up his arms, looking up to the heavens covered with Patalot's branches. Silvus cannot help but chuckle. The way Nardo speaks is the typical Creston behavior.

Silvus gratefully puts the golden feathers into his cloak to thank him once again. He turns around to see Ico, Fi, and Ocia walking up to him.

"So what now, Silvus?" Ocia asks him.

Silvus takes out the package to make sure it is okay, and tells them, "We do what we came here for." He turns around at the giant tree. "We head to the royal palace."

—••((•))••—

As much as Silvus wants to enjoy the city, he has to keep focus on the task at claw. After requesting Nardo to continue taking care of the Snaguanas, he makes his way through the market district, followed by two of his friends, Fi and Ocia, as well as his cousin Ico. Fi is following behind Ico, gazing around looking like she is going to faint, while Ico is busy keeping an eye out for the knights of the Mist. Ocia walks beside Silvus, looking around with amazement, acting like a total history buff, spouting facts like the city is actually of Precursor origin.

For being a big city, it proves to be an overwhelming walk for Silvus. He has to pass through hordes of Raptors crowding the streets. Both in the nice neighborhoods and shopping centers he tries to ask for directions, but the Raptors are too busy minding their own business, passing through him, making him groan in annoyance. At least being in a city covered in plant life, he can admire the forested theme around him, hoping to ease some stress. Getting closer to the palace, Silvus decides to lead his party to search for a place to rest up, feeling himself getting thirsty.

They decide to sit on a table outside near a tavern selling Maglo cuisine. Silvus picked it personally due to being a reminder of his home. Instead of food, they are having lotus bloom tea. Lotus bloom tea is a drink brewed from a yellow flower native to Maglo, lotus bloom. What is good about the tea is that it serves to calm the nerves. For walking a long distance, Silvus himself really needs it.

A waiter from the tavern comes out with a tray of four cups and a tea pot. The waiter places the tray in the middle of the table, then Silvus reaches into his bag giving the waiter the appropriate amount of Golden Feathers to pay. Silvus decides to stand up, picking up the pot to serve the tea for Ocia and Fi first, believing in the saying, "Ladies first." Then he serves Ico and himself before sitting back down.

"So what do you think the royal palace looks like, Silvus?" Ocia asks, sipping some of her tea.

Taking a sip of his own tea, Silvus faces her now. Looking calm, he responds, "If we ever make it there, I bet it is even bigger than the ones we lived in."

"By the Root, if this palace is another ginormous thing, I might not wake up on my next faint!"

All eyes go to Fi, who is pouring herself another round. The poor little Kobold lass developed a habit of fainting over giant things. She hopes that by drinking as much tea as she can, she could prevent another episode. That is, until Ico opens his snout.

"Princess, we are talking about the home to the highest authority of all Raptor-kind." Ico drinks his tea, looking smug, and leans his head near her. "Of course, the royal palace is going to be huge."

"NOT. HELPING. ICY!" Fi stammers with a glare at Ico, who just makes a playful grin. Thinking his grin is so funny, Fi cannot help but laugh instead of staying mad. To both Silvus and Ocia, it is becoming clear that the two are getting along well. Perhaps they could be the first Raptor and Kobold to potentially fall in love around the past the number of years since the last time Raptors ever contacted the Kobolds.

While Fi and Ico continue to speak, Ocia turns her attention to Silvus, looking curious, and asks him, "So how far do you think we are?"

"I honestly don't know. This is my first time ever being in this historical city." Silvus lifts his head, turning to his left, hoping to find help from one of the Raptors that continue to pass by in the streets. What seems odd to him is that they don't seem to be worried about the ongoing war at all. Probably they do not care much, as long as the war does not come to them. Further scanning around the streets, he eventually spots a guard standing by the Magnus statue. He gets off his seat to approach the guard, hoping he will be of more help than the average citizen.

"Excuse me, sir. Do you know how far we are from the palace?"

"For what purpose, citizen?" the guard asks him in a stereotypical deep guard voice, looking at him with a serious face as he is trained to do. Silvus responds by telling the guard that he has an urgent task to meet with the arch-sage on behalf of his mother. The guard slowly points to the north road, to show them they are not far.

The guard seems to be holding back a worried expression on his face while he points. Silvus takes notice and asks the guard what the problem is. The guard tells him, "If you all are really planning to get to the palace, I recommend you make an appointment with a member of the watch. There is an angry mob right now."

"An angry mob?!" Silvus perks up, shocked. He knows there have been many angry mobs formed across the kingdom, like the one he saw back home. He could bet that it is mostly anti-Mistatorium rhetoric, as usual. Beside him, he hears Ocia gasp, walking up next to him while covering her snout with a fearful look.

"By the spirits, how bad is it?" she asks.

"In a place like this, I think it is better I show you hatchlings." The guard gestures them to follow him. Silvus looks to Ocia who looks at him back with a worried look as Fi and Ico walk to him, wondering what is going on. Silvus explains what the guard told him. Then he has them follow along to catch up with the guard.

Chapter 19
The Empty Throne

A large angry mob of Raptors is seen holding picket signs crowded in front of the royal palace gates, guarded by a swarm of royal guards trying to keep them away. The mob looks like they are mostly Omegas, due to the lack of the nobility scarf. The signs they carry reads "Justice for Sulthur," "Mistatorium are oppressive killers," and "Don't trend of sneck," whatever that means. The guards themselves are holding tower shields lined up covering the lower grand staircase while archers are seeing with bows drawn. Silvus is in shock, seeing how large the mob is. He feels his claw grabbed by Ocia, who is scared by the sight.

"Dude, this Sulthur guy must be very popular with these Raptors," Ico states, reading the signs from the mob.

"Icy is right, and what does one of them mean by 'Don't trend on Sneck'? Sounds very silly," Fi adds, also attempting to read the signs, trying not to laugh.

The guard in front who led them gives a sigh in exhaustion. He turns around to face the trio, telling them, "One thing I know about Sulthur is that he made a lot of promises to the Omegas."

"What sort of promises?" Silvus asks the guard, curious about the promises by Sulthur.

"I was a young recruit when he was still alive. Before he was even crowned Alpha-King, Sulthur was already a very popular fellow. Perhaps while his father Alpha-King Ultamar Sylvain III was Ill, Sulthur started acting as if he is Alpha-King already even though he is still Alpha-Prince. His popularity might have to do with the promise of more freedoms to the Omegas, like the right to self-employment."

"You mean the right for Raptors of all castes to own businesses independently?"

"Sulthur was not like any Alpha-Prince. In his speeches, he always spoke about how the hard- working Omega folk have the potential to be a great as a Delta to benefit the economy. He even claims that the privilege of marrying nobles is one such example." The guard shrugs. "I bet it has to do with his mother being an Omega. Perhaps he is doing it for financial reasons."

"I think it is great to recognize the potential of Omegas and their hard work. Omegas and Deltas owning their own businesses and working together. No wonder a lot of Raptors love him!" Silvus beams at the idea of what Sulthur planned. At the same time, he ignores Fi's muttering about how insane it would be if the Raptor nobility were willing to defile their noble blood.

"Indeed. Sadly the Alpha-King is dead. Many Raptors are blaming the Mistatorium that the promises of new freedoms will never come," the guard replies, sounding disappointed.

Silvus looks back at the mob. They all have expressions of betrayal and suspicion. Seeing how angry they are, he decides to ask the guard for an appointment, so he doesn't have to deal with them. He reaches into his cloak, hoping to find parchment and a quill pen. With parchment and pen, Silvus leans down on the ground and writes his full name, the Mistatorium member he is requesting, and the reason. He stands back up and gives the parchment to the guard.

The guard looks through the parchment to see that everything is in order. With a nod he tells them to rest up at an inn while he takes it to the arch-sage. As the guard finds his way through the mob, Ico walks up to Silvus from behind and nudges his shoulder.

"Did you really carry a paper and pen the entire journey?" Ico gives Silvus a half-eyed look.

With a cheeky smile, Silvus tells him, "You may never know if you want to learn a thing or two!"

"Silvy is right! There is always something to learn worth recording! Perhaps I would have done the same myself." Ocia defends his action.

Ico and Fi exchange weird looks and both agree that Silvus and Ocia are total nerds.

Silvus finds himself sitting on a bed near a window inside a local inn at nightfall. Around him are his companions, sleeping on their associated beds. Instead of sleeping, he is gazing at the window, enjoying the view of the city at night. The city streets are empty due to the residents making their way to their homes, making the streets peaceful, except for the guards with torches who patrols for the night shift. Even if he could not enjoy the stars being blocked by Patalot's colossal branches, the wisps flying around the city like fireflies make good substitute. He watches one batch of wisps fly around a flower garden where the statue of Magnus is.

Silvus breaks his gaze to turn his head back into the room to watch over his cousin and friends who are sleeping peacefully. In truth, he is keeping an eye out for a guard or two to come find him. He reaches to his right to pick up the package he is supposed to deliver. He wanders if the guard even made it to the arch-sage. *I hope we get to see Arkus soon; my mother is depending on me.*

A tear falls from his eye. Just thinking about his mother makes him more worried than ever. Believing that the guard is not coming, he puts down the package to get some sleep. Suddenly, a sound of knocking on the door is heard, waking up Silvus with a deep gasp. He looks around to see his companions are waking up too, due to the loud sounds.

"This is the guard. Is there a Vessel Silvus here?" the voice calls out, followed by more knocking.

Silvus exchanges looks with his tired companions and gets off his bed. He walks up to the door and slowly opens it to see a team of three guards waiting. They all look at him with serious faces, as they are trained to do.

"Is something the matter?" Silvus asks them.

"Are you the one who made the appointment to meet the arch-sage?"

"Why yes! It is I!" Silvus makes a hopeful smile. It turns out his appointment went through after all.

"You made a smart move to schedule an appointment, young sir. With all the mobs gathering these days, you would have got mixed into trouble. Right now, the mob has gone home, so this is a perfect time for you and your companions to come with us right now!"

With that, Silvus happily agrees, allowing the guards to wait around the entrance. He tells his party that the guards have arrived to collect them. Wasting no time, the party collect all their belongings and rush out of their room, meeting up with the guards who are waiting for them outside.

⟞•⟝

Led into the grand royal courtyard, the palace keep is exactly how Silvus imagined it. The walls are teal stone in color, the keep big enough to cover Patalot's stump area, and by the spirits, the castle has this temple like architecture meant for worshiping the one true God. While he follows the guards, Silvus turns his head to check on his companions who are following along. He sees Ico with a surprised face mouthing "Holy powers of mist!" Fi's face is in a shocked trance, doing her best not to faint. And Ocia is acting like a young girl who discovered her own dream castle, looking at the gardens in the palace. Turning his gaze back to the guards, Silvus sees that they are being led into the entrance hall through a pair of large onyx doors.

Inside the grand entrance hall, Silvus immediately takes his chance to look around the spacious room for any sign of Arkus as he follows along the black carpet with silver edges. So far, he can see only the drones keeping the room clean, and the guards standing around like mannequins keeping an eye out for anything suspicious. Above the grand staircase he spots the Raptor he is looking for. Silvus sees Arkus standing in front of a large pair of doors in between two arching stairways in the scales. The sight of him makes his inner fanboy swell up in his chest as if he were meeting his hero Magnus himself. The elderly age, the purple scales, the center-parted long white feathered mane, and wearing a robe of utmost authority—that is Arkus, alright, and in his tired light-blue eyes look stressed.

Approaching the old Raptor, the guards make their respectful bows, telling him, "Good evening, Arch-Sage, we have collected the adventurers as you ordered."

Arkus looks past the guards to see Silvus standing with his companions. He orders the guards to leave them, then turns his attention back to the Silvus with a smile.

"Young Silvus. I would never have thought to see you here," Arkus greets him with a friendly grandfatherly voice. Silvus cannot help but grab one of Arkus's claws, shaking it very hard with a relieved smile.

"Arch-Sage Arkus, you cannot imagine how much of an honor it is to finally meet you in Raptor rather than a hologram!"

Arkus makes a chuckle and replies while letting go of his claws. "Same as I, young Silvus. I believe, according to your note, you are here on behalf of your mother Silviera?"

With a nod, Silvus takes the package from his back and gives it to Arkus, telling him, "My mother told me to give this to you believing that it could save the kingdom."

"Did she?" Arkus raises a brow, examining the package in his arms. When he spots the seal, his eyes widen. He slightly opens it up to peek inside and closes it again.

"Did she tell you how she got this?"

"She did not, as we were in a middle of an invasion," Silvus tells Arkus, bowing to show respect.

Arkus looks up at the ceiling, deep in thought. With a snap of his claws, he gets an idea. He looks past Silvus, using his free claw to point to one of the drones tending to one of the large portraits of the past Alpha-Kings or Queens and calls him out. He orders the drone to give Silvus' companions a tour around the palace, then escort them to the guest chambers when done.

Followed with a bow, the male drone calls for Ocia, Fi, and Ico to come with him, but Silvus is told to remain with Arkus. The erone leads the three up the stairs to the east wing, leaving Silvus and Arkus behind.

Silvus lifts himself up back on his feet wondering what Arkus is going to do next. With a gesture to follow, Arkus begins to climb up the stairs to the west wing with the package still in his arms. Silvus follows suit, climbing up the stairs, following Arkus to the second floor of the west wing.

Silvus finds himself in a fancy hall, looking around the various portraits of the past Alpha-Kings and Queens like the ones by the entrance hall. What is interesting is that they are all silver scaled like himself.

"I sense you have questions," he hears Arkus call out. Silvus turns his attention to the old Mistcaster beside him to his right looking at him with his tired eyes. Arkus is holding an enchanting staff like a cane on one claw, while is holding the package on the other.

"Um," Silvus struggles in his mind what to ask. He has a lot of questions that he really wants to ask the leader of the legendary Mistatorium. Suddenly he thinks about the invasion by Targon, especially the argument between Targon and his mother. "Actually! Before I was forced out of my home, Mom and Targon were arguing about the election of a new Alpha-King. Why is it you guys have not picked one yet? Do you know of the ongoing war up north?" he asks the old Mistcaster, who makes a tired sigh, stopping by a portrait of Sulthur.

"Young hatchling, I have indeed heard of the fighting up north. The Sage of Monchester told us everything after coming here since his exile."

"You mean the Sage of Monchester?"

"Oh yes, my boy, Sage Gorm has clarified our suspicions that Beta-Lord Anvar Targon has begun open rebellion against us, starting with the invasion of Maglo. Sage Fernus of Maglo of course was heartbroken to hear of the news," Arkus sighs. "As much as we want to send help to Tricia, we have our claws tied trying to regain order here in Suaronian Heart. Perhaps I have been hearing riots in one of the towns at the Terrian Valley to the southwest!"

"And the election of The Alpha-King? It is why many Raptors are believing you killed Sulthur," Silvus asks, walking up to the portrait of Sulthur, who seems familiar to him. Arkus turns around, looking a bit defensive, like how Ocia reacted when confronted about Monchester.

"I assure you we did no such thing!" Then Arkus calms down with an uneasy expression. "I am afraid it is not that simple… perhaps you caught me in a very odd time, as we have nobles right now at the throne room waiting to be tested with the other sages."

"Tested?" Silvus turns his gaze away from the portrait. Arkus, realizing he let one cat out of the bag, widens his eyes and closes them. Then he looks at Silvus for a closer look to inspect him, making the latter step back a bit. Then Arkus looks to the package in thought.

"I have said too much…what about we put this relic that your mother wanted to give me in the armory, and I'll take you to the throne room with the others," Arkus offers, guiding Silvus to the armory.

———— ⊙ ————

Back to the entrance hall through the large doors in between the stairways, Arkus leads Silvus into the most enchanting garden he has ever seen. Walking across the cobblestone walkway, Silvus sees that the garden is filled with various plant life from all the Betadoms, mixed together with Miststreams flowing through radiating Mist fog, giving the garden a rainforest feel. Across the path, he sees rows of statues of the Raptor heroes, including his ancestor Vessel Atheros, with utmost admiration.

"Enjoying the Gardens of Odyssey, I see?" Silvus hears Arkus ask as he continues to follow.

"I never seen anything like this!" Silvus states, beaming, continuing to look around the plant life, new and old, with glowing flowers blending together.

"Haha, your mother had a similar reaction when she came here for the first time," Arkus adds, earning Silvus' attention about his mother.

The mention of his mother makes him remember that she once told him that Arkus was her old mentor. To come and think of it, he wonders what his mother was like when she was a young hatchling. With a smile Silvus asks as he continues to follow, "What was she like when she was younger?"

"Your mother was a very shy lass when she was young. She was more into reading books rather than socializing with friends."

Silvus feels himself blush, hearing how much in common he has with her. Arkus continues, "Well, that is until she met one of my greatest pupils, the young Sulthur himself."

"My mother knew the Alpha-King?!" Silvus perks up, surprised. His mother never mentioned ever knowing the Alpha-King in her youth.

"Why, yes. Before my promotion to Arch-Sage, your mother was one of my best students, along with the Alpha-Prince and his good friend Raspute Bylark."

Raspute Bylark? Did Ocia mention him before? Silvus asks to himself after hearing Akrus mention the name. He remembers when talking with Ocia about him being a new court Mistcaster. Perhaps the figure he saw with Targon could be him. He is going to ask Arkus about Bylark until he pauses at the sight of a large stump with an opening, making his jaw drop slowly. With eyes of shock, Silvus scans the stump upwards seeing the rest of the wellspring of Patalot up close in the middle of the gardens of Odyssey. By the spirits, no wonder Patalot is also named the world tree.

Arkus looks at him with a smile, pointing with his now free right claw into the opening. He tells him, "Into the throne room we go."

<hr />

Walking through the tunnel with torch lights hanging on wall, Silvus is guided by Arkus all the way to the throne room itself located inside the center of Patalot. The room is a circular space with a high ceiling shaped like a dome, with glowing crystals giving the room light. On the wooden floor is the same black carpet with the kingdom symbol that stretches all the way to a large platform. On the platform are the five symbols of the known Betadoms: the Rook Tower of Monchester, the Crescent moon of Creston, the Sun of Sherrasic, the Trident of Tricia, and the Star of Maglo.

Silvus turns his gaze up the platform made out of Patalot's emerald-colored wood all the way up to see the Alpha's throne itself, the amber throne with three gems carved on top of the three triangle edges on top—one blue, one red, and in the middle shiny white. Looking down, he sees five members of the Mistatoruim. The sages are all gathered, with two noble Raptors standing in front of the platform waiting for a Raptor. Silvus can hear talk among them as he gets close with Arkus.

"By the spirits, what is taking so long?!" one noble who is male demands with his arms crossed, tapping his taloned foot rapidly.

"Um… Delta Citro is right…this wait is taking so long!" the female noble moans, showing that she is very nervous by the way she stutters and shakes her body.

"Aren't you a Delta from Sherrasic? I though you all are supposed to be brave hunters, Delta Jezera?" Citro looks at her with narrowed eyes, earning her a shriek.

"Patience, Delta Citro; once the arch-sage comes we will begin 'The Anointing' at once," a female middle-aged sage wearing purple robes tries to reason.

Silvus looks over to Arkus as they get close and whispers, "What is the Anointing?"

"I will explain everything; just be patient," Akrus whispers back as they approach the other sages and the two nobles. The female in purple robe walks up to them, looking serious.

"About time ya showed up, Arch-Sage! Our candidates here are getting anxious about the Anointing," the Female sage tells Arkus with her fisted claws to her hips. She turns her eyes, noticing Silvus with a gasp. In return, Silvus makes a nervous smile with a small wave.

"Aren't ya Vessel Silvus? The Newly Caster of the Mist?" the sage asks, taking a closer look at him.

"Why yes I am, Lady Sage. And I am guessing by your seaside accent you're from Tricia?" Silvus asks her, making a soft bow. The Lady Sage makes a hearty elderly lady laugh and offers her claw. Silvus takes the claw and gently shakes it and gives it a gentle male kiss, making her blush a bit.

"Indeed I am, you polite lad. I am Ariella, Sage of Tricia. As much as I want to get acquainted with ye, I believe there is a task at claw."

"She is correct, young Silvus." Arkus comes in between them, putting a claw on Silvus' shoulder and announces, "Which is why as Arch-Sage of the Mistatorium, I nominate you as another candidate!"

Silvus beams as the sages and the nobles all gasp. He never thought of himself being Alpha-King. Perhaps he is so used to being Beta-Lord that he thought it would not be worth it. One of the other sages, a middle male wearing Maglo blue, walks up with concern.

"Are you serious, Arch-Sage? As much as it pleases me that a candidate comes from my representing Betadom, did you ever tell him what is going on?"

"I am getting there, Sage Fernus. If you remember, He shows a promising gift to learn Mistcraft like a master. I say it is a sign." Arkus turns his head to Silvus and tells him, "Would you walk with your fellow candidates, Silvus, so we can proceed?"

With a nod, Silvus walks up to the other candidates. One candidate, Citro, is looking at him as a rival while Jezara only shakes in fear for her life. All three, with the other sages behind, watch Arkus walk toward the front of the platform. With a few coughs he explains, "Now that we are all here, welcome to the Anointing. It is said in the old text, to defeat the world gone mad with Dark Mist, the champion needed the blessing from the spirits in order to face the corrupted Precursors, the first of the Dark Mistcasters. To receive such blessing, the champion is said to have drunk from the Mist core of Patalot itself!"

"And what does that have to do with us becoming the new ruler?!" Cirto complains, wanting to get to the point. Arkus walks around the platform and points for all Raptors present to a large fountain in the middle of a Mistpool behind.

"Before his betrayel by Necros, the champion had told the first of the Mistatorium that if by any point his royal line dies out, one must also drink from the Mist core of Patalot in order to determine if the spirits find you worthy to rule."

"Um, you mean we have to drink from that fountain? That does not sound bad?" Jezara comments, looking somewhat confident. Arkus stays serious, looking at Jezara uneasily.

"The Ultamar clan have lived for so long, we have not done this for many years. With the death of Sulthur without an heir, we looked through the scrolls to figure out what we need to do. Finding out about the ritual, we wasted no time looking for candidates and making them keep it a secret."

"Why keep it a secret?" Silvus asks with concern in his voice. He knows there has to be more than just drinking the Miststream from the core of Patalot.

"The Mist core is the very source where the wellsprings radiate their power, as it is their very heart. The streams you see outside the wellsprings are just weakened Mist, but inside near the core is pure and powerful. When a Mistcaster drinks directly from it, he or she will gain a unique ability, if he or she is not overwhelmed by simply fainting with a small chest ache. Patalot is a special case. As the firstborn child, the Mist from its core is so old and powerful, it could overwhelm its drinker and die."

The cannidates, including Silvus, all gasp at the revelation. The thought of risking one's life to become ruler did not sound real to

Silvus. No wonder that the ritual is a secret. To even imagine any Raptor hearing about it would mean drastic results. "You mean… IT WILL KILL US?!" he hears Jezara shriek as Cirto yawned, not believing such a thing.

"The champion was the only known individual who was ever to survive Patalot's taint in order to be allowed to sit upon the throne. This is why we keep it a secret. It is how the spirits determine not only who is worthy of being their voice but also purge those tainted with too much darkness in their hearts. To start a new royal line is to be the heralds of the spirits themselves."

Arkus closes his eyes, looking down with a worried expression. Silvus can tell that Arkus is very hesitant to go forward with the ritual. There is no telling how many cannidates they have collected only for them to die. No wonder they have not chosen a new ruler yet. Looking back up with a serious face, Arkus tells them, "It is time!"

Arkus looks to one of the knights guarding the entrance and orders, "Knight! Hand me the chalice!"

The knight from the post walks past the sages and the nobles and kneels on one knee, giving a sapphire chalice with silver beads to Aruks. Arkus collects the chalice and walks up to the pool where the fountain is spewing the liquid Mist, and cups some of it up. With the filled chalice, he turns around and returns to the front of the throne platform and calls out with an authoritative tone, "Citro, step forth!"

With a huff, Citro throws his scarf to the side and walks up like a snob. He takes the chalice from Arkus's claws and drinks from it. Returning it to Arkus, he takes a few steps back, expecting something to happen. Suddenly, he feels something in his chest, clutching it with his two claws, making painful screams of agony. Citro first drops to his knees; then his entire body is on the ground, shaking around as if he is having a seizure, tail and limbs all twitching. Silvus and Jezara can only watch in horror while Citro helplessly cries in pain. Suddenly cracks begin to form around his body, with glowing energy coming out. His eyes snap open, revealing them to be glowing, and he raises his arm in plea toward Arkus, who in turn looks at him with an apologetic face. "I am sorry, Cirto," is all Arkus says before the latter blows up into energy with no trace.

"Delta Jezara... step forth," Arkus calls next, but Jezara takes out a dagger from her cloak, looking too terrified.

"I...I...I have a family...this is insane...I DON'T WANT TO DIE!"

"There is no turning back, Jezara," Arkus warns her as more knights begin to move up to her with swords drawn in case things get ugly. It is also a reminder that the ritual must be kept a secret.

"This is madness! I did not sign up for this! Why do we need this insanity to begin with?!" She rushes up the staircase, passing Arkus, all the way up to the throne, keeping her dagger drawn. "If I sit down, I'll show you all you don't need that mumbo-jumbo!"

"You don't want to do that!" Arkus warns her, but with worry this time. Oddly, the knights do not chase her up. Instead, they just stand by the stairway. In defiance, Jezara sits on the throne with a prideful smile, thinking her plan will work.

"SEE I TOLD YOU SO!" she cowardly mocks until the throne starts to glow red, making a big flash. The flash is so big, Silvus has to cover his eyes with his poncho, along with the others. Her screams of agony can be heard while the flash dies down.

The flash fades away. Silvus uncovers his eyes to see Jezara gone, vanished without a trace just like Citro. He puts on a face of horror witnessing the death of two foolish Raptors. The ritual is not done yet. He sees Arkus now approaching him with the chalice wiping it with a cloth.

"Silvus...you're next."

Silvus takes the chalice gently. He looks into the glowing mist that flows inside it. As beautiful as it looks, it could potentially be poisonous. With nervous gulp, he drinks it and returns it to Arkus. All eyes look at him, hoping he will survive his trial of ordeal. Silvus braces himself for something to happen. But nothing is happening. Instead, the sound of the fountain behind the throne continues to echo through the entire room.

All the sages except Arkus huddle up talking among each other debating why nothing is happening to him. Silvus looks to the side listening to what they are saying.

"By the spirits, nothing is happening to the lad!"

"Does that mean he passed?"

"You don't think he has the taint already, does he?"

"Preposterous! That could only mean…"

The sages stop arguing, turning their attention to Silvus who only stares looking confused. Arkus, on the other claw, looks at him with a hopeful smile. Tears are seen coming out of his eyes.

"By the spirits…Master Silvus…would you climb up the stairs and sit on the throne?"

Silvus turns his gaze to the empty throne standing on top of the platform, looking uneasy. He looks back at Arkus, who only motions him to go on with his free claw. With that, he slowly approaches the stairs. He puts one foot on one of the steps, looking at the throne with a fearful expression. The glow he has witnessed made him paranoid due to his fear of fire. He is afraid that the throne will incinerate him like Jezara. Taking one glance at his gloved claw, he mutters, "Here goes nothing."

Silvus is about to take another step, only for a voice to call out. "ARCH-SAGE!"

All eyes turn to a royal guard rushing into the throne room, making a bow of respect.

"What is the meaning of this interruption?!" Arkus demands the.

"We have report of an army attacking a nearby hamlet of the

Terrain Grasslands. I fear they are rebels loyal to Targon, beginning to invade!"

"By the spirits, why at a time like this!" Arkus rants, slamming his staff, making sparks below.

Arkus looks at Silvus, who is standing on one of the steps with a disappointed face. He looks back at the guard and tells him, "Meet me by the main gates. We'd better put a stop to this before it is too late."

With that, the guard salutes and rushes out. Arkus turns his attention to Silvus and tells him, "I am afraid we have to continue this the next sunrise. I'll have a drone escort you to the guest chambers where your companions should be sleeping."

Chapter 20
Captured

S ilvus finds himself trying to sleep on a bed of the guest chambers. He cannot stop thinking about what happened in the throne room. He learned the secret of the selection of a new Alpha-King. Why is it that the Miststream of Patalot has no effect on him? The only clue he can remember, lying on the luxurious bed in the middle of the spacious fancy room, is that one of the sages mentioned already having the taint. *What could that mean?* he wonders, as he continues to gaze at the ceiling until he hears footsteps.

He lifts himself up, turning his head to his left at the door where the sound of feet can be heard. Silvus quietly gets off his bed and slowly opens the door. Peeking out from the door, he sees Ocia walking in the middle of the hall. Curious about what she is up to, Silvus decides to follow her.

Without being seen, Silvus follows Ocia all the way to the garden doors, which are surprisingly still open. In the garden he continues to follow her all the way back to the throne room where he sees her staring at the amber throne. He walks up behind her and calls out, "Ocia?"

She is startled, but not drastically like in York. Recognizing his friendly voice, she looks at him, putting on a relieved face with her claw to her chest with the amulet on. "Oh, Silvus! You almost scared me there!"

"What are you doing awake at this time of night?"

"I just could not help myself. I wanted to see this legendary throne myself." She turns her gaze back at the throne while Silvus gets closer to her. "Looks so amazing, doesn't it?"

"Indeed," Silvus softly answers. Both Raptors continue to look at the throne until Ocia breaks the ice.

"It is amazing that we are taught about the Precursor race as hatchlings, yet they never really tell us who they are. I mean our cities, this throne, and the name of our kingdom were made by them! Thinking back about how beautiful the city is, do you really think all Precursors at the time were that evil?"

"What are you implying?" Silvus raises a brow, looking at her.

Ocia turns around facing Silvus, now looking serious. Not that she is mad or anything.

"The reason why I love history so much is because I want to uncover hidden secrets our ancestors hid from us. As a hatchling, I always suspected that there was something fishy about what we are taught. Like why would the spirits bestow the gift of Mistcraft to the Precursor race knowing that they would betray them? Doesn't that make you a wee bit suspicious?"

"Now that you mention it, some stories that we are taught do have loopholes, like never knowing who this champion is!" Silvus adds, scratching his chin, making Ocia gasp.

"OMG, you're right! That is exactly what I mean. It is possible that some stories might have some kind a fabrication to them, don't you think?"

She made a good point. Silvus looks back at the amber throne, nicely preserved. With a closer look, the size of the throne looks like it is built for a creature who could be three feet taller than them. Makes him wonder.

"Ocia?"

"Yeah, Silvus?"

"Do you think it is possible that the champion might be--"

"STOP RIGHT THERE!" a female voice calls out, getting the attention of the two Raptors. Behind them is a familiar she-Raptor that Silvus knows very well. It is Clara, the headmistress of the Maglo Monastery chapter, followed by a squad of Monchester rebels, along with the black hooded figures who had been hunting him.

"Clara?! What is going on?" Silvus demands, igniting his claws with sparks of electricity.

"Ha ha ha, let's just say thanks to the snake, here we managed to track you here." Clara laughs, pointing to Ocia with mockery, "Isn't that right, Ocia?"

Silvus turns his head to Ocia, who in turn looks confused. "Ocia...what is going on?" he asks her with a voice in disbelief. She looks at him, both scared and confused, holding her two claws together while tears form in her eyes.

"I swear to the spirits, I do not know what she is talking about!" Ocia pleads, only for a lightning bolt coming from Clara to shock Silvus out cold on the ground, making Ocia scream, while the Monchester guard rushes to apprehend her.

"SILVUS!" was all Silvus could hear from her as Clara walks up in front of him. As he loses consciousness, he sees Clara turn around to Ocia with a smirk.

"Don't worry, First-Delta Anvar Ocia, he will be safe for the moment. That is, until he meets your brother for the first time, ha ha ha ha."

First-Delta? Anvar? Ocia? Brother? Silvus thinks, as he drifts into a coma.

———— ◉ ————

He slowly opens his eyes back in the waking world. Silvus feels himself being dragged across a messy dungeon. He slowly looks to the right, only to see part of the Monchester guard grabbing one of his arms while the other does the same to the other. He hears sounds of screaming prisoners in the rows of dirty cells passing by. Some are protesting their innocence while others are pleading for mercy. He cannot see better, due to his vision being a little foggy from a distance.

Of all the cells, they come across one toward the end of the dungeon tunnel where Silvus can faintly see a familiar figure standing right by the cell looking at him. Whoever is carrying him makes a brief stop and greets the figure. He tries his best to listen, despite having murky hearing at the moment. Whatever the figure might be saying, he sees him talking to a guard, pointing at him, hinting that he is asking if he is the one. The guard nods and the figure orders him by jabbing his claw, now pointing to the cell.

The two guards drag Silvus into the cell with a pair of cuffs loosely hanging in the middle. Strapping them tightly on two of his wrists, Silvus now feels himself hanging. Looking down, he sees that his belongings have been stripped off. He checks his left claw to see it ungloved, exposing his burn. Without the glove, he can feel the pain on his left wrist, due to the cuff grabbing tight. All chained up, the guards leave his cell allowing the figure to come in. Silvus cannot look up to see him and feels himself fall back into unconsciousness. The only thing he can hear from the figure is an old, sinister voice telling him, "When you wake, we will speak."

His eyes shoot back open as he gasps for air. Silvus looks around to see he is inside the cell with a small opening high up upon the wall to his left giving the cell barely any light. He tries to use his Mist power to escape, but it is not responding. All he can feel is a static shock from both his wrists. He looks up to see that he is bound to cuffs hanging from the ceiling made of Mythril, making him groan in frustration. Mythril, as he remembers, is a rare stone that dwells inside a secret mine deep within Maglo. It makes a strange radiation known to ward off Mist. It is used by various guards and the knights of the Mist in order to deal with roque Mistcasters who would dare to misuse their powers.

"You're awake," a cranky old voice calls out. Silvus turns his attention in front to see the same figure walking toward him in black robes with strange purple markings, using a familiar staff as a cane. Two cloaked Raptors wearing black metal armor follow the figure behind. One of the cloaked Raptors takes out a ring of keys from his cloak and opens the cell, allowing the figure to enter. The figure orders the two escorting Raptors to keep guard while he uses his levitation power to call forth a nearby stool from the corner and sits in front of the bound Silvus, who is hissing at him with anger.

"At last we meet, Vessel Silvus." The figure puts down his hood, revealing a bald-headed chocolate-brown Raptor with red eyes and a large scar around his left. While the guest gets comfortable, Silvus keeps his snarling face, knowing that his unwelcome guest is trouble.

"Who are you? How do you know my name? And where is my MOTHER?!" Silvus threatens, showing off his sharp teeth as he tries to free himself, shaking the cuffs, making a rattling noise of metal.

"Your mother is safe at the moment. As for who I am, I am Raspute Bylark. I am the current Mist advisor to Anvar Targon," Bylark says, impressively polite for a sinister-looking old fellow as he lays his staff onto his lap. "I have been watching you for a while now. Ever since you met the young lass…Ocia, you call her."

Silvus' expression changes from a snarl to shock at the mention of Ocia, remembering that before he got kidnapped by Clara, she called her Anvar Ocia. His face changes into denial. He can't imagine Ocia being a sibling to the Beta-Lord who invaded his Betadom. Even worse, Ocia turns out to be some kind of spy, but he doesn't understand how.

"Don't you recall that amulet she is wearing, hmm? I am surprised a smart young hatchling such as yourself did not realize it," Bylark remarks, leaning forward, giving Silvus a mocking stink eye.

Silvus closes his eyes, thinking about what he meant. When he first met Ocia, she had an emerald amulet. Seeing her again back at the bandit encampment, she wore it there, too. Then it hit him, gasping at the obvious revalation. "You don't mean?!"

"Oh yes, boy, the same amulet that was forged by a Monchester Beta-Lord as a means to spy on a rebel base, the Amulet of the Basilisk's Eye." Bylark takes out the same snake-eyed amulet that Ocia was wearing, along with a crystal ball magically showing the amulet's current perspective—a humiliated Silvus hanging by the Mythril cuffs.

"The original purpose of sending her to Maglo was to allow us to search for weaknesses within. That is, until she met you." Bylark narrows his eyes.

"What does that have to do with me?" Silvus weakly demands, still gazing at his humiliated reflection from the ball. Bylark puts the ball and the amulet away into his robe and gets off his stool with claws behind his back.

"You see, boy, I am part of an old group dedicated to bringing this the world back to the days when Raptors like me, or Dark Mistcasters as you and the other fools for the Mistatorium call us, were respected and not branded as fiends," Bylark explains as he begins to circle around Silvus. "In order to achieve such a goal, we need to purify this world by bringing it into war. To start, we needed to get rid of the royal family."

"Why kill the royal family? Why are you doing all this?" Silvus barks, as Bylark stops circling and stands facing him with the smirky smile.

"In history, the royal family is a symbol of stability and leadership. For millennia, the Raptors have been dependent on the Ultamars. By killing the Alpha-King with no heirs, his death allowed us to pin blame on the Mistatorium by spreading rumors in order to distract the Omega fools while we prepared for the purifying by war. And for me."

Bylark begins to grow angry, as if he is about to say something personal. He takes a deep breath and explains, "I was once a great student of the Patalot chapter of Monastery. Like all students of Monastery, I wanted to be a great Mistcaster for a purpose. I wanted to use my powers to benefit my family mining business back at Emerald Mountains. That is, until by my fifth winter, the arch-sage Arkus learned of my talents and wanted me to be his personal pupil, alongside Ultamar Sulthur himself.

"Sulthur and I became great friends during our time training under Arkus. He always liked to brag about wanting to be the best Alpha-King one day, like a cliché knight in shining armor, and wanting to better the lives of the Omegas, believing they have potential, he told me. Then Arkus brought in your mother as another private pupil. I did not really speak with your mother much, because she was never one to talk, but Sulthur somehow managed to get her talking to him. Regardless, the three of us trained under Arkus for at least two more winters."

Bylark's claws begin to tighten as his face forms a snarl, which terrifies Silvus. He sees Bylark look at him with frowning eyes, teeth drawn from his snout.

"One day I believed I needed to be better. I felt that I was falling behind when I sparred with Sulthur. He would best me every time. Not only that, he managed to learn Mist powers quicker than both me and your mother. I went to the palace library to learn what I could do to become a better Mistcaster. Then I came across the forbidden sector. I started to learn about the nature of Dark Mist. I got intrigued by its power, so I decided to dabble in the art, hoping to use it to prevail against Sulthur. However, he caught me first and RATTED ME OUT TO THE MISTATORIUM!!!!!"

Bylark fumes in rage, flaring his fire Mist from both his claws raised up high, while his eyes glow red, followed by a raging screech coming out his snout. Silvus turns his head away, closing his eyes to brace himself, even though he is still cuffed. Bylark calms down, taking some breaths as the Mist wisps turn visible, seeping into him, recharging him and making his eyes flash blue. Bylark sits back down on the stool, making a few coughs into his claw.

"Forgive my outburst; I am usually the more polite Dark Caster compared to the others you faced. Where was I? Oh yes, after being ratted out, the Mistatorium kicked me out and I was humiliated. My own family disowned me for bringing shame to them. But I was not alone. A group called out to me. They helped me gain a new purpose as long as I joined them. In return, I personally volunteered… to poison Alpha-King Sulthur as revenge for what he did to me. Hahahaha!"

Bylark laughs, feeling no guilt, like a sociopath. He just confessed to Silvus that it was he who poisoned the Alpha-King for vengeance. Whoever that group is, they are responsible for the war that is going on. Speaking of the war, Silvus wonders if Targon is a part of Bylark's group. "What about Anvar Targon? Is he a part of it?" he asks.

Bylark scoffs, "Targon is just a tool for our plans. He is only doing this to bring order, as he believes. I assure you, his usefulness will eventually fade away."

"I KNEW IT, YOU MONSTER!" a voice of a familiar female calls out from behind. Bylark turns around as Silvus tilts his head to the side to see Ocia running out of the shadows of the prison hall with two claws radiating an illusion spell aura, only for her to be restrained by two of Bylark's guards who are guarding the cell. As Ocia attempts to break free from the guards' grasp, Bylark makes a mocking small laugh, getting up from his stool. He walks up to her looking unamused, with both claws to his back. Silvus can only helplessly watch as he tries to break free from his bonds.

"Dear little hatchling, I thought you were supposed to be with your big brother?" Bylark mocks Ocia who only hisses in return still being restrained by the two guards.

"I knew there was something shady about you! You are trying to use my brother to destroy the kingdom!" Ocia screeches, only to hear another familiar voice.

"OCIA!"

All eyes turn to the back to see an armored male Raptor around Silvus' age with an orange cape walking toward them, with two Monchester guards following. He is Anvar Targon, Beta-Lord of Monchester, and without his helmet Silvus could finally see what he looks like. Targon looks almost exactly like Ocia, with the orca-patterned scale color. He has a white short mane, and pale white serpent eyes. His face looks serious as he approaches Ocia, who turns out to be his younger sister, gasping at the sight of him.

"Big brother! I--"

"You were supposed to be at your quarters resting to head back to Rookingrad," Targon speaks with a serious tone, cutting her off for a few momenets.

"Targon! Bylark is a Dark Mistcaster the whole time! He is up to no--"

"I know," Targon cuts off Ocia again.

"W-what?" Ocia makes a shocked gasp.

Silvus does too, overhearing the conversation between the two sibblings.

"You...you...know? ...why?"

Tears begin to flow out of Ocia's eyes. Her face slowly changes into an expression of one whose heart is about to break. Targon only looks down and gives her his back. After a long pause, he breaks the silence. "Little sister, our kingdom is suffering. To restore order, desperate actions are needed. Bylark told me a way to achieve this. He promised to use his powers to aid us in our ambitions."

"HE IS A DARK MISTCASTER! He is trying to manipulate you to destroy Avalonia, like many others in the old stories!" Ocia cuts her brother off, trying to get him to listen to her. Yet Targon persists in further arguing, showing how closed-minded he is.

He turns his face back to his sister, telling her, "He helped us get rid of the bandits in Monchester, Ocia."

"HE KILLED THE ALPHA-KING! HE STARTED THE SUFFERING TO BAIT US!" Ocia shrieks in full tears, turning her head back, glaring at a confident Bylark. Targon, however, looks at him with an inquisitive look on his face.

"Is my sister speaking truth?" he demands.

"Such strong accusation your dear sister made. She must have hung out with the boy behind me too long. She forgets that as a Dark Mistcaster, I am not allowed into the palace," Bylark calmly claims with an evil smile.

———◗◖◗———

Silvus continues to listen to the entire conversation while he is still chained up. He makes a soft hissing sound, knowing that Bylark flat-out lied to defend himself from Ocia's accusation. He watches Ocia turn her head back to Targon, and pleads with him to believe her.

Targon does not say another word. He only turns to his guards, ordering them to take her from the robed one's grasp to escort her to her private guest quarters. He briefly stops them so he can whisper into Ocia's ear that they will discuses the matter later.

As the guards continue to take Ocia away, who is still crying as she struggles to break free, Targon turns his attention to Silvus, still chained up, who is giving him a soft glare. He walks past Bylark and the robed guards, approaching Silvus to inspect him. "So you're the male that my sister told me about?" Targon asks.

Silvus can only keep glaring at him. A part of him is still upset that Targon led an invasion to his Betadom. Another part tells him that he is only being used as a puppet to Bylark due to whatever feelings he has left for Ocia. Silvus decides to warn him, "You better listen to your sister, Targon. You know what happens when a Raptor is foolish enough to make a deal with a Dark Mistcaster."

"Better that than to be a blind puppet to a group of Casters who are just corrupt fools who do nothing for their subjects, only to seize power for themselves."

"Those are lies, Targon! They are still trying to find a new heir. They are doing it by some kind of secret ritual. I was there; they told me everything!" Silvus counters, hoping to spark some sense.

Targon gets up back onto his feet, turning to Bylark, asking what Silvus meant by this. Bylark only tells him that he should head to the war room to discuse the war effort. With that, Targon and his guards walk out of the dungeon hall, leaving Bylark and his goons behind.

Bylark takes one more look at Silvus and tells him, "You better get comfortable, boy; as for tomorrow, you are going to be sent to my masters in order to deal with you." He makes a neck slice gesture, hinting to Silvus that his masters are planning to kill him before he himself walks out with one robed guard, leaving the other to close Silvus' cell and keep guard.

Act V

Chapter 21
The Great Escape

S ilvus is still chained up, humiliated, with his head hanging down
and his eyes shut. He does not know how long he will be kept
that way. What is known is the poor young Raptor is going to be
taken to whoever Bylark's masters are. A robed guard in front keeps
watch, making sure Silvus does not escape or another Raptor tries
to break him out, as ordered. The guard continues to watch down
the hall of cells filled with sleeping prisoners until he sees a hooded
figure come out of the shadows. "Stop right there! You are not allowed here--"

The new figure raises his or her claws glowing green at the guards'
eyes and whispers in a gentle female voice, "Sleep." The guard's eyes flash
green, making him go dizzy and fall down by the female's feet, asleep.

The thumping sound of the guard wakes Silvus up in shock. He
sees that the guard has fallen down sleeping in front of the figure
who kneels down, searching him. The figure uses her claws to search
around the guard's cloak and takes out a ring of keys. With one key,
the figure unlocks the cell and switches to another key to release
Silvus down for him to be carefully caught by his hooded rescuer.

"Who are you? What is going on?" he asks as he is placed back
on the ground standing.

"We are getting out here. We have no time," the figure says with a familiar sweet voice. Silvus turns around, flexing his wrists, facing the figure looking directly into her hood to see her face.

"Ocia," Silvus says sternly, giving her a look, not trusting her.

The figure puts down her hood, revealing herself to be Ocia, looking guilty. "I know you are mad at me right now, but one, I swear to the spirits I did not know I was being used as a spy and two, I'll explain everything when we get out of here."

"And why should I trust you this time?" Silvus softly demands.

"Because she helped me, son," a familiar exhausted voice of a mid-age lady says.

Silvus tilts his body to see his mother, Silviera, coming out the shadows. She does not look well, as her once beautiful light-blue mane is dirty and messy. She is not wearing her Beta-Lady cloak and crown and jewelry, with the exception of the locket around her neck. She carries a wooden staff, trying to keep herself up. As she gets close, she begins to lose her balance.

"MOTHER!" Silvus rushes past Ocia and catches his mother before she falls on the ground, dropping her staff.

Silvus holds his mother in his arms, seeing her turn her head weakly looking at him panting with a smile. "My son—you're here." She puts a claw onto Silvus' cheek, who in turn has a hopeful smile, looking at her with tears. He is so glad to see her again after being separated for so long.

"I made it to Patalot, Mom," he sobs, "I was going to get help from Arkus, but I got kidnapped," he tells her, with more tears.

"Your special friend told me everything while releasing me from my cell to rescue you. I could not be any prouder," Silviera softly tells him as she gets back up, using her staff like a cane. She turns her gaze to Ocia with a grateful smile.

Silvus sees Ocia blush nervously looking side to side. "I don't mean to interrupt the reunion, but we really have to get out of here," she reminds them.

Knowing she is right, Silvus exchanges a quick look with his mother, nodding with her. Then he lifts his mother into his arms to carry her, believing she is not in any condition to keep moving. With his mother in his arms, Silvus follows Ocia, believing she knows her way around the dungeon.

Toward the end of the hall, they stop by a sturdy stone door with bars for Ocia to peek through. She uses another of the keys to open it up, while Silvus continues to hold his mother.

"Why…we…stop?" Silviera asks weakly, still holding on to her son.

"I believe you guys need to get back your things," Ocia answers as she opens the door for Silvus and Silviera to enter.

Turns out it is the evidence room where a prinsoner's belongs are confiscated. The room is a large square filled with chests. Silvus gently lays his mother against a wall right by the entrance and tells Ocia, who gives him the keys, to stay by her to keep watch.

Silvus searches through the wooden chests one by one, using the keys that Ocia gave him. With each chest opened, all he can find is mostly clothing or possibly stolen items. He finally opens a chest with his belongings: a black leather cuirass, gauntlets, and a long blue hooded poncho.

Silvus quickly puts on his equipment and runs back to his mother, who is resting on the wall while Ocia stands by the entrance, holding the staff she collected from Silviera, keeping watch. He picks up his mother again, letting Ocia know that he found what he was looking for. All three head to another door where they must climb down a circle of stairs down.

—————«(●)»—————

The climb down the stairs is long due to the dungeon being at least ten stories tall. The trio makes it to the ground floor only to be meet by three Monchester guards who are patrolling the hall, forcing them to stop in their tracks. The guards draw their spears and are about to alert the others, only to be pushed off to the walls by a gravitational force by Ocia, who thrusts out both her claws to knock them out. However, they hear a shouting voice from the other sides of the hall and turn their gazes.

"THE PRISONERS ARE ESCAPING!"

A swarm of guards is seen charging at them from all sides with spears at the ready. Ocia tells Silvus and Silviera to head back to the circular staircase, believing she knows a secret escape route at the third floor. As they run up back on the stairs, they can hear running feet of the guards on their tail. When they enter the third floor, Silvus takes a sniff of terrible smell. Wherever the awful smell is coming from might be coming through the metal bars on the rows of stone doors.

"Yuck, where are we that this hall smells so bad?"

"This is the sewage hall where we do our…business." Ocia covers her nose looking sick as she guides Silvus and his mother further down to another door which will lead them to the dungeon sewers. Ocia opens the door to reveal a tunnel entrance resembling a giant pipe. Silvus, still holding his mother, peeks inside the tunnel looking uneasy, along with Ocia, who joins as well.

"This pipe is going to take us down to the sewers, is it?" Silvus asks, looking disgusted, smelling more of the stink inside. He would cover his nose, but he has to hold on to his mother who is in his arms, looking fatigued.

"Unless you want us to get captured…we have no choice," Ocia states just as uneasily, looking like she is going to vomit from the smell.

The two take a quick look into the pipe, hesitant until they hear the voice of the guards shouting, "HERE THEY ARE! DON'T LET THEM ESCAPE!"

Both Raptors turn their heads in shock to see the guards running down toward them fast. With no options, they jump into the pipe, sliding down into the smelly sewers. The guards who were chasing them stop in their tracks, hesitating to go after them, not wanting to fall into the sewers. Instead, they decide to find Targon and warn him.

⸺ ◉ ⸺

From the outside the dungeon, Silvus and Ocia find themselves coming out of the sewer tunnel to be greeted by a wide grassland filled with patches of tall grass with glowing flowers, while the Mist wisps are seen flying around the night sky filled with bright stars. A pair of green mountains can be seen from a distance, which borders between where they are and Maglo. They are in Monchester, Ocia's home Betadom and the land of Enchanting, a school of Mistcraft involving using Mist to craft mystical objects.

Ocia and Silvus have their breaths held coming out of the sewers. They both gasp in relief as they can finally breathe the fresh air. Silvus begins to feel movement in his arms, getting his attention.

"By the spirits…what was that awful smell?" the voice of Silviera is heard as she squirms in Silvus' arms.

Silvus looks down to see his mother slowly open her eyes halfway, looking at him. He makes a nervous smile and tells her that they just came out of the sewers to escape, which only makes her squirm, looking disgusted.

"Do you know a quick way back the capital?" Silvus asks Ocia.

Ocia scans around the grassland to figure out where they are, with a claw to her squinted eyes. All she can see are sleeping herds of Stegos and Maias gathered around, either sleeping or eating the tall grass and wild fern trees, until she sees the world tree of Patalot from a distance. Beaming, she tells Silvus to look and points at the tree with the staff in her claw.

Silvus walks up to her, carrying his mother, to see the tree with a hopeful smile. The biggest blessing of a capital city being built under a giant tree is being able to find it when not following the Miststream. Silvus whispers to his mother that things are going to be okay and is about to walk off with Ocia until a familiar serious male voice calls out.

"OCIA!"

Silvus and Ocia stop in their tracks to see Targon above the wall of the main gates of the prison with a swarm of guards, and Bylark with him. Targon has a mixed expression of anger and disappointment. Ocia walks past Silvus and his mother to face her brother, looking like she is about to cry.

"YOU USED ME! I BELIEVED YOU! I DEFENDED YOU WHEN COUSIN AND SILVUS TOLD ME THAT YOU LED A HOSTILE INVASION BY FORCE!" Ocia shouts with tears coming out of her eyes, showing how heartbroken she is.

Cousin? I was not the only one who told her? Silvus thought as he watches Ocia giving a piece of her mind, calling out her brother's actions. He continues to hold on to to his weakened mother, at the same time continuing to listen to the siblings' argument. Targon and Ocia go on and on, justifying each other's actions. Targon looks like he truly believes that he wants to bring back order to Avalonia, yet Ocia keeps pointing out that he is only causing more suffering in the kingdom.

"I AM DOING THIS TO BRING THIS KINGDOM BACK TO NORMAL!" shouts Targon.

"BY MAKING A DEAL WITH AN EVIL DARK MIST-CASTER. ALLOWING HIS GOONS TO HARRASS OTH-ER RAPTORS?" Ocia sobs and wipes her tears with a piece of her cloak. "I CAN'T KEEP FOLLOWING YOUR MISGUIDED

AMBITION ANYMORE! SAGE GORM, AUNTIE DOE, COUSIN BUCK, AND SILVUS WERE RIGHT!"

"Sister…" Targon gently says, slowly turning his face in a form of guilt. Silvus can see that Targon is also heartbroken by Ocia's words. Targon must be getting pressured on what to do with his own sister. He turns around with eyes closed, looking down. The guards take notice and check on their Beta-Lord to see if he is okay. Ocia also turns around, still putting a hurt face, returning to Silvus and Silviera.

"Are you going to be okay, Ocia?" Silvus asks her. Ocia only closes her eyes, taking one more peek at her brother and the guards while Bylark only looks at them. She turns her gaze back to Silvus, telling him that she just wants to get away from the dungeon as soon as possible. With that, the two with Silviera still in Silvus' arms begin their journey back to the royal capital.

—«◉»—

While they leave further into the grasslands, Bylark turns his stern face to Targon who is looking down, conflicted in his feelings. Bylark warns him that the prisoners are getting away but Targon just shouts, "YOU DEAL WITH THEM!" and turns around to retreat into the keep.

The dumbfounded guards turn their attention to Bylark, who is waiting as if he has his own orders. Bylark turns his gaze back at the fleeing prisoners, making a sinister smile, ordering them, "Release the Carnotaurs."

—«◉»—

Since escaping, Silvus finds himself leading back to the Patalot at a rapid pace with his mother resting in his arms. Ocia follows suit, keeping up the pace ever since she decided to leave her brother. There is no telling how long the trio have been crossing the grasslands, but at least twenty-one sunrises have passed. Traveling without mounts proves to be tiring. One moonrise, the trio decides to make camp right by a lake surrounded by herds of herbivore dinosaurs who are just sleeping around, guarding their nests.

Sitting around the campfire, Silvus sits next to his mother, who does not look better, lying on a pile of grass. He finds himself keeping an eye on her, worried, stroking her head with his unburned claw. Her once beautiful teal scales have turned dull. Whatever Bylark and his goons have done to her seems to be affecting her health. He looks to Ocia, who sits opposite from him by the campfire looking down, guilty.

The poor girl must think Silvus is still mad at her for unknowingly deceiving him. He cannot completely blame her for being used as a tool. Ocia had her eyes raised up looking like a shamed puppy, making her look adorable. The tears slowly coming out shows she is not fooling. She is truly sorry for what has happened to him, and she does not have the amulet anymore, so Targon and Bylark won't track them. "Silvus..." she whimpers slowly.

Silvus slowly looks back to his mother who is slowly breathing, barely.

"So you're part of the Anvar clan...why did you not ever tell me?" he softly demands, still keeping his eyes on his mother.

"I wanted to tell you," she sobs. "But my brother, Targon made me vow to never tell any Raptor outside Monchester about our connection." She keeps sobbing. "He is my brother, took care of me when my father died when I was young... I trusted him."

Silvus slowly turns his gaze still looking serious away from his mother. He watches Ocia break into tears, still heartbroken. He has a bit of a hard time believing her, yet the emotion is real. It sums that she really did not know that she was being used as a spy by not only Bylark but her own brother. He wonders if Targon was always the strict male that he is today. So he asks her, "What was Targon like before all this?"

Ocia stops her crying looking up to Silvus. She still has tears coming out and is making a few sniffs.

"He...wasn't always that closed-minded, you know. When my father was still alive, Targon was a very chivalrous male. He always looked up to Father. He wanted to be a great knight, just like him. When I was bullied by other Raptor nobles, he would always rush to my aid like a knight of old would do."

Ocia makes a small smile, looking at the night sky filled with stars.

"One day when I turned seven...Father went on a mission to stop a bandit attack. Targon took care of me until he returned. A messenger came by with grave news that Father...fell in battle. Targon was devastated as was, I since Father was the only parent I knew.

Ocia saddens, looking down back at Silvus, who is still looking at her back, keeping his claw on his mother's head.

"After Father's funeral, Targon, being next in line for Beta-Lord's throne, was coordinated by the end of the seventh sunrise. As long he did not have heirs, it leaves me taking his place as First-Delta. He did not look happy when he took the mantle as the new Beta-Lord of Monchester. Probably he could not get his mind off the death of both Father and Mother. I did not know Mother personally, but my aunt Anvar Doe, my father's younger sister, became like a mother figure to me. She told me to give Targon space to get over his grief.

"So I took Auntie Doe's advice and gave Targon space. Things looked better, as he performed his Beta-Lord duties well. But once in a while, I see him stressed after doing requests involving fighting bandits. The more he fights crime, the more he shows that he is getting frustrated with the lack of aid from the Mistatorium. I even overheard him rant about it in his quarters one night, praying to the spirits for a solution.

"One day at a court session, a Mistcaster visited us, claiming to have a solution to the problem. That Mistcaster was Bylark, and he looked friendly at first from the way he spoke at court. Targon seemed intrigued, but I sensed some dark aura within him. I sensed it when Bylark came up to me to give me that accursed amulet as a gift. Sage Gorm probably did too, as he tried to warn my brother about it. Targon ignored his warning and decided to let Bylark prove his worth.

"Since then, I have been hearing that crime is starting to fall in Monchester. Whatever Bylark did, it pleased my brother, but the sage did not like it. One night I overheard arguing between Targon and Gorm about Bylark. I was worried about what Bylark did that upset Gorm.

Ocia makes a shiver through her spine and continues on with her story.

"The next sunrise during court, Targon announced that he exiled Sage Gorm, to be replaced by Bylark as the new court Mistcaster. Since then, I have seen Targon preparing a massive army with Bylark's help. I saw him make a speech to all the Raptors of Rookingrad about his ambition to bring Avalonia back together, and claiming that the Mistatorium is corrupt, pleasing many Raptors, as there was a lot of anti-Mistatorium rhetoric."

"Sounds like Bylark was trying to get close to your brother in order to convince him to turn on the Mistatorium," Silvus butts in, earning a nod from Ocia in agreement. She explains the rest of her story to him. Her brother eventually came up to her, telling her about his great ambition to restore order in Avalonia. She even tells him how Targon eventually had her go to Athera for an errand, which is how she and Silvus met without her knowing she was being used as a spy.

Seeing that it is getting late, Silvus and Ocia decide to sleep, until the ground begins to shake under them. Silvus looks around to see a stampede of frightened Stegos running from a hill. They seem to be running away from a predator native to Monchester.

Squinting his eyes, Silvus spots a pack of four large Theropods that almost look like a Tyranno Rex except they have longer arms and a pair of long horns on their on their brows. They also wear armor, showing that they are domesticated for war by the way they are sniffing for a specific target.

Silvus looks to Ocia, who in turn slowly walks up to his side with bulging eyes of fear at the sight. "Ocia…we better run. WAR CARNOS!" he shouts, rushing to his mother, scooping her up into his arms and running as fast as he could with Ocia following suit, terrified.

The shouting sound of Silvus' voice causes the war Carnos to spot them. The one leading rises up, making a brief roar; then they all begin their chase for the targets they are trained to hunt. Being domesticated war dinos, they ignore the nearby frightened herbivores, keeping focused on chasing Silvus and Ocia, who are running for their lives.

Running for his life, Silvus holds onto his mother tightly, not wanting to leave her behind. He looks behind to see Ocia running along, panting with each step. Behind her he sees the Carnos in the open continuing to chase after them, making his heart race fast in fear. He and Ocia continue to run, avoiding the frightened herbivores that run along in middle.

"CAN'T YOU USE YOUR MISTCRAFT TO FIGHT THEM?!" Silvus shouts to Ocia.

"I ONLY KNOW NON-LETHAL POWERS LIKE GRAVITATION, ILLUSIONARY, AND LIFE-MENDING. I NEVER REALLY LIKED LEARNING POWERS TO TAKE LIVES!" Ocia shouts back, taking one more peek behind, seeing the Carnos. "WHY CAN'T YOU USE YOUR POWER?"

"MY CLAWS ARE OCCUPIED HOLDING MY MOTH-ER RIGHT NOW," Silvus yells. As much as he wants to use his powers to defend himself, he cannot risk hurting his mother.

They run into a border wall to Suaronian Heart with no gate at sight. Silvus and Ocia are cornered, turning their heads to see that the Carnos are about to catch them. Silvus gently leans his mother down against the wall; then he flares electricity in his claws, preparing to zap the Carnos while Ocia runs behind him, looking helpless.

One of the Carnos is about to strike Silvus until it gets hit by a long purple Mist arrow through its head, killing it. The Carnos turn their gaze while Silvus and Ocia turn their heads to the left to see where the arrow came from. In their sight, they smile at a cavalry of ten armored Raptor knights to their rescue, riding on their mounts. They are the knights of the Mist. They all have their associated Mist weapons drawn, like the one with a bow and arrow at the ready, shooting another at the other Carno by the eye, staggering it, while the other nine take out the three by Snaguana back. One knight throws a Misted halberd like a javelin right at a Carno's heart, killing it directly. Another knight leaps off his mount, using his Misted sword to impale it right on the head of the one with the arrow to the eye. The final Carno tries to swish its tail at the knight with a Misted claymore only for the knight to dodge it; he counters by slicing the tail off. The Carno screeches in agony only to be finished off by an arrow to the neck, and falls down to the ground, making a big thumping sound.

The knights approach Silvus and Ocia, who in turn look relieved. They have covered helmets with a bush of sky-blue feathers on top, not knowing which knight is who. One knight with a bow walks up to Silvus on a familiar-colored Snaguana, telling him, "Looks like this is the third time I had to save your tail, cousin."

The particular knight's voice sounds familiar. Silvus gasps with a smile both glad and disbelieving, knowing who the knight is. "Ico?!" he guesses.

The knight gets off his mount, walking up to Silvus. He takes off his helmet to reveal the familiar teal-faced Raptor with a shorter brushed-back blue mane with a beaming face. "That's Sir Vessel Ico, kind sir, as I have officially joined the knights of the Mist!"

Chapter 22
Revalations

Being rescued by the knights of the Mist, Silvus did not expect his cousin to be among them. His reason for joining Silvus' adventure was to join the knights in the first place. And there he is wearing the white plated armor with the symbol of the knights itself, a dark-blue sword in the middle of a light-blue comet coming down, looking proud while the other nine knights came forth. Another question in Silvus' mind is how Ico and the knights knew he was kidnapped.

"How did you guys find us?"

Ico makes a charming smile, posing like hero with his folded claws to his hips, telling him, "Well, Cousin, it's a long story. While you were with Arkus, I came across the knights themselves during the tour and I convinced them to sign me up--"

Ico pauses at the sight of a sick-looking Silviera leaning against the wall making a small gasp. "Whats wrong with Auntie Silviera?! She looks like she needs a healer?!"

Silvus sees his mother groaning by the wall, looking worse. He runs up to her, putting a hidden ear to her chest to make sure she is still breathing. Turning to the knights he says with a worried tone, "A Dark Mistcaster did something to her! And she really needs help, and fast!"

"That is why we are here, my lord." One of the knights steps forward. "You're lucky that your cousin spotted you being taken away to tell us. If not, we would have never learned of your situation and I'll say, your cousin has proven himself to be a great addition!"

The knight pats Ico on the back, making the latter smile at the compliment. Ico walks up to Silvus and tells him, "What about I tell you everything while we head back, so we can save your mother as soon as possible?"

Silvus looks behind to his sleeping mother. Without hesitation, he nods in agreement, and he scoops her back into his arms, approaching Ico, telling him, "Then let's go, Sir Ico."

———※◈※———

In the middle of Terrian Valley southwest of Suaronian Heart, Silvus is being escorted by the knights accross the main road in rows of two. He rode on an extra Snaguana they brought with them while Ocia is mounted behind him holding onto his waist. He looks at a carriage being pulled by two knights at the back where his mother is lying inside. At first it did not feel right to him to place her in a carriage supposed to be meant for supplies. But the knights insist it is better for her to lie down and rest. Riding beside Silvus to his left is Ico, who is telling him how managed to join the knights.

Ico explains how during the tour he eventually met up with the knights, who allowed him to prove his worth by demonstrating his skill with the bow and arrow, and telling them his father was one of them. The knights were so impressed that they signed him up as a squire, a knight in training under the tutelage of one of the knight-captains. Then he tells him how he learned of his kidnapping.

"So the night after my official training, I was trying to sleep, but

I was so excited to train more, yet I couldn't, but instead I heard footsteps. Being curious, I took a peek out the door to see Clara escorting something out from the throne room with two shady guys. At first, I did not get involved, not knowing what was going on, so I went back to sleep. The next morning, I was training with the knights with Fi, watching until Arkus burst in, and man he was scared, telling us that you and Ocia were missing.

Ico makes a big gasp for air, talking so fast, making Silvus and Ocia exchange surprised looks, shocked how far a snarky Raptor like Ico managed to explain. He continues.

"Then it hit me. I realized that Clara and her goons were escorting you guys, so I told him and the knights everything. So Arkus had Clara apprehended and interrogated her to find out where you guys were. After getting some intel, Arkus had the knights go on a rescue mission to save you guys in Monchester. But before they went, they wanted me to tag along by becoming a full knight, by learning that cool spell you and Dad know!"

Guess that explains why it took twenty-one sunrises to find me, Silvus thinks. He remembers from his uncle that the Mist weapon spell usually takes weeks to master. Thanks to his gift, he managed to learn his in less than a few minutes. As much as he wants to scold Ico for not saving him sooner, he is grateful that he eventually did so. He turns his gaze to one of the knights, asking how far they are from Patalot.

The knight tells Silvus that the journey might take a while longer, which worries him. He is worried that his mother might not have much time. All he can do is ease his worries by turning his head to the right, seeing a herd of Brontos gathered around a lake in the middle while a flock of Petadons are seen flying south, where another kingdom called Olympadonia is located. For the rest of the ride, he focuses forward, following the knights to Patalot with his mother's health in mind.

Back in the palace front courtyard, Silvus walks alongside a carriage being pulled by the knights while Ocia and Ico are behind. Looking in the carriage, he sees that his mother's scales have gotten even paler. Fi, Arkus, and the other sages are seen standing by, waiting for them by the main gates.

Fi, who is now wearing a nice leather cloak, runs up with a big smile on her face. She runs past Ocia, Silvus, and the knights to Ico. Ico scoops her up into his arms, giving her a passionate kiss on the lips, as it turns out they have become a couple during Silvus' absence. Breaking the kiss, Ico tells her what happened, pointing to the knights pulling the carriage of Silvus' mother, making the latter gasp.

Arkus, among the sages, runs up to the group, demanding to know what happened.

Silvus steps up with pressure swelling in his chest, telling him, "MY MOTHER NEEDS HELP! Something must have happened to her!" He points to the carriage held by the knights.

Arkus runs up to the carriage to see Silviera's critical condition, making him anxious. He orders the knights to head to the healers' champers immediately. The knights do as they are ordered and pull Silviera into the palace in a rush.

Silvus watches his mother being pulled by the knights into the palace with an expression of anxiety, as a tear flows down his cheek. Ocia walks up beside him holding onto his arm in comfort, looking just as worried. Ico with Fi, in his arms, walk to him too, joining the anxiety.

In the royal living room, Silvus sits on one of the three regal couches looking tense below a large candlelit chandelier. He just sits looking at his cup filled with tea, anxious for his mother's health. The anxious Raptor is told that his mother is currently in the royal healer's room being taken care of. The sound of a nearby grandfather clock continues to tick and tock. He closes his eyes, praying to the spirits that his mother will be okay.

Ocia sits beside Silvus and has her claw on his shoulder, giving him comfort while her other claw is in her lap. Ico and Fi are seen holding claws, looking just as worried for the silver Raptor.

A pair of large doors opens up, gaining the party of four's attention to see Arkus and the female healer wearing a white robe and a red necklace coming in with sad faces. Silvus gets up with a face of more worry. Every Raptor knows that when a healer is not looking happy, it means something is wrong. He runs up to the two with his attention directly to the healer and asks, "Is my mother okay?"

The healer looks to Arkus, wanting to know if she should tell him. Earning an approving nod from the latter, the healer walks up to Silvus to place a claw on his shoulder with an uneasy face.

"It's hard for me to say this, young master, but I am afraid your mother is afflicted by some unusual poison."

"My mother is poisoned?! Can't you help her?!"" Silvus worriedly exclaims.

"We tried, young master, but the poison in her body came from a form of Dark Mist for so long she is beyond any healing," the healer sadly explains.

"Poison Mist," Silvus mutters in anger. Usually any poison can be healed by anti-Venom, but poison coming from the forbidden Mistcraft makes anti-Venom useless, due to coming from an unknown source.

"Can I help? I know a Mist power that could heal Poison Mist?!" Ocia offers rushing up next to Silvus flaring golden aura from her claws called Anti Body, the Life Mend spell that is supposed to heal any affliction, whether a virus or some incurable disease.

"It is true that the only way to cure Poison Mist is by the use of the Anti Body spell, but I am afraid the poison infected her too long, and using such spell would not be effective anymore," Arkus sadly states. The spell that Ocia mentioned can only heal Poison Mist when the poison is in the early stage, before at least the minimum of ten sunrises. It shatters Silvus' heart.

Silvus drops to his knees slowly breaking into tears to say with a breaking voice, "You mean there is nothing we can do?!"

Arkus walks up to Silvus, placing a claw onto his shoulder with a disappointed sigh. Silvus, however, keeps his face down on the carpet, pounding his fisted gloved claw and tail at the same time, spouting, "NO, NO, NO" before he breaks into tears, trying to hold it back.

"We could take you to your mother; she still has some breath to tell us that she wants to see you," the healer adds, making Silvus get up still in tears.

<hr />

Silvus is greeted by a rectangular room filled with potions, medicine, and herbs around the counters and shelves while rows of beds are to the left. Silvus is escorted all the way to the end of the room where his mother is still lying, looking peaceful.

With the healer waiting outside the room, Silvus sits on a stool right next to his dying mother covered in white covers. He softly strokes his mother's face, looking at her with a tear-streaked face. In his sight, he sees her locket on a nightstand to his left.

Curious, Silvus picks it up, taking a closer look. He sees a switch and opens it to reveal what looks like a silver ring with a diamond in the middle.

"It is the wedding ring your father gave me when we got married. He tells me it is his family heirloom," a weak voice calls out, startling Silvus a little, almost dropping the ring.

He looks at his mother to see her slowly turning her head, looking at him with a small smile.

"I even wore the same ring when he and I finally conceived you," she adds with a cough, making Silvus reach out to her in response.

"Mother! Save your breath. Things will be--"

"I know I am dying, my son," his mother cuts him off. "Bylark did a lot of Dark Mistcraft to me in order to get information, but I refused. Before your special friend released me, Bylark used a Poison Mist spell at me."

I knew it! Silvus thinks, making a small hiss to himself, clenching his eyes shut. He then opens his eyes, looking at his dying mother again and tells her, "I am so sorry I did not save you sooner...but things got in the way and--"

Silvus is cut off by his mother's talon to his lips with a "shhhh" sound, telling him, "You did save me, Son. With the help of your friend, you both freed me from further torment. At least I get to see you with my own eyes one last time...listen."

Silviera motions for Silvus to pay attention to what she is about to say. "I don't have much time, but I believe it is time I tell you who your father is. But I want you to make a new vow," she tells him.

"Anything, Mother!" Silvus grabs his mother's claw, listening to her. He will do anything to fulfill a dying wish for his mother.

With a few more coughs she tells him, "There is an evil presence lurking in the shadows trying to destroy our way of life. For whatever reason, I assume it is for revenge long ago. You, my son, have a greater destiny than simply being Beta-Lord. It is why this hidden evil is trying to hunt you down. You must save Avalonia, my dear son. You must stop this war, or else Bylark and his masters will win. If they do, darkness will spread not only in Avalonia but also the rest of Cretatia." She makes a few more coughs, turning her head and looking at the ceiling.

"I will, Mother! I will save Avalonia for you and all the good Raptors!" Silvus closely holds onto his mother's claw. "Who is my father?"

Taking one more breath, his mother, Vessel Silviera finally tells him, "Ultamar Sulthur...is...your...father." Then she passes out on her pillow, lifeless.

"Mother? MOTHER!" Silvus calls out to her, shaking her lifeless body. He breaks into tears and sobs right onto her body. He hears footsteps approaching him from behind. He lifts up his head to see Ocia looking at him with an apologetic face with claws held together holding back tears.

"I heard everything," she tells him and kneels, giving him a comforting yet affectionate hug. Silvus could not help but hug her back. He truly needs it. He can feel her claw stroking his back as he continues to cry on top of her shoulder.

Chapter 23
The Lost Alpha-PrinceRrises

Silvus stands alone in the throne room in front of the stairway to the throne itself looking depressed. He holds a locket he collected from his mother, who passed away. Turns out it is a ring she received from his father, who is the Alpha-King Sulthur himself. He continues to look at the ring with a lot on his mind. Since his father is Sulthur, that means he is an Ultamar, heir to the throne above. As much as he wants to be happy at such a revelation, he cannot, as the death of his mother weighs heavy in his mind.

The fountain of the Mist core continues to echo like the sound of a waterfall in the room. Ocia, Ico, and Fi are seen standing by the throne entrance tunnel, looking at Silvus with worried looks. Ocia holds her claws together with a conflicted expression, while Ico and Fi hold claws, still keeping their gazes on the lone Raptor in the middle of the room.

"Poor Silvus. He must be so broken, losing his mother...I know such a feeling from when I lost Daddy," Fi comments, beginning to sob, knowing Silvus' pain as she tightens her grip on Ico's claw.

"Auntie Silviera was his only parent. Well, my dad is like a father to him, but still...damn," Ico replies, while keeping his eyes on his depressed cousin who just stands there.

"Do you guys think we should do something for him?" Ocia

blurts out, forming a heartbreaking tear in one of her eyes, worrying about Silvus' well-being.

"I am afraid the best you hatchlings can do is give him space."

All three turn their gazes to see Arkus approaching them with his staff, making them bow, including Fi, in respect.

"Arch-Sage! We are just worried about my cousin, as he really wanted to save Auntie throughout his journey to meet you," Ico tries to explain like a professional to his boss or lord.

"No need for formalities, Sir Vessel Ico. However, how about you go with your fellow knights and train while you, Fi--"

"I want go with Ikie and see him train!" Fi finishes for Arkus, standing up, who in turn looks at Ico with a raised brow. Ico tells Arkus that he and Fi became a "questionable" couple due to being different creatures, before Arkus gives him an awkward yet approving nod for them to flee. Arkus turns his attention to Ocia, who is looking at him waiting for what he has to say to her.

"As for you, young Anvar Ocia, how about you join with Sage Gorm and tell him what is going on, as he was your one-time private tutor before being replaced by another."

"With all due respect, Arch-Sage, I am still worried about Silvus." Ocia turns her head to Silvus, looking guilty." I just can't help but feel responsible for what he is going through."

"How so?"

"The reason he was taken is because I was used as a spy by not only my own brother but the Dark Mistcaster Bylark," Ocia explains to Arkus, lowering her head in shame.

"Bylark?" Arkus repeats the name with a heartbreaking voice. Ocia seems to have picked up as she lifts her head looking at him concerned.

"You know Bylark?" she asks him.

"It's a long story, my lady. Go meet with Gorm, and I'll see if I can help the young Silvus alone."

Ocia takes one more glance at Silvus, looking hesitant. Hoping to put her trust in Arkus, she nods and walks slowly past him to find Gorm leaving the ladder behind with Silvus.

Silvus slowly looks up at the throne. All his life, he always wanted to know who his father was. But he never wanted to find out at the deathbed of his mother. He is curious to know if she is telling the truth, not that he doubts her. She would never steer him worng. He puts away the locket in a carrier bag and walks up the steps to the throne for a closer look.

The throne itself is so big, as if it were built for one who is at least ten feet tall, three feet taller than average Raptor. He places a claw on one of the throne's arms to feel the smoothness of the stonework made out of clear amber. He looks up at the three triangles with the colored stones resembling the three paths of the Alpha-Monarch: red for tyranny, white for neutrality, and blue for benevolence.

With a deep breath, Silvus turns around to finally sit on the throne. He closes his eyes expecting to be incinerated like what happened to one of the candidates from the Anointing. But nothing happens; instead, the throne begins to glow bright. Silvus is amazed at the glow surrounding him, as if the spirits are giving him their own blessing. It can mean only one thing. He is truly the lost son of Alpha-King Sulthur himself. Another question in his mind is why his mother kept it a secret, until a familiar grandfatherly voice calls out interrupting his thoughts.

"Your father meant the world to your mother, you dnow."

Silvus sees Arkus walking up to him, climbing up the steps with a sympathetic look on his face. He even has his claws behind his back.

"When I first saw you, I always had this feeling that you were not only the son of Vessel Silviera but also the son of Ultamar Sulthur." Arkus chuckles as he stops in front of Silvus, who remains sitting on the throne. "They must have conceived you immediately after they were wedded."

"You knew!" Silvus blurts, surprised that the arch-sage knew about his parents' relationship.

"Oh yes, perhaps it was I who wedded them," Arkus replies with a proud smile. "Why they wanted to be a secret I do not know, but all that your father told me is that he wanted to protect your mother." Arkus shrugs his shoulders with his eyes closed, "Perhaps your father sensed something amiss."

"You said that my father meant the world to my mother. What where they like?" Silvus sadly asks, wanting to know more about his parents.

With a smile, the old Raptor Arkus tells him, "Well, Alpha-Prince. Long ago during my early years since becoming the arch-sage of the Mistatorium I was also a private tutor to your father, since it is part of the sacred duty of all arch-sages, my predecessors, to train future Alpha-Kings and Queens in not only Mistcraft but also to give a proper education.

"Your father was a very bright lad with big dreams, always telling me that he hoped to be a great leader. Just like how you wanted to be a great Beta-Lord and a hero with the same optimism, your mother used to tell me."

Silvus feels himself getting red with an awkward smile, imagining his mother comparing him to his father. Turns out he inherited his positive optimism from his father. Arkus sure knows how to have this sense of humor by the way he chuckles at his reaction, continuing his story.

"Just like you, your father was able to learn Mistcraft quickly due to the taint of Patalot that all the Ultamars have. You, Silvus, an Ultamar, have the same taint since the blessing of the champion."

Come to think of it, since Sulthur is his father, that means the legendary champion and the hero Magnus are his ancestors. He feels almost giddy at the thought. Right now, he needs to focus, learnning more of his parents, especialy his mother in her younger years. Silvus reminds Arkus by asking, "What about my mother?"

Arkus's expression becomes sorrowful. "When your mother was younger, she was very socially awkward. She was never the type to socialize with other Raptors due to her fears of being made fun of. Despite her social awkwardness, she proved to be a very good student, so I decided to take her in as another private student."

Arkus forms a small smile, turning his attention back to Silvus.

"When your mother first laid eyes on your father, she hid right behind me. But that seemed to encourage your father's sense of nobility to believe it was his sacred duty to help her. Surprisingly, he was a very patient around her: he helped her with her studies, practiced Mist spells with her, and he even helped her learn how to talk with other Raptors. Yet your mother wanted only to be around your father.

"The more your parents spent time together, it seemed your mother was falling more in love with your father with each year, from the way she looked at him. You would not believe how she reacted when your father gave her a unique flower native to here. I even got letters from her father, your grandfather, that your mother would not stop talking about your father."

Arkus takes a breath after having a jolly laugh. Silvus looks at him as if he is some crazy grandfather he did not know he had. Perhaps, it seems that Arkus really likes to include humor when telling his stories.

"Of course, another pupil of mine, Bylark, was a different story," Arkus mentions with a heartbreaking tone in his voice.

The mention of Bylark makes Silvus growl through his teeth. He would never forget that sinister face. Whether he is the one who poisoned his mother or not, he is the one who poisoned his father and started the war up north. One thing for sure is that Silvus needs to stop him, as he promised his mother to save Avalonia. With a saddened face, Silvus turns to Arkus, asking him, "Is it true that my father was friends with Bylark?"

"I am afraid that is true," Arkus responds with a sigh. He proceeds to explain to Silvus that long ago Bylark used to be a respected member of Clan Raspute, the Delta clan that owned the Emerald Mountain mines, wanting to be a great Mistcaster for family business.

Arkus further tells Silvus that Bylark showed great promise in Mistcraft, to the point he wanted him to be his private student alongside his father, who in turn became great friends with Bylark, to the point of becoming spiritual brothers. He mentions the only time they would ever fight would be the topic of Omegas. The more Arkus speaks about Bylark, the more depressed he seems to be getting. Silvus senses that he must be getting to the point where things are getting dark.

Yet Arkus does not stop further explaining that one day Bylark began to show signs of jealousy toward his father after each sparring session where he would lose to him—so jealous that Bylark would eventually get seduced to Dark Mistcraft, where his father catches him in the act. The old Raptor turns his gaze away from Silvus with one arm to his back with a staff on the other. He concludes his story with a heartbreaking tear coming from his eye.

"Bylark was like another son to me. The day I had no choice but to expel him was the most heartbreaking choice I have ever made. As the arch-sage, it is part of my duty to make sure no Mistcaster abuses their power. Sometimes I feel responsible for his downfall. By the spirits. I could have prevented it."

Arkus says no more, lowering his head in shame, believing himself to be guilty of Bylark's downfall. Silvus cannot help but feel bad for the poor old male. Raptors sure have this habit of hiding sensitive emotions in order to not feel weak. Then another question comes to mind.

Silvus reaches into his bag to take out the dagger he carries. He calls out to Arkus, who turns his gaze to him. The former asks, "Do you know of this symbol? I believe Bylark is a part of this group who might be the ones responsible?"

Silvus shows the dagger for Arkus to examine. The reaction of the latter is complete shock with a gasp, grabbing it from Silvus' claw. Arkus looks at the dagger, specificly the purple skull symbol on the pommel. "Where did you get this?!" the old Raptor asks, eyes still glued on the symbol.

"I got this from a crazed Kobold princess who turns out to be working for them. I have been seeing this symbol among bandit camps and rebels. Back at Tricia, I read a book that explains it was used on a flag during the time of Second Ava—mmph!" Silvus tries to explain only for Arkus to grab his snout shut looking at him very seriously with frowning brows.

"With all due respect, your highness, we don't ever mention that period by name," Arkus tells him sternly before letting go of Silvus' snout. "But you are telling me that you have been seeing this symbol?"

Silvus nods and tells him everything he knows connected to the symbol. The bandit groups, mysterious riders who tried to chase him, and a crazy Kobold princess. He even tells him that he came across a Dark Mistcaster leading a rebel gang.

Arkus is at a loss for words, looking horrified. He turns his gaze back to the dagger for a few moments and mutters, "This is worse than I thought."

"Pardon?" Silvus asks, looking concerned.

Arkus finally turns back to Silvus, looking serious.

"During the past twenty-four winters, the other sages and I have been sensing Dark Mist growing around ever since your father died. Turns out our suspicions were right. This war is the work of Dark Mistcasters, organizing our downfall from the shadows."

"Do you know who they are?" Silvus asks, wanting answers. He expects Arkus to know, since he is the arch-sage.

"I am afraid not. We were too busy bringing order in this Beta-dom as well as trying to find a new Alpha-King. We never had any time to look into it, yet we did keep our eyes out for anything out of the ordinary," Arkus claims, looking back at the dagger.

Silvus gets into deep thought. Now that he knows there is a mysterious group of Raptors in the shadows causing trouble, he must think of a way to stop them. One thing he does know is the first step in stopping them is to stop the war that is occurring above. He taps his chin, wondering where he can get more information, while Arkus continues to study the dagger. Then he remembers Ico telling him about Clara.

"Where is Clara?" Silvus stands up from the throne with a face of seriousness.

※

Silvus follows Arkus and two royal guards across the palace dungeon hall in search of a mutal acquaintance. They stop around one cell to see Clara sitting on a stone bed by the wall on the left with her arms tied up with Mythril cuffs to keep her from using her powers. The burgundy female looks a bit surprised at the sight of Silvus, not expecting him to survive at all. One of the guards uses a key to open up a cell to allow Silvus entry.

Silvus enters the cell with caution, approaching the former headmistress, who in turn lowers her brows with a scoffing sound through her lips.

"You escaped. Here to gloat, are you, young boy?"

Clara is obviously mocking Silvus. The latter turns his head to see Arkus and the guards keeping watch, then back at her, looking a bit nervous. In truth, he has never interrogated a prisoner before. Yet he is willing to get all the information he needs if he wants to save Avalonia from this shady organization. With a deep breath, he begins the interrogation.

"I am here to get information," he begins. "I know there is a group of Dark Mistcasters like yourself behind all this. I demand to know who exactly you guys are and why are all doing this?!"

The old hag just laughs like a witch and replies, "HE HE hee, you foolish boy. I guess you deserve to know some of our secrets. Not to mention, our plan has already been in motion for so long you won't be able to stop it."

She even keeps a smirk on her face, making Silvus suspicious, wondering whether she could be lying or plotting a trick. But he needs to look strong if he is ever to go anywhere. He can always use a spell, if anything is needed.

"My little group of friends has been around for like a millennium. We were founded with the purpose of revenge."

"Revenge for what?" Silvus threatens, keeping a serious face with lowered brows, only for the witch in front to snicker.

"Revenge against the fools who demonized us for years! Our master has promised to bring back the glory days. We are called the Necromancers.

"The Necromancers are an old organization of Dark Mistcasters, as you call us, under the great teachings of our master named Necrosis. I will not tell you who Necrosis is, as I will not betray the most important secrets."

"Then what exactly are you Raptors hoping to gain in this war you created?" Silvus demands further.

"To weaken your kingdom, of course," Clara says, as if Silvus already knows the answer. "Well, Bylark is doing this for his own agenda, but he too is a good asset to our cause."

"And I am guessing you wanted me dead because I am royal blood?" Silvus crosses his arms.

Clara once again laughs like a wicked witch, telling him that it is not just she who wants him dead but her group, the Necromancers. Then she goes on to tell him that they know who he is and states that his being related to the champion of old makes him a threat to her masters, until a voice calls out, interrupting them.

"ARCH-SAGE, I HAVE DIRE NEWS!"

Silvus turns his head around to see Arkus and the two guards turn their attention to a messenger running up to them, looking exhausted.

"What is the meaning of this? Don't you see we are in a middle of interrogation?" Arkus rants like an old male, slamming his staff on the ground.

The messenger kneels before Arkus and tells him, "I fear that Tricia is on the verge of being conquered!"

"WHAT?!" all the Raptors present gasp while Clara only laughs, mocking the males in front, earning a glare from Silvus.

"HEHEHE! As I said, boy. You are too late to stop it!"

"Not that I have something to say about it," Silvus mutters, ignoring the boast from Clara as he follows Arkus and the guards, who in turn lock up the cell to make sure the prisoner does not escape.

—◦—

Located down the first floor of the north wing of the palace is a grand circular chamber where members of the Mistatorium conduct their meetings. All the known high-ranking Mistcasters, wearing different-colored robes, are sitting on the stone benches while at the center round table sit Silvus, Arkus, and the other sages. They all have their eyes on the messenger, who stands by the round table explaining Tricia's plight.

The messenger tells the Mistatorium that despite the might of the Tricia's forces for being a big Betadom, Monchester forces are still able to slowly gain territory for being better equipped. The current state of the war as of now is that Monchester rebels now holds half of Tricia, putting Sherrasic at risk. It does not sit well with Silvus.

The Mistatorium speak among themselves with voices of anxiety. They fear if the rebels manage to conquer the entire Eastern Betadoms, they will be next. The Mistcasters who wore purple for Tricia, Red for Creston, and Green for Sherrasic where more anxious, worried for the loved ones. The ones who wore Maglo blue and Monchester Orange stay quite with uneasy faces since their Betadoms are already conquered.

Done with delivering the message, the messenger is allowed to leave, with two knights guarding the doors, opening them and letting the messenger through.

Akrus who sat on the largest chair by Silvus spoke up, "Fellow members of the Mistatorium. Not only that we have underestimated the rebels but there is even more dire news."

Silvus could hear all the mutters from the other members of the Mistatorium filling the chamber with an atmosphere of fear. Can't say he blames them, based on what they have heard. He looks around to the sages who also show faces of fear, yet stay silent, allowing Arkus to speak.

"For the past twenty-four winters, we have sensed a dark presence rising in the kingdom. Based on the information that our esteemed guest has provided to me," Arkus getures his claw to Silvus, who in turn makes a small bow while the non-sage members are just wondering who exactly he is.

"As it turns out, an old enemy of ours are emerging from the shadows. Everything that is happening in our kingdom is the work of Dark Mistcasters!" Arkus announces as the entire room gasps in horror.

"HE IS SPEAKING TRUTH!" Silvus speaks up, earning attention from the crowd.

"And how do you know of this?" Sage Fernus of Maglo asks him.

In response, Silvus gets up from his seat, walking to the front of the round table so he can be seen by all the members present. Before he makes his speech, he debates whether he should tell them that he is the son of Sulthur. He decides to keep his birthright a secret for now in order to avoid unwanted attention. He clears his throat and procedes to address the Mistatorium with what he knows.

"To all who do not know me, I am Vessel Silvus, son of the late Beta-Lady Vessel Silviera. I was forced out of my home by the same rebels who are taking over Tricia. To make my long story short, I was tasked with delivering an important package given to me by my mother, believing it to be a key to save the kingdom itself. While you all were distracted with finding a new ruler, I went on a journey, learning many secrets, coming across the bandits, rebels, and a hidden society. I can confirm that a group of Dark Mistcasters was behind this entire crisis!"

"And what proof do yah have, Master Silvus?" Sage Ariella of Tricia questions, looking anxious as her representing Betadom is on the verge.

Silvus reaches into his carrier bag to take out the dagger that Arkus returned to him and shows to all the members the pommel, where they can see the familiar symbol. They all gasp in shock at the sight, except for Arkus, who has already seen it.

"I got this dagger from a crazed princess who was working with them. The same symbol you see here was used by the rebels. When I was in the Tricia castle library, I learned that this same symbol was used during the time of you all know what!

"Upon interrogating the traitor, Clara, I learned that the group of Dark Mistcasters call themselves the Necromancers. Not only were they responsible for the attacks, but they also were the ones who poisoned the Alpha-King, knowing they could easily spread rumors about you guys to tarnish your reputation! By doing so, they have manipulated the Beta-Lord Anvar Targon to amass an army in order to further weaken the kingdom!"

Silvus did not expect himself to make such a speech. The way the Mistatorium speak to each other, with faces mixed in fear and seriousness, it is a good start. Among the sages, Fernus gets up.

"Then what do you think we should do? Since you seem to have more knowledge on this issue. I say impressive for a mere hatchling such as yourself."

Believing this is his moment to shine like a true hero, Silvus makes a proud smile. He straightens his posture and responds in glee.

"I say we have turned a blind eye for too long. I will not lie, I spent most of my life stuck in a castle reading books, learning Mistcraft, and as a First-Delta prepared for my set destiny to become Beta-Lord. The reason I studied Mistcraft in the first place was because I wanted to help my fellow Raptors. But it turns out I have an even greater destiny.

"I learned if I want to help Raptors, I did not need to learn only from a book or a classroom. I could help Raptors by using what I learned by literally getting out there and doing something in the real world instead of sitting around a bedroom or reading in a library.

"I'll admit, politics is a really complicated subject to me. But I do know if we all stay around doing nothing and letting the rebels win, it will be the Necromancers who are the true winners! And if the Necromancers win, we are about to see history repeating itself, and we can't let that happen! So who's with me?!" Silvus raises his gloved claw high up in a fist, waiting for a response.

The council chambers stand quiet. The members of the Mistatorium do not know how to respond. Arkus, on the other claw, listened to the entire speech; then he gets off his chair and walks up to Silvus with a proud smile. The old Raptor puts a claw to his shoulder and replies, "Young Silvus, on behalf of the Mistatorium, I say you are right. We can't afford to let our old enemy win."

Arkus turns around, facing the rest of the council, and announces, "It is time to contact the royal army so we can send aid to our remaining allies!"

The entire crowd goes wild, giving Silvus a round of applause, booming with the sounds of clapping filling the entire chamber. During the applause, Arkus leans toward Silvus' head and whispers why he had not told them of his connection to the royal family. The only response Silvus gives the old purple Raptor is that they need to start focusing on the bigger picture instead of being distracted by politics.

Chapter 24
Return to Sendar

"Truth be told, young Silvus, we have been attempting to contact the royal army to maintain order for the past ten winters, yet we received no word from them," Arkus explains to Silvus, now back in the throne room with the other sages and high-ranking knights, including Ico, gathered in the center. Ocia and Fi also stand with them, with special permission to listen to what is going on.

"So you are saying the royal army is not following orders somehow?" Silvus responds, looking somewhat surprised. It explains why the royal army has done nothing since the surge of crime.

Arkus nods, confirming that Silvus is correct. He further explains that during the early years since Sulthur's death, the state of the kingdom ran smoothly. The royal guard did their job, allowing the Mistatorium to focus on searching for a new successor. Then he further tells him that when anti- Mistatorium rumors begin to spread like the plague, the royal guard suddenly stopped patrolling the frontier, allowing crime to rise, causing the Raptors of all castes to further blame them. Once it got out of control, Arkus himself tried to send letters to the army but never got a response.

"Did you ever try confronting them?" Silvus asks, looking suspicious. He finds it very odd that a force who are supposed to protect innocent Raptors would suddenly stop doing their job. The old Raptor in front continues to explain.

"Because we were too busy trying to find a successor at the time. We sent a knight or two to confront them on our behalf."

"And what happened to the knights?" Ico butts in, walking up to Silvus' side. Now that he is a knight, it makes sense to be concerned for one's kin.

Arkus looks to his sages, who are all putting on nervous faces, holding their staffs tight. That does not spell good news for Silvus, who knows it can only mean bad news. Closing his eyes, Arkus tells them softly, "They never returned…four winters ago."

Silvus gasps, along with the girls present.

Ico, however, seems to be taking it personally, from the way he makes a gritting face. "With all due respect, Arch-Sage…you guys had four winters to solve what was going on and yet never bothered to investigate what happened to them?!" he accuses, yet seems to be trying to not raise voice.

Silvus gets worried that Ico is looking for a fight with the arch-sage. However, he cannot help but agree with his cousin that it is strange that the Mistatorium did not bother investigating the royal army. Yet he sees Arkus merely sigh, looking up to Ico with a guilty look, responding, "I understand your sudden suspicion, Sir Ico, but truly, we really wanted to investigate but the riots in the city and the entire Betadom were getting worse. We had no choice but to keep focused on restoring order with our remaining knights and city watch."

"As much as I agree with Ico, with the royal army refusing your orders, what do you think it means?" Silvus asks, regaining Arkus's attention. He wants to focus on the point.

"I believe something is troubling back at Fort Gallagar, the main headquarters of the royal army. But now that we have found an heir to the throne, we can finally focus our attention on getting the army back to the fold…your fold, your highness." Arkus makes a wink with a smile at Silvus, earning confused looks from Ico and Fi, as they do not know of Silvus's heritage.

Ocia, who already knows due to overhearing a conversation between Silvus and his mother, leans toward Fi with a smile, whispering the revelation to her, making the latter gasp, constricting her pupils as thin as a thread. Ico turns to Silvus, still looking confused, wanting to know what Arkus meant and what Ocia whispered to his unique female friend. Silvus turns his attention to Ico with a nervous chuckle and tells him, "Oh yeah, turns out my father is Alpha-King Sulthur."

"SAY WHAT?!" Ico makes a face of shock, dropping his lower jaw, freezing in place. Fi walks up to Ico, looking worried, tugging one of his arms, asking if he is okay. The sages also gasp, turning their eyes to Arkus, demanding to know if it is true. With a smile, Arkus confirms that Silvus is the lost legitimate son of Sulthur, and that is why he survived the taint during the Anointing.

"Um, well…with that out of the way, we better not waste any time. The remainder of my family is depending on us!" Silvus excitedly shouts with light in his eyes, along with a heroic smile, making Ocia giggle in response.

"Before you go, I think you will need two things." Arkus turns his head and snaps his fingers. From the throne entrance, a female drone walks up with a familiar package in her arms. It is the package that Silvus had delivered during his journey. The drone continues to walk all the way to Silvus to kneel and bow at the same time, lifting up the package for him to take.

Silvus turns his head to Arkus, giving him a curious look. With the latter telling him to open it, Silvus slowly uses his claws to unwrap the package and gasps. It turns out to be a big long sword. The hilt of the sword looks like it was forged from an odd creature's skull with some horns on the sides, while the one in the middle serves as the handle. The shining blade seems to be carved into a shape looking like flames are coming out of the skull's mouth.

Silvus picks up the sword, admiring its unique look. Suddenly the sword begins to glow white at his touch, startling him a bit. He carefully makes a few test swings, making him giddy. Despite its size, the sword feels like he is holding a thin stick.

"We called it The Sword of Ultamar. It is the same sword that betrayed Necros and accepted Magnus as his master to defeat him," Arkus explains, gaining Silvus' attention. "Since then, the Ultamar family has used the sword for many generations. Oddly enough, only an Ultamar can use its true power. The way I see it, it is not only that your mother was entrusted with it by your father, but wanted you to deliver it to us, to show that you are indeed an Ultamar."

Arkus and his fellow sages bow to Silvus, greeting him as their new Alpha-Prince who could eventually become the new Alpha-King. Silvus cannot help but feel a bit awkward. It is still hard for him to grasp the reality that he has been the lost heir the entire time.

"I know you guys are excited about my cousin being the heir and all, but what about the second thing you want to discuss?" Ico blurts, out recovering from his trance.

Arkus and the sages stand back up. The former turns his attention to Ico with a smile, commenting that he is glad he asked.

━━━•《●》•━━━

As the daylight shines upon the main road in the Neon Forest, Silvus is riding in his usual traveling garments with the sword of Ultamar on his back. On the same mount Ocia sits behind him, holding onto him carefully, while Ico rides next to him, talking non-stop about his cousin's claim to the throne. Fi, who is mounted on Ico's mount, gazes at giant glowing mushrooms, which remind her of the Glowing Roots back at her home. Also joining the gang is a battalion of fifty Knights of the Mist, requested by Arkus to follow them to Fort Gallagar in case something happened.

It makes sense that Arkus would have the knights travel along since the mysterious disappearance last time. Among the fifty knights, a female with a short sword gallops up between the pair, turning her face to Silvus, asking, "Is it true what my father said? Are you really the lost Ultamar heir?" The knight's voice sounds like she is middle-aged, with hint of a tomboyish tone. With her helmet covering up her face, all that Silvus could see is a pair of feminine pale white eyes.

"Why yes it is, lady knight, and you are...?" Silvus confirms and asks back, wondering who the particular knight is. The knight takes off her helmet revealing a purple scaled she-Raptor with a long light-purple mane brushed to the side.

"Madam Pendra Gwynie VII at your service. Knight-Captain of this platoon and daughter of the arch-sage himself!" the knight Gwynie brags a bit with a grin, pointing at herself.

"Arkus is your father? He never told me he has a daughter." Silvus wonders calmly, keeping his gaze on Gwynie who chuckles in response.

"Did you even ask? And yeah, my dad does not like brag about his clan mates."

"Spirits! First I learn that my cousin is the lost Alpha-Prince and Arkus, technically my Delta-Lord, has a daughter who is also my superior?!" Ico blurts out to his fellow knight and superior.

"I also have two daughters and a husband back home working as a bartender. And I say he is really good at his job!" Gwynie adds, licking her lips, probably thinking about her husband's goods.

Traveling farther north, Silvus continues to speak with Gwynie, who in turn likes to tell him about herself. She loves to brag about her clan having a lineage filled with Gwynies who were all knights, just like her. She even mentions that her first hatched daughter is Gwynie VIII as part of the family tradition.

They continue to travel, passing by the herds of Brontos and Tritops feasting on the trees and bushes as well as various colorfull bug life buzzing around. So far, no Tyrannos or Spinos are seen. Instead, a large fortress, almost as big as a mountain is seen by the distance.

It is Fort Gallagar, alright. The fort itself looks more like a Roman aesthetic temple in the middle of the forest clearing. The kingdom's flags are shown waving proudly, indicating that the fort is still occupied by the royal army.

Stopping in front of the main gates made of hard iron, Silvus can feel Ocia shaking in excitement. He turns his head to see her staring in awe, holding back her instinct with her lips held together tightly. "What is wrong with her?" Gwynie asks Silvus, holding back some laughter.

With a few chuckles, Silvus replies, "She is fanatically in love with history."

"And you're not?" Ico adds with a smirk on his face.

"Not at the fanatical level, dinosaur-lover," Silvus teases back, looking confident with a cheeky smile, acknowledging Ico's knowledge of dinosaurs. The cousin only mutters "Haha very funny" in a more mature way, showing how mature he has gotten since joining the knights.

From behind, Ocia begins to spew out a lot of what she knows about Fort Gallagar, like a young female who just finished reading a very popular romance book. "Did you guys know this fort was made as a response to fight against invading raiders?!"

"Are you referring to 'the Goliath of the north,' the story about

Sentinel Gallagar's campaign to repel the Raptors of Fenheim?" Silvus perks up, interested out of nowhere, earning a moan from Ico.

With glee, Ocia is about to spew out another fact until a voice calls out.

"WHO GOES THERE?!"

All eyes turn up to the top of the main gates to see a royal guardsman looking right at them, wearing the black feathered helmet they are known for.

"WE NEED TO SPEAK WITH THE SENTINEL! THIS IS URGENT!" Silvus shouts, hoping the guard hears him.

"UNDER WHOSE AUTHORITY?!" the guard shouts back.

"BY THE AUTHORITY OF THE MISTATORIUM!" Silvus points to the fifty Knights of the Mist. The guard puts on a nervous face at the sight, with a small gulp. He must be afraid, knowing that the knights are very good fighters. Rumors has it that a team of five hundred of them took out a large force twice their size during a one battle war against the Raptors of Olympdonia.

"STAY WHERE YOU ARE AND I'LL ASK A NEARBY WARDEN OR SENTINEL TO LET YOU ALL IN!" the guard shouts as he runs back to find the supposed warden or sentinel.

While waiting, Fi, who is sitting behind Ico, asks, "I assume this sentinel is the head of your royal army, but what is a warden?"

"A warden is an officer ranking under the sentinel. Six of them exist to oversee a division in a Betadom," Silvus replies.

"How did you know that?" Ocia asks him.

"I have some friends that I used to spar with when I was little," Silvus answers Ocia as the doors begin to open. He turns his gaze to see the doors revealing an entire courtyard filled with busy royal guardsmen roaming around. In the middle of the gate entrance are three officers standing right by. They are more armored than the ones who are training from behind, as it is a tradition for Raptors of the army to earn a piece of armor when achieving a new rank. The more armored, the higher the rank.

———

The officer in the middle without a helmet on is a male who looks around the same age as Silvus. His scale color is ruby red with a sergeant-style green mane and tail tip. He is standing looking at them with his lime-green eyes scanning them. When the middle officer spots Silvus, he rubs his eyes as if his vision is being deceived. "By the spirits, Silvus, is that you?!" the officer calls out in excitement with a deeper voice.

Silvus looks at the guard who calls out his name, takes a closer look at him, then realizes that the particular officer is an old friend of his. Feeling excited, he gets off his mount and runs up to the officer who in turn also runs up. "By my Mist-tainted blood, Leon! It is great to see you again!"

The two old friends shake their claws like bros, glad they are able see each other again. The two other officers ask Leon if he knows Silvus. Leon tells them that he is an old friend and can be trusted and commands them to go back to their business. Turning his attention back to Silvus, he replies back, looking proud, "Damn right, brother; it has been winters since me and my brother left Maglo to join the royal army!"

"Guess time flies when you are student of Mistcraft like myself," Silvus points to himself, looking proud, earning a small laugh from Leon. Then Leon tells him to follow him in along with the other guests. Silvus turns his head to his friends and knights, gesturing his arm, signaling them to follow suit. They all enter the fort, closing the gates shut.

They pass through the main courtyard crowded by royal soldiers training in the fields or patrolling the grounds. Silvus speaks with Leon about what is going on with the kingdom due to the lack of presence of the guard themselves without telling him of his heritage, not wanting to draw unwanted attention. Looking frustrated, Leon puts a claw to his forehead as they stop by a large bronze statue of Sentinel Gallagar. Silvus can hear Ocia gasp in amazement at her first sight of it, earning a pair of eye-rolls from Fi, who stands beside her.

"Oh, I heard about the crime alright. Since becoming warden, the sentinel for some reason is telling us to not get involved, which is odd." Leon speaks with suspicion in his voice, crossing his arms.

"You're a warden already?!" Silvus blurts out, a bit shocked at his friend being a warden at such a young age, earning a smile from the red Raptor in front.

"You could say during the early years I proved myself to be a capable leader for my fellow soldiers." Leon looks up to the nearby keep of the fort with his claws to his hips. "Or maybe the sentinel is desperate to fill up the seats as soon as possible."

"Then you must be very proud of yourself?" Silvus comments with a smile. He remembers thatt when they were young, Leon was always the charismatic type, compared to his timid younger brother. Despite his comment, Leon's expression turns a bit sour, killing the mood.

"I was, my old friend, but since the sentinel has us stay put like sitting Velocis, all we do is train, patrol, or sometimes we scout outside to get some supplies. I tried expressing my concern to the sentinel but he just tells me that things are fine, yet the others say otherwise. Makes me feel that my promotion is empty...meaningless." Leon shrugs.

"Well, that is why we are here. We came on behalf of the Mistatorium to get you guys to help us defeat the rebels up north!" Silvus tries to reason, looking behind to check on his companions. Ocia is still gazing at the statue. Fi is checking out some the royal soldiers with black dots on their snouts, wondering what they are.

A royal guardsman walks up to Fi and explains that the ones with the dots are extra-borns as part of a recruitment program to be raised into the military. It involves a controversial breeding law thea applies only to Omegas, who can have only have two hatchlings per family, while Deltas and Betas are allowed four, and the Alphas can have as many as they want. The only time an Omega can have more is to marry a higher caste mate.

If Silvus can remember what his old friend told him about military history long ago, the kingdom would force Raptor families to give up a certain number of eggs until they fall to the legal limit. Such a law was made by Alpha-Queen Nora, the daughter of Magnus, in order to refill the military ranks in order to fight the Fenheim Raptors. It does break his heart thinking about it.

Not wanting to listen anymore, he checks on Ico, Gywnie, and the knights, who are met by royal guardsmen, asking for combat advice or autographs.

"Is that so? Well, you guys are not the first ones who came by," Leon states snapping Silvus back to his attention.

"You mean a group of knights four winters ago," Silvus guess softly, remembering what Arkus told him.

With a nod, Leon explains, "When I was still captain, the same knights came by, telling us they need to see the sentinel on behalf of the Mistatorium. So the sentinel complied, taking them to his office, only for them to somehow disappear the next day." Leon gets into thought scratching his head, "Come to think of it, I wonder if the sentinel has something to do…"

Leon pauses his thought. His face seems to be best described as confused. Silvus asks him what is wrong, looking concerned. Only telling him that he is fine, Leon decides to take Silvus alone with him to meet with the sentinel, while the others are told to wait around the courtyard. Gwynie, however, wants to join up with the boys to see the sentinel herself. As knight-captain, she probably believes it is her responsibility to ensure the safety of her fellow knights—especially the ones who disappeared.

Leon leads Silvus and Gwyine into the main keep to be greeted by a large rectangular room with hanging black flags and tapestries of Avalonia filled with high-ranking guards.

As they cross the room to a circular staircase, Silvus scans around the hordes of guardsmen, hoping to find a particular Raptor. All he can see are faces on the guardsmen, looking nervous. Some take notice of him, whispering to each other, wondering who he is. Turning his gaze back to Leon, he asks, "Where's Nidus?"

Climbing up to the third floor where the sentinel's office and quarters is located, with a worried face Leon replies as they walk through the hall, "I honestly do not know. What I do know is that he and I were both getting suspicious about not getting orders to help innocent Raptors. Then the next morning, my brother vanished."

"Just like that?" Silvus asks Leon.

"I do not know. When I ask a fellow officer, he told me that the sentinel needed him last night. Demanding answers, I was going to confront him until I heard you guys near the gates."

Leon's face is filled with worry. As an older brother, it makes sense for him to feel so. It is like what Silvus used to feel when trying to save his mother.

"Interesting. Just like the knights, your little brother was taken to the sentinel, never to return." Gywnie makes a connection looking up scratching her chin. To the two friends, she makes a good point. Perhaps to Silvus, maybe the sentinel could be involved not only with the disappearances but maybe the lack of enforcement.

They all approach the door to the sentinel's office, where they briefly stop. Leon knocks on the door, hoping the sentinel is around.

"WHO IS THIS!" a grumpy old male voice calls out from the

doors. Whoever the current sentinel is, he does not seem like he wants any visitors.

"This is Warden Leon. I come here with guests seeking to meet with you."

"FINE, GET IN HERE NOW!"

Leon opens the door, letting Silvus and Gywnie enter. The office itself is loaded with hanging dino trophy heads on the walls, while the sentinel himself stands by his desk in front of a large map of the kingdom.

The sentinel is best described as a bald, middle-aged grey male, looking upset, with his claws behind his back. As the sentinel, he is loaded with armor with a black cape to display the sentinel's authority, answering directly only to the monarch.

"This better be important, Warden, and I swear if this is another complaint about how I run things, get lost!"

From the sentinel's tone of voice, Silvus immediately does not like him. He questions how a Raptor like him got the position in the first place.

"Um… Sentinel, sir, this is an old friend of mine and a Knight of the Mist who have come here on behalf of the Mistatorium to reque-"

"Who exactly are you, boy?!" the sentinel cuts off Leon, rushing up to Silvus, giving him the stink eye. Gwynie puts her claw on the hilt of her short sword in case trouble happens to Silvus. But the latter raises his claw, telling her that it's okay.

"My name is Silvus, sir. I have come on behalf of the Mistatorium to request aid in stopping the rebels."

"Do they?" The sentinel scratches his chin, sounding unamused, yet seems surprised that Silvus did not get intimidated. Instead, he speaks calmly like a professional—or maybe it's simply a Mistcaster's trick. He only scoffs, walking back to the large map behind his desk.

"Can you tell me why I should follow a group that killed the Alpha-King?"

"Because they are innocent!" Silvus says defensively. He is tired of hearing Raptors making false assumptions about the Mistatorium. Turns out the sentinel believes the rumors as well. There is one thing that he can do to prove their innocence, and it is on his back. So he draws the Sword of Ultamar to show the stubborn fool, hoping he has heard the legend.

The blade of the sword makes the same white glow at his touch. Two of the three military Raptors are in shock.

"Is that the sword of Ultamar?!" Leon gasps in awe.

"That's right, soldier boy. Our mutual friend here is the lost son of the the Alpha-King," Gywnie confirms with a big smile and her claws to her hips, standing proud.

While Leon struggles to find the right words, Silvus notices a strange form of behavior from the sentinel is making. He seems to be more nervous, rather than awed. Sweat is seen coming out of his forehead, as he is muttering something. Squinting his eyes, Silvus could swear he hears the words "This is impossible" from the sentinel's snout. Silvus senses that he is hiding something.

The sentinel moves his eyes side to side and stammers, "Even if...you are the Alpha-Prince...what do you even know of the safety of our troops?"

Silvus sheaths his sword and looks to Leon, giving him an idea. "Speaking of the safety of one's troops, do you know of a guardsman by the name of Nidus?" he demands.

"Beg your pardon?" The sentinel stiffens as Silvus looks back to Leon, nodding for him to stand forward.

"He is my little brother. A guard told me that you needed to see him a few hours ago. Speaking not only as a concerned warden but also an elder brother, I have the right to know where he is, RIGHT NOW?!" Leon pounds his fist on the desk with anger, causing the piles of books and parchments to shake.

Looking intimidated himself, the sentinel cowardly turns around facing the map while Silvus, Gwynie, and Leon wait for an answer. Unexpectedly, the sentinel perks up as if he has an idea. He turns around looking proud, too proud, telling them, "I believe you're right! Recently there was a sighting of Fenheim soldiers crossing the border. As it is our duty, I sent Palladin Nidus and a few men to deal with them."

"YOU SENT MY LITTLE BROTHER TO FIGHT FEN- HEIM RATPORS!" Leon shouts in panic while Silvus drops his jaw in shock, Gywnie gasps, covering her snout with both claws.

Every Raptor knows stories about the kingdom of Fenheim. It is filled with brutal Raptor warriors who will not show mercy. It is known by the recordings of Gallagar that Fenheim Raptors have a survival of the fittest mentality, believing that the weak are to be either purged or enslaved. Making things even stranger is how they even managed to get through Maglo or Tricia?

"Correct, Warden." The sentinel turns his eyes to Silvus, ignoring the growling Leon, who is obviously angry. "What about if you go up north and save my men? I might consider joining up—deal?"

The sentinel raises his claw for Silvus to shake. Silvus hesitates at first, being suspicious. He looks at Leon, who keeps his snarling face, while Gywnie nods for him to play along.

"You swear if we save your troops from Fenheim, you'll help us?"

"My word indeed."

"Deal." Silvus shakes the sentinel's claws while at the same time looking at him sternly. He still does not trust the sentinel, yet he is willing to save another old friend who is about to be butchered by fierce pagan warriors.

When Silvus, Gwynie, and Leon leave the office, what they do not know is that the sentinel has his talons crossed behind his back.

Chapter 25
Battle of Neon Woods

Traveling deeper into the forest, Silvus travels with Leon, Ico, and a band of ten knights and other guardsmen searching for Nidus and his squad in order to save him as fast as they can. Gwyine, Ocia, Fi, and the other remaining knights stay behind at the fort in order to keep an eye on the sentinel in case something happens behind their backs. Silvus turns his gaze to Leon to check on him. Leon looks anxious, gripping his sword and shield tightly, worried about his brother's safety.

"Hey man, are you okay?" Ico asks, walking beside Leon to his left.

"I don't know, brah. We must be heading to some kinda--OF COURSE I AM NOT OKAY! MY LITTLE BROTHER IS IN DANGER OUT THERE!" Leon shouts at Ico's obvious question, making the former and some of the guards and knights flinch.

Silvus knows that Ico did not mean to offend. Probably he wanted to brighten the mood before heading to the grand battle, where they might not see another day. Suddenly, Silvus hears sounds of blades clashing and battle cries, signaling his claw for his companions to stop. Using his hidden ears, Silvus tracks the noise eastward.

"That noise? NIDUS!" Leon sprints past Silvus, who in turn tries to grab his tail to stop him from being suicidal.

Shaking his head side to side, Silvus runs after Leon while the others follow suit. Running up to a cliff, the group, including Leon, stop by the edge to see a battle going on between the Fenheim Raptor army and the Avalonia Raptor army. The Fenheim Raptors are easily identifiable by their bodies being covered almost completely by feathers, except for their faces, due to coming from a cold environment. Also, their soldiers wear horned helmets in comparison to the Avalonian feathered helmets.

Silvus scans around the battlefield to see at least twenty Fenheim compared to the outnumbered ten Avalonians. Or at least there were fifteen, looking at the five corpses of the Avalonians fallen in battle. Thank the spirits that none of them were Nidus. Silvus looks to his right to see Leon looking around in panic hoping to find his brother still fighting.

Back at the battlefield, Silvus spots one high-ranking guardsman wielding a halberd like a pole axe, taking out two Fenheim Raptors with two swings. One of the Fenheim soldiers kicks the guardsmen from behind, knocking off his helmet to reveal a familiar younger red Raptor but with a darker green mane, looking up to see the same Fenheim brute running at him with dual wielding axes, shouting, "CREHALLA!!!!!!"

The young officer quickly picks up his weapon and jabs it right at the brute's chest like a spear, and throws him off. He gets back on his feet to see his fellow Avalonian guardsman get axed in the face by a more armored Fenheim solider wearing a helmet with huge horns. The large brute turns his gaze toward the red guardsmen. The red guardsmen prepares himself as the heavy brute begins to charge.

"LOOK, IT'S NIDUS!" Leon shouts, pointing at the young red Raptor almost resembling him, who is engaging in battle with the larger enemy. "We've got to help them now!"

Leon is right. Silvus knows if the battle keeps up, the royal soldiers, Avalonia soldiers, will get wiped out. He looks around to see a slope they can run down to in order to launch a surprise ambush.

"Every Raptor on me. SPIRITS WILL IT!" Silvus draws his sword, leading his troops down the slope.

Joining the fight, Silvus and his group begin their battle cries, gaining the attention of both the Fenheim soldiers and the other guardsmen. The royal guardsmen, led by Nidus, begin to cheer, waving their weapons at the sight of reinforcements boosting their morale. Caught off guard, the Fenheim soldiers find themselves overpowered by the unexpected reinforcements.

While Silvus uses his sword to fight off the Fenheims, he spots Leon rushing to Nidus' aid. Turns out Nidus re-enaged back into battle with the large Fenheim brute. Nidus tries to deflect the attacks but the blows by the Fenheim prove to be so powerful that he disarms the former and kicks his chest, pushing him on the ground. The Fenheim is about to make the finishing blow, only to be stabbed from behind by Leon, saving Nidus' life.

"THE SKIRMISHER IS DOWN! RETREAT, MY BROTHERS!" one of the remaining Fenheim Raptors shrieks, witnessing the death of the large brute. The Fenheim Raptors rush out up north in retreat, giving the Avalonians the battle. The latter all cheer with victory croaks, and raise their weapons up high.

Silvus looks around the remainder of the royal army to see Leon helping up Nidus and embraces him in a hug, telling him how worried he was, in tears. With a heart-melting smile, Silvus walks up to the brothers and greets them. Nidus turns around, gasping at the sight of him.

"S-S-Silvus?!" Nidus stammers and looks to Leon, who smiles in response.

"It is great to see you again too, Nidus," Silvus replies, regaining Nidus' attention.

"Dude, I don't know what to say, other than to thank you guys both for saving me!" Nidus grabs Silvus' claw and shakes it. "I honestly did not expect any reinforcements at all!"

"What do you mean by that?" Silvus asks him, looking serious.

"Well, the sentinel told me that this mission was supposed to be a secret, with only a few guardsmen."

Both Silvus and Leon exchange confused looks when Nidus mentions that his mission is supposed to be a secret. That does not make sense—why would the head of the royal army make such a shady move?

"YO, GUYS, LOOK AT THIS!" The voice of Ico calls their attention.

Ico is seen searching around the corpse of the leading Fenheim to take out what looks like a rolled-up parchment. He walks up to three and shows it to Silvus, who in turn takes it.

Silvus opens the parchment up to see a royal seal above on the left claw corner and reads,

To Alpha-King Ragnark Lokiir of Fenheim,

Two of my soldiers are starting to ask too many questions about the way I operate. So without further ado, I need your aid to take two of the leading conspirators one by one per day. I am sending the first target in this position. He is a young soldier, so you should not have any trouble. After you deal with them both, I will pay you all handsomely with at least 10,000 Golden Feathers, as long as you all keep this operation a secret.

Sincerely, Sentinel Judar Bernic of Avalonia

The note that Silvus reads turns out to be some kind of contract to have the brothers killed. He gives it to the two brothers for them to read it themselves.

Reading the parchment, Leon's expression begins to turn sour, realizing that the sentinel is trying to get both him and Nidus killed for asking too many questions. Nidus asks Leon how it is possible the sentinel knew of their concerns. Leon responds to Nidus that the sentinel probably overheard them.

Believing the others could be in danger, Silvus gets every Raptor's attention. "If this is true, we better head back to Fort Gallagar. Our friends could be in danger!"

With that the entire squad, guardsmen and knights, follow Silvus to head back to the Fort. The sentinel himself has a lot to answer for.

―――――◆―――――

Silvus and the gang are greeted by a large crowd of guardsmen back at the fort, looking nervous. One of them runs up to Silvus telling him, "Are you Silvus, my lord?"

Silvus nods.

"Lady Gwynie is in critical condition!"

"Gwynie is WHAT?!" Silvus hears Ico step up when the guard mention the knight-captain. The guard only tells them that they had better come with him to the infirmary where Gwynie is being held.

In the infirmary are rows beds with wounded guards. They are being tended by healers who are all females due to their stronger use of Healing Mist. Ocia, who is helping them, spots Silvus and his group, looking relieved.

Ocia runs up to latch Silvus into a quick hug, telling him that she is glad he came back safe.

"Where's Gwynie?!" Silvus asks without hesitation.

Ocia turns around, pointing to the end of the room, looking uneasy. "She is over there, resting. Thank the spirits I saw her in time and healed her wound, but she is still barely conscious."

Ocia leads Silvus, Ico, Leon, and Nidus all the way to end where Gwynie is moaning on the bed, putting one of her claws on her stomach like a cramp, with Fi sitting on a stool next to her, keeping an eye out. Fi looks up with a gasp and rushes to Ico, jumping into his arms.

Silvus, followed by Leon to his right, walks up next to Gwynie to check on her. Gwynie looks to the side with her claw still on her stomach, yet she manages to put a forced smile at the sight of a familiar friendly face.

"Succeeded in heroic mission?" she asks with a groan, wincing in pain from her stomach, tightening her grasp.

"What happened?!" Silvus softly demands, while Ico joins to his left. After further groaning, Gwynie speaks, struggling with her pain.

"While you guys were gone, I was investigating what happened to the missing knights. I attempted to sneak back into the sentinel's office to search for clues. The door was wide open and I caught the sentinel practicing Blood Mist."

"By the spirits! This is worse than I thought!" Leon comments out loud.

"That's why he wanted us to do nothing!" Nidus guesses, looking stern.

"And what did that guy do to you, Cap?!" Ico buts in.

I bet he is with the Necromancers, Silvus thinks to himself, still listening to Gwynie's story.

"As a Knight of the Mist, it is my duty to bring those who misuse their Mist powers, especially Dark Casters, to justice. So I drew my Mythril sword, telling him that he was under arrest. But the old fart fought back and managed to do a number on my gut. Instead of finishing me off, he jumped through a window like a coward when he heard footsteps coming—it turned out be to Ocia, who immediately healed my wound and called out for nearby healers. Then I fainted and woke up here." She coughs.

To Silvus, Gwynie is very lucky Ocia was around. A stabbing strike at the gut would have killed her in a matter of seconds unless treated quickly by Healing Mist.

Suddenly a guardsman bursts through the door in panic. Silvus turns his head to see the guard running up to him, standing up straight with a salute.

"My lords! There is an army heading this way!"

"What army?! Explain, soldier!" Leon steps up sounding like Ki back at Shima.

"I think it is best I show you, Warden," the guard recommends and leads the group out.

<hr />

Silvus and gang are led by the guard all the way up to the ledge of the front gates filled with other guardsmen with bows and arrows drawn.

In Silvus' view, he sees a swarm of unknown rebels wearing a mix of black and purple armor raising familiar flags with purple skulls marching through the Neon Forest. Some are riding on Carnotaurs as mounts. They must be the Necromancers. They look too organized to be simple rebels or bandits. Leading the entire group is the traitor sentinel himself, wearing the matching black/purple armor with a sinister look on his face.

Whatever they are planning, Silvus can only guess that they might be plotting to wipe out the royal army. They must have been plotting it for a long time, to muster such a force. Sensing tension in the air, he looks around at the guardsmen, who are looking intimidated. Silvus needs to think fast, or he will lose the army who can help him.

Silvus looks around to see a Ballista on both corners of the fortress, getting an idea. He looks to Leon, who is snarling at the invaders, and tells him, "How many are we exactly?"

Leon turns his attention to Silvus and answers, "At least 49,994. The last time I looked at the records we were at least 50,000 here, being a gigantic fortress with an underground cavern—why?"

Silvus tells Leon to gather the troops in the main courtyard so they can meet in order to deal with the invaders that marches farther.

Silvus stands in front of the statue of Gallagar, delivering a speech to a crowd of royal guardsmen, hoping to rally them to follow with the knights standing behind him. Igniting his fanboy instincts, he exaggerates the tales of the bravery of Magnus' soldiers whom defeated Necros as well as Gallagar's stand against the Fenheims. One of the Guardsmen steps up with his arms crossed looking unamused.

"Even if it's true boy, the better question is why should we follow you?"

Silvus makes a frustrating groan needing a better way to convince the royal Army to follow him. He hoped to not reveal his heritage to not get attention. He has no choice. Like what he did at the sentinel's office, he draws his sword making it glow earning gasps from the army getting their full attention.

"THAT SWORD!" one guard shrieks.

"THE SWORD OF ULTAMAR!" another blurts out.

Silvus lowers his arm, still grasping the sword, telling them, "My real name is Ultamar Silvus! The lost son of Alpha-King Ultamar Sulthur! I will not lie, I have been through a lot! I fought an army underground, I faced giant insects, I fought a horde of rebels, and I even fought a Dark Caster! If I could do all that…you guys can, too. You are the royal army of Avalonia, the bravest warriors of all the three Raptor kingdoms of Cretatia!"

The royal army gives approving nods to each other, agreeing with what Silvus is saying. Nidus looks to his brother, asking if what he is saying is true. Silvus is not done yet.

"I might know much about leading a huge army, but I do know that if we stand around and do nothing, not only we will be dead, but all our families are going to suffer! So I ask you all again. ARE... YOU...WITH ME!" Silvus raises his sword high and proud.

Leon steps up, telling them, "Raptors of the royal army, as testimony I can confirm that my old friend here is a great fighter and leader. We fought together. He led us head on to save my brother and your fellow country Raptors from a horde of savages. So what do you all say? Will we give him a chance?"

Among the crowd of soldiers, Nidus is the first to step forward and kneel before Silvus with his halberd drawn on the ground.

"If my brother trusts him, then I shall too!"

Soon other guardsmen, including the other wardens, follow suit, vowing to give Silvus a chance to deal with the invaders.

As the invading army gets closer, Silvus finds himself in the war room, wearing a unique black armor set with glowing white runes and a silver leather cape. After his speech, he is requested by Leon and Nidus to the armory in order to give him a unique set of armor worn by many Alpha-Kings in the past. As royalty leading the army, it will be symbolic for Silvus to wear it.

Gathered around a large stone round table in the middle, using a sheet of paper, Silvus is drawing a strategy plan to best deal with the invaders, not only to all the wardens, but also his companions who want to help the best they can, except for Gwynie, who is not in the best condition to fight, so she appointed Ico in her stead as acting captain. When asked how he knows the plan will work by an unnamed warden, Silvus tells him that he is using a tactic once used by the hero Sentinel Gallagar himself in a book he read, earning a face palm by Ico.

For the tactic to work as it did according to the old story, Silvus will be in the front line fighting alongside Ico, Nidus, and Leon, whom Silvus nominated as the new sentinel, as well as the various Knights of the Mist who are ready to fight alongside the royal guardsmen. Ocia, who is wearing female- style light royal armor with her cloak, will be in charge of leading a group of healers to collect any wounded allies who need help. Fi, alongside a captain, will be leading a group of archers. Learning of tamed Tyranno Rexes, Silvus thinks they could be useful for a counter ambush. The plan is called "Trap and attack."

———⹀《◉》⹀———

Outside, Silvus is seen wearing his helmet covering his face with silver feathers on top, leading the royal army to the gates. "Open up," he commands, making the doors open to reveal an army of the invaders in view through the large trees.

The royal army forms their positions in front of the fort entrance in a long rectangle with Silvus, the knights, Ico, Nidus, and Leon on the front lines. Fi and another Archer captain gather as much archers as they could above the main gates getting ready to support their allies below.

"I would never have imagined myself fighting alongside you, old friend," Leon whispers through his helmet with a smile to Silvus at his right.

"Same here! It is like old times when we were little." Nidus stands proudly to Silvus' left

"Of all the things we have been through, Cousin, this is going to be the best time of my life as a knight!" Ico comments, earning a chuckle from Silvus.

Tritus is so going to be jealous about this! Silvus mentally jokes to himself, making a quick thought about his best friend's reaction. He shakes his head to refocus on the battle at claw.

As both sides wait for the first moves, tension fills the air. The invading troops draw their weapons as the ex-sentinel blows his horn, signaling his troops to begin the first charge. With cries of battle, the invading army ran like a stampede of Brontos shaking the ground while the Carnotaur riders follow suit.

This is the moment of truth. This is Silvus' chance to start acting like an Alpha-King in the midst of battle. He could feel the tension swelling up in his chest as the troops in the front line draw their sword and shields, at the same time watching the enemy running toward them. With a deep breath, he looks up behind him and shouts, "ARCHERS!"

One captain who leads the archers on one side, and Fi who leads the other, commands their groups to draw their arrows at the same time preparing ballistas to be aimed at the Carnotaur riders.

With the invaders halfway to the royal ground forces, the captain makes the first signal with his claw, unleashing a swarm of arrows, striking down the invading forces by the right while the ballistas shoot down the enemy Carnotaurs with ginormous javelins. Fi follows suit on the left, weakening the invaders, yet they still charge.

"TYRANNOS!" Silvus shouts, causing hidden doors to open up. From the hidden doors, the DinoMasters in charge release at least ten armored Tyranno Rexes to sprint past the royal ground troops, making their way to the enemy. They use their massive teeth to chop down any enemy Raptor, squishing them with their massive feet, or swatting them off with their large tails. Many even take down nearby enemy Carnotaur riders. Some Tyrannos sadly are killed by nearby pike men and surviving Carnotaur riders.

With the enemy weakened, Silvus draws his sword, commanding his troops to follow. Leon draws his sword and shield, Ico takes out his bow and arrow, and Nidus draws his halberd. With the army at the ready, Silvus takes a deep breath and shouts, "AS THE SPIR-ITS WILL IT! FOR AVALONIA!"

Silvus leads the charge. The knights and the royal army all roar in high spirits as they run toward the struggling invaders, either becoming Tryanno chow or taken out by more arrow and ballista fire. With their associated weapons, the royal forces and the knights clash making sounds of metal clashing with each other.

The Sword of Ultamar proves to be a very powerful fighting tool for Silvus as he takes out each invader like butter while dodging attacks at the same time. He sees an invader about to attack Ico, so he thrusts his claw to shoot a lightning bolt, saving his cousin, who is using his bow and arrow like a pro. Then he sees Leon fighting together with his brother Nidus, taking out invaders like a team.

Silvus scans around the battlefield through the hordes of his own soldiers doing well to see the main target. The ex-sentinel is taking out a few royal soldiers like it is nothing. With a puff from his nose, Silvus raises his sword to make the charge. The ex-sentinel takes out one more royal solider by the chest with his sword before he spots Silvus making a leap attack toward him.

Engaged in battle, Silvus clashes his sword with the ex-sentinel's, with fierce faces. The ex-sentinel makes a few offensive swings while Silvus uses the parrying technique to deflect each one. Even for an old Raptor, the ex-sentinel proves himself to be a unique fighter. Probably that is how he managed to become a sentinel in the first place.

As the battle goes on around them, Ocia leads a team of heal-ers protected by a few soldiers rushing out of the fort toward a pile of bodies away from the fighting, in search of any royal soldier or knight still alive. While the healers begin to drag out a first wave of wounded soldiers, Ocia gets up, scaning around the battlefield in front of her, worried for Silvus, who is currently engaged in fighting.

The ex-sentinel begins to show fatigue as each strike is deflected by his opponent, who shows none. He tries one more swing, only for Silvus to use his sword to cut off his claw to disarm him. The ex-sentinel cries out in pain, looking around to see his forces getting creamed by the royal forces and the Knights of the Mist. He even sees many of his troops beginning to retreat like a bunch of cowards, while enemy healers are seen helping their wounded.

"Give up, Bernic. You lost!" Silvus demands, shouting the ex-sentinel's real name, which he learned from a note.

The ex-sentinel only gets angry and uses his wound to form a blood spear, allowing him to get up. "YOU SHOULD HAVE BEEN KILLED BY THE FENHEIM RAPTORS!" he shouts before making a reckless yet desperate charge, only for Silvus to side-step and stab him from behind, killing the old ex-sentinel.

Silvus stands in place, taking deep breaths. He takes off his helmet and looks around the forest turned battlefield to see that his troops have won the battle. Among them he sees his cousin, looking giddy, as well as Leon, who is carrying Nidus, catching breaths—not that he is hurt, but tired of fighting. Silvus turns his head to the right to see Ocia being followed by healers, looking relieved. Fi too runs with her team of archers with a face as if she just came from the most amazing party of her life.

Silvus looks down at the lifeless body of the ex-sentinel. He kneels down and uses his claw to flip the body around and gently closes his eyes. Even though he is a Dark Mistcaster, he is still another of the misguided. "May the spirits rest your soul," Silvus mutters, to show respect to his opponent.

Silvus lifts himself up with the sword of Ultamar in claw. He thrusts his sword high in the sky, making his allies chant, "ALL HAIL ULTAMAR SILVUS! ALL HAIL THE TRUE ALPHA-KING!"

Silvus cannot help but feel a sense of hope and excitement that dwells inside his chest as he just lived like a hero, like Magnus, defeating many odds. This battle in history will forever be known as The Battle of Neon Woods. The tides are beginning to turn.

Act VI

Chapter 26
The Royal Alliance

S ilvus now has full control of the royal army. The first thing he does is promote Leon as the permanent new sentinel, while Nidus takes his brother's spot as a new warden. Second, he begins to coordinate efforts to bolster the numbers of the royal army by having them go on missions to aid the nearby settlements to encourage recruitment, and also to show that the royal army has returned. Third, he has Ico and Fi to carefully travel to Shima in order to request reinforcements from his new friend, King Ki of the Kobolds.

Right now, Silvus is inside the private king's room and office, sitting near a fancy desk. He is writing a letter to Arkus, letting him know that the royal army is back under control as well as telling him what happened in detail. Putting the quill back into the ink, Silvus gets up from his leather chair to walk up toward a Petradon (Pterodactly), a flying dinosaur trained to deliever letters. He gives the Petradon the letter and enchants a spell to ensure it knows where to go, and releases it outside through the window.

Silvus walks up outside on the balcony to check on the troops. He can see the wardens, including Nidus, training the troops in the middle of the night. Now that Leon is the new sentinel, Silvus hears that he has been working on the organization of missions for the soldiers to carry out from time to time to enforce the law. Since then, he has been hearing that crime, at least in Suaronian Heart, is beginning to decrease. The next step is to wait for the arrival of his cousin and Fi with reinforcements, in order to muster enough power to save Tricia in time. He cannot help but admire the sight.

With a tired sigh, Silvus walks back into the quarters, approaching a mirror to check himself out still wearing the royal armor and cape. Then he walks up to the bed where he sits to take off one of his gauntlets, exposing his wound. He hears a gasping sound from the front door of the room. He quickly turns his head to see Ocia looking at his wound with two claws covering her mouth.

"Ocia?" Silvus calls out calmly, hiding his claw behind his back. "What brings you here?"

Ocia slowly walks into the quarters, looking apologetic. "I am so sorry for intruding. I came here to tell you that Gwynie is feeling better, so she will be able to lead the knights again tomorrow morning-and I say for an old lady like her, she sure knows how to brighten the mood despite what she has been through!"

"You got that right," Silvus agrees calmly. It is good to know that a new friend is feeling better. Gwynie looked like the kind of Raptor who knows how to handle almost anything, even at death's door. Or she is simply blessed by the spirits, giving her a lot of sheer luck.

"You were very amazing today!" Ocia perks up developing a blush on her cheeks.

Silvus cannot help but feel himself blush too, getting nervous. He turns his head slightly away, commenting, "Oh shucks, I thought you did well, too."

"Oh, Silvus, all I did was lead healers," Ocia giggles, turning her gaze to Silvus' wound, looking worried. Catching Silvus by surprise, Ocia gently picks up his burned claw, making him flinch in pain, yet he does not retract it.

"You poor baby. What happened?" Ocia scans Silvus' burned claw with her beautiful eyes.

Believing he can trust her now, he decides to tell her what he remembers. Considering what they have both been through, Silvus thinks she deserves to know how he got such a wound.

"When I was a young hatchling, I was practicing Mist spells in order to gain entry to Monastery." Silvus sighs and turns his gaze at the open balcony, staring at the stars. "One day in the middle of my old castle's courtyard, I was demonstrating a fireball spell with Sulphie. The fireball spell, as you know, is an advanced spell that is not suitable for beginners. Sulphie tried to warn me, but I was foolish enough to try it anyway. When I got distracted by the smell of crab biscuits from Tricia, the fireball suddenly burst in front of me, catching my left arm on fire."

Silvus turns his gaze back to Ocia who has a shocked expression with sympathetic eyes.

"Luckily, a drone was nearby carrying a bucket of water and used it to extinguish my arm. I was immediately taken to the castle infirmary, feeling very traumatized, with my eyes glued to my arm. Since then, I have developed this fear of fire to the point that not only do I refuse spells that deal with fire, but also avoid areas with fire in them."

"You poor thing. And you're still afraid of fire after all these years?" Ocia asks after Silvus finishes his story confirming his pyrophobia. "Can healing Mist treat it?"

"The healers told me that the burn is so great, not even healing Mist could completely heal it." Silvus gets up from the bed and puts back the gauntlet, wincing in pain. "The best I can do is wear left- clawed gloves or gauntlets, to not only hide my wound but also shield it from getting touched. Now you know why I wore that when we first met," Silvus clarifies as a guard bursts into the room, getting the attention of both him and Ocia.

"Your highness! There is a group of soldiers heading this way!" the guard says directly to Silvus with a salute.

"What banners do they hold?" Silvus asks the guard.

"Light blue background with a green Tritop head in the middle, with green swirling roots on the border."

Silvus widens his eyes, knowing what the guard described. "Go find the sentinel and tell him to round up the royal soldiers to wait near the gates!" he orders the guard.

The guard salutes again with a bow and rushes to find the sentinel.

"Is it the Kobolds you spoke about?!" Ocia jumps off the bed with a squeal, excited to learn about a new society.

"There is only way to find out," Silvus answers with a smile as they both leave the room to meet up with the others.

<hr/>

All the royal guards stand by the main gates as ordered. Leon stands proud, wearing the black cape of a sentinel. Seeing Silvus enter the walkway with Ocia following suit, Leon shouts, "Royalty at the bridge!" followed by a salute.

The guardsmen greet him by bowing as Silvus pass through. Approaching Leon, Silvus tells him to order a gate guard to open the gates. The former does as he is ordered and gives the command.

The gates open. Silvus sees Ico return, riding his Carnotaur, along with Fi, who is now wearing the light-blue female-style Oriental armor of her kingdom, with a big smile.

"Well, Raptor boys, meet the most fab army of my people!" Fi points behind her as an army of Kobolds in their associated armor marches up in a distance. They all wear their Oriental armor with different colors to represent their clan lords. Leading them all is the familiar dark-blue-scaled male wearing his shining black armor with a nice cape, riding on the skinklike creature. He takes off his helmet, revealing the blue-scaled face of Ki, looking proud. "Permission to enter, sir?" he asks with the familiar soldier's tone.

Silvus walks out the gates with Leon and Ocia following behind, passing Ico and Fi. Approaching the now fellow royal shorter than him, Silvus extends his claw. Ki grabs the former's claw and shakes. "It is great to see you again, King Ki Jin," Silvus greets him.

"Likewise, Soldier—or shall I address you as your majesty?" Ki asks, letting go of their claws at the same time, making Silvus chuckle. Ico and Fi must have told him his heritage.

"I am not Alpha-King officially yet, not without proper ceremony. For now, I am simply Alpha-Prince at this point." Silvus turns his gaze to his Kobold friend's army all standing proud. Then he tells Ki to follow him with the Kobold army following suit. He orders the others to wait for him in the war room.

As Silvus walks alongside Ki, he can hear whispers among his royal army talking about their Kobold guests. He hears one guardsman comment how small the Kobolds are, while some try not to laugh.

"So how is Shima going along now that you're king?" Silvus asks, ignoring the whispers.

"Well, my friend, I have been working on efforts to find a way to finally take back parts of the Outer Roads. With my sister and your cousin requesting me to send aid, I could not help but agree to fight by your side again."

"Who is watching over your kingdom while you're gone?" Silvus asks Ki as they are about to stop by the main keep.

"My wife volunteered to be regent," Ki responds

"You have a wife?" Silvus raises an eyebrow.

"We have been married for a while now. I apologize for not mentioning that earlier, as we were too busy finding my sister," Ki apologizes as Silvus opens up the doors for both of them to enter, leaving the two royal armies to mingle.

Both Raptors and Kobolds gather in the war room. Silvus stands at the round table with a map of Avalonia placed in the middle, discussing the next course of action. All officers, both Avalonia and Shima, gather around to listen. Sentinel Leon stands next to Silvus to his right, while King Ki stands to the left. Gwynie is also there with Ico, representing the knights.

"Now that we are all here, let me make sure we are all on the same page." Silvus looks to King Ki. "Did Fi and Ico update you about what is going on?"

Ki nods and says, "Affirmative, they told me that you are planning to liberate this place called Tricia. I'll admit, I agreed to this alliance not only because we owed you, but also because the entrance of my kingdom is around that territory, which means if Tricia falls to the rebels, they will come for Shima as well."

"Well then," Silvus replies with a confirming nod and places a talon onto the map specifically on Tricia, getting the attention of all the officers present. He tells them that based on news from a messenger, Tricia is about to be conqured by the Monchester rebels.

The plan is that he will need to form two teams of scouts. One will patrol into Tricia in order to navigate the safest route through the royal border so they can launch a surprise attack and save what is left of Tricia. Because Kobolds are not known among Raptors, Ki volunteers to send a few of his troops to scout in. Another patrol will make a journey into Creston in order to request even more reinforcements by the next sunrise. Silvus stands up straight and asks if any Raptor or Kobold has questions.

One warden raises a claw and asks, while scanning, the Kobold Shima officers, "Apologies, your majesty, but I believe my fellow wardens and I would like to know a bit more about our Kobold comrades and why they will be fighting with us?"

Taken by surprise, Silvus gives an awkward glance at Ki, who tells him that it might be necessary to explain to his soldiers about the Kobolds and an old promise made by his father.

"It's a long story," Silvus nervously responds, making the Raptor Avalonia wardens and the Kolbold Shima officers exchange looks.

⸺◦⟨◉⟩◦⸺

The time has come. Both armies of Avalonian Raptor and Kobold march out of the fort, making thumping sounds echoing in the forest. The marching is so loud that Raptors in nearby hamlets cannot help but gaze with curiosity or fear. Silvus leads the two armies on his Carnotaur, northeast from the fort where Tricia is located.

When they approach the border gates not taken over by the rebels yet, they are greeted by an army of Raptors in guard militia uniform, wearing helmets with red feathers on top. They are the Creston militia forces.

The sight of them gives Silvus a hopeful smile, believing that they have agreed to join up with him. Even better, he sees that the militia is being led by a familiar golden Raptor wearing an artist's cap on his head while wearing very artistic steel armor. First-Delta Davinchio Nardo is riding on his Carnotaur in a fancy manner, with a big smile on his face, spotting Silvus in sight.

"Silvus, my dear friend. What a great pleasure to see you again!" Nardo greets him as the two armies get close to each other.

"Likewise, Nardo." Silvus scans around the Creston militia, noticing that the Beta-Lord is not present. "Where is your uncle? Is he not joining us?"

Nardo's expression changes from joy to sorrow. He closes his eyes, telling him, "As much as my uncle would love to aid you in this glorious war for saving my life, yet he caught such a dreadful fever. So he had me go on his stead."

A chuckle can be heard from Ico, earning an eye roll from Silvus. Probably he still thinks how much of a drama king Nardo is. Shaking it off, Silvus tells him, looking proud, "Well then, I assume the scout told you the details?"

"Oh yes he did! Is it really true that you yourself are the fabled lost heir of the mighty Ultamars?" Nardo asks with a shocked gasp. His puts on a face of utmost glee, beaming his eyes.

"It is true, First-Delta. Silvy here might as well be some prophesized hero that we did not know we need," Ocia, who is sitting behind Silvus, confirms, grabbing him into a hug, making the nearby soldiers make small laughs to themselves. Silvus does not mind, as he keeps his smile, staying focused for the task at claw.

"Then let this be like the heroes of old and be out to vanquish those fiends who have been terrorizing this mystical land for all these years." Nardo pounds a claw to his chest. The gates beside them begin to open, revealing a Kobold scouting party of four running up to them.

The Kobold scouting party approaches between Silvus and Ki and kneels to their king directly.

"Report, soldiers!" Ki demands to his scouts.

"The Raptors in orange are approaching a wooden city defended by those in purple," one Kobold scout says.

"The ones in purple seems to be very desperate, as they have lots of barricades set up with at least five catapults set up," another Kobold Scout adds.

Nardo scoffs as if what he heard meant nothing to him and brags, "Still using catapults? My fellow Raptors of Creston made this!" He points toward his troops and orders them to make way, showing them ten ballistas on wheels, one of the various inventions that the Avalonian Raptors of Creston like to take pride in.

Regardless, Silvus does not want to waste any time, so he has the entire army, now including Creston, move forward, approaching the border gates into the swamp.

———— ⬤ ————

The royal alliance marches farther into the swamp. So far, there has been no sighting of an enemy or two. No predator seems interested in attacking, since they are a massive force. Around the front lines, Ico gallops up next to Silvus looking uneasy.

"Hey Silvus…do you think my dad is still okay?"

"I hope so," Silvus replies, and noticing that his cousin is sweating out of nervousness, he asks, "Are you okay?"

"Yeah…kinda, because I just realized I never told my dad that I joined you!" Ico freaks out.

Silvus remembers, looking just as uneasy for his cousin. Knowing his uncle, he would probably get furious at Ico for running away.

"You mean you ran away!" Ocia butts in, surprised, earning a nod from Ico.

"Getting in trouble with your daddy, I hear?" The voice of Fi is heard. Ico turns his head around to see Fi looking smugly at him, riding with her brother Ki. Ico groans, turning his attention back in front.

Speaking of his uncle, Silvus cannot help think about him, his best friend Tritus, and also Sulphie and the unborn Raptors she is expecting. Being out of Tricia for so long, he can only pray to the spirits for their safety.

His thoughts are interrupted by sounds of familiar beating drums from a distance. Silvus orders the alliance to stop and listen. He looks to the east and commands all his soldiers to keep moving in caution. Following the sound, they find themselves greeted by a besieged port city of Atlantra.

The city itself is surrounded by barricades and catapults throwing fireballs at the invading rebels who are trying to swarm in. From the city of Atlantra, the Trician militia forces make their desperate charge and clash with the greater numbered rebels turning the beachside into an intense battlefeild.

Hidden by a wall of trees, Silvus uses a telescope to examine the battlefield. He is looking around hoping to see his uncle and Tritus still alive. So far, he cannot, making his heart beat fast. "Are you okay, your highness?" Leon asks, looking concerned.

Silvus lowers his telescope and replies, "I'm just worried for family," then gives the telescope to Leon so he can gallop in front of the alliance with the army leaders at the front lines. Sentinel Leon of the royal Avalonian army, King Ki Jin of the Shima Kobold army, Knight-Captain Gwynie of the Knights of the Mist present, and First-Delta Nardo of the Creston Militia are all mounted, standing proud, awaiting Silvus' word.

Silvus nods for Ocia to dismount and join up with the healers so she can be at a safe distance. With a few coughs, Silvus speaks.

"Raptors and Kobolds, today we are about to make history. It is true that we are going to fight the ones in orange, but they are not really the enemy. The true enemy is a group of Raptors called the Necromancers! Whoever they are, let this be a message that we will no longer stand by and let them destroy our way of life! As true as I say, right now we need to stop the misguided Monchesteons or else the Necromancers will win!"

Silvus draws his sword of Ultamar and points to the battlefield with the rebels and Tricians fighting.

"Raptors and Kobolds! ARE YOU READY?!"

Both Raptors and Kobolds draw their weapons and prepare the ballistas and catapults.

"SPIRIT WILLS IT!!!!!!"

The entire alliance begins to sprint out of the forest down the hillside in a stampede along the beachside. Weapons are raised, wheeled ballistas are pushed, and tame Tyrannos roar with all their might as they approach the first wave of rebels.

In the middle of the battlefield, both rebels and Tricians briefly stop, turning their gazes, surprised to see an army of Raptors and strange little Kobolds running toward them.

Silvus leads the charge, raising his sword, and twirls it like a wand, igniting electricity, and thrusts it at a group of rebels, making the first strike. Then he fires another at another group of rebels, earning cheers from the Tricians.

Getting close, Silvus orders his army to split in two. He, Ki, and Gwynie move to merge in with the Tricians to reinforce them and show that they are on their side. The other team being led by Leon and Nardo turns to the rear, flanking the rebels from behind. Nardo heavily uses his wheeled ballistas, mowing down a lot of rebels, while Leon leaps off his mount looking cool as he joins his troops, slicing through each rebel. One rebel is about to strike, only to be stopped by a halberd from Nidus.

By the front, Silvus fights in line with his troops, using his sword to strike down each rebel that gets dangerously close, while using a mix of lightning and frost spells to attack in range. He sees Ki and his Kobold troops fight with their curved longswords, mixing different fighting styles depending on what weapon a rebel wields. Thanks to their small size, it is difficult for the rebels to properly see them. Then he sees Gwynie fighting with her short sword, making fast swings at the correct areas. When a rebel attempts a leap, he gets shot by Ico's arrow, saving Gwynie.

Silvus continues to fight on and hears a pair of doors open from Atlantra. Turning his gaze, he sees Tritus wearing his armor, looking very happy, along with the rest of the Trician defenders with him. He raises his golden trident in the air and shouts, "NOW THAT IS WHAT YA CALL A WORTHY CREW! SPIRITS, YE WILL IT!"

Tritus thrusts his trident forward, rushing out of the city along with the rest of his own troops raising cutlasses, following suit with cries of glory. Seeing his best friend whole and well, with the exception of his eye patch, makes Silvus smile proud, and he quickly raises his sword before he returns back to fighting the rebels. Tritus rushes to his side now, fighting side by side, pushing the rebels deeper to the other royal team who are fighting from behind.

Sandwicged, the rebels begin to get overwhelmed, showing signs of demoralization as they lose even more of their troops. The commander leading the rebel troops scans around and spots Silvus getting closer to him, slicing and blasting through. Then he turns around to see the enemy from the rear getting closer. Knowing that he is going to lose, he shouts, "STOP! WE SURRENDER!"

Both sides stop fighting. The remaining rebel troops drop their weapons, going onto their knees with their claws behind their backs. Silvus walks up toward the rebel commander, telling him that he accepts their surrender, earning cheers from both his troops and the Tricians, earning them their long- awaited victory.

Silvus turns around to see Tritus walking up to him with a jolly smile and pats him on the back. "About time you join this fight! Me and my crew were about to get crushed like the legendary Kraken."

Silvus shares a laugh with Tritus on his pirate-like comments. He looks around to see Ico speaking with Gwynie. Gwynie seems to be proud of his cousin for saving her life. That is, until he finally spots his uncle Orezyme wearing his old Knight of the Mist armor, storming up to Ico and looking very angry.

Ico turns around with a gulp, knowing that he is in big trouble. Gwynie backs away, not wanting to get involved.

Approaching Ico, Orezyme furiously slaps him in the face at least ten times. "WHERE HAVE YOU BEEN?! Your sister and I have been worried sick, believing that you were killed by bandits or worse!"

Ico does not moan or complain. Instead, he puts on a guilty face, knowing that he deserves it for running away with Silvus.

"I wanted to show that I could grow up, Dad. I know what I did was wrong to run like that, but I just…want to finally make you proud." Ico closes his eyes looking down.

Orezyme wants to give him another slap, but he notices the armor Ico is wearing, looking surprised. "Son…did you join the Knights of the Mist?"

"I thought by joining it could help me learn to be more mature, and they did." Ico perks up.

"He is right, Sir Orezyme," Gwynie joins in, confirming Ico's experience. "He proved himself to be a very capable member of our order."

"Is he?" Orezyme scratches his chin. "I'll speak of your punishment later, but right now, where's Silvus?!"

Hearing that he is asksing for him, Silvus tells Tritus to wait so he can approach his uncle. Passing through the cheering guards, he gets his uncle's attention with a few coughs. Orezyme turns around to see Silvus wearing the royal armor with smile.

"Nephew! You made it alive!" Orezyme runs up, embracing him into a quick hug. Breaking the hug, Orezyme looks around hoping to find a particular Raptor. Looking concerned, he asks, "Where is your mother?"

Silvus turns his expression from joy to sadness. He looks down at the ground with a tear coming down from his eye.

"Silvus?" Orezyme looks at his only nephew, worried.

Silvus looks back up still with a face of mild sadness, telling his uncle, "Mother is in a better place."

Chapter 27
The Battle of Maglo

Following the victory of Atlantra with the sun still shining bright, the royal alliance sets up camp in front of the city across the beach side. While most train or keep watch, skirmish parties are set up to be carefully coordinated into the swamp to liberate the nearby settlements from rebel influence. Most skirmish parties consist of mainly royal army troops, assisted by militia and Kobold allies. The Monchester rebels who were captured are being held in POW cages guarded by royal army guards. The rebels sit around looking upset that they lost. All they can do is wait for whatever punishment awaits them. As the royal alliance awaits the next move, Silvus requests to meet with his family in private in Castle Atlantra.

⊷⊷⧉⊷⊷

Inside the living room filled with ocean-themed decorations, located at the second floor of the castle, Silvus sits with his maternal family, consisting of only his uncle Orezyme, his two cousins Sulphie and Ico, and cousin in law Tritus. He tells his family what has happened throughout his journey, leading to how his mother Silviera passed away. Sulphie is breaking into tears while the boys give sympathies, except for Orezyme, who gets off the couch, walking up to a nearby fireplace.

Silvus can hear his uncle breaking into tears, muttering to himself that it is his fault for holding back his nephew. He wipes off his tears with his scarf and asks in a sobbing voice, "Before she died... did she say anything?"

Without looking at his uncle, Silvus closes his eyes with his face looking at the purple carpet.

"She made me promise to save Avalonia, or else Crestetia will fall into darkness." Silvus looks up at the ceiling, directly at the chandelier giving the room light. "Also, she finally told me that my father is the Alpha-King, the whole time making me the heir to Alpha-King's throne."

"SAY WHAT?!" Sulphie shrieks, while Tritus spits out his rum at the news. Ico laughs, mostly at his sister, remembering his own reaction upon finding out.

Orezyme does not react. Except he only continues to stand in front of the fireplace, no longer in tears, and says, "I know."

"You knew?!" Silvus perks up, looking surprised. Aside from Arkus, he cannot believe that his uncle knew as well.

"Yes, Silvus," Orezyme turns his head halfway, looking at Silvus with one eye. "I knew who your father was. When I was young, before joining up with the knights, your mother would talk non-stop about your father. A week later, after your father died during the celebration of Third Avalonia's birth, your mother would not leave her room. When she finally left the room, your grandparents and I were all shocked to learn that she was with egg by an unknown father. I asked who the father was, but she refused to answer. Yet I suspected it was Sulthur. Your mother never really had any other friends close to her."

Orezyme turns around fully, looking at Silvus with a serious look. He wipes off a tear from his face and tells him, "Enough of that. Your mother would never want us to sit around and mourn forever. If her dying wish is for you to save Avalonia, then I will be honored to aid you the best I can. I owe her that much."

Orezyme makes a small bow. Silvus guesses that his uncle still believes himself to be guilty for holding Silvus back for the sake of his own family. At least he is willing to take responsibility by helping him. A coughing sound is heard from Tritus, earning Silvus' attention.

"I don't mean to intrude but I have to say, yer life is filled with surprises." Tritus sips more of his rum. "Discovering a hidden society, fighting dark Mistcasters, finding out you're the Alpha-Prince, and now ya have yer own army?! Hahaha! You must be some kind of prophesied hero er somethin'?"

"I don't think I'm this prophesied hero thing. I am just a young Raptor who wants this kingdom to get back to normal. Whatever it takes." Silvus takes out his mother's locket, showing it to his family. "I still made a promise to my mother before she died. And I will fulfill it!"

"Your mother used to tell me that you sound just like your father," Orezyme adds with a smile, sitting back down on a nearby couch next to Ico.

"As happy as I am for saving us and my crazy husband trying to make me a widow," Sulphie jabs an elbow at Tritus, making him flinch and grunt in annoyance, "What you are going to do next?"

Silvus gets up from his seat and answers her with a voice of enthusiasm, "I say once I get news that Tricia is completely liberated, we are going to take back Maglo next!"

He makes an arm pump to look heroic, earning playful laughs from both Tritus and Sulphie while Ico smiles, turning his head side to side, and Orezyme looks at his nephew with a smile, knowing he is right. Taking back Maglo is the next priority, yet one more question remains.

"As much as I admire your enthusiasm, Nephew, don't you think your troops should rest up? I believe there were some wounded?"

Orezyme is right about that. Silvus remembers that there are some wounded troops being tended by healers. Then he thinks about another opportunity before taking back Maglo. He looks to his uncle and asks, "Do you know your way around Sherrasic?"

"Why, yes, I do. I am married to a Raptor living in Sherrasic right now—why?"

"To think of it, in order to take down the rest of the rebellion in this state, I am hoping you could make the journey to Sherrasic and request their aid. Their skill in archery can be useful!"

Silvus sees his uncle smile and get up from his couch, telling him that he would love to do so. He did say he would aid him the best he could, to honor his mother. Ico volunteers to go with his father, as he wants to see his mother, Oria. Sulphie, however, states that as much as she wants to go with them, she is still expecting eggs that are still in her belly and the journey could be dangerous.

So as agreed, Orezyme and Ico head off to Sherrasic with some knights following along. Fi is also seen riding with Ico, who also volunteered, in order not only to be with Ico, but also to meet his mother, having lots of questions of her own—probably something to do with the blood relations.

Silvus hosts a meeting with his allies in the Atlantra war room to pass some time waiting for his uncle to return. Compared to Gallagar, Atlantra's looks more like a pirate captain's cabin, with more seaside décor and a flag of Tricia hanging. The meeting is mostly about skirmish updates, status of the army, and a plan to liberate Maglo. The meeting is cut short by the sound of fast knocking on the wooden door gaing all the attention of all the Raptors and Ko-bolds in the room.

"Come in?" Silvus orders with a questioning look, wondering what the commontion is.

The door opens, revealing a very eager Ocia rushing in with a very happy face. She scans around the room very fast until she lands her wide-open eyes on Silvus.

"By the spirits, Silvus! You gotta come with me! We've got guests!" Ocia runs up to Silvus, grabs him by the claw, and drags him out of the war room, leaving dumbfounded members of the royal alliance wondering what happened.

Ocia drags Silvus all the way up on the ridges of the main gates, crowded by guards with their bows and arrows drawn. In the middle, Ocia shows Silvus what she saw by pointing a claw forward. He looks down below, scanning through the allied soldiers gathered around the barricades upwards all the way to a group of Raptors of fifty, wearing Monchester colors, except they have black paint covering half.

Among the crowd an armored male carrying a claymore on his back and not wearing his helmet steps up, presumably in charge. His scale color looks like Ocia's and Targon's except his eye and feather color are yellow. His mane is brushed in a spiky back position. The leading male takes a deep breath and shouts, "ARE YOU THE ONE WHO DEFEATED THE REBELS HERE?"

"INDEED I AM! WHO ARE YOU AND WHAT IS YOUR BUSINESS HERE?" Silvus shouts back with both his claws to his snout.

"I AM ANVAR BUCK! I HAVE COME HERE TO JOIN YOUR ALLIANCE!"

Silvus is about to ask why he should trust him until he hears Ocia gasp beside him.

"Oh my goodness! Silvus, he is my cousin! He's one of the few Raptors who spoke out against my brother." She pauses, and her expression becomes guilty. "Which is before I learned of my brother's treachery."

If Ocia could trust this Buck, then he would, too. He needs all the help he can get. So Silvus orders the guards to let them through. With the troops moving out of the way, the main gates open, allowing the leading male named Buck, who tells his troops to stay with the allied troops and mingle while he walks into the city as Silvus and Ocia climb down the ridge.

Silvus sees Ocia run past him very fast and embrace her cousin into a big hug, like a hatchling and parent reuniting with each other. He can tell they missed each other by seeing a tear or two that falls from both their faces. A smile forms on his face watching the two cousins continue to have their warm moment—an experience he had hoped for when reuniting with his mother.

"Cousin Ocia...I am so glad to see you again!" Buck says with a heartfelt voice. Hearing his voice, Silvus guesses he is at least one or two winters younger than himself.

"Me too, Buck." Ocia pulls back from her cousin. "I am even gladder to see that not all my family are closed-minded."

Buck chuckles in response and ruffles his cousin's long feathered mane and jokes, "Actually I thought you were closed-minded when you defended your brother when Mother and I tried to warn you."

The mention of Buck's mother perks up Ocia, making her turn to the side, looking around the Monchesteons he brought, speaking with the allied troops for a particular Raptor. "Where is Auntie Doe?"

Buck's expression turns sour at the question. He looks down at the ground, causing Ocia to worry. Buck looks up, still looking sour, and tells her, "She stayed behind."

"What do you mean, stayed behind? Did something happen at Monchester? Particularly Rookingrad?" Silvus butts in, wanting to know more about the supposed Anvar ally.

Buck and Ocia turn their gazes to Silvus. Buck walks up to him and greets him, "You must be Silvus? The supposed Alpha-Prince I overheard your troops speaking about?"

"Indeed I am." Silvus briefly shakes Buck's claw. "What about you explain as we walk back to the castle. I was actually in the middle of preparing to take back Maglo from…"

"Rebel claws," Buck finishes for Silvus sternly. Whatever happened between him and Targon must have been personal. "And yeah, I will be happy to explain, and I must warn you both, it is a very long and painful story."

The tone of Buck's voice hints at something tragic. Wasting no time, Silvus escorts the two Anvar cousins through the streets. Along the way, Buck tells them that the ongoing war is beginning to take its toll on the Betadom. Food is becoming scarce, causing hunger riots due to heavy distribution. Working conditions at both the smithies and the mines are getting more dangerous, causing workers themselves to strike. And now complaints are being made that Dark Mistcasters are kidnapping their own to perform horrific experiments. When any of the issues were addressed, Targon would instantly execute them and brand them as traitors, causing Ocia to gasp in horror.

"What about Auntie Doe? As the steward and member of the Anvar clan, she must have spoken up to him?"

"She did, causing a deeper rift between Targon and her. Mother tried to convince him that this war is going too far, but he…assaulted her, threatening her to never tell him what to do."

Buck tightens his fists, growling, as his tail begins to shake. The three stop in the middle of the castle courtyard as Buck continues his story. "Not standing his leadership anymore, my mother tried to organize a coup to remove him as Beta-Lord, but Targon has so many spies. My mother and many of her associates got arrested, except for me and the troops I brought."

"And how did you escape?" Silvus asks.

"And after Auntie Doe was captured?" Ocia asks after.

Buck closes his eyes, turning around, making a few steps toward the main keep and answers, "I don't know what exactly happened to Mother, but the last time saw I her was when she ordered me and the men to escape through a secret tunnel to buy us time. Since then, we have been trying to find help from the royal army, only to see you leading them with a strange group of small creatures. In case you saw us as enemies, we followed you at a distance, which is how we witnessed your victory."

Buck finishes looking very hopeful.

"Well then. One, the strange creatures you mentioned are called Kobolds, and they are helping us stop Targon. And two, this war is really about stopping Bylark. Targon is just a puppet for his own gains," Silvus states with his arms crossed.

"Bylark? You mean that manipulating Dark Mistcaster! Mom and I suspected he is the one who twisted Targon's mind!" Buck speaks out in anger. Ocia puts a claw on his shoulder, calming him down.

"You are correct, Cousin. Bylark is the one who managed to fool not only my brother, but many other Raptors who follow him."

Silvus walks up closer to Buck, who is an inch shorter, and tells him, "What about we meet up with the others in the war room? They are going to want to meet you."

Buck nods in agreement with a determined frown. So Silvus leads the cousins into the castle to meet with the others.

≈•((◉))•≈

Stopping by a pair of large doors in the wooden hallway, Silvus has the Anvar cousins stop for a moment. When Buck asks why, Silvus turns around and tells him, "I better get in first; they might think you're a rebel spy, so they might attack you."

Buck is about to protest, but Ocia convinces him otherwise. With a hesitant nod, Buck allows Silvus to enter the war room first.

Every Raptor and Kobold is seen talking among themselves in the room. Leon and Ki are talking about war stuff, both being soldier boys. Tritus butts in, between joining into the conversation discussing his own stories of his hunting adventures. Nardo tries to flirt with Gwynie, but she tells him that she already has a husband and two daughters, making the former flinch in embarrassment. Silvus calls them out, gaining their attention.

"Your Highness! About time you came back; we almost thought you went out to get married to that girl," Gwynie jokes, as all eyes go to Silvus.

"No, I did not. But I want you all to have open minds, as we have a new questionable ally you all must meet."

"What do ya mean, questionable?" Tritus raises his brow at Silvus.

Silvus opens up the door slowly and motions for Buck to come in. Seeing that he is wearing a Monchester-colored cape, both Raptors and Kobolds almost rush to draw their weapons, only for Silvus to raise his claw, telling them to halt.

"Bro, what is the meaning of this?" Leon demands, sounding overprotective. Perhaps he has been very overprotective ever since he almost lost his brother.

Keeping his cool, Silvus replies, "Every Raptor and Kobold, this is Anvar Buck. He is a defector from Monchester. He wishes to join us."

"And how do ya know he won't be one of them back-stabbing crew members?!" Tritus questions, folding his arms.

Buck steps up and answers, looking defensive, "Because my mother and I tried to overthrow him but we failed."

"So you and your mother tried a coup? How did it ever so dreadfully fail?" Nardo asks, scratching his chin.

"And you mentioned you are an Anvar? Are you related to the enemy leader?" Ki follows, keeping his green eyes on him squinted in suspicion.

Buck looks to Nardo to answer him first.

"We did, but there were so many spies. Many of us got arrested yet some of us managed to escape." Buck turns his head to Ki. "To answer you, I am the son of Anvar Doe, younger sister of Targon's father and steward, which makes Targon and Ocia my first cousins."

All Raptors and Kobolds in the room gasp. Tritus gets up and blurts out with a jab of his talon, "Ha! So you are Targon's kin, which means you might be a back-stabbing spy!"

"Did I not mention that my mother and I tried overthrow him?! And also, not all Monchesteons are against the Mistatorium! A lot of Raptors back home are starting to up rise against him, for crying out loud!" Buck shouts back defensively, like an angry teen, which is natural for his age.

"Oh boy," Silvus mutters to himself with a face palm. He better convince his allies that Buck is friendly before things get ugly. So he tells them to give Buck a chance, reminding them that Ocia, a Monchester native herself, helped him escape. He even tells them to use Buck as an opportunity to win hearts and minds when they head to Monchester itself. Skeptical at first, they eventually agree to let Buck help, but they will be watching him.

⸺∘《◉》∘⸺

For the rest of the day, Silvus takes his time training his skills in order to prepare. First he spars with his friends, especially Leon and Nidus, to practice more with his sword skills. Then he goes to pair of practice dummies, where he demonstrates his offensive spells, like his favorite, the lightning shock, to zap five dummies with one claw. Sometimes he would go to a quiet place like the library to meditate on all the spells he knows.

Eventually news of Orezyme's return with reinforcements from Sherrasic is heard by Silvus' hidden ear. From the castle balcony, Silvus spots his uncle bringing in Sherrasic militia, led by their Beta-Lady. He smiles at the sight, knowing he is prepared for the battle ahead.

In the middle of the night with skies filled with stars and a full moon shining bright above the forest of Maglo, the beautiful city of Athera is being heavily patrolled by rebel occupiers. Lots of rebel guards keep eyes out along the wall ridge due to hearing the news that their army is defeated in Tricia. In response, their Beta has ordered a heavy presence to prepare for a possible counter attack. The only setback is the difficulty of watching into the large forest eastward, due to the darkness of night. It is the only place they suspected where the rumored royal alliance is going to attack.

A swarm of objects glowing orange is seen flying up out of the tall trees. With a closer look, they all seem to be flying toward them, revealing that they are firebombs. One the rebels guard shouts, "LOOK OUT!" too late as the first barrage of firebombs collides on the ridges, blowing up the nearby troops.

The sound of marching feet is heard inside the forest. Coming out is a massive legion of the royal army leading their allies with large tower shields up, giant pikes raised, and flags of Avalonia hanging. A battering ram is seen in the middle being pushed toward the wall. The rebels fire arrows, hoping to stop their advance, but the royal army ground forces carry ladders nearby and manage to get close and raise them up. A royal army soldier leaps off from one of the ladders with a claymore, taking out a nearby rebel, making a war screech followed by another.

With the ladders latched onto the top ridges, the royal army and their allies quickly climb up to take out the defending rebel archers who are trying to stop the battering ram from getting close. From the south, a horde of rebel forces attempts to reach the city to assist, only to be flanked by a barrage of arrows flying out of the forest nearby. Out of the same place Shima, Tricia, and Sherrasic forces swarm out being led by King Ki, Beta-Lord Tritus, and Crova Zira, the Beta-Lady of Sherrasic. They all lead the charge with the backing of the remaining royal army troops led by Nidus, in order to flank the extra rebel troops to ensure that the main royal army can breach the city behind.

More royal army troops flood up to the ridges, taking out the defenders. This allows the battering ram to reach its destination. The troops operating it turn the lever, raising the ram back far, and releases it to pound the wall with a massive force at least three times. With the fourth time, the wall finally shatters, allowing the royal army to rush in. With the city breached and the extra rebels taken care of, the allied army focuses its attention on the city, as the Creston and Monchester defector forces join in the battle. The royal alliance floods into the city, taking out nearby rebel guards, and Silvus is seen hopping in alongside Leon; Nardo, who is wielding a crescent-style halberd; Buck, who wields a claymore; and Orezyme, who is wearing his old Knights of the Mist armor, wielding his Mist spear.

Silvus looks around to see that they are in the Omega district. He can tell by the lower-class wooden buildings clumped together.

"THE ENEMY BREACHED IN!" Silvus hears a pair of rebel troops retreating into another district. But that is not his target. As more troops run past him through the hole, he turns his head northward to gaze upon the towering cathedral-like building in the distance: Castle Athera, his old home.

Whoever took his mother's place must answer for siding with the rebels during the invasion. Silvus turns to his companions to give them orders.

"Uncle, you lead some troops to reclaim the Delta and Monastery districts. Leon, you used to know your way around the Omega and Market Districts, so you are in charge of that. Nardo, you will be in charge of guarding this position for the others and telling them that Tritus and Zira are to join Orezyme while Ki and Nidus are to join Leon. I will storm the castle with Buck and some troops, got it?!"

All heads nod. Silvus looks to Buck, who in turn looks eager. He motions for Buck to follow, along with at least five hundred of the royal army troops and other Monchester defectors who are now at least one hundred, due to those who were prisoners being convinced to join up.

⸺◈⸺

Silvus and his allies fight all the way to the castle district to find it guarded by more rebels, forcing them to fight through. The royal-defector troops distract the rebels guarding the castle courtyard, engaging them in battle. This allows Silvus and Buck to slip by to the castle entrance door. Silvus slowly opens up, taking a peek to see the entrance hall is empty, suspecting a trap. He turns to Buck and orders, "Help the men fight off the rebels while I scout ahead. I don't want us to land in an ambush."

"YOU CRAZY! What if something happens to you?" Buck protests.

Silvus does not know what to say, honestly. Instead, he tells Buck to simply trust him. Buck looks hesitant, not wanting Silvus to head into a trap. So he trusts him and decides to run off to help the troops as ordered. Silvus runs into the castle empty as expected. While the sounds of war are still heard from the outside, Silvus proceeds to keep his guard up, running through the hall all the way to main throne room doors. He suspects the pretender might be waiting for him. He uses his gravity Mist power to slowly open the pair of doors to see the throne room with the wellspring in sight. Silvus slowly walks into the candlelit room to see the Beta him or herself. Turns out the pretender is a Beta-Lady, a plump- looking she-Raptor with yellow scales, red eyes, and long red mane and tail. She is wearing the Beta-Lady cloak and silver crown, staring at him shivering in fear.

"S-S-Silvus?! I am surprised that you are the one who leading this invasion?" the pretender stammers with a cheeky smile, looking at him in fear. Silvus knows who she is. He stares at her, looking somewhat surprised and confused. Of all the nobility within Maglo, they chose her? True, she was never a friend of Clan Vessel, but she is part of a very unpopular clan. Not to mention she used to be very spoiled and cared for nothing but fancy jewelry.

"Bula Jezza? They picked you?"

"Well…they were very desperate for a new Beta in charge, so I stepped up. I'm here as long as I do as they say." Jezza shrugs until another voice calls out behind Silvus with a sound of a sword being drawn.

"And you are going to step away from her."

Silvus turns his around to see a familiar light-blue-scaled male Raptor with long white mane and tail tip, wearing steel chest armor and an orange cape. He looks at Silvus with a stern expression with his dark-green eyes. Silvus gasps at the sight of him.

"Posious?! You are one of the rebels?"

Posious, as Silvus calls him, used to be his mother's bodyguard as part of Raptor tradition for the nobility to have a bodyguard of opposite gender. Posious begins to circle around him while Jezza runs behind the throne like a coward fearing for her life.

"That's right. I betrayed your mother for something better."

"Guess that's why you were absent before the invasion," Silvus assumes, beginning to circle along. "Why did you do this?"

"When I first laid eyes on your mother, I thought she was the most beautiful thing ever. I tried to talk to her, but she refused to even acknowledge me! I thought being a bodyguard would allow me to get close, only to have my heart shattered when she told me that she was with another male! All that changed when the rebels took over. But now you have returned to ruin everything!"

"You don't have to do this, Posious," Silvus tries to plead but the heartsick male will not listen. Instead he raises his sword with a screech, running at him, forcing him to fight.

While Silvus and Posious clash swords, Jezza peeks out, rooting for Posious to defeat Silvus so she can stay in power. Posious uses one of his feet to push Silvus to crash into nearby mannequin in armor. He tries to get up, but Posious has him pinned and is about to make another strike to finish him off until Jezza shouts, "WATCH OUT!"

A claymore comes out of nowhere, slicing off Posious's claw, disarming him. Screaming in pain, he gets off Silvus and lands on his knees, holding onto his cut wound. In rage, Posious looks to his right to see Buck witih the claymore covered in his blood. "YOU ARE SO DEAD!" Posious rants, only to be yoinked by the tail. Silvus is using a gravity spell, levitating him up in mid air with one claw.

Silvus uses his one claw to spin Posious around very fast and slams him onto the ground in front of Jezza, who screams behind the throne. With the crazy bodyguard out cold, Silvus gets up, recovering a lot of Mist quickly, thanks to the presence of the wellspring. He turns his gaze around to see Buck with a smile giving him a thumbs-up.

"I owe you one!"

"Anything for a special friend of Ocia," Buck replies, sheathing his sword on his back.

Sounds of footsteps are heard coming into the throne room to see all members of the royal alliance, led by Orezyme with a smile on his face. "Good news, Nephew! With the help of eager civilians, the city is all ours!"

The troops behind all raise their weapons, screeching in cheer as Silvus smiles at the sight. He turns his attention to see Jezza still hiding behind the throne with her unconscious bodyguard still lying in front. Silvus orders some of the troops to apprehend them to the dungeons to await judgment. As ordered, the troops rush in to take Jezza, who struggles and begs to be released along with the bodyguard. Silvus walks up to the throne looking up at the wellspring of Maglo. He smiles, shedding a small tear coming down from his right eye and whispers, "I'm back home, Mother."

Chapter 28
Cretacian Hearts Bloom

Athera is finally free from rebel control. The royal alliance wastes no time in making skirmish parties to wipe out remaining rebel influence in Maglo, just as they did in Tricia. Massive repairs are being done for the city, like fixing the eastern wall where the battering ram made its hole. Lots of Raptors who live in Athera express their gratitude to their liberators. Many tell them stories of their families being dragged out by Dark Mistcasters while the rebels acted like thugs, while resources were getting scarce due to having no control. To organize the efforts, Silvus places many of his allies in charge, with Orezyme as the head and acting Beta-Lord of Maglo.

———⋘◉⋙———

Silvus finds himself walking through the private quarters hall of his old castle. Since the return, he has been walking around the castle to catch some memories. He stops by his own private quarters to see it surprisingly still intact. Closing the door, he decides to walk to another door leading to his mother's old quarters, hoping Jezza did not mess up anything.

His mother's old quarters. The same place his mother took him before his escape. Thank the spirits it is not out of place. Silvus searches around the wizard-style room, hoping to find something his mother left behind. He searches through a bookshelf and he spots what looks a rusty old diary. Since his mother is gone, he hopes she will not mind if he reads it. Taking the diary, the young Raptor walks up to the king-sized bed to sit where he can read.

He opens up the diary, reading through the pages which are most-ly about his mother's hatchlinghood. Her favorite books, places, and being giddy with new spells—yet she learns nothing about friends, being anti-social as Arkus described her. The closest thing the diary mentions about other Raptors are her family, like his grandfather having her sent to Arkus for private tutoring. Eventually the diary begins to talk about his mother's experience with his father, Sulthur, starting with her arrival in Patalot chapter of Monastery. The diary reads:

Winter's Birth 23, 1424

Today is my first day of private tutelage with Arkus, the arch-sage himself! I overheard many Raptors telling me that he is very nice and funny. It is hard for me to believe that an arch-sage, the head of the Mistatorium and second to the Alpha-King, would poses such a manner. When I finally arrived at the main campus in Patalot, there he was. Arch-Sage Pendra Arkus. I thought he would be one of those strict teachers who would harshly scold you, yet he had a friendly aura around him. He made a playful laugh and told me not to be afraid.

The other students are both boy Raptors. One is silver and the other is chocolate brown. The silver one seems to be very eccentric and always loves to look proud. He was the first one to see me, looking very happy, and he walked up hoping to greet me. When he told me his name was Ultamar Sulthur, I got even more nervous that my fellow student is the

Alpha-Prince himself. Yet he has this sense of chivalry, to the point that he respected personal space and offered if I ever needed help. I ease up a bit sensing a large amount of light inside of him, which means he is okay.

The other one, Bylark he calls himself, did not seem interested in me at all. But I could sense a rising darkness inside of him. All he cared about is trying to be a good Mistcaster.

The first six pages are mostly about Silvus' mother being a student under Arkus's tutelage. As he reads on, he begins to read that his mother is starting to talk more about his father. That gets him interested. Looking around to make sure he is still alone, he reads on.

Winter's ReBirth 10, 1425

Throughout my time as a private Student, Sulfy has been such a good help! I know I might be repeating myself, but he always seems to enjoy spending time with me, studying together. The more I spend time with him, I'm starting to feel this weird feeling in my chest when I am around him. One time he invited me to his palace, and by the spirits, it is so enchanting! He even introduced me to his father Alpha-King Sylvain III, who seems to be kind of ill. The poor male must be very old.

During my stay, Sulfy really wants to teach me how to make friends, as he introduced me to some of his own like Pendra Gwynie, a Knight of the Mist and Arkus' daughter!

"Gwynie knew my mom and dad?!" Silvus thought out loud. He is surprised that Gwynie, the knight he had traveled to Fort Gallagar with, knew his parents the whole time. Maybe after the war is over, he can ask her a few things. He continues to read through the diary until he comes across a hanging Crystal key on the page where his father has just proposed to his mother.

He picks up the key, taking a closer look at it. The key itself looks very regal and nicely carved. Silvus looks around the room, hoping to find a chest or something that the key might open. Next to the wall right by a window to the bed's left, he sees a large wardrobe-like shelf with strange runes on it. Getting off the bed, he approaches the wardrobe and uses the key to open it up to reveal a caster's staff, nicely preserved.

Looking at it with awe, Silvus takes the staff by the metal handle for a closer look. The wood of the staff is colored navy blue. A large crystal Mist Orb is placed on top, where Mist casting is performed. Looking below, he sees a long Mythril blade attached to it. Whoever forged the staff must be clever enough to divide it between the metal handle, or else Mist casting would be impossible. It is not just any staff. According to the legend, this particular staff that Silvus is gazing at was carved from the branches of the wellspring. "The staff of Maglo," Silvus says to the staff.

Out of nowhere, a knocking sound is heard, snapping him back in reality. "Who is it?!" Silvus calls out.

"It's me, Ocia! May I come in?" the voice calls back.

Ocia! What is she doing here? Silvus think to himself as he gently puts the staff away into the wardrobe. He could have sworn he sent her back in Tricia to be safe. Then he walks up to the door and opens it up, and he gets tackled into a hug by a tearful Ocia.

"Oh, Silvy! I was so worried for you!" The she-Raptor buries her head into his chest.

Silvus gently pushes her away to look into her eyes with a smile and asks with his brow raised, "How and why did you come here?"

"Buck came to me and escorted me back here. He told me that you guys finally took back Maglo," she replies back with light in her eyes.

So Buck went back to Tricia and brought her here? Silvus guesses as Ocia stands in front looking at him with a smile until she gasps, looking around the bedroom behind him.

"Is this...?" she guesses as Silvus lets her in. She must be enjoying the wizardly aesthetic room, which is a scholar's paradise. He finds it cute to watch her look around the place. Silvus tells her that they are in his mother's old room, which belonged to all Beta-Lords in the past. He even shows her three nice bookshelves placed around one corner, knowing she will smile at the sight of it. Speaking of books, Ocia takes notice of one particular book that Silvus is holding, so she asks him what it is and points at it. Silvus turns around, wondering what she means, until he sees that he is still holding his mother's diary.

"Oh, this? This is my mother's old diary. I was reading it to find some answers, like why my parents kept their marriage a secret."

"You were reading about your mother and father? Can I read it with you, please?" Ocia puts her claws together looking at him with puppy eyes, and her tail is beginning to wag side to side. Silvus looks at her, a bit hesitant. For what she has been through with him, maybe she earned it. With a smile, he leads her to the bed and they sit together; he reads her the rest of the diary.

Reading the entire diary, Ocia seems to be enjoying the romance parts between his parents, by the way she tears up with a smile. Silvus guesses that it could be a female thing, making him silently chuckle at the thought. He continues to read the diary with her, all the way to the part where he believes there might be the answer. It reads:

Spring's Seeding 11, 1426

Since our special night after our secret wedding with my mentor being the witness, even for so long, I still could not fathom the idea of being married to the now Alpha-King Sulthur. However, I began to feel strange around my belly. I thought at first it was a simple tummy ache. As time went by, I began to see my tummy rounding for each passing day. I went to the castle healer and have confirmed that I am with egg!

By the spirits, I am going to be a mother! At that moment I was going to tell my secret husband about it. Maybe it could convince him to finally reveal our marriage to the public as I always tried to convince him. I mean I myself never understood why he wants our marriage to be a secret. I always assumed it has to do with Bylark. He tells me that there is dark presence growing around the kingdom and he simply wants to keep me safe.

Spring's Seeding 17, 1426

By the spirits! I have never been so heartbroken in all my life! The love of my life, Sulthur, just died during the Rebirth celebration. I don't know what to do! It breaks my heart that my unborn hatchling will never know who his or her father is. It is even worse that my love would never get a chance to see our hatchling grow up!

Ocia is beginning to cry at this part. Silvus feels himself saddened as he continues to read further. He is also at the same time frustrated by the fact he only learned half the answer that he is looking for. All he got is the simple "to protect his mother" statement, like what Arkus told him. Not bearing any more, he decides to close the diary, earning a disappointing aww from Ocia who is actually enjoying it. Looking depressed, Silvus gets off the bed and walks toward the window, leaving a concerned Ocia, who just watches him look out. Silvus leans to the side to gaze up upon the stars, revealing that it is nigh fall. Looking at the stars with his arms crossed on the edge, he gazes with a heavy heart in his chest. Remembering the old story his mother once told him, he whispers, "Are you up there, Mother? Is Father with you?"

"You still miss her, do you?" he hears Ocia ask him as he hears her coming toward him. Silvus only nods, keeping his eyes glued to the stars above. More tears come out of his face. Ocia gently uses her talon to wipe one of his tears away. After a long pause, Silvus finally speaks.

"Losing my mother is just so hard, you know." Silvus takes a deep breath and wipes off his own tears. "The best I can do is just gaze at the stars, hoping my mother is up there with my father."

"Do you think my mom and dad are up there too?" Ocia asks him as she begins to hold his claw and nuzzles his neck. The mention of Ocia's parents makes Silvus wonder. He remembers her telling him that she was raised only by her father. He guides her back to the bed.

He asks her, "So you have no idea what your mom is like?"

"Well," Ocia falls into thought. "My father used to tell me that I am more like my mother."

"Really?"

"Oh yes, he tells me that my mother loved history as much as I do. Guess that could be due to the fact my mother is from Maglo."

"Your mother is from Maglo?!" Silvus perks up, surprised. No wonder that Ocia is such an intellectual sweetheart.

"That's right, at the time my father visited Maglo, he met my mother in a nearby settlement. Perhaps she is actually a daughter of a Delta-Lord of the settlement. Daddy used to tell me that my mom loved to lecture him about history stuff." She giggles to herself. "Makes me wonder how Targon felt when Mom did the same."

Silvus sees her expression turn sour at the mention of Targon. She faces him and asks, "Do you think there is any hope for him to see reason?"

The poor girl seems to be conflicted. Despite what happened, deep down Ocia still cares for her brother. She cares so much that she hopes to redeem him somehow. In response, Silvus wraps his arm around her to give her some comfort. He struggles for the right words to cheer her up. When he first saw Targon, he seemed set with his ambition to reunite Avalonia under his rule, yet misguided. In the end this whole war was not completely Targon's fault, as he is simply a puppet to Bylark, who wants revenge against the kingdom on behalf of the mysterious Necromancers.

Come to think of it, he remembers Ocia's testimony about Targon's change when losing his father. He wonders if Targon is being more motivated by grief, wanting to be a great Beta-Lord just like his father. In thought, Silvus begins to wonder if he himself is at risk of ending up like Targon. Like him, they both lost their precious parent, motivating them to do what they do: uniting Avalonia with the purpose of getting things back to normal yet in two different paths. Targon is following a Dark Mistcaster as he himself continues to be faithful to the Mistatorium. Silvus turns his head to Ocia and asks, "What do you think? He is your brother, after all."

Ocia takes a small breath, turning her gaze to the alchemy garden, admiring the beautiful flowers.

"I believe my brother is only doing this because he believes has no choice. He truly believes that he is helping Raptors." Ocia turns her gaze back to Silvus. "Yet now he is being used by Bylark for his own gains."

Ocia is beginning to cry. Thinking of the fate of her brother must be very heartbreaking for her. By instinct, Silvus grabs her into a hug and strokes her mane softly, letting her tears flow down on his chest.

After a long pause, Silvus gently moves her face to his eyes and tells her, "You and I both know that your brother had committed atrocities in the kingdom, yet his heart is in the right place." Silvus closes his eyes briefly and opens them again and continues, "Bylark is the one to blame for twisting his mind, so I will promise you if given the chance, I will spare him when possible."

"Really?" Ocia's face begins to form a small smile, still with her sad eyes.

Instead of words for an answer, Silvus moves in and kisses her on the lips. He feels his heart beating fast in his chest. The female with him does not fight it, yet she welcomes it. Kissing back, she gently moves her arms around his neck. Their tails begin to intertwine, wrapping each other affectionately. With red cheeks, the two young Raptors retreat from each other for a moment for Silvus to say, "I owe you a lot. I will do anything to keep you happy...I love you."

"Silvy I... love you too!" Ocia replies and kisses him back again.

Throughout his entire life, Silvus could never imagine himself ever finding the female of his dreams. He feels his cheeks get even redder and his heart beats even faster. After all the kissing, Ocia begins to nuzzle affectionately into his neck as he nuzzles her back on her cheeks. For the rest of the night, they continue to embrace the love they have for each other.

⸺≈«(◦)»≈⸺

The next morning, Silvus finds himself lying in his mother's bed, slowly waking up. He looks around to see Ocia lying on top of him, cuddled up, still sleeping with a smile. She looks very cute, the way she sleeps. Silvus puts on an affectionate smile, watching her make small snoozes as her body continues to slowly move up and down. He makes a few strokes on her mane and gently gets out of the bed, not wanting to wake her up.

Silvus walks to a nearby window to see the sunrise. Gazing at the calm mystical forest up north, he thinks about the next plan of the war. This is the moment. He is going to lead his troops to Monchester. He remembers he has promised the female he loves that he will not kill Targon if given the chance. He looks around the room to see his mother's private shrine in the corner. He walks up to it and kneels like a chicken, putting his claws together in prayer to the spirits for guidance, hoping that he will not only end the war as soon as possible but also fulfill the promise he made to Ocia.

"What ya doing?" The sound of a tired Ocia is heard. Silvus turns his head to see her getting up with a yawn, showing her sharp teeth as she stretches her limbs and tail.

"I am doing a quick a prayer to the spirits before I head out for you know what," Silvus replies, admiring how beautiful the female on the bed is. With a giggle, Ocia gets off her bed and walks up beside him and asks if she can join the prayer. Silvus nods yes and shifts to the side allowing her to kneel in the same chicken-like position. She puts her claws together, joining in. They both make their prayers for good health and fortune, and more importantly, for the war to finally be over.

Finishing his prayer, Silvus gets up and waits for Ocia to finish hers. While he waits, he thinks about her safety. She might not be much of a fighter, but she does need some form of protection if something bad happens to him. Seeing her finish her prayer, Silvus asks her, getting an idea, "Have you ever used a staff before?"

Ocia looks at him curious and replies, "I think I did as part of my tutoring. Why do you ask?"

Silvus gestures her to follow him to the wardrobe. He opens it up and takes out the staff of Maglo and shows it to her, making gasp in awe. "If anything happens to me, Ocia, I know you don't like to commit violence, but you still need something to defend yourself, which is why I would like to give this to you," he tells her, giving her the staff. He sees her admire the staff with the same look he had when first laid eyes up on it.

She scans the staff up and down with her eyes and looks at Silvus and says, "You really think I could use this? Isn't this your family heirloom?"

Silvus walks up to her, giving her a small hug and peck on her snout, and tells her, "For what we have been through, at this point you became like family to me, so I am trusting you to use it to protect yourself. There is no telling whether a Dark Mistcaster, or worse, might come to do you harm."

Looking hesitant at first, Ocia eventually accepts it with a smile that Silvus trusts her with it. They are going to give each other another kiss until knocking is heard, interrupting them.

"Yo, Cousin, it's me, Ico! Whatever you and Ocia are doing in there, we gotta get going. It's time!"

"I'll be there in a sec!" Silvus calls out, looking disappointed, hearing footsteps run off. He turns his head to Ocia and asks her if she is ready. She nods with an uneasy smile, not only wanting to be with Silvus but also to confront her brother, tightening her grip on the staff he gave her.

⇒«◈»⇐

The sun raises high in all its might. In the Maglo, forest the entire royal alliance marches along, with Silvus taking the helm wearing his royal armor proud now riding on a grey-scaled Carnotaur. With him is Ocia, wearing blue-painted armor with a small cape that Silviera used to wear. Behind her back is the same staff that Silvus gave her. Also with him are his inner circle.

Leon commands the main royal army, Orezyme commands the rebuilt Maglo militia in blue colors with Ico following beside, Tritus commands the Tricians in purple, Zira commands Sherrasic in green, Nardo commands Creston in red, Ki the Kobold king leads a mix of royal forces and Rotting Ronin, and Buck, who commands Monchester defectors wearing a mix of orange and black to differ themselves from their rebel counterparts. All seven of Silvus' trusted allies and useful commanders follow his lead deep south of the forest filled with herds of Stegos minding their own business, eating the nearby bushes, while packs of Velocis are seen watching with curiosity like small puppies.

At least five sunrises pass by. The royal alliance approaches the southern Maglo border now reclaimed by the royal army. The border gates slowly open to reveal a mountain path to Monchester—the Emerald Mountains, a row of ginormous lush green mountains which are also used to border between the two western Betadoms. Silvus takes a look back to check on his troops to see they are all alright before refocusing back to the path ahead.

Silvus and his army continue to cross into Hephestion, taking seven more sunrises. They come to the northern grasslands of Monchester, a wondrous lush valley filled with bright green grass with patches of bushes around a cliff with a large cactus or two. So far, the enemy did not try to ambush them. All Silvus can see are more native dinosaur herds like the Mayas (Maiasaura) gathered around a lake to drink water while more Petradons are seen flying in the skies. One night, the army decides to make camp, resting up.

In the middle of the camp, a royal scout with a scroll in his claw makes his way through the tents, earning concerned stares from nearby mingling troops who are either sharping their weapons or training for the battle ahead. The scout makes his way to the largest tent, where Silvus is seen having a meeting with his inner circle. Into the tent the scout gains the attention of all the eyes present. The scout makes a quick salute and says, "Your highness! While I was scouting, I was approached by a group of Monchesteons, with Targon himself telling me to deliver you this message!"

"A message from Targon? Please give it to me!" Silvus orders, raising his claw for the scout to approach him and give him the message. With the scroll in claw, Silvus opens it up and reads through.

"What is the message?" Buck calls out while Silvus continues to read.

The more Silvus reads the scroll, his face begins to turn into a face of concern. He looks to all his allies giving him worried looks—especially Ocia when it comes to her brother.

"Guys... Targon is challenging me to the royal duel." Silvus turns the scroll for all to read. The scroll reads,

To the one who calls himself Ultamar Silvus,

You are starting to prove to be an utter nuisance in my ambition to reunify the kingdom. However, I hear from my surviving soldiers that you showed mercy to those with honor. If you don't seek any more bloodshed, I Beta–Lord Anvar Targon herby challenge you to the royal duel taking place in my castle throne room. If you accept, let it be you and I fight till either the death or submission. The one who loses must immediately surrender the war.

The royal duel, as Silvus remembers, is when one noble challenges another, and they fight in claw-to-claw combat until one either submits or dies. Usually it happens when peaceful debates fail. All Raptors present in the tent begin to argue whether Silvus should accept the duel. Ocia, Leon, Ki, and Buck believe Silvus should decline, not wanting to risk not only his life but the entire war. Fi, Ico, Tritus, and Nidus believe Silvus should accept, due having faith in him to win, since it would mean winning the war without more causalties. Orezyme only stands next to Silvus, who both watch them arguing, with uneasy faces.

"I accept," Silvus blurts out, stopping the argument.

All eyes turn to him in shock. When asked by Ocia why he would accept Silvus, walks in between his group and tells them, "To tell you all the truth, I am getting tired of all the fighting. This duel may be our only chance to stop this war for good without bloodshed. If I am going to be Alpha-King, then I must learn to take big risks."

"That is true." Orezyme walks up next to Silvus. "All rulers of old, especially the Ultamars, are always faced with hard decisions and must take big risks for the greater good."

All Raptors present agree with his uncle's point. Some, like Ocia, are a bit hesitant, getting a bad feeling. Silvus takes notice and walks up to her and asks if she is okay. She tells him that she has a bad feeling about the duel and is worried that it will result in someone's death.

———————

The royal alliance approaches the city of Rookingrad itself in the middle of the green valley with even more cactuses around it while dawn approaches. It is a large stone city similar to Athera, except the buildings have a more square appearance. Above the main gates are the orange flags with the rook symbols. Hordes of rebels are gathered around the main gates, armed. They all have their eyes on the royal army to keep watch.

The royal alliance continue their march until they are at least ten feet apart from each other. Silvus commands the troops to stand by and gets off his Carnotaur, allowing Ocia and Buck to come with him, as it is their home, after all. He gets closer to the horde of rebels, keeping watch if anything happens. Leading the rebel force is a white-scaled armored female with a purple feathered mane and tail. Her mane is in a ponytail style due to how long it is. Looking at him seriously, the female briefly squints her magenta eyes in suspicion.

"Are you the one called Ultamar Silvus?" she asks with a serious tone in her voice, hinting that she is in her late twenties.

"I am indeed, and I," he shows her the scroll, "accept your Beta-Lord's challenge."

The female takes the scroll and reads over it. Giving it to a nearby rebel, she greets her guests with a bow. "I am Gem, serving sentinel of the Monchester forces and bodyguard of Anvar Targon. I am pleased that you accepted his challenge." Gem lifts herself up and gives further instructions.

"Before I take you in, my Beta-Lord demands that you bring only two companions. The rest of your royal army must stay."

Silvus gives her an inquisitive look, suspicious if there is some kind a trap. Taking notice of his look, Gem assures him that Targon is honorable and will not go back on his word. Silvus looks to the Anvar cousins to clarify if Gem is telling the truth. Ocia tells him that being his sister, she can confirm that Targon holds a sense of honor despite his state. So Silvus agrees to go in with the Anvar cousins, since they know more of the city better than any other Raptor. Gem motions for them to follow into Rookingrad.

With Gem leading, Silvus and his chosen group pass through the rebel horde who are all making way for them to approach the gates opening up slowly. Silvus follows into the main street to see a crowd of unhappy Raptors gathered in between the walkway being blocked by rows of guards. As much as he wants to admire the stonecraft of both the buildings and the statues, he cannot ignore the faces of depression being sensed from the Raptors. He can even see signs of starvation from the Raptors, due to how thin they look.

"I was not kidding when I said the war is taking its toll," Buck whispers into Silvus' ear.

"How could my brother let this happen?" Ocia sobs, trying to hold back a tear.

The best that Silvus and the gang can do is gaze as they continue to follow Gem to the castle.

Chapter 29
The Royal Duel

Rookingrad castle. It is where Silvus is going to face Targon for the duel taking place. As risky the terms are, he would do anything to stop further bloodshed. First he needs to focus instead of distracting himself with theorizing thoughts. They pass through the spacious square courtyard all the way to the main keep.

The entrance hall is filled with guards all lined up on the orange carpet, keeping watch. The room itself looks more like a military hall, filled with stuffed hunted dinosaurs as trophies, and Monchester color tapestries. A big cactus or two can be seen around the corners to reflect the entire lands of the Betadom. In front of the party is a large door leading to the throne room, with two staircases in between being blocked by the guards. Gem gestures one of her claws up for Silvus and his companions to stop. She turns around, taking a brief look at Buck with a sad expression, and then at Silvus, looking serious.

"I need you three to wait here as I head to the throne room, to let my Beta-Lord know of your arrival."

Gem snaps her talons, causing nearby guards to turn around facing the three. They have their weapons ready with their eyes all on Silvus to make sure he does not leave. Gem leaves them behind to go through the doors, leaving him by himself with the two Anvar cousins.

Silvus turns to Buck with an inquisitive look and asks, "What was that?"

"What was what?"

"The way Gem looked at you. Was there something between you two?" Silvus raises one of his brows while Buck closes his eyes briefly, looking down.

"She and I were very close. I first met her at the blacksmithing academy where she showed me the ropes." Buck looks back up with cheeks beginning to turn red, moving a claw behind his head, making Ocia giggle behind Silvus. "You could say eventually we became more than just friends."

"A blacksmithing academy? So you were training to be a blacksmith?" Silvus asks, changing the subject, making Buck perk up with a smile.

"Oh yes! I am acutally an enthusiast of different weapons and armor and how they are crafted, like your sword." Buck points to Silvus' sword on his back. "When I was a hatchling, I always admired my dad's work as a blacksmith, watching all the weapons and armor being made."

"So you want to be more like your dad?" Silvus asks.

"Not just to be like my dad. But I want to prove that blacksmithing is not an Omega's only job!"

Buck finishes, pumping two arms proudly with a lot of enthusiasm. He sounds very dedicated to breaking the stereotype of certain positions meant for a particular caste. Silvus looks to Ocia, who giggles in response. "It's true, Silvy. He has a grand collection of replicas of weapons and armor in his private quarters. When I took Buck to the castle library, he would immediately try finding any books related to weapon styles of the kingdoms of Cretatia."

"And find out if any Beta-Lords were blacksmiths!" Buck finishes rudely for Ocia, who glares at him, causing the former to make an apologetic face. "Well...I eventually found out from the books that Anvar Rook, the first Beta-Lord of Monchester, was actually a blacksmith! So I ran to my parents and used it to convince them to sign me up to the academy."

Buck grins proudly until Silvus asks him, "Then what happened, since you are no longer in the blacksmithing academy?"

Buck went sour, lowering his head and shoulders, telling him, "This war happened, that is what. Cousin Targon wanted to form a private army, since we thought at the time the Mistatiorum were corrupt. Me, Gem, and a few others were taken out of the academy because he believes Raptors like myself belong into the battlefield. So I trained to be a soldier alongside Gem."

Buck looks back up with a shrug.

"At first things were well. I became a captain of my own unit, as it turns out I have leadership skills I did not know I had. Gem too is a good leader, but Targon believed her to be worthy enough to be not only his new bodyguard but also sentinel of his rebel forces."

"Why did Targon not have you as his sentinel?" Silvus asks, looking suspicious.

Buck looks side to side uneasily and continues, "That is when my mother started to call out Targon for relying on a Dark Mistcaster. He might have believed that if I became sentinel I would command the entire army to turn on him, which I would. You remember the story I told you on the day we met, right?"

Silvus nods, confirming that he remembers. Taking a chance to learn about Targon, he asks, "Speaking of Targon, how good is he in claw-to-claw combat?"

"Big brother is a very good fighter, Silvy!" Ocia speaks up, earning Silvus' attention. He sees her looking very worried with her claws together as if she is praying.

"Really?"

"Oh yes, I used to watch him spar with Daddy in our hatchling years. Before I was even sent to Maglo, he faced off with three of his wardens in claw combat!"

That does not sit well with Silvus. It makes him nervous, learning how skilled in battle Targon is. He looks down at his own claws covered in gauntlets to check them out. He closes his eyes to imagine himself fighting Targon one on one. His thoughts get interrupted by the sound of doors opening. Silvus sees Gem walking back toward them, telling them that it is time, and guides them into the throne room.

Rookingrad's throne room is a large square temple-like room filled with a crowd of Raptor nobility wearing their orange scarfs or cloaks. They are all gathered around two dining tables in be-tween the center. They all have eyes glued on Silvus walking along following Gem as they approach Targon himself, who sits on his throne in front of a giant glittering cactus, which is the wellspring of Monchester.

Targon looks at his guest or opponent with a stern face, while Bylark stands next to him, uptight, with a smile on his face. Gem tells Silvus and his companions to stop in their tracks in the middle of the room. She walks up to Targon with a quick bow before walk-ing up next to the opposite side.

"We meet again," Targon says, looking at Silvus. "I see that you also brought my sister and cousin."

Silvus looks behind, seeing Ocia looking at Targon with hurt eyes while hearing Buck making soft growling sounds.

"Where is my mother?!" Buck demands, rushing up to Silvus' side. Targon looks to Gem, then to Bylark, who nods for him to tell them of Doe's fate.

"Cousin, your mother was a traitor to our cause. You were there on the day we captured her and her accomplices plotting to over-throw me as Beta-Lord, destroying everything we worked hard for."

"RAPTORS WERE STARVING AND DYING! Yet you choose to ignore the needs of your Raptors in favor of your ignorance letting your mind be twisted by that vile fiend!" Buck butts in, pointing an accusing finger at Bylark, who just stands calmly, making the crowd of nobles gasp.

"Big brother...please tell us what happened to Auntie Doe!" Ocia begs her brother with tears flowing out of her eyes.

"Looks like your sister and cousin have the right to know what happened to your own aunt," Silvus says. He crosses his arms, looking serious.

Targon gets up from his throne, keeping his frown, and tells them, "For committing treason...Anvar Doe was sentenced to be fed to the Tarbos(Tarbosuarous) we captured from Fenheim."

Ocia drops down to her knees crying at what she just heard. Silvus remembers Ocia telling him that her aunt is like a mother to her. He can sympathize with her pain in her heart, the same feeling he had when losing his mother. Ocia continues to weep, muttering, "How could you." She swings her tail to her face, grabbing her feathered tip, burying her face and crying into it like a pillow.

Buck is taking this very personally, tightening his fists while showing his teeth and shouting, "YOU EXCECUTED MY MOTHER!" He is so angry he almost draws his claymore, but Silvus stops him as the nearby guards rush with their spears to ensure Buck does not try to assault the Beta-Lord. Seeing Gem getting ready with a hurt expression, Buck reluctantly steps back, keeping his anger toward his fallen cousin for what he did to his mother.

Silvus walks a few more steps toward Targon. He puts on a face of determination and seriousness. Despite how fallen he is, Silvus still believes he can appeal to him. "You could stop this right now, you know. No more Raptors have to die."

Targon does not look amused. Bylark makes a mocking huff and says, "How pitiful, still believing peace is possible. Typical belief coming from a snout of a young hatchling who spent most of his life reading books."

Bylark turns his attention to Targon advising him, "Perhaps this duel is a waste of time. Why not just kill him alre--"

"This duel must be done for sake of our cause. Killing Silvus prematurely will just make him a martyr. As potential Alpha-King, I must appear strong for any Raptor who serves me. Or have you forgotten who is in charge?" Targon cuts off Bylark, looking suspicious, with a glare. Bylark backpedals a bit with a nervous look, allowing him to go on with a huff, and mutters how annoying nobles are with their sense of honor.

Targon climbs down the steps, approaching Silvus face to face. Being the same ages, the two male Raptors are of equal height. They lock eyes with each other, creating tension between them. The nobles present whisper among themselves, wondering what is going to happen.

"You know why you're here?" Targon asks, keeping his frowning eyes on Silvus'.

"Yeah," Silvus replies sternly.

"Well then, many of my troops that you showed mercy to told me of your supposed lineage. If it's true, I believe it is only fair for me to finally test you to see if you are indeed the Ultamar heir."

Silvus does not responed. Instead, he continues to stand his ground, keeping his glare on the orca-patterned male in front of him—the same misguided Beta-Lord who believes he has the best intentions, yet is ignorant of those around him. Targon looks at one of the drones and orders them to disarm Silvus.

The drone walks up to Silvus, raising his claws, telling the silver prince to relinquish his weapon. It is the rule of the royal duel for two Raptors to use their natural weapons: claws and teeth. Gauntlets are an exception. Silvus gives the drone his sword while the other drone gives him a Mythril ring to wear so he won't use his Mist powers to cheat.

The nobles present, including Ocia and Buck, are being ordered by the guards to spread apart. The crowd lines up, surrounding the two Raptors in a squared space. The royal duel is about to begin. The main rule is simple: if one of them either faints or dies, he will lose.

———◆———

The two male Raptors begin to circle around snarling with various hissing. They position themselves, looking like Velocis surrounding their prey, getting ready to attack. Among the anxious crowd, Ocia is seen conflicted, looking to Targon and then to Silvus, worried for them both—one being her brother and the other being the love of her life. Buck stands next to her, putting a comforting claw on her shoulder, hoping to relax her a bit as he watches the duel between his new friend and his cousin.

With a vicious squawk, Silvus makes the first move by leaping in the air to make a leap attack, only for Targon to dodge it, followed by an uppercut, scratching Silvus' face. He kicks him on the ground by the side. Silvus quickly gets up, placing a claw on his face to feel blood coming out the side of his snout. He tries another swing with his claws, but Targon sidesteps, making another slash and kick, but Silvus recovers his balance this time. Desperate to land an attack, Silvus makes three swipes with his claws, but Targon dodges each one and performs a claw fake and uses his other claw to punch Silvus in the face between his eyes.

The impact causes Silvus to wince in pain, grabbing his head with both his claws as if he has a big headache. He endures the pain, looking back at Targon, who is doing side hops, waiting for Silvus to make the next move. Desperate, he looks around to see Ocia worried while the crowd is cheering for Targon, not by choice, but simply not wanting to upset their Beta-Lord. Silvus needs to find a new strategy if he is going to win. Getting back in position, he looks to his gauntlet-covered claws, getting an idea. Targon gets impatient and attempts a vertical claw swipe down, only for Silvus to use his both his claws to deflect them, staggering the latter.

Silvus looks down his gauntlets to take a quick look at the plates. It turns out he can use them to deflect Targon's attacks. Instead of attacking, he decides to switch to a defensive position so he can attempt to tire out Targon as well as study his moves. In a rage, Targon attempts to uses claws to attack, only for Silvus to start using his gauntlets to deflect each one. Silvus' strategy seems to only annoy his opponent rather than tiring him out.

Being a veteran fighter, Targon proves himself to have lots of stamina, yet he puts on an annoyed face as he continues to attack offensively while being blocked By Silvus' gauntlets. Targon makes one double leap attack only to be blocked once again, but his time he tries to put pressure on Silvus, hoping to break his guard.

"Why don't you attack?!" Targon demands with frustration in his voice.

Silvus does not answer, but instead he struggles to push off his opponent with his arms. He refuses to answer, not wanting to expose his plan. With his teeth gritting together in rage, Silvus slowly lifts himself up and pushes off Targon, making him stagger. Taking advantage, Silvus makes a quick horizontal spin kick attack at the face, pushing Targon to the floor, causing the crowd to gasp.

Targon gets up feeling pain right at his snout as if a bone or two shattered. Whatever pain he is feeling, he is angry and continues to attack Silvus, only to be deflected. No matter how much Targon strikes, Silvus shows great reflexes, still using the plate area of his gauntlets to parry each move while learning the skills. Tired of playing games, Targon tries to swing his tail to whip him off balance, only for Silvus to make a quick hop and stomp on Targon's tail, making him scream in pain, followed by another hop with a brief stomp on the face in the eye area, blinding Targon in the process.

Hopping off, Silvus sees Targon placing a claw on his left eye in pain. Silvus gets an idea, seeing that he created a blind spot. Targon is so enraged, he makes a desperate leap, only for Silvus to sidestep the attack toward the blind spot, allowing him to do an uppercut attack at the face, and high kicks him in the head.

Targon struggles to get up despite not being in a good condition. Back on his feet, Targon attempts to charge at Silvus for a bite attack, only for the latter to sidestep again at the blind spot and uses his teeth on Targon's neck. He swings him around and slams him vertically on the ground, making one big impact. The crowd gasps, either in awe or fear.

Silvus keeps his distance as Targon tries to get up, but he can't. He begins to cough a lot of blood. He lifts his head up to see Silvus walking up to him.

"What are yo- waiting for? Finish me!" Targon taunts, but Silvus does nothing but pant.

Silvus looks around at the crowd with faces of anxiety while Ocia is seen shaking, worried what Silvus is going to do to her brother. He looks down at Targon to notice a tear coming out of his only good eye. Carefully listening, he can hear Targon muttering about how he just wanted to be a good Beta-Lord like his father. As Silvus expected, Targon is just another misguided fool with good intentions. Instead of finishing the kill, Silvus crouches and says, "I won't kill you," causing the audience, including Bylark, to gasp.

Targon lifts his head once again, looking surprised. "After all I've done, you would spare my life?!"

"Targon…do you really believe you are doing any better?" Silvus asks him.

Targon lifts his head up again, telling him in a sobbing voice, "I just want to make things back to normal! I just…want to be a great Beta-Lord, just like my father before he died!"

Now Targon is starting to cry, but not in a drastic female-like manner. He grits his teeth, allowing tears to come out of his face. "I promised help to make Avalonia a better place. Bylark told me that his powers can be used for good!"

"It is how he is deceiving you, Targon. Just like an assassin would appeal to a noble's goodwill in order to get close." Silvus points to the crowd, directly to Ocia and Buck. "Look how the Dark Mistcaster is ruining your relationship with your family!"

Targon looks to the side to see Buck looking at him, disappointed, while Ocia cries begging her brother to accept the surrender. Targon looks back to Silvus and asks, "Are you really the one who could put everything back together?"

"Honestly, I don't really care what my status is. I just want things to get back to normal as much as you do." Silvus looks around the crowd. "We all want to make the world a better place. The better question is how far you will be going. It does not mean, however, that you will be excused from facing the consequences of your actions. Have you even seen your Raptors?"

"What do you mean?" Targon perks up, confused.

"When I got into the city, I saw a lot of the Omegas miserable and starving to death," Silvus answered, looking back at Targon.

"Buck and Auntie Doe were right! What have I done?!" Targon blurts out, getting up on his knees. Silvus offers a claw for Targon to accept. Without hesitation, Targon grabs Silvus' claw and gets up back on his feet, announcing, "I surrender—you won."

The crowd cheers, not because their Beta-Lord lost, but because he accepted an appropriate surrender, meaning that the war is over. Silvus takes off his Mythril ring while Ocia runs up to him latching him into a hug with tears of happiness, while Targon walks up to Buck, begging for forgiveness for what he did to his mother. Buck tells Targon that he will never forget what he did to his mom, but he will try to forgive.

"Oh, Silvus! Thank you for sparing my brother and saving him!" Ocia gratefully thanks him, looking at him with tears of joy.

Silvus is going to say something, but he hears Targon call out. The two Raptors turn their heads to Targon to see him looking at them with a heartwarming smile. He looks to Ocia, telling her, "My dear sister, I am so sorry for all I have done! Will you ever forgive me?"

For an answer, Ocia grabs Targon into a hug, telling him that she forgives him on one condition. He must deal with Bylark. So Targon turns around, facing Bylark, who still stands by his throne looking furious. With an angry face, Targon walks up to Bylark, telling him, "You ruined my family! You manipulated me into doing horrendous crimes. For that, you will be banished from my court forever!"

Out of nowhere, Bylark only makes a small laugh, earning a raised eyebrow from Targon.

"Well then, your usefulness is no longer needed, which is why I have a plan B!"

Bylark grabs Targon by the throat, igniting his energy drain spell.

"TARGON!" Silvus, Ocia, Buck shout out while the crowd all gasp in horror as they watch their Beta-Lord being drained.

"LORD BETA!" Gem draws her sword and tries to rush to Targon's aid, as it is her job as bodyguard, only to be force pushed by Bylark's spell as he continues to drain Targon's life. The guards attempt to stop Bylark, but they too get pushed off.

"You...traitor!" Targon struggles while Blyark continues to admire draining his victim with a sinister grin on his snout.

"While you were busy fighting those pests, I have been collecting Raptors to drain them of their energy to fuel full power to my potential to destroy this kingdom for the glory of my masters! Perhaps, with such power, I don't need my masters anymore! HAHAHAHAHAHA"

Bylark throws Targon to Silvus and the crowd right at their feet, looking lifeless. Ocia drops down, begging for Targon to get up. Silvus quickly uses his levitation spell to call back his sword to his claw.

Buck draws his claymore, getting ready to fight the true enemy. The entire noble crowd only trembles in fear.

Bylark begins to turn red as he being to grow large in size; spikes are seen growing from his shoulders, horns stick out from his head, pair of fangs grows from his teeth, and large leathery wings stick out from his back. He opens his eyes, revealing that they have turned glowing red.

The nobles present all begin to flee the throne room, fearing for their lives. Silvus looks to Buck and Ocia, telling them to flee while he deals with Bylark. But the cousins, especially Ocia, beg to stay and help, but Silvus insists that they flee for their safety. So they do, carrying Targons's body. As they run out of the castle, Ocia stops in her tracks and turns around, facing the throne room where Silvus is facing Bylark.

Ocia takes out the staff from her back that Silvus has given her. She looks at it, meditating on what to do. Silvus stands his ground, grasping his sword on one claw while at the same time igniting a lightning spell on the other. The transformed Bylark turns around, looking like some draconic creature from the underworld, gazing his glowing red eyes at Silvus below with a sinister grin on his face.

"With the Mist energy of a descendant of the mighty five heroes of Magnus, I have become the most powerful Mistcaster of all Cretatia! HAHAHAHAHHA!"

The transformed Bylark continues to do his evil laugh as he thrusts his claws up high, igniting purple miasma-like energy from his claws, piercing through the rooftop, performing some kind of Necromancy spell in full power.

Chapter 30
The Final Showdown

The Miasma energy is so powerful it pierces through the ceiling above. As the room rumbles beneath his feet like an earthquake, Silvus watches the Miasma fly up into the sky with wide eyes as it starts to cover the beautiful blue sky with dark purple clouds, unleashing purple lightning bolts outside. Whatever spell the transformed Bylark performed must not be good for the outside. Silvus looks back down to see the fiend in front finish his spell, turning his head down with a sinister look.

"What did you do?!" Silvus demands as he gets his sword and spell ready for a fight of his life.

Bylark makes a brief laugh and ignites his two claws on fire.

"Let's just say your friends will die when I finally get rid of you, Ultamar Silvus!"

Blyark thrusts his arms forward, igniting a flamethrower, causing Silvus to dodge out of the way and counter with a lightning bolt spell at the head. Bylark only flinches a bit, wiping his face with one claw. The monstrous being puts on a mocking smile, revealing the fangs among his sharp teeth.

"Is that the best you got?"

Silvus puts his sword back and desperately performs an ice spear from his claws and throws it like a javelin, only to be caught by one of Bylark's grown red-lined claws and melts it with his fire aura. Then the latter counters it by igniting sparking shadow balls from his claws and throws them. Silvus dodges one and gets hit by the other, sending him flying into a nearby wall.

Silvus quickly gets up and desperately tries another lightning spell in a form of a large ball and throws it at Bylark right at the chest, pushing him this time. Bylark flies all the way to the wall only to quickly recover, leaping off and landing on his feet.

Bylark thrusts one of his claws up and creates a shadow disc and throws it, only for Silvus to dodge it by doing a somersault, landing back on his feet. Instead of firing another elemental spell, Silvus looks around the room hoping to find something he can use to fight. He looks to the wellspring with large needles, giving him an idea. Thrusting one claw, he uses his levitation spell to pluck out tons of long sharp needless off the wellspring and commands them to fly toward Bylark like a horde of spears.

The wellspring's needles all pierce through Bylark's torso, making him wince in pain. He uses his own levitation spell to remove the needles off his body and quickly uses his healing spell to close his wounds followed by a smile mocking Silvus for making such an attempt.

Silvus does not give up. He continues to use the levitation spell to levitate various objects to attack Bylark. He even levitates nearby dropped weapons dropped from the guards to inflict more damage to Bylark. Then Silvus draws his sword from his back and sprints toward his enemy while the demonic Raptor is distracted, trying to remove the spears off his body. Silvus leaps into the air and is about to plunge his sword right at Bylark's chest, but he gets grabbed by the neck.

With Silvus in his grasp, Bylark spins his arm and throws Silvus right back at the wall. Bylark once again levitates the spears off his body and heals. Then he raises his claw and levitates Silvus by the neck and throws him around the room, slamming him against the walls, the furniture, and also the throne itself.

The impact of the throw is so great, the Sword of Ultamar flies off Silvus' claw, disarming him. Silvus tries to get back up, but Bylark spreads his new wings and flies at him, grabbing him by the tail, and flies up in the purple-stormed sky. Silvus struggles to break free from Bylark's grasp by shooting lightning bolts or ice spears, but they do not have much effect. Bylark proves himself to be very powerful compared to the others he faced. He is currently hanging in the sky as Bylark keeps his grasp on his tail.

Silvus looks around to see they are above Rookingrand. Then he looks to the main gates to see a horrific sight. It turns out the spell that Bylark used earlier is to raise an army of undead Raptors engaged with both his allied army and Rebels working together. They are comprised mostly of Raptor skeletons in armor and wielding weapons. There are also skeletons of Tyrannos and Carnotaurs being used in the middle.

Both the royal alliance and the rebels are fighting with all their might to take down as many skeletons as they can. Ico is seen fighting alongside his father Orezyme. Fi is fighting alongside her Brother Ki, using their katanas. Leon and Nidus, as usual, fight side by side. And Tritus is seen fighting alongside Beta-Lady Zira of Sherrasic and First-Delta Nardo of Creston. So far Silvus does not see Buck or Ocia. Instead Silvus looks to the city to see Buck himself with the recovered Gem leading the Monchester troops, fighting off skeletons who emerged from within the city. Still no Ocia in sight, making him worried for her wellbeing.

"You see that, boy?" Bylark mocks as Silvus turns his head, looking at Bylark in anger while helplessly hanging around.

"Your friends, your family are all going to die with my new army! HAHAHA!"

As Blyark laughs, Silvus continues to see brave Raptors holding their ground, clashing weapons at the skeletons. A cry or two can be heard from the soldiers slain by the skeletons nearby. Bylark's dreadful transformation and the skeleton army are true proof of how dangerous Dark Mistcraft can be. It is the reason why Dark Mistcraft is feared by all Raptors in not only Avalonia but all of Cretatia.

The manic laughter dies down. Bylark lets go of Silvus' tail, dropping him back into the castle. To break his fall, Silvus thrusts his two claws together to form a shield, making him bounce off the ground, landing on his back near the throne. He slowly tries to get up, with cramps around his body, but a large foot of Bylark pins him on the ground, preventing him from escaping.

Silvus struggles to get out, but Bylark keeps his glowing eyes at him like a predator who captured his prey. Believing that he won, Bylark is about to use one of the sharp nails on his feet, only to freeze in place.

"GAAAAH!"

Bylark screams in pain, forcing him to get off Silvus. The confused silver prince lifts himself up to see Bylark circling around trying to use his arms to reach his back where the pain is. Bylark shows his back, and Silvus spots the Staff of Maglo pierced right the center of his back by the Mythril blade. Turning his head to the side, he sees Ocia herself taking breaths. Turns out she just saved his life by throwing the staff.

In rage, Bylark turns around, spotting Ocia with blood lust in his eyes. Ocia gets spooked and attempts to run away only to trip on her own tail, falling backwards, and attempts to crawl away.

"YOU WILL PAY FOR THIS!" the enraged Bylark threatens as he thrusts one of his claws to perform a spell, but nothing happenes. Instead, a spark of pain is inflicted, causing Bylark to flinch, grabbing his wrist. Turns out with the Mythril blade stuck on his back, he is unable to use his Mist powers. But that does not stop him from trying to use his physical claws to attempt to attack Ocia, who in turn tries to get up. Bylark begins to growl in anger as he slowly makes small stomping steps toward the defenseless female. He prepares his enlarged claws to make his kill.

Taking his chance, Silvus looks around to see his sword and calls it back with his levitation spell. Back on his feet, Silvus takes a deep breath, using his other claw to create the Mist sword that his uncle taught him back at Atlantra. He sprints as fast as he can as the sword of Ultamar begins to glow white. Then he leaps up into the sky and plunges both swords directly at the top of Bylark's head before the beast can harm Ocia.

With the swords pierced through his head, Bylark's face is in a state of shock—widened eyes with his jaw open, twitching. Thanks to the Mythril blade, he cannot use his healing powers. His talons and eyes twitch a few more times before Bylark slowly falls forward. Ocia quickly side rolls out of the way as the now dead Bylark lands on the ground with Silvus still having his swords pierced on the head.

━━━━━━◄◉►━━━━━━

With Bylark dead, the sky begins to turn blue again, with rays of sunlight shining through the ceiling directly at Silvus as he recalls the Mist sword and slowly stands up. He almost faints to the side, to be caught by a worried Ocia. She quickly uses her healing Mist to heal Silvus' major wounds, making him gasp for breath.

Silvus opens his eyes to see Ocia looking at him, crying in relief. "Good throw," he tells her.

Instead of saying a word, Ocia buries her face into Silvus' chest and cries that she is glad that he is alive. Giving her a few soft strokes on her silky mane, Silvus slowly gets up while holding Ocia's claw.

The two turn their gazes at the lifeless body of Bylark, making sure it's over.

"So…we won?" Ocia softly asks, leaning herself against Silvus' body as he wraps an arm around her, looking serious, with a neutral expression.

"For now, at least." Silvus looks up at the blue sky through ceiling, "They are still out there. Plotting their next move."

"What do we do now?" Ocia asks with a worried tone.

Silvus is going to answer until he hears a weak moaning sound from the entrance. The two Raptors turn their gazes to see the body of Targon leaning against the wall. They both run up to him seeing that he is not in good condition. He looks more like a shriveled-up corpse, beyond healing, due to the draining by Bylark. Targon turns his head to Ocia with tears in his eyes.

"Sister…I am so sorry for what I have done."

Ocia herself begin to cry as she grabs onto one of Targon's claws getting cold. "I forgive you, Big Brother," she sobs. "If only you had listened to Auntie Doe, Cousin Buck, and me."

Targon slowly looks to Silvus and says, "You have done the impossible, Ultamar Silvus." He coughs. "I see that my sister cares for you a lot. Before I die, please promise me that not only you protect her, but please do not make the same mistakes as I did! And don't you ever dare trust a Dark Mistcaster even if they act helpful like a devious Pompy who fools you into believing they are innocent to lead you to their traps."

"You have my word, Anvar Targon," Silvus clarifies, making Targon smile one last time.

"May the spirits, guide your reign…Alpha-King." And he falls to the side, now lifeless. Ocia begins to cry near him while Silvus puts on a comforting claw on her shoulder.

"YO, SILVUS!" a voice calls out, gaining the attention of the two mourning Raptors to see Ico and Fi running up to them with the rest of their friends and family and troops running with them.

"Dude! You guys would not believe what happened?!" Ico blurts out with shock in his eyes. "Whatever happened to you guys, there was a massive army of skeletons coming out of the ground."

"OH...my...gosh! It is like a spooky campfire story coming to LIFE! As soon as the skies turned blue again, the skeletons just vanished, turning into dust," Fi finishes for Ico until she spots the large lifeless body of Bylark. Her face turns green and she points at it with a shaky finger. "What is that?!"

Silvus and Ocia turn their attention to see that the Kobold princess is referring to the large lifeless body of the demonic Bylark, then exchange weird looks. Then they both share a laugh, knowing what Fi is talking about, as the Kobold faints at the sight of large things, making Ico catch her in his arms.

Silvus keeps his arm around Ocia, looking very happy, and tells the crowd, "Well, guys, it is a long story."

⸻ ◆ ⸻

In the darkest hour of Avalonia's history, who would have known that a young noble who spent most of his life isolated with books would be the one to save the kingdom on the brink of collapse? It all started when the young Silvus is recently forced out of his home to go on a quest to Patalot in order to save his mother. Throughout his entire journey, Silvus learns that he needs to grow out of his shell in order to achieve, resulting in him growing into a wise leader that he is today. By doing so, he eventually learns of his heritage, discovering that he is the lost heir to the Amber Throne as Ultamar Silvus.

With the defeat of Anvar Targon, the Monchester rebels surrender to the royal forces, thus ending the Avalonian Civil War. With the war over, Raptors of all walks of life can finally return to their normal lives with their families. The royal army is stronger than ever, and crime goes down, stabilizing the kingdom as various merchant groups safely return to their trading routes. Travelers begin to wander the forests and valleys of the kingdom, while hunters and meat farmers return to maintaining the food stock. As life slowly gets back to normal, a new Alpha-King is about to emerge.

——◦《◉》◦——

In the middle of a strange grassy field, Silvus sits in the middle looking up at the ocean of stars shining brightly. He is wearing what looks like royal black cape with silver patterns along with a pair of black royal leather gloves. He gazes at the stars, putting on a depressed face, even though he achieved in saving the kingdom. In truth, he still misses his mother dearly.

Silvus still wishes he could have done more in order to save her. So he looks down with a face of sadness until a familiar voice calls out. He perks up, turning his head, and gasps to see a white-robed figure. It is the spirit that saved him from the temptation from the evil spirit. The spirit walks up to Silvus, making the latter stand up.

"I am so proud of you," the spirit speaks in a calm male voice.

"You...are?" Silvus stutters, nervous at the appearance of an actual spirit coming to greet him.

The spirit makes a small chuckle, telling him, "Indeed, you have accomplished the impossible. You saved this kingdom from a possible destruction. But this is only the beginning."

"What do you mean? What can you tell me?"

"By defeating Bylark, you only prolonged the inevitable. There will be a time, the enemy of our world will one day re-emerge from the shadows. When that day comes, you must be prepared."

Silvus still has many questions that he wants to ask the spirit. Of all the questions he wants to ask, he goes with one about his mother. "Is my mother among you?"

A tear comes out from his eye. The spirit places a ghostly claw on his shoulder.

"Look behind me and find out."

Silvus turns to the side to see another robed figure with her hood down, revealing his mother, Silviera, smiling at him.

"MOTHER!" Silvus shouts happily and runs up to her to embrace her in a hug.

His spirit mother returns the hug, allowing Silvus to cry onto her shoulder, telling her how much he misses her.

"Oh, Mother…I am so sorry I did not save you sooner."

"There is no need to apologize, my son," Silviera makes another stroke on Silvus' head. "As I said on my deathbed, you did save me. Not only that but you honored your promise and saved Avalonia from the clutches of Bylark."

Silvus slowly breaks off from her hug looking at her with tears of joy that he can see her in his dream. But Silviera is not finished yet.

"But your father is right. Bylark is only the beginning."

"Father?" Silvus questions, seeing his mother point over him. He turns around to see the spirit put down his hood to reveal a silver face similar to his. Alpha-King Sulthur, his father.

With a gasp, Silvus blurts out happily, "Y-y-y-you're my father!"

The spirit Sulthur walks past Silvus, standing beside Silviera, and wraps his arm around her, telling him, "Indeed, my son, It is such a shame that I was never able to see you grow up in the scales. But at least I could watch over you, guide you to the coming days. But you should not be worried as of now. You are going to be an Alpha-King and you will have the responsibility to govern your fellow Raptors as you see fit. Just don't abuse it, will you?"

"I promise I won't, Father, but I have one more question for you both…will I ever see you two again?" Silvus tearfully asks the spirits of his parents.

"When that time comes, it will be revealed. Just don't worry too much about us, Son. But we must also warn you that there are a lot of secrets to uncover of our world. It is way bigger than we realize," Sulthur explains. earning a confused look from Silvus.

"What do you mean?"

"That is for you to find out. You did your part in your tale in scale," Silviera states, giving her son a wink as she begins to walk with Sulthur back to the afterlife, leaving a confused Silvus behind, who begs for them not to go.

"Wait! Don't go! I still have so many questions!"

And he is blinded by a flash of light, returning to the waking world.

Chapter 31
The Return of the Alpha-King

I n the middle of the top stairway of the entrance hall stands Silvus, wearing his royal cape and gloves. In front of him is a pair of large doors waiting to be opened.

"Are you ready, your majesty?" a voice calls out from the other side.

"Yes, Guard, you may open," Silvus confirms with a smile, making the doors open. As they open, he takes a deep breath and begins to march into a familiar sight.

Through the doors, Silvus is greeted by a large crowd of noble Raptors from all the Betadoms gathered in the gardens of Odyssey gazing upon him in awe with smiles and cheer. Musical sounds of trumpets can be heard blowing from a distance. Silvus continues to walk along the path. Each of the royal guards places a spear and kneels to greet their new monarch. Silvus greets them all with a smiling wave at the same time he continues to walk down the path into the giant tree where the throne room is.

In the throne room, Silvus is greeted by more nobles and guards awaiting him as he crosses closer to the throne itself. In his sight is the stairway where he would climb up to the throne with Arkus holding a large silver crown, along with the sages awaiting. In front of the stairway are all the Beta-Lords and

-Ladies, new and old, all wearing their smaller crowns. Vessel Orezyme of Maglo, Anvar Buck of Monchester, Sidon Tritus of Tricia, Crova Zira of Sherrasic, and finally Davinchious Nardo of Creston. He climbs up the steps. Silvus gazes around the crowd to see Ico with Gwynie and the Knights of the Mist rooting for him, while Fi and Ki stand around with other Kobold nobles, all observing with smiles.

Silvus makes a brief stop on the throne platform. He makes one more peek at the audience to see one female he is looking for, Ocia herself, standing around with Monchester lords smiling affectionately at him, happy at what he has become. With a heartwarming smile, Silvus walks up to the throne where he kneels in front of Arkus who continues to hold the crown.

"Do you swear to uphold the values of the spirits?!" Arkus begins.

"I do."

"Do you swear to bear all the responsibilities laid out before you?!"

"I do."

"Then by my right as Arch-Sage, I enact the ancient rite of the holy blessing of the spirits themselves and proclaim you Alpha-King of Avalonia, voice of the spirits and protector of the Raptors of Avalonia."

Arkus places the large silver crown with three gems upon Silvus' head and moves to the side. Silvus walks up to the throne and sits upon it. Arkus turns around, facing the crowd along with the sages, and shouts, "RAPTORS OF AVALONIA! WE GIVE YOU ALPHA-KING ULTAMAR SIVLUS!"

And the crowd goes wild with cheering as Silvus continues to sit on his new throne, looking up at the ceiling. He would never have thought that he himself would be destined to be a greater power other than Beta-Lord. More importantly, in his heart, both his parents would be proud of him.

On the following night, a party is being hosted to celebrate the coronation of Silvus. The city of Patalot is filled with decorations. The Raptors themselves fill the streets to celebrate the special day like a festival. In the palace, an even bigger party is taking place in the middle of the grand ballroom with various nobles mingling or dancing to the wonderful music being played from Creston. Silvus, however, is not around, to a certain cousin's annoyance.

Silvus is with Ocia walking along the Gardens of Odyssey instead of at the party. It is a perfect place to get away from the large crowd so they can be together all by themselves. Holding claws, they walk along a stone path in between various flora that glows beautifully at night. They eventually stop by a grand fountain with statues of the six heroes placed around.

"So what will you do now?" Silvus asks Ocia as they halt in front of the fountain, holding Ocia by two claws.

"I honestly do not know. One thing is for sure; I really do not want to be Beta-Lady due to what happened to my brother. Which is why I let my cousin take the throne instead of me." Ocia turns her head to the side, looking at the fountain flowing lots of water gracefully.

"Maybe I will sign up to be a teacher for Monastery, unless something comes to mind," Ocia further states, giving Silvus an idea or a chance.

He lets go of Ocia's claws and kneels on one knee. Ocia's expression turns confused about what Silvus is doing until he takes out a locket belonged to his mother, showing it to her. When he opens it up, she gasps, throwing her claws, covering up her lips at the sight of a silver ring.

"Isn't that your mother's wedding ring?!"

Silvus nods and says, "Anvar Ocia, throughout my journey you have always been at my side. Since the day we first met, I had this feeling that I was going to want to be with you for the rest of my life. So I ask, Anvar Ocia, will you marry me as my lawfully wedded Beta-Queen?"

Ocia puts on a face of absolute joy. She looks like she is going to scream at any moment by the way she wiggles her arms. She grabs Silvus into a very tight hug with tears coming out of her eyes and answers, "OH, SILVY! OF COURSE I WILL MARRY YOU!"

When Ocia breaks off the hug, Silvus feels his heart beating aflutter, with a big happy face forming on his snout. With one claw, he gently grabs Ocia's claw and places the silver ring onto one of the talon fingers. It is a perfect fit. She checks out the ring on her finger with a smile, only to get caught off guard by Silvus scooping her up into his arms, telling her, "You just made me the happiest male in the world."

Silvus happily swings her around a few times, making Ocia giggle in even more happiness. The young couple lock their eyes to each other then they slowly lock their lips against their snouts, embracing each other's love for the rest of the night to come. Above them are the various stars above the night blue sky. Among them a pair of two stars shines greatly, as if the spirits themselves are giving a welcoming sign.

—⊙—

As the new Alpha-King, Ultamar Silvus focuses his reign in efforts on both restoration and fulfilling old promises once made by his late father, like allowing the Omegas independent autonomy with their business without the intense interference from the crown, as long as they don't violate Raptor rights. The Omegas rejoice with cheer while the nobility at first skeptical but eventually they see the worth of the Omegas to the point they are willing work together as fellow Raptors. By doing so earns him the title, Alpha-King Silvus the wise fulfiller.

Under Sentinel Leon, the royal army is stronger and more unified than ever. Crime is down in the frontier, making the roads safe for merchant caravans and travelers to travel in safe distances. The royal army under Leon is so successful; a lot of young Raptors begin to volunteer to fill their ranks. Luckily, the army has more volunteers than extra-borns.

Since the war ended, instead of getting a new Beta-Lord right away, the Monchesteons, with the help of the royal guard and their allies, rebuild the damages from Bylark's wake. Because Ocia is now living with Silvus as Beta-Queen, Anvar Buck is chosen to be the new Beta-Lord of Monchester with Gem as his bodyguard, just as she once served Targon. Rumor has it that Buck and Gem are getting very close.

Vessel Orezyme becomes the new Beta-Lord of Maglo with his only son as First-Delta. Under his leadership, the Raptors of Maglo rejoiced in the restoration efforts. His wife Oria is picked to be his bodyguard where they could finally have peace together.

Returning to Tricia, Sidon Tritus makes it in time to witness that his wife Sulphie has laid three wonderful eggs. With the war over, Tritus can finally settle from his reckless days so he and Sulphie can watching their hatchlings hatch together as parents.

Vessel Ico, for all his efforts, becomes the most respected member of the Knights of the Mist, fulfilling his father's legacy. Eventually he will be promoted as the new captain after Pendra Gwynie's retirement to live with her husband and her two daughters. Today, Vessel Ico is married to Princess Fi Jin with Ki's blessing. Surprisingly, Ico and Fi have eight hatchlings—seven Kobold daughters and one Raptor son?!

Fulfilling his promise, Silvus sends as many troops as he can to Shima, where they aid the Kobolds in reclaiming the old Claves in the outer roads. Effectively it saves Shima from impending doom. After restoring Shima, King Ki and Alpha-King Silvus make new trading deals to allow Kobolds and Raptors alike to open trade with each other.

With the restoration efforts all but complete, Ultamar Silvus can finally be at peace with his wife and Beta-Queen Ultamar Ocia and their three wonderful hatchlings—two sons and one daughter.

Epilogue
Invasion by Fire

Twenty-one winters later

I n the middle of the night, a group of seven hooded riders is seen galloping to an old ruin that looks like a rundown fortress of an unknown location somewhere in the swamp. Among the riders, one is carrying a prisoner with a bag over his or her head while the claws are bounded by Mythril cuffs. Inside the fortress, they all dismount their Snaguanas, hitching them up to a nearby post, and with two dragging the prisoner, they approach a pair of old rusty gates. The leading rider raises one claw and chants an old spell in a sinister tone, making a pair of strange runes appear on each door of the gates, allowing them to open slowly by themselves.

The figures enter the building into a deserted hallway with torches lightning up purple flames revealing cobwebs as the pass by. Behind them the gates behind slam shut, making a booming sound, causing dust to blow. The figures approach the end of the hall and open another door to be greeted by a massive circular room crowded with more hooded figures waiting for them.

They are all gathered around a large round table, with various tapestries of the mysterious purple skull representing the group, hanging above. The seven figures make way to a round table with a purple stone in the middle. The leading figure raises both claws, making them glow purple, followed by the others. They chant a spell, making the purple stone glow, and reveal a magical hologram, revealing yet another figure in the shadows.

The prisoner is thrown off and caught by the leading figure and removes the bag revealing a terrified Clara, who turns out to be freed from her prison some time ago. She looks around in fear, knowing that she is in trouble, then freezes at the sight of the spectre. The figure looks at her with a pair of large frowning purple eyes visible from the shadows.

"WHAT HAPPENED?!" the figure in the hologram booms, with his voice filled with authority. There is also a hint of disappointment.

Clara, still with her claws bound, struggles, trying to come up with an excuse for her failure.

"M-m-m-my lord! I swear that the kingdom was about to be cleansed as you wanted, but there was a complication."

"WHAT COMPLICATION?! YOU AND BYLARK WERE TASKED WITH DISMATLING THE KINGDOM FOR US TO TAKE?!"

The figure, who seems to be the leader of the Necromancers, has no patience for petty excuses. Clara, however, who continues to shake in fear, tries to defend her actions once again.

"Master Necrosis! Please show some mercy! It is true that we believed that we got rid of the royal family!"

"BELIEVED?!" the figure raises a brow, knowing a hint of failure in Clara's tone.

"T-T-T-Turns out there was another heir of Ultamar under our noses the whole time! We tried to hunt him down, but we have underestimated him, costing Bylark's life!"

The figure makes a blood lust roar, causing the room to shake, as the Necromancers cower in fear, except the leading rider, who stands his ground. A pair of wings is heard popping out from behind the leader. Then they retract the leader finishes his roar gazing back at cowering Burgundy she Raptor.

"Bylark was a very prominent member of our cause. Yet you remained allowing yourself to be humiliated while the entire plan got ruined!"

"I WAS SURROUNDED! I had no choice!" Clara loudly claims

"YOU were still foolish enough to act without knowing you were being watched! Not to mention I heard from my agents that you revealed some of our secrets."

The figure, Necrosis, leans forward out of the shadows to reveal a draconic face: black scales with dark purple runes, narrowish yet broad long snout, large frilled cheekbones, and four long horns sticking out backward from the back of his head. Turns out Necrosis is a dragon, and he is not happy, from the way he fumes from his nostrils making threating growls revealing his sharp teeth and fangs.

"Regardless of what you did, you and Bylark still failed in your task and I do not tolerate failure!" Necrosis jabs a clawed finger at Clara. He looks to the leading figure and orders, "Take her to be executed!"

"It will be done, Master." The leading figure bows to Necrosis and commands two of the Necromancers to grab Clara and violently take her to another chamber. She begs Necrosis for mercy.

The leading figure takes the hood down, revealing a she-Raptor having the same scale color and eye color as Necrosis, with a messy purple mane, looking young, but with a serious face. She turns to her master and asks, "What will you do now, Master?"

"Hearing that we suffered heavy losses thanks to another fool, Bernic, I have sent some of my kin to reinforce you all while the rest of you should be prepared. You, however, proved yourself to be very loyal to me, which is why I promote you as the new head of this chapter, Nera," Necrosis announces pointing to the Raptor namef Nera, who in turn makes a small bow.

"I am honored, Father," Nera says, looking up at Necrosis, who turns out to be her dragon father.

"Good. Your new task is to prepare our followers. Recruit if you have to, and await my kin for another task at claw."

With that, the specter vanishes, leaving Nera in the care of the Necromancers in Avalonia.

━━━━►◄(◍)►◄━━━━

Around the shores of Tricia lies a decent-sized fishing hamlet built on top of the shorelines. It is one of the grand fisheries built around Tricia to catch fish to harvest them for food. In one of the three large sheds built around the hamlet, a group of Omega fishermen is seen gathered around the decks inside, collecting the dead mackerel, scooping them with large nets. With every net full they gathered from the pool in the middle, they place the dead mackerel in one of the row's wagons.

Turns out the fishermen Raptors of the hamlet took advantage of the mackerel breeding habits by building the fisheries in the middle of their nesting grounds, knowing they return to mate. When tons of fish enter the shack, the Raptors would close the channel gates, trapping the fish so when they lay their eggs and perish after without drifting away into the ocean so the Raptors could scoop them up from the deck inside. With all the fish collected, the Raptors reopen the channel gates leading to the ocean so newborn Mackerel can swim free and grow up until the next mating season or harvest to the Raptors.

With one of the wagons filled with fresh mackerel, one of the male fishermen pulls it out of the shed to take it into the hamlet.

The fisherman stops by the main gates to wipe sweat from his head and looks around the ocean scenery with a relaxing breath. That is, until he spots something in the distance, widening his eyes along with a big gasp. Whatever he sees makes him rush into the hamlet without the wagon of fish.

⟫⟪◍⟫⟪

Across the ocean, a fleet of giant ships is seen in a distance with large sails opened to their full strength. Above the ships are golden flags hanging on the center pole with a white symbol in the middle. Operating the ships are multi-colored large reptiles called dragons, working the decks, walking around like Theropods.

They have horns while some have frills on lower sides of their heads, spines from head to tail with a blade at the tip, a pair of leathery wings folded on their backs, a pair of arms and claws being used to maintain the ship, padded underbellies from under their necks to the under tail, and they also have snouts, either broad or narrow. Males are seen to be more muscular, while the females are mostly slender.

On the main ship, various dragon sailors work the decks while being watched by the armored guards. The guards wear gold-scaled metal chest armor, bracers, and helmets that resemble those of the Roman Empire.

Coming out of the main cabin is a young male dragon wearing a golden chest armor and bracers on his wrists. He is primarily black-scaled with a red padded underbelly from his neck to tail and a red padded face in between his orange eyes. A pair of large orange horns is seen sticking out behind his head upward with two smaller ones below. And rows of orange spines can be seen behind his back all the way to his tail with a blade shaped like a scythe.

The male black dragon closes his eyes and stretches out his black wings, revealing dark-red membranes. Then he stretches his arms, making him yawn, revealing his sharp teeth and fangs beneath his snout. Hearing his yawn, a female guard captain standing by the front of the ship shouts, "Imperial highness at the decks!" making all soldiers and sailors huddle up in two rows with the female guard in the middle.

The male dragon chuckles, nodding his head side to side, wanting to tell them that formalities are not necessary. Yet he plays along as he walks along the deck, earning salutes from the dragon soldiers and sailors alike, all the way to the white-scaled middle-aged female not wearing her helmet, showing her blue eyes, small teal horns, and her snout with upper lips resembling icicles. White fluffy feathers are seen wrapped around her neck area. She even has a smooth teal underbelly and padded face.

"Enjoyed your rest, imperial highness?" the beautiful female for her age asks with a small smile, standing straight with her claws behind her back.

"Ha ha, you don't have to keep calling me imperial highness. Captain Halla," the royal male says with a smile. "Just call me Ignus."

"Forgive me, High-King Ignus, but as your loyal bodyguard and captain of the watch of this expedition, it is my duty to be professional to you, since you're the High-King, which means--"

"I become the emperor after my dad," High-King Ignus finishes for his bodyguard and captain with a hint of disappointment. Not that he isn't looking forward to being emperor, but he just wants to be treated like a normal dragon.

"Of course." Halla bows to show respect. "However, I have good news!"

"Really?!" Ignus perks up, looking excited.

Captain Halla takes High-King Ignus all the way to the front of the ship giving him a telescope. With the relescope, Ignus uses it to see a pile of land that they have been looking for, with a gleam in his eyes. He lowers down the telescope, giving it back to Halla, shouting, "LAND AHOY!"

The invasion by fire begins...